Passion
& Purpose

St. Peter, Clement of Rome, and Struggles in the Early Church

GENE VANDERZANDEN

CreateSpace

Seattle

PASSION & PURPOSE: St. Peter, Clement of Rome, and Struggles in the Early Church

ISBN-10: 978-1973866374
ISBN-13: 1973866374

PRAISE FOR PASSION & PURPOSE

In his second historical novel, Vanderzanden brings to life the personalities of Peter, Paul, Clement, and others, and the character of the world in which the Christian faith received its foundations. Exciting, romantic and inspiring!"
—Fr. Phil Bloom, Pastor, St. Mary of the Valley parish, Archdiocese of Seattle

"A fabulous walk through first century history with deep insight into the lives of our heroes in the faith. Clement's romantic life and his passion for the gospel weave throughout the narrative to make a very clear 'read between the lines' of his growing faith that is inspiring, imaginative and alive."
—Fr. Jim Dalton, Senior Priest of the Archdiocese of Seattle

"Passion & Purpose is delightfully informative and helps deepen our awareness of the nuanced relationships among key leaders of the early Christian Church. Deacon Gene successfully weaves together tales of true human love and actual historical events into a well-researched and fact-based narrative that explores the motivations and dedication of these saintly men and women. Recommended to any modern faith-seeker looking for a believable, historically accurate and refreshing story that encourages the best in faithful human decision-making and fruitful dedication to Christ."
—Deacon Pat Moynihan, Archdiocese of Seattle

The historical events depicted in this book are factual, and all of the named individuals are real people, except for the family and friends of Clement that history does not remember, two Christians from the east, and the characters from Egypt, who are creations of the author.

You will learn a great deal about the origins of the gospels and the realities of life faced by the early Christians. The names of actual people and places are usually shown in their English spelling, and I avoided archaic language to help you enjoy the story.

To see illustrations, links and maps that relate to the first century events and to learn more about what New Testament scholars are saying today, go to the author's website at www.markspassion.com.

And check out the free educational videos on YouTube at our Mark's Passion channel.

WHAT HAPPENED TO ST. PETER?

According to the Acts of the Apostles, Peter left Jerusalem in about 41 AD and 'went to another place,' which some scholars think was Antioch in Syria. Then a year later, historical sources tell us, he sailed to Rome, where he led the Church until he met his death during the persecutions of Nero in 64-65 AD.

Nothing remains in writing from the time about what the great Christian did during those two decades of widespread growth of the Church. The effects of his leadership are known from the many later documentary sources and archeological finds that substantiate his presence in the eternal city and characterize him as the first pope.

WHO WAS CLEMENT?

St. Clement of Rome was a grandson or relative of a freed slave whose family continued to serve the imperial palace. He was ordained a presbyter by Peter during the early 60s and became the fourth bishop in about 88 AD.

Despite the many legends that surfaced in later centuries, to which scholars are reluctant to give credence, history has left us one valuable insight into his personality and interests—a lengthy letter to the Christian community in Corinth that dealt with issues of disunity, church governance, and other theological and practical matters. The story of Clement is an account of the events that shaped the Church in the second half of the first century and an exploration of the passion and purpose of the fourth pope.

Along the way Jesus asked his disciples, "Who do people say that I am?"
They said in reply, "John the Baptist, others Elijah, still others one of the prophets."
And he asked them, "But who do you say that I am?"
Peter said to him in reply, "You are the Messiah."

Mark 8: 27-29

1

The question came as a total surprise, "Clement, would you like to go on a trip with me?"

The youth's eyes bulged wide, "Do you mean it, Peter? Where are we going?"

"I need to attend a council in Jerusalem, and I'd like to stop by Alexandria on the way."

In his seventeen years, Clement had never traveled beyond Pompeii. He had waded in the sea, but never sailed on it. His imagination stirred with images of adventure. "How soon will we leave?"

"We need to get underway fairly soon, but it will take some time to get ready." The leader of the Church knew he needed to get the funds to finance the trip. He hoped that Clement's father would pay their way.

"I can be ready tomorrow," the youth shouted impetuously.

"Well, not that soon," Peter cautioned. "Let me talk with your parents. Don't say a word to them until after I do."

"Oh. They'll let me go." The lad's father had spent liberally on his son's education—more than on both of his older brothers combined. Now they were successfully helping in his business, and he looked forward to Clement doing the same.

"I will speak with your father at midday. I'll tell him that a journey to the Holy City will round out your education."

Clement nodded his head, but he already was feeling the maritime wind carrying him to new horizons.

Peter had come up with the plan a few days earlier when he received a letter from Jerusalem saying that Paul was traveling there to debate a recurrent question that kept dividing the Church. Some Christians from the Holy City, under the direction of James, had been in Antioch saying that all who sought to become Christians must first be circumcised and submit to the law of Moses. This was not a problem in Judea, but Paul was dealing with Gentile converts, not Jews. He knew the requirements were too big of an obstacle to successfully evangelize in the other provinces. The two were very strong personalities, and it was not likely that the issue could be settled without Peter getting personally involved.

Peter figured he could get Clement's father to fund the trip. Urbanus owned a thriving business, and probably could handle the cost of the voyage. Since arriving in Rome six years earlier, Peter continually had to ask for money. He was the head of the Church, but he couldn't afford his own home and seldom took his wife to a trattoria for a meal. He was grateful for the generosity shown by some of the families, but he hated to always have to ask.

"I have serious matters to attend to, Clement, but we should have time to do some sightseeing while we are there." He liked the boy—he saw potential in him. Clement was intelligent, personable, and passionate about things that interested him. Peter thought the youth might make a good presbyter.

"What will we see?"

"In Jerusalem? Well, Jesus finished his life's work there, and the temple is one of the most magnificent in the world."

"But they killed him there."

"Yes. And I can show you the place. It proved how much he loves us."

Clement grew up in a Christian household, but he hadn't yet matured in his understanding. It bothered him that Jesus was crucified like a common criminal.

"I'll show you the garden where he prayed the night they arrested him. It's a beautiful place in the moonlight. Jesus could have just walked away, but he stayed."

The young man paused and pondered the image. He didn't fully understand Jesus, but it impressed him that he was so passionate about his purpose that he allowed the guards to take him.

Peter noticed the look in Clement's eyes and resolved to show him the places where Jesus walked.

"Did Jesus have a wife?"

The question surprised Peter. He thought Clement knew. "No. He loved all people."

"Did he ever have a girlfriend?"

"No. He was good friends with a woman from Magdala. Her name was

Mary like his mother."

"Was she pretty?" The lad wanted to know.

"She was kind of pretty. Not outstanding, but most would say she was good-looking. Why do you ask?"

"I am going to have the most beautiful wife in the world!"

Peter didn't know how to respond to such a remark, but he noticed that Clement seemed lost in his dreams.

2

At midday Peter strolled partway up the Capitoline Hill to a stone house with an arched doorway leading into a spacious courtyard. He had been to see Clement's father many times and always felt welcome. The middle-aged businessman was seated at a table, looking at some papers. He had the strong features of a man who spent many years on his feet, although he was gathering a soft roll around his belly as his black curly hair began to grey. His attention was so focused on the papers that he didn't notice his visitor.

"Ah. Good morning, Urbanus."

"Oh, Peter. Welcome! What brings you out on this beautiful day?"

"It's too nice to stay home. How is business?" He knew this was the merchant's favorite topic.

"Oh. Fine, fine. Everybody wants eggs." Urbanus held the contract for providing eggs to the emperor's household, and over the years the palace staff had grown into the thousands. His father started the operation as a slave under Tiberius, and after being freed by the emperor for loyal service he continued it as an independent contractor. Urbanus managed to stay on good terms with the palace staff, even though that was tricky while Caligula was in power. Now with Claudius on the throne and two sons helping run the operation, things were getting easier as well as more profitable.

"That's good. You are a very smart businessman."

"Look at these numbers. We are delivering thousands of eggs every day. It's my sons who are making it prosper."

"Cassius and Horus are fine young men."

"Oh my. That's an understatement. Cassius has honed the transportation process to the peak of efficiency, and Horus has masterfully refined the delivery and billing. We now get paid for almost every crate. There is very little theft or breakage. I am very proud of them."

"You have every reason to be proud."

"Yes. And do you know the best part? Now that they both are married, they are even more settled and focused. I am gaining business, and soon they will be giving me grandsons! What could be better?"

"God has blessed your house, Urbanus."

"Yes—well—what brings you here?" Although the businessman was dutiful about attending the Sunday morning gathering of Christians, he didn't give the faith much attention during the week.

Peter thought he may as well blurt it out. "I have an idea, Urbanus. I need to go to Jerusalem for a council, and maybe Clement should go with me. I'd like to stop in Alexandria, too, if that works out. Clement is a fine young man, and a journey like this could round out his education."

The merchant instantly understood the financial aspect of the proposal, which was not a problem. He voiced a reservation though, "He is not like his brothers. They were working in the business when they were barely old enough to drive a cart. Clement hasn't shown much interest."

"He has great potential."

"Oh yes. Clement has great potential," he said with a frown. "He's intelligent. I've seen to it that he has gained a fine education. He can speak and write in Latin and Greek. He knows the philosophers and has mastered Aristotle and Cicero. But he is seventeen years old and hasn't worked a full day in his life!"

"Well, maybe when he comes back from the trip, he'll be ready to settle down."

"Maybe he will. Then maybe he won't. He may come back with even more wild dreams than when he left."

"I will look after him."

"You, Peter, I trust. It's Clement that I can't count on." Urbanus had decided while he was complaining to let his son go on the voyage, but he enjoyed voicing his concerns to a receptive listener. "I will speak with his mother this evening. If she says he can go, then he can go."

"That sounds good, Urbanus."

"Yes. Now, let's have something to eat."

"The bishop paid us a visit today," the businessman told his wife after dinner. "He wants to take Clement on a voyage to Jerusalem. I said I would talk with you before giving my approval."

Cordula was a short woman with greying hair who had added a bit of weight with age. She generally went along with whatever her husband wanted, but she knew how to slip her ideas into his mind. "Would he see the holy sites?" she asked. "It might make him a better follower of the Way."

"I suppose so. We didn't talk about that."

"What did you talk about?"

"Peter said he needed to go to a council. I told him it is time for Clement to settle down. He's not a child anymore. My concern is that a voyage may turn him into even more of a dreamer than he already is."

"The boy deserves to dream, dear. He has many years ahead of him to work."

"When I was his age, I knew the egg business inside and out."

"Yes, you did. But things are different now. And who said that all of our sons should go into business? Maybe one of them could do something different."

"Like what?" Urbanus had little imagination for nonbusiness pursuits.

"Oh. I don't know. Perhaps he could become an artist or a presbyter."

"An artist or a presbyter! How is he going to make a living doing that?"

The mother of three could see that the line of conversation was not going in a helpful direction. "Well—we don't need to plan such things now, dear. Let's just let him go and see how it works out."

Clement was thrilled at the news. When he came to breakfast his mother shared with him how his father had agreed. Urbanus had already gone out with Cassius and Horus, who lived nearby and usually met with him each morning.

The youth ran to find Peter. "I can go! I can go! Both Father and Mama said I can."

A look of great relief spread over the church leader's face, which melted into a big broad grin. "We will have a good time. I've been thinking about the places I will take you to see."

"Like where? Tell me."

"Well, yesterday after I spoke with your father, I located a ship heading for Alexandria, and the captain said he could arrange passage on to Caesarea. It's leaving in three days. We will have two nights in Egypt, where I need to meet with Bishop Marcus, and then we're off to the Holy City."

"Three days! I can hardly wait." The youth didn't hear the entire itinerary. His heart was beating too loudly. "How long will we be there?"

"That depends upon how long the council takes. The meeting may end quickly, or it may go on and on. But I have no need to rush back to Rome."

"Nor do I," the youth said in reply. His horizon didn't go past the immediate adventure.

"Good. Let's get together tomorrow morning and talk about what we need to bring."

That evening at dinner Peter broke the news to his wife. He was blunt. "I am going to Jerusalem. James and Paul need me to work out some problems."

"And what are your daughter and I supposed to do? Just sit here while you are gone."

"You will be fine."

"Who is paying for this?"

"Urbanus. I am taking Clement along."

"So, you had all the details worked out before you even spoke with me."

"I have to go."

"When are you leaving?"

"The ship leaves in three days."

"You know, Husband, I hate it when you say nothing about these trips until you are ready to leave."

Peter did do that. She knew his pattern. When he had to go, he went. It started when Jesus came to their city in Galilee and said, "Come, follow me." Peter just dropped his fish net and went. He didn't know how long he'd be gone, and he didn't even tell his wife. She thought it was very unfair. She believed in Jesus, but she didn't like how he constantly called her husband away. After Christ ascended into heaven, she thought their relationship might become more mutual, but the demands on Peter only grew greater. Now she had no choice but to put up with it.

The next day Peter reviewed with Clement what he needed to bring. "The most important thing to carry on a ship is a good cushion. The decks are hard, and the longer you are on them the harder they get. And a heavy blanket is important at night. Bring a couple of extra tunics, a toga, and a towel. The captain will provide food and water, but treats are on us—and wine, too. Whatever you like, put it in your bag."

"Will do."

Peter was at home on the water, but he was concerned about Clement's first voyage. "Do you get seasick? There is a lot of motion."

"Actually, I don't know."

"Well, ask your mother if she has any remedies for it. The weather can get rough out there."

"Will we make stops?"

"Of course. We'll stop for supplies in Syracuse and Cyrene. Each leg will take a few days, depending on the wind."

Clement said good-bye to his envious friends, and when the day came the whole household got up early to see him off.

"Now you stay close to Peter, and don't wander away and get into trouble," warned his father.

Cassius embraced him. "Good luck, Brother. This is a great opportunity for you."

His mother gave him a long, warm hug. "I'll pray for you every day, my son. God may have something in store for you that you will learn in the Holy Land. Watch and listen for clues. May Christ open your heart and deepen your faith."

"Thank you, Mother. I will do as you say."

"All right. Get in the cart," ordered Horus, "if you want to get to the dock on time."

As Clement climbed onto the cart beside his brother, Cordula pressed an object into his hand. "Take this. Remember us, and remember who you are." It was a small bronze ichthys—two intersecting arcs that formed the outline of a fish—an identifying symbol that many Christians used throughout the Mediterranean world.

Clement leaned down and kissed his mother tenderly.

3

Peter was already on the ship waving when they reached the docks. Horus helped his brother bring his things on board, then quickly left for work.

Clement's blood stirred as the ship eased away from its moorings. *We are on our way to exotic lands!* he mused.

The two travelers said little as they gazed at familiar sights along the Tiber, noticing how the perspective differed when seen from the river. As they passed Ostia, where city leaders were talking about dredging a bigger harbor, and headed out onto the open sea, the crew put up all the sails. With the wind carrying them along, everyone began to relax. Peter struck up a conversation with the captain.

As the two spoke about places they'd sailed, Clement went up to the bow. He stared at the waves, noticing the broad wake where the bow was cutting the water, and feeling the strong breeze on the back of his neck. He began pondering what the future might bring.

Perhaps I will meet the girl with the golden hair, he imagined.

In his dreams, he often had pictured meeting a beautiful girl with hair that glistened with streaks of gold. He had seen blondes from the north and liked how they differed from those in Rome, whose hair was so ordinary, but the girl in his dreams was unique. Her hair was the color of cinnamon with highlights that sparkled like darts of gold. Her skin was as smooth as fresh cream, and her lips were full and sensuous like the slave girls from Nubia. Her eyes revealed a love so deep that she sensed his every wish and responded with all her heart. When he touched her back with the tips of his fingers, she leaned toward him, circling his neck with her slender arms and touching her tender breasts to his chest.

The attraction was powerful, like the current of a raging river. After caressing her soft shoulders and supple neck, he reached around her back—so lithe, so young—and drew her even closer. Their lips met, and the blood in his veins surged. Their bodies melted into one as their passion welled up with the power of a restless volcano.

Two white birds suddenly began to call, as if wanting his attention. Briefly realizing where he was, he tried to ignore them, but the heat of the vision had passed. He watched the birds flying together, closely in unison, and wondered if it was a sign of his future.

That afternoon, under a clear sky, Peter mentioned to Clement, "You seem to be handling the waves quite well."

"Yes. I got a little tightness in my stomach after we ate, but it went away."

"You'll get used to the motion."

"I believe so."

"You seemed to be thinking hard, up on the bow this morning."

"Oh, just the normal things," he lied. Then he asked, "Do you miss your wife when you take trips?"

"Umm. Why do you ask? We are both used to it."

"Weren't you married when Jesus first called you to follow him?"

"Yes. Several years."

"And you just left your home and your wife and went."

"I didn't go by myself. My brother and two of our friends went too. We followed him together."

"What was it about Jesus that made you go?"

The apostle rubbed his beard as he thought about the question. "There were several things. Even before he had done any mighty deeds in our city, we could tell he was a holy man. His eyes showed great understanding, and his words were gentle and loving. And he announced, 'The kingdom of God is at hand.' Our people had been waiting many years for the Savior to come—the one who had been foretold by the prophets. We thought he might be him."

"Was there anything else?"

"One thing more: The Master said, 'I will make you fishers of men.' I had fished all my life—for fish. I wasn't sure what he meant when he said 'fishers of men,' but I was intrigued. He seemed to be offering something with more purpose than just hauling in fish for the tables of the rich."

Clement rubbed his bare chin while his mentor gave him space. "That's kind of how I feel. My brothers are making a good living delivering eggs to the emperor's staff, but I can't imagine spending my whole life doing that."

Peter laughed. "For some people, making a good living is all they want."

"Not me. I'm not like that. I want to do something great!"

Seeing the youth's eyes light up, the bishop posed an option, "The Church will do great things."

"I thought about becoming a famous philosopher, like Cicero. I don't think they make much money, though."

"Money isn't everything, lad. In fact, sometimes it can get in the way of our freedom to accomplish our mission in life."

"I wish I knew my mission in life."

"You are only seventeen. In time you will know."

"I hope so," sighed the dreamer. "When we get back, my father will put a lot of pressure on me. I know it's coming."

9

4

When they arrived in Syracuse, Clement was not impressed. The city, founded by Greeks, had a long history, and the mathematician Archimedes was born there. But it looked like most port towns—dirty and cluttered with low buildings that catered to the needs of sailors. "I wouldn't want to live here," muttered the young man.

"We're only going to be here a couple of hours," the captain advised, "no loading of cargo—just water and food. Don't try to go into town. It's not safe for travelers like you. The gangs will take your money." When both passengers showed their disappointment, he added, "Cyrene will be better. It's a much nicer place."

Clement wanted to get his feet on solid ground. Peter watched the harbor activities, but the youth laid down on his cushion like he was napping. Myriads of visions churned in his mind.

That evening, at sea again, Clement questioned his bishop, "You mentioned as we left Rome that the Church will do great things. What kind of things will it do?"

Happy that the youth had given thought to his promptings, the older man answered, "Well—we are already doing important things. We are spreading the gospel. The faith has followers now in most all of the major cities."

"Why is that important?"

"Because God is the Lord of the whole world, and Jesus sent us out to all nations."

"He said that?"

"Yes. At first we only went to the villages of Galilee. But later he made it clear that our mission was to the entire world. Just before he ascended into heaven he told us, 'Go forth to all nations, baptizing them in the name of the Father, and of the Son, and of the Holy Spirit. Teach them to obey all that I have commanded you and know that I am with you always, even to the end of the age.'"

"Amazing. How is Jesus with you?"

"I feel his presence every day, and we receive him in the breaking of the bread. Many times we prayed to him for things we needed in order to spread the faith, and they happened!"

"Amazing."

"I don't tell this to many people—but a little while after he challenged us to spread the gospel, John and I were going up to the temple to pray when we saw a man who was crippled from birth, begging for alms. I looked at him and said, 'I have neither silver nor gold, but what I do have I give you. In the name of Jesus Christ the Nazorean, rise and walk!' I took him by the hand and raised him, and immediately his feet and ankles grew strong. He leaped up, stood, and walked around, and went into the temple with us, walking and jumping and praising God!"

"You did that?"

"Jesus did it. I was the instrument he used."

"That's astounding!"

"If it were only one incident, that would be astounding enough. But I have seen so many of these healings and mighty deeds over the years that I know he is with us and answers our prayers."

"I'm beginning to understand. But what difference will it make if the whole world has faith in him?"

"It will make a great difference. Everyone will treat one another with respect. There will be no wars, no lies, no injustice. No one will take from another—everyone will have enough. Would you like that?"

"Yes, certainly. That's quite a vision. My father says I'm a dreamer, but you are a dreamer too."

"It's a dream that will become a reality—not in one day—perhaps not in my lifetime—but it will happen. I'm convinced of it."

"Is that what keeps you going—following your mission?"

"That's what keeps me going. I've been at it since I was a young man, and I'll keep doing what I can until my last day on earth."

"I'm impressed with your dedication. I really am. You've given me a lot to think about."

The leader of the Church wanted to offer more, but the youth pulled his blanket around him and rolled over on his cushion. "That's enough for now," the bishop supposed. "Faith grows in stages."

Later that night Clement was awakened by the sound of the creaking mast. Gazing at the starry sky he thought, *Peter and I are so different. He is tall and strong, while I am average. He grows his beard, and I shave. He was a Jew, and I am a Roman. I am accustomed to living in ease, but he seems to care little about money. And he is so dedicated to the Lord and the Church, while I am not dedicated to anything. Yet, out of all the people I know in life, this man impresses me the most. He makes my spirit stir within me.*

Ancient Cyrene was a Greek city located on the north coast of Africa, a few miles in from the sea, named for the beautiful daughter of a king in one of the many legends of Apollo's love affairs with young women. Greeks from the island of Thera sought the advice of the oracle of Delphi on what to do about their rapidly rising population and declining food supply. They were told to send an expedition to the region of Libya to found a colony. With the help of friendly residents, they located a suitable site with gushing springs of fresh water. The city became the home of the Cyrenaic school of philosophy, started by Aristippus, a disciple of Socrates.

With abundant water and a long growing season, the region became prosperous. When the Romans came into power, they made the city a metropolitan center. Its strategic location jutting out toward the island of Crete made it a favorite stopping point for ships sailing the southern coast of the Mediterranean.

On the evening before the ship reached the port, Peter overheard one of the crewmen shout that he was getting close to home. He asked the man, "Are you from this region?" The captain and the others were from Alexandria.

"Yes. Cyrene is my birthplace. My wife and children are there."

"You are from a famous city."

"Oh yes. And a beautiful city it is."

"My name is Peter. What's yours?"

"Marcellus. My parents gave me a Roman name. It means 'from the sea.'" The seaman was short and stocky with weathered skin from many years in the sun and wind. He seemed honest and sincere, and dedicated to his profession.

"Well, Marcellus, did you know a farmer from Cyrene named Simon?" Peter asked.

"A Jewish farmer? I don't know many Jews. They don't come around the docks."

"He is a fine man. He became a Christian."

"Oh really. Do you know much about the one they called Jesus?"

"I followed him," said the apostle. "I was one of his disciples."

Clement leaned back on his cushion and listened, taking in how easily his mentor could turn a friendly greeting into an opportunity to evangelize.

"Oh, then you knew him well. I've heard some amazing stories about him. Is this Simon a disciple too?"

"Yes. Simon is a farmer now living in a village near Jerusalem. He has two sons—Alexander and Rufus. It was quite a coincidence how he came into contact with Jesus. Our Master was a holy man and a teacher, who got into conflict with the chief priests and scribes of the temple."

"I heard that they got the Roman governor to crucify him, but you Christians say he was not guilty."

"He was a man of peace. He had compassion and love for everyone."

"Why did they turn against him?"

"They had grown rich, but Jesus tried to lift up the common people."

"It's the same everywhere. The rich keep getting richer, and the poor just get poorer."

"Well, Jesus wanted to change that. He proclaimed a kingdom of justice and righteousness."

"I wish it was like that. I have to spend many months each year away from my family just to make a living."

"We who follow Jesus believe that he was the Son of God, and we do what we can to make his kingdom grow."

"Where is this kingdom? How can I get there?" the seaman asked.

"It's not far away. Jesus taught that the kingdom of God is in our midst. It is wherever we live our lives with mercy and love."

"What do you have to do when you belong to this kingdom?"

"We each have a role. We each do what we can. Would you like to hear what Simon did?"

"Sure."

"As I said, it was a coincidence. The guards beat Jesus so brutally that it left him half dead. Then they made him carry the heavy cross out of the fortress, through the city streets and up the hill to the place of execution. When he fell, they whipped him until he got up and continued on. And just when Jesus couldn't carry the cross any longer, Simon passed by on his way in from the fields. The guards pressed him into service, and he carried it the rest of the way."

"Oh! How unlucky."

"Not really. Simon was the most fortunate of the unfortunates who were there that day. He became the one who helped Jesus the most, by carrying the awful weight of the cross on his shoulders."

"Oh, I see."

"Simon suffered a little, while Jesus suffered greatly and died. We accept some suffering because Jesus gave his life for us."

13

"So in the kingdom of God, you live as Jesus taught."

"We live as Jesus taught, and he makes our joy complete."

"I sure would like to live there."

"There is a Christian community in Cyrene. If you ask around, someone will help you find them."

"And what then?"

"They will tell you everything you need to know. It will change your life. You can live in God's kingdom right in Cyrene."

"I might do that," the seaman avowed with a smile. "I'll look for them when I am home."

Both men stood up and embraced one another. Clement was impressed at how easily Peter was able to introduce people to Christ.

"You are a master at telling people about Jesus," the youth declared.

Turning his attention to the smiling eyes, the apostle answered, "I've had plenty of practice—nearly two decades."

"I know. But still, that took courage. The man might have hated Christians or belonged to a cult."

"We don't know how people will react, but when you share your faith, remember to have a smile on your face. A little friendliness is usually returned."

"I'll remember that when I am ready to do it. You make friends so easily."

"I just asked if he knew Simon. That started the conversation."

"Do you do that often?"

"What do you mean?"

"I mean, was Simon a real person, or did you make him up?"

The big man looked shocked. Then he raised his hand to slap the youth across the face, but restrained himself. "We don't make anything up! We never do that. We don't need to do that. The truth about Jesus is all we need to say." Shaking his fist he added, "Don't you ever make up a story about Christ. You learn! And after you learn, you tell what you know!"

"I'm sorry."

Lowering his fist, the big man picked up his cushion and blanket and stormed to a different part of the ship.

Clement pulled his blanket around him. It was getting cold.

The youth rehearsed an apology, and in the morning found his mentor.

Seeing him coming, Peter confessed, "I'm sorry I got angry with you last night."

"I'm sorry too," the youth admitted, surprised that his elder spoke first.

"It's just that the truth is such an important part of the kingdom of God."

"I know. I can see that."

"I want you to grow to be an upright man."

"I'll try. I will always remember this lesson."

"Good. Now let's just put it in the past."

"You may punish me. I will accept it."

"I will not punish you. That's the farthest thing from my mind. I just want to help you."

"Thank you," Clement whispered, grateful that the man of God was so forgiving.

A few minutes later shouts rang out from the crew, "Land ahead—there's the port!"

The two travelers turned to where all the eyes were looking. They could see some low buildings, but not a city.

"Where is the civic center?" Clement asked.

Marcellus answered, "It's up on the hill. You'll see it soon."

Clement stared in the direction he was pointing.

"Do you see the low hill with the mountain behind it? The city is there. It's not far. Only a few miles."

"Oh, I hope we can go into the city."

"There is probably time," remarked the seaman. "They have to load some cargo for Alexandria. That will take a few hours. I doubt that the captain will leave before the morning tide."

"How will we find our way?"

"Oh. I can take you. My house is on the other side. I can show you some places on the way. Then you can walk back."

Clement was anxious to stretch his legs after the long voyage. The captain confirmed that the ship would remain at the dock overnight and that the route was safe to walk. Peter advised him to be back by the evening meal, and as soon as Marcellus had finished his duties, the two jumped onto the dock and headed uphill.

After an hour on the road, Clement began to tire.

"There is a spring at milepost IV. It's not much farther," the seaman advised. Clement understood. The Romans had constructed roads all throughout the empire, primarily to move armies when they needed to. A mile was a thousand paces, counted each time the right foot hit the ground.

The mariner seemed to be in better condition than Clement and was not puffing, even though he was carrying a heavy pack. "There is the spring. Let's stop and fill our jugs."

The young man was grateful for the respite, but when his guide nodded he stood up and followed.

The city was more beautiful than Clement imagined. Just inside the gate they came to a gushing fountain—a welcome sight to travelers. Enjoying the shade of a colonnaded street, Marcellus proudly pointed out a large marble statue of Apollo, a bronze bust of the mythical Cyrene, and an exquisite statue of Venus.

People were strolling in and out of shops, all of them smiling, revealing their civic pride and sense of security. No one showed even the slightest hint of anxiety. *This is a fine city*, Clement assured himself.

"The school of philosophy is just ahead," noted Marcellus. "I want to say hello to a friend first. I won't be long—you can look around. I'll meet you here by the statue."

"That will be fine. I'll just look in a couple of shops."

The young man peered into a sandal shop, but realized he didn't need any shoes. Then he spied a place selling gifts and artifacts. *This might be interesting*, he thought.

Inside he smiled at the shopkeeper and picked up a figurine of a horse. It was remarkably realistic. Putting it down, his eyes caught a glint from the next table. It came from a crystal star with curving points that conveyed a sense of cosmic wonder. Taking it into his hands, he admired the fine workmanship and noted how fragile the object was. *Whoever made this had steady hands*, he mused.

"May I help you?" the shopkeeper offered.

Not expecting the question, the youth jolted abruptly. His hands became as limp as wet feathers, and his eyes glared in horror as the star fell from his grasp, the pieces making a crackling sound as they bounced across the hard floor.

"Oh my!" exclaimed the shopkeeper.

"I'm so sorry—I wasn't expecting you to speak."

"That's fine. Don't worry." The shopkeeper found a broom and swept the pieces into a small box.

"I will repay you, of course," said the startled youth.

"Of course. That will be eight denarii."

"Certainly. However, my money is on the ship. I have only one coin with me."

"Hmm. That is a problem. Do you have anything to offer in security?"

"No. I'm just here for the day. Our ship is leaving tomorrow morning."

"Then how can I expect you to return with the money?" The shopkeeper was polite, but was not about to trust the young foreigner.

"There must be a way. I'll think of something."

Sighing gently, the shopkeeper stepped out the door and blew a whistle sharply, three times. "The magistrate will be here in a moment," he said—again very politely.

The officer appeared before Clement could say another word. "What's going on?" he asked.

The shopkeeper explained, "This young man broke a valuable item and offered to pay for it, but he has no money."

"That's defrauding a merchant," the officer charged. "I'll take you to the jail until we figure this out."

"But I can't go. My ship is leaving."

"You should have thought of that before you defrauded a merchant. We are very honest in our city. We cannot permit anyone to commit a crime."

"But..."

"Come with me."

The cell was small with no window, but Clement could see light from the office in front. The circulation was poor, and the place smelled like it had held a few drunks and vagrants.

Several hours passed, then Clement noticed that the light was growing dimmer and he was getting hungry. "What am I going to do?" he muttered. "Oh God, what am I going to do?" He needed to get word to the ship, but he didn't see how. The magistrate didn't seem to care. He acted bored, like this was just one more nuisance in his long day.

If they keep me all night, I'll miss the ship, he complained to himself. *Peter will be mad at me, and—Oh God—if my father has to bail me out of this situation, he will have me totally in his grip.* Clement sat on his cot with his head in his hands. *What am I going to do?*

Pacing the floor didn't help—there wasn't much space to walk anyway. At one point he started pulling his hair, but all that proved was that he wasn't dreaming.

Calling for the magistrate, he pleaded again, "Is there not some way for me to get the money from the ship? My traveling companion has money too. We have plenty to pay the bill."

"Your bill now is nine denarii, you know. Eight for the star and one for your incarceration."

"But..."

17

"And tomorrow you will owe ten."

Shocked and dismayed, the youth dropped onto the cot and cried.

5

When it was getting dark, Clement heard voices. Someone was speaking with the magistrate. The voice seemed familiar. Then Marcellus appeared.

"I looked all over for you. Why didn't you stay by the statue?"

"I just went into one shop."

"Yes. And it took me hours to find the right one. The shopkeeper told me the story. I settled your bill. Thank the gods that I just got paid and had enough on me."

"Oh, thank you, Marcellus. You are a good friend. Thank you."

"You still can get to the ship. There will be moonlight. Just follow the road. I want to get home now. My wife will worry."

"Certainly. But I need to repay you."

"Leave the money with the dock master. I will get it there."

"Do you trust me? No one else in this city does."

"You are a Christian—right? So you must be trustworthy."

Clement embraced the considerate seaman and sobbed on his shoulders. Then they both raced to their destinations.

Peter was suspicious when Clement didn't return until after dark. He didn't say anything, though, until morning, when he saw the youth get off the ship and speak briefly with the dock master.

"What business did you have with the dock master?" he asked.

"I left some coins with him for Marcellus."

"Hmm. How much?"

"I owed him nine—and gave him ten." The boy was honest.

"Why did you owe him so much? What did you buy?"

Knowing better than to try to test Peter again, Clement poured out the whole story. The apostle listened intently about the issue with the shopkeeper, broke into a broad grin on hearing how he whistled for the magistrate, and laughed out loud as the youth described his torments in the jail cell.

"Don't you care that I was stuck in that jail and almost missed the ship?"

The older man laughed again. "You are learning so much on this voyage. I am pleased for you."

"Pleased! Why?"

"You are becoming baptized in the Christian life."

"What?"

"You are learning that things do not always go as you hope and what to do when they don't."

"I didn't know what to do. If Marcellus hadn't gone into the right shop, I'd still be locked up."

"What did you do while you were in the cell?"

"Nothing. I just paced and worried."

"Did you pray?"

"Huh?"

"Did you pray? A jail cell is an excellent place to pray."

"Are you teasing me?"

"No. You were in serious trouble. Why didn't you turn to Jesus?"

"I didn't think of praying. I was too busy…"

"You were too busy panicking. Wouldn't it have been better to spend your time asking Christ for help?"

"Yes. I guess so."

"It's not a guess. It's our experience. Jesus helps us when we turn to him."

"I haven't had that experience."

"No—not yet. You are just getting started in the life. In time you will have much experience, and you will know. You won't just believe, you'll know."

"I'm beginning to understand."

"I remember the first time I was put in prison," Peter recalled. "It was right after the crippled beggar that I told you about was healed. All the people who saw it were amazed, and I told them it was by the power of Christ that the man was cured. Then I called on them to repent and be converted, and their sins would be wiped away."

"What happened then?"

"The captain of the temple guard took us into custody until the next day, where we were to be tried by the *Sanhedrin*—the high council. We prayed all night. The next day they brought us before the high priest and the whole priestly class who asked, 'By what power have you done this?'"

"Were you not afraid?"

"Yes. Certainly. But I felt a strength within me that I didn't know I had. I just stood there and lectured them. Words flowed from my mouth like I had never spoken before. I said, 'If we are being examined today about a good deed done to a cripple, then all of you and all the people of Israel should know that it was in the name of Jesus Christ the Nazorean whom you crucified, and whom God raised from the dead, that this man was healed. Jesus is the stone rejected by you, the builders, which has become the cornerstone. There is no salvation through anyone else, nor is there any other name under heaven given to the human race by which we are to be saved.'"

"Amazing! What did they do?"

"They let us go! They were afraid to punish us in front of the people—they were more afraid of the people than we were of them. So, they just ordered us not to speak or teach about Jesus and kicked us out."

"That's remarkable! Then what did you do?"

"First we prayed together as a community in thanksgiving for the divine aid, and then we just kept on teaching the people. They wanted to hear more."

Clement laughed.

"It was an excellent time to teach. The people saw us confront earthly power with heavenly power."

"That's amazing. I never knew."

"You are learning much on this trip, my son."

"Yes. Yes, I am."

"Good. Now, let's have breakfast. I bet you are hungry."

After the long-overdue meal, Clement took the bronze ichthys from his bag and went up to the bow by himself. Caressing the image of the fish gently in his hands, he thanked the Lord for the experiences he was gaining. Then remembering how his mother had pressed the object into his hand as they left for the docks of Rome, he brought it to his lips and kissed it.

6

Alexandria—where the Nile River meets the Mediterranean Sea—was founded in 331 BC by Alexander the Great. He envisioned a glorious city with wide streets laid out in the pattern of a grid. The full expansion came under the direction of his general, Ptolemy I. After Alexander's death in 323 BC,

Ptolemy brought his body back to Alexandria to be entombed.

Under his descendants, the city sprang into eminence, accumulating culture and wealth, and becoming the most powerful metropolis of its time, controlling the lucrative trade with India and Arabia. The supportive environment attracted scholars from far and wide. Eratosthenes calculated the circumference of the earth to within fifty miles at Alexandria, and the great mathematicians Euclid and Archimedes taught at the university there. Ptolemy II completed the Temple of Serapis, which contained seventy thousand papyrus scrolls. Books were purchased or confiscated until, over time, more buildings were required and the library of Alexandria contained as many as a half of a million books.

The *Septuagint*—the Greek translation of the Jewish scriptures—was composed in Alexandria, where there was a large Jewish population. Some say that Ptolemy II commissioned the work on the first five books. Seventy scholars worked seventy days, coming up with translations that were essentially identical.

With the advent of Christianity, conversions also came in great numbers. Peter wanted to stop at the city and visit with their bishop to make sure that all was going well for the growing Church.

The dominant feature when approaching the city from any direction was an enormous structure looming above the harbor—the Pharos lighthouse, considered one of the seven wonders of the ancient world.

"It's huge!" exclaimed Clement.

"And a welcome sight," said the captain. "In daylight or dark, when I see the fires burning, I know we are coming home."

"I've never seen anything so tall."

After securing the ship and dismissing the crew, the captain told Peter, "You and the lad take only what you need for two nights. The rest of your things I will put on the ship to Caesarea."

"That's perfect," two voices echoed.

"But you must be here early Thursday morning. The ship cannot wait."

"We will."

The apostle and his companion picked up their light packs and walked through the wide, shaded promenades toward the house of the local bishop. Peter knew the way.

"Pomegranates! Lemons! Apricots!" barked a street vendor. Clement eyed the fresh fruit—more appealing than the dried figs and dates they carried on the sea.

21

Peter cautioned him not to pick up anything, but the youth hardly heard. He was taking in so many exotic sights and sounds and smells.

"Silks from the Orient!" exclaimed another.

Clement shook his head.

"Something nice for your girlfriend?" A shopkeeper held out tiny canisters of oils and perfumes, waving them in the lad's face.

He turned away. "I wish I had a girlfriend," he muttered.

The bishop's house was not far—an older but stately mud-brick structure that needed a new coat of plaster. They entered the courtyard just as Bishop Marcus was walking out of the living area with two other men.

"Aha! Peter! Peter my friend. I am so glad that you came."

Peter threw his arms around his colleague in the faith. "It's good to see you!"

"I think it's been four years. That's too long."

"Much too long. We have much to talk about. I can stay two nights."

"Wonderful. Oh! Let me introduce you to these two fine men. This is Kenamon, one of our prominent citizens, and Anianus, a presbyter here."

"Good to meet you," replied the Galilean. "And this is Clement, the son of one our most successful merchants in Rome."

Clement blushed. He wasn't accustomed to such lavish introductions.

"And, oh, Kenamon, Anianus—this is Peter, the leader of the apostles. He was with Jesus for three years."

"The Peter that I have heard about?" asked the Egyptian. "What a pleasure it is to meet you,"

"Thank you."

The bishop continued, "Kenamon is becoming a Christian. We have just given him his third lesson."

"You are well along," the apostle replied. "You will be happy as you follow the Way."

"I believe I will. I'm quite sure I will." Then, with his face lighting up, the Egyptian exclaimed, "I have an idea! Can you come to dinner with us while you are here? I have so many questions about Jesus that you could answer."

"We will only be here for two nights. Our ship leaves on Thursday."

"Then come this evening. I believe in doing things right away."

"Well—if that is all right with you, Marcus."

"Yes. Fine. But I can't go with you this evening. Can you accompany them, Anianus?"

The presbyter nodded. "That will give me some time with Peter also."

"Then it's settled." Kenamon agreed. "Tonight it is. And just come as you are—nothing formal."

When the Egyptian left the courtyard, Marcus invited the two travelers to freshen up and sit down for a cool drink. The rest of the day Clement listened as the three churchmen chatted about the growth of the faith in Alexandria.

That evening, as the sun was setting, Anianus led the travelers to a neighborhood on a low hill with newer and larger homes. He paused at the gate of an impressive structure, commenting, "This is it! Kenamon has done well in the ivory trade."

"He certainly has," remarked the bishop of modest means.

Clement added, "I bet they have quite a view. It looks like they get a panorama from here."

"They do," the presbyter affirmed. "It's amazing from the balcony. You can see most of the city. It's flat, as you would expect on a river delta, except for a few high places."

"The land alone must have cost a fortune."

"I'm sure it did. Shall we go in?"

Inside the gate, Clement and Peter were studying the numerous vases and stele that adorned the courtyard when their host came out. "Welcome. Welcome. I see you are noticing our Egyptian gods. You are looking at Anubis, who has the body of a man and the head of a jackal. And this is Isis. She represented the ideal mother and wife. We don't worship them anymore, but when we have visitors from up the Nile they like to see them."

Kenamon was heavy and flabby, clean-shaven with short black hair on the sides of his head and a large bald area across the top. "Let's sit out here. There's a nice breeze. Would you like beer or wine?" A servant appeared with both.

As the visitors took a seat and a beverage, their host continued, "The old gods are losing their appeal. That's why so many of us are turning to your God and his son, Jesus."

"Yes," remarked Peter. "Marcus was telling us today how so many are coming into the faith."

"More Egyptians than Jews," Anianus added. "Many Jews, but even greater numbers of Egyptians."

"We had too many gods," the host declared. "I believe that if there is only one high god, then the rest are superfluous."

The presbyter agreed. "We learned that from the Jews. They were right on that."

"You know, we Egyptians tried once to progress to monotheism. It was just before your Moses escaped with his people. Amenhotep IV took a bold and revolutionary step to replace the old system. He abolished the traditional practices and promoted worship of the sun, Aten. He built a new capital city between the upper and lower sections of the Nile, which was totally dedicated to the Sun. The pharaoh even changed his own name to Akhenaten, which meant 'beneficial to Aten,' the sun."

"What happened?" asked Peter.

"It didn't work. He found out that even the Pharaoh can't change people when they don't want to change. The traditional priesthood resisted, and the common people were afraid that it could bring on the wrath of the other gods. After his death, our country returned to its former ways."

"I didn't know that," Peter commented. "When I lived in Galilee, Egypt seemed far, far away."

"Travel and commerce are bringing us closer."

"Yes."

"You know," added Kenamon, "I like everything I've heard about Jesus, but I have one reservation."

"What is that?" Peter asked.

"Well it's about—you know."

"What?"

"You know—the cutting."

"Do you mean circumcision?"

"That's it! I mean—how coarse and primitive, in this day and age. And I'm told it's painful for grown men."

Peter laughed. "That's why I'm going to Jerusalem. We are holding a council on that very matter. Before you are ready to be received into the Church, the whole matter may be resolved."

"Oh! How relieved am I to hear that. And my friends think it's ridiculous."

"Don't worry too much about it. We'll see what we can do."

All eyes turned as Kenamon's wife came out to where they were. She was younger than her husband and quite trim. She was wearing the traditional figure-hugging, semitransparent linen dress of Egyptian women and quite a bit of kohl around her eyes and ochre on her cheeks. "Ah…Redji. Come meet these fine men."

As the introductions were made, Clement studied the woman's hair. It was light brown with highlights that were almost golden—very non-Egyptian. "I can't help noticing your hair," the youth blurted. Then realizing the indiscretion added, "I'm sorry if I was too forward."

"That's all right," his host assured him. "Redji's mother was European—a slave from where, we do not know. My wife is both Egyptian and European."

"My mother had beautiful hair," the woman added. Her master named her Sati, which means 'sunbeam.' She died when I was ten."

"And he took very good care of Redji—until I came along."

The woman blushed. "You have been good to me too, my Husband."

"We only have each other, now that my parents also have passed on. We are happy together—and with our daughter. She will join us for dinner."

At that moment their daughter emerged from the doorway—a radiant young maiden with cheeks as smooth as fresh cream. Clement could not even breathe. Her hair was the color of cinnamon with highlights of gold.

"Peter—Clement—this is Sati. We named her after her grandmother."

7

Clement could hardly contain himself. When they sat down for dinner he was placed across from Sati, and he could catch glimpses of her without staring. Her complexion was as smooth as silk with only a hint of color brushed on her cheeks and a thin trace outlining her eyes.

He wanted to speak to her, but his tongue was frozen. When she looked his way, he smiled—which she modestly returned.

Did she smile at me? he wondered. *I'll have to wait until she looks this way again to be sure. Oh, what a goddess she is. Even in my dreams I never imagined anyone so beautiful. Is this real, or am I dreaming again?*

Oh. Did she glance my way? Clement wasn't sure.

The meal was a blur. The servant brought courses of fine local fare: cormorants, flamingos, apricots, vegetables, dates, and different types of bread. The youth accepted the delicacies, but hardly ate a thing.

Clement wasn't even listening to the table conversation, which was focused on Jesus. Kenamon, as he had said, had many questions. Peter was answering them as rapidly as his host was asking.

As they finished the meal, the lady of the house remarked, "I'd like to know about Jesus's mother. It reveals a great deal about a man."

"Certainly." Peter replied. "Her name was Miryam—we translate that as Mary. She was of a priestly family, but both of her parents died when she was a little girl. They had consecrated her to the Lord, and she was living in the temple quarters. She was a very devout child."

"What happened then?" Redji asked.

"When she got a little older, they placed her in the care of a man named Joseph, who was of the line of David, our most glorious king. Joseph lived in Galilee, in the hills just part way around the lake from where I was born. Joseph and Mary became betrothed, and soon after that an angel came to her."

"An angel!"

"Yes, a messenger from God. The angel told her that she was chosen by God to bear his son. She had no relations with Joseph or any other man and asked, 'How can this be?' The angel said, 'The Holy Spirit will come upon you, and the power of the Most High will overshadow you. Therefore, the child to be born will be called Holy, Son of God.'"

"What did Mary say?"

"Mary was very decisive. She simply bowed her head and said, 'I am the handmaid of the Lord. May it be done to me according to your word.'"

"Was she not afraid?" asked Sati, who was listening attentively.

"Perhaps—I don't actually know. I was told she left immediately to visit her kinswoman, who was older and also with child. She stayed several months before returning."

"Was Joseph surprised?" Kenamon interjected.

"Of course. She was quite far along."

"And what did he do?"

"Joseph was an upright man and thought of divorcing her quietly. But an angel of the Lord appeared to him in a dream and told him to accept the child and to take Mary as his wife. They loved each other and were very good parents for Jesus. His mother taught him his prayers, and Joseph brought him to the rabbis for instruction."

"That is all so reassuring," said Redji. "With so good of a mother, I'm sure she raised a fine son."

"Oh yes."

Kenamon had many more questions, but his wife stood up to withdraw to the interior of the house. When Sati rose as well, Clement quickly sputtered, "I would love to see the view. Do you have a balcony?"

As the men turned back to their discussion, Redji waved, "Show him, dear."

The view was spectacular. A bright moon illuminated the city, a thousand stars sparkled in the heavens, and a faint pink glow clung to the western horizon. As they gazed out toward the harbor they saw a myriad of ships peacefully rocking and bobbing as if under the care and protection of the lighthouse, like a giant hen looking after her chicks.

Sati pointed toward another magnificent structure, "That's the Temple of Serapis—where the first collection of books are held—and the other buildings house the rest of our great library."

"It's so beautiful," Clement exclaimed.

"And there, you can see the Temple of Saturn, near the theater."

"Oh, yes," he sighed, looking down her slender arm and off the tips of her graceful fingers. "And those obelisks are so tall."

"They're the ones we have left. You Romans took the others."

The young man gulped. He had seen several of the tall monuments in his city and knew of their origin. "Some of us in Rome are not like the ones who conquered."

"Oh. So you are not a typical Roman?"

"Not really. Actually, I'm just learning who I am."

"On this journey? Why are you traveling with your bishop?"

"Peter asked me to come. I'm learning a lot. I know I don't want to go into business with my father."

"Is it a bad business?"

"It's probably all right. He provides eggs to the household of the emperor. He and my brothers are making a good profit, but I can't stand the thought of doing that the rest of my life."

"I hate my father's business," Sati confided.

"Why? Doesn't he handle ivory? So many beautiful objects are made from it."

"They kill the elephants and cut off the tusks. Then they just leave the carcasses to rot in the sun. He doesn't want me to know those things, but I found out."

"How awful."

"The native people up the river do it. My father just buys the tusks and resells them. But to me, that only makes it worse. Elephants are such magnificent animals. It seems so senseless for such gentle creatures to live their whole lives only to be killed for their tusks. The gods must cringe when they see it."

"I see—when you put it that way."

"I care about such things. I hunger for goodness and truth."

"So do I," Clement exclaimed. "I want to have a purpose in life, and I'm hoping to find it on this trip."

"Finding your purpose is important. Will you serve in the Church?"

"I don't know. I studied philosophy, but I don't have a passion for it. I'm not sure what church leaders do, but I certainly am impressed with Peter. He is one of the finest men I've ever met."

"You will find your purpose. I'm sure you will."

Clement didn't reply. For a moment he just stood there gazing at the view. Then he turned toward her and revealed his greatest secret, "I've dreamed of meeting a girl like you."

Sati blushed. "Am I so special?"

"I've dreamt of your hair and your eyes and your lips and…"

The girl put her fingers to his mouth, "How can you say that? You just met me."

"It's true! On the bow of the ship I had a vision of you—exactly you—until two white birds called and broke the spell."

"Oh, Clement."

He reached his right hand around her back and gently touched it with his fingertips. She seemed to move toward him an imperceptible distance. Increasing the pressure he pulled her closer, and she did not resist. He looked deep into her eyes, now filled with awe and wonder.

He could feel her warm breath and inhaled the sweet scent she wore. Leaning toward her even more, his left hand found her shoulder—soft and supple like a baby's cheek. Then as his fingers moved up her neck, she arched it and yielded an almost silent sigh that seemed to ask for more. He responded by caressing her neck with touches so soft and gentle that she wiggled her head and giggled.

Moving his head closer and circling her further with his right arm, he brought her so close that her tender breasts brushed against his chest, sending a sensuous tingle through his entire body. He felt a force—new and masculine—telling him that he was no longer a boy and propelling him to bring his lips to hers.

She still was looking into his eyes when their lips met, but then she closed them and put her arms around his ribs. For a moment time stood still and the cosmos slowed to a halt, as if they were the only two on this planet—drinking in the wonder of the other. He pulled her body to his and caressed up her neck into her hair. Then feeling unfathomable power surging through his veins, he kissed her harder and felt the soft folds of her smooth lips press onto his. Nothing could separate them. It was if his whole life had prepared him for this moment, and he was giving himself to it fully.

He didn't breathe. He couldn't. Squeezing her tighter, he ran his left hand further into her hair and pressed her head until their teeth met with a click. Then he drew back and gasped for air.

Her eyes opened and she gazed at him with astonishment for what seemed like minutes. Then she brought her hands up to his cheeks and held them tight while she returned his kiss with a boldness she had never imagined. She didn't let go of them until her lips hurt and she felt a bond with him that could last a lifetime.

Pulling apart they both grinned—and then chuckled out loud with joy.

"We must go in," she said.

"I know."

8

Clement could not possibly sleep. He was too delighted to even consider it. And he also wrestled over and over with his tormenting dilemma—how to pursue his new love when he and Peter were sailing away after only one more day. The situation seemed impossible.

An hour before dawn he remembered the advice the apostle gave him after his near disaster with the shopkeeper in Cyrene. He almost could hear the words out loud, "Did you pray about it?"

Dropping to his knees, the youth presented his difficulty to Christ. "Jesus, my Savior and my Lord, I bow before you with a terrible predicament. You know how I feel about Sati, and you know how my life at this point does not permit me to leave Peter and go to her. I don't know what to do, so I am turning to you. Help me to find the way. Help me to see through the fog that clouds my life. Help me to be faithful to Sati and to my family and to you. You are my only hope at this hour. Please, please heed my prayer."

Then he relaxed into a deep, but brief, period of sleep.

At breakfast Peter asked him, "Did you sleep well?"

"Fairly well," he lied.

"Maybe you didn't eat enough last night. You seemed lost in a cloud through the meal."

"I'm all right. What are our plans for the day?"

Bishop Marcus answered, "We are going to see our largest gathering place and then come back and talk some more. Will you come with us?"

"Perhaps. Will Anianus be here?"

"I think that's him I hear now. Yes, it's him. Hello, Anianus—would you like something?"

"Thank you, but I had a full meal at home."

When he had the opportunity, Clement whispered to the presbyter, "Can you stay here? I'd like to speak with you. It's a private matter."

Anianus nodded.

When the bishops were ready to leave, the presbyter said, "Why don't the two of you go look at the building. I'll stay here and swap stories with Clement."

After they had gone, Clement explained, "I really appreciate your staying. I need to talk with someone and I don't think Peter will understand."

"Why not?" asked the presbyter.

"Because it's about a woman."

"Peter is a married man."

"Yes, but he's a man's man. I need to talk with someone who might help me."

"I see. And do I know the woman?"

"It's Sati."

"Oh."

Clement poured out the story of their visit to the balcony, how they seemed to have so much in common, and how he felt after the kiss. "I don't know what to do," he cried.

The older man put his arm around Clement's shoulder, "Well. Let's see how we can approach this."

"I will lose her if I leave this city."

"You are not yet grown, and you don't have a job. You are in no position to ask for a girl's love."

"That's the problem. By the time I am old enough, she may be married to someone else."

"Hmm. You have to go with Peter, you know. There is no other option."

"I know. But I don't want to lose her. I believe that she is the love of my life."

"How can you say that after just one kiss?"

Clement revealed how he had envisioned her on the ship. He told the whole story, including the part about the two white birds flying in unison.

"I wouldn't put too much stock in two white birds being a sign from Christ, but I can see how sincere you are. Maybe we should consider another option. What if you wrote a message to her? I can deliver it for you. You can state your feelings, and if she wants to have you return at a later date, then perhaps that will work out."

"And if she doesn't want to wait…"

"Well, if that is the case, you will have to accept it. Won't you?"

"It seems risky."

"I think it seems adult! You are on your way to becoming a man. You need to approach this like one."

Clement looked at the presbyter long and hard. "You are a good friend, Anianus. And you are right. If anything is to come of this, then both Sati and I will have to be patient."

"Do you love her enough to do that?"

"Yes. I believe I do."

"All right. And there is one more thing that you must promise before I deliver your message."

"What is that?"

"You must tell Peter the whole story."

"But he won't understand."

"He may not. But you are in his charge, and if you want me to do this for you, you must agree to explain it all to Peter, leaving nothing out and having everything said. You must tell the entire truth and get it out in the open. Will you promise that?"

"I love Sati, and I must let her know. So yes, I promise. I will tell Peter before we reach Caesarea."

In his room, Clement penned his message:

To Sati, my sunbeam, who holds the key to my heart—from Clement, your traveling admirer, who hates to leave your city: greetings.

If circumstances were different, I would never leave Alexandria until I had either won your love or knew that you cast me aside. I would come to your house daily, pledging my dedication to you and endeavoring to gain the confidence of your fine mother and father. But those are not my circumstances; those are not our circumstances.

Anianus helped me to see that now is not the time for me to pursue any woman. I have not reached a proper age, nor have I the means to live out such a decision. I must go on to Jerusalem with Peter and return to my parents in Rome. My hope is that in not too long of a time, I will be able to return to you and seek your love. I cannot ask you to wait for me. Your feelings may not be the same as mine. But I want you to know that I love you with all of my heart. From the moment I first laid eyes on you, I knew that you are the one for me, the girl of my dreams, and no other will ever take your place.

I am glad that we had the time to talk about our purposes in life. I believe that one of mine is to love you and to make you happy. My other purpose—how I serve others—will hopefully become clear soon. I have the best role model: Jesus Christ, who gave his life for all humanity. And I have the best of friends to support me along the way.

Please tell your parents that I plan to return as soon as I am able. I want them to understand my feelings and know that I will always do the best I can for their wonderful daughter.

While I have nothing tangible to offer you at this time, I am enclosing this simple token. The ichthys in the shape of a fish is an identifying symbol to those who follow the Christian life. Please keep it as a memento from me, the one who has no other words to convey except, I love you.

The next morning, after giving the letter to Anianus, Clement walked to the ship with Peter, holding his head high and praying that the God of Life would watch over his love until he could return.

9

The first day at sea, Clement decided he'd better do it. He had promised Anianus that he'd tell Peter the whole story and felt that he may as well get it over with. After the midday meal he just blurted it out. "I have something that I need to tell you. Is this a good time?"

They were relaxing on their cushions. Peter nodded.

"Well…it's about Sati and me."

The apostle looked at him with a blank stare.

"It makes me nervous to share this with you. You see—I am in love with her."

"I thought something was going on. You've been acting odd since the dinner with the ivory dealer."

Clement cleared his throat and spelled out everything that happened—the vision on the ship, the shock on meeting Sati, their discussion on the balcony, the kiss, and how he got Anianus to deliver the message. When he finished, he was shaking.

"So, what are you going to do now?"

"I'm going to try to pursue this with responsibility. I'll go with you to Jerusalem and when we get home, I'll share it with my parents. Anianus helped me to see that I need to take an adult approach. This will take a great deal of patience."

"You can say that again. How old are you now—seventeen? How are you going to get the money to come back here? Will you work for your father?" he asked.

"I will do what I have to do. I love Sati, and I want her to spend her life with me. I hope she will wait for me, but if she doesn't, then I will have to go on without her. In the meantime, I will pray to Jesus for guidance and try to approach everything with maturity."

"What do you mean by that?"

"I mean you don't need to concern yourself with this unless you want to. I'd like to just not talk too much about it and do the things we were planning to do. I've thought about it. Sati may be one of my purposes in life, but you have taught me so much on this trip. I'm hoping that I also will get more clarity on my vocational purpose. I respect you, Peter, and you inspire me. My mother hopes that I will grow closer to Christ on this voyage. Will you still help make that happen?"

The blank stare continued for what seemed interminable. Then the apostle broke out in a big wide grin and laughed out loud. "I think you are growing up, my son. Yes—you are growing up. Let's make the best of this opportunity."

"Thank you, Peter. You are a good friend."

"Yes, and by the way, you can talk to me about Sati anytime you want."

The next day Clement asked Peter to explain the issue that they would be discussing in Jerusalem.

Peter was glad that the young man was showing interest. "It has to do with what should be required of people who want to convert to the faith. This shouldn't be a complicated issue, but it depends upon where you are coming from. Jesus was a good Jew, and those who were Jews feel that the laws of the Jews are the foundation—they are God's laws, which apply to everyone. Those who have never been Jews see no logic in that. They are attracted not to the old covenant, but to Jesus, the new covenant."

"So how they feel depends upon their past experience."

"Exactly."

"How can you resolve it?"

"Both Paul and James are very stubborn. I don't think either will budge. They each are thinking of their people and what they believe is best for them. I'm hoping to find a middle ground, some reasonable compromise that we all can agree to."

"Have you thought of one?"

"Not exactly. But I've been thinking about the vision I had in Joppa."

"You had a vision too?"

"Yes. Two men were on their way to the city to tell me that a centurion in Caesarea named Cornelius wanted me to come and dine with him. He was God-fearing and good to the Jews. About noon I went up to the roof to pray. I was hungry and wanted to eat, but I fell into a trance. I saw heaven open and something resembling a large sheet coming down, lowered to the ground by its four corners. In it were all the earth's four-legged animals and reptiles and the birds of the sky. A voice said, 'Get up, Peter. Slaughter and eat.' I said, 'Certainly not. For never have I eaten anything profane and unclean.' Then the voice said, 'What God has made clean, you are not to call profane.' This happened three times, and then the object was taken up into the sky."

"Amazing! What did you do?"

"I didn't know what it meant. But as I was pondering it, the men came and asked me to go with them to the house of the centurion. I went, and when we got there I said to them, 'In truth, I see that God shows no partiality. Rather, in every nation whoever fears God and acts uprightly is acceptable to him.' Then I began relating all that Jesus had done that proved he was the Son of God, and while I was speaking the Holy Spirit fell upon all who were listening. So I ordered them to be baptized in the name of Jesus Christ, and they invited me to stay a few more days."

"Did that settle the issue?

"Well, the brothers in Judea got word of it, and when I went up to Jerusalem they confronted me saying, 'You entered the house of uncircumcised people and ate with them.' So I explained the whole thing, step by step. I said, 'I saw how the Holy Spirit came upon them. If God gave them the same gift he gave to us when we came to believe in Jesus, who was I to hinder God.' The matter seemed settled at the time. That was over ten years ago. And since then Paul has gone on a long missionary journey and has gained many converts."

"Then why is the issue coming up again?"

"A lot has happened since then." Peter paused and thought about what he should share. "Paul was very successful in his travels, but in Judea we were having many struggles. About seven years ago, King Herod began persecuting us. He had James, the brother of John, killed by the sword. And I was put in prison again."

"How did you get out?"

"I'll tell you that story later—angels helped free me. But James, the brother of the Lord, had by that time assumed a great deal of the leadership in the Jerusalem community. I felt liberated, actually, not just from prison, but from Jerusalem. I told those I was with to tell James I was released, and I left the city. I had to get away from Herod; it was too dangerous for me to stay. So I went to another place."

"Where did you go?"

"To Antioch."

"Did the persecution last long?"

"Not too much longer."

"Did you go back?"

"No. I've not been back. After a little while in Antioch, I realized that I had been too focused on Jerusalem. If the Church was to go forth to all nations, then I needed to broaden my perspective as well. Jerusalem was in the hands of James. There was a good leader in Antioch—Evodius. So I left him in charge there and came to Rome. That was in the second year of Claudius."

"You make it sound like you were pushed out of your country."

"In a way, I was. But that is often how the Lord works."

"What do you mean?"

"I mean—we who follow Christ don't make our decisions in isolation. Sometimes it seems as though we are led. I didn't want to leave my country, but it turned out for the better. When Jesus calls us to something new, we don't necessarily hear him speak in words. Most of the time the circumstances push us to where he wants us to go. It's like he makes use of the circumstances to move us."

"Amazing! I had no idea. Do you think I will be led?"

"You very likely will be."

It was sunny, as usual, when the ship arrived in Caesarea, which the Romans used as a hub to control the region.

The beautiful city and harbor were built by King Herod the Great in honor of Augustus, his patron. Originally dubbed Caesarea Palestinea, the city soon came to be known as Caesarea Maritima for its location on the sea routes between Alexandria and Antioch.

The harbor was the largest artificial facility ever built in the open sea, with two immense jetties, the largest over a quarter mile long. Breakwaters were made of lime and *pozzolana*, a type of volcanic ash carried by ship from Pozzuoli, Italy, set into an underwater concrete. It is estimated that the project required at least seventeen thousand tons of the ash along with a vast amount of rubble and lime.

Both the theater and oblong racetrack faced the sea, where spectators could watch the festivities while enjoying the cool sea breeze and observing the movements of the ships.

Caesarea became the civilian and military capital of the Palestine Province and the official residence of the Roman procurator Antonius Felix and prefect Pontius Pilate.

Peter was overjoyed to be back in his homeland. As soon as he got his feet on solid ground he dropped his bag, stretched out his arms, and danced to the music of his youth he heard ringing in his head.

Clement laughed. It was good to see his friend so happy. *"I love this man,"* he snickered as he tried to picture the older man at his own age.

The Galilean led the way. "It's getting on in the day, and we should look for an inn. Is it all right with you, if we go to a Jewish one? I am hungry for the tastes and smells of my homeland."

"Certainly. Does Caesarea have both?"

"Yes. The Jewish ones are not far."

That evening Peter talked nonstop about the food, the wine, and the many Jewish customs. He ate quite a lot, savoring every bite, and drank more than he should have. It was not long before he fell fast asleep.

Clement, not as accustomed to the flavors, did not take as much, and he stayed wide awake. His thoughts soon centered on the girl with the golden hair. For a long while he simply laid on his cot, picturing her beauty and imagining what she might be doing at that hour. Then he lifted his thoughts to Christ and prayed in a whisper, "Jesus, my Lord, you know how I love Sati and you know how I am trying to be as responsible as possible in these times. I entrust her to you. Take care of her and help her to know how devoted I am to her. Make the pathway easy for her family to approach the waters of baptism. See that she does not lose heart as she waits for me to return. Thank you, Jesus. I trust in you."

10

Anianus arranged to see Sati privately. They met just inside of the main entrance of one of the library buildings and moved to a quiet spot, public enough that it would not arouse suspicion and private enough that they would not be overheard.

"Thank you for coming, Sati. Were you told that I have a message from Clement?"

"Yes," she said nervously.

"It's about his feelings for you and his responsibilities in these circumstances."

"Tell me! Tell me! I've been sobbing all night since Thursday."

"I am here to do precisely that, but first I must ask you to agree to one condition. Will you share with your parents how I came to deliver the message to you?"

"Why do they need to know?"

"I made Clement make the same promise. He may have told Peter by now. You both are not yet grown, and as a presbyter, I do not sneak behind the parents' back to deliver messages to their children."

"I see. All right, I agree."

"Good. In Alexandria it is customary for young people to choose their lovers, and they often use another trusted person to deliver private messages. However, that is not a role that we presbyters customarily fill."

"I can understand that. What did he say?"

"Clement sent you a letter. It's in his own handwriting."

Taking the letter in her trembling hands and looking it over, she recognized only some of the words and asked Anianus to read it. He read it slowly and gently, pausing at the important points. When he finished the last line, she dropped to the floor, sobbing.

"Please rise and compose yourself. This is a public place."

She reached up, and he took her hand to help her to her feet. He smiled, and she fell crying against his chest.

"There, there," he comforted her. "You will get through this."

"I love him. I love him with all my heart. I can't stand the thought of being

37

apart from him."

"This may require you to be patient. I told Clement the same thing."

His words made her break down again in deep, anguishing sobs. Her tears were wetting his garment, but he was more concerned about someone seeing them and getting the wrong idea. "Please pull yourself together. If you love each other as you profess, then you both will need to act prudently. It may require much patience."

"I know," she cried. "But does he know how I feel? I want him to know."

"Clement is not sure how you feel, as he says in the letter."

"But he must know. I will be in anguish until he knows. Will you tell him for me?"

The presbyter paused for a moment, pondering the options. "If you write a letter to Clement—I don't know how to get it to him in Jerusalem, but I can forward it to him in Rome. I'll send it via Peter."

"If that is the only way, then that is what we must do. My heart is breaking."

"All right. What day can you meet me here again? I'll take your letter and send it to Rome."

"Can you write it for me, if I tell you what to say?"

"Yes. I will do that."

"Thank you," she sobbed. "I can return here in two days."

"Good. And by the way, here is the bronze image that Clement mentioned in his letter."

Sati took the ichthys in her shaking hands and pressed it to her lips. She wanted to reply but could only break out again in a flood of tears.

"And pray, my child. Pray to Jesus." Anianus bowed to her sincerely and left the building.

Two days later Sati returned to the library. She waited calmly for Anianus, who appeared soon.

"Hello, Sati. How are you today?"

"Thanks for coming. I miss Clement, but I'm accepting the fact that we may have a long wait."

"I'm glad that you see it that way. You and Clement may have a long future together. You'll just have to see."

"Yes."

"Let's sit over there, where I can take some notes for your letter. What would you like to say to him?"

"Can I just say the words to you?"

"Yes, of course. But go slowly so that I can write them."

"Please write this:

From Sati, your faithful friend in Alexandria—to Clement of Rome, my love forever: greetings.

I received your message and was very moved that you spoke so boldly of your feelings. I love you as well. I am getting more certain each passing day.

It will be difficult for me to wait through all the uncertainty. In addition to your not knowing how soon you will be in a position to return, I also may be receiving pressure from my parents to become betrothed. Although the choice should be mine, I am getting to the age where such things are expected.

I love the ichthys you gave me, and I will treasure it always. Kissing it makes me feel close to you. It also reminds me of your faith, which will become my faith, as I wish to become a Christian as soon as possible. I know that your God, our God, is smiling on our love. I will ask Anianus to teach me to pray, and I will pray for you and for us every day until we are again in each other's arms. I believe that we can overcome all obstacles if we remain faithful in our love and steadfast in our dedication.

I am enclosing a small gift to you. When you look at it or kiss it, or when you see what is inside, remember how I kissed you on the balcony and how I want to smother you with my kisses so much again.

I love you with all my heart."

"That's a beautiful letter," whispered Anianus. "I'm sure that Clement will love it."

"Thank you for all that you are doing for us. Here is my gift to him. It's an ivory locket."

"How exquisite. It's lovely."

"Can you teach me to pray?"

"Of course. Christian prayer is not difficult. You just focus your mind on the Lord and say what is in your heart, either silently or out loud. Can you do that?"

"Yes. I will do that every day."

After pausing for a moment, the presbyter added, "When are you planning to share this with your parents?"

"I won't put it off. I don't know how they will feel, but I want to do it within the next few days."

Anianus folded the page and picked up the locket. Then he sighed and smiled.

Sati stood up, smiled, and patted him on the cheek. "You are a good man. And I am becoming a…a good woman."

11

During its long history, Jerusalem has been attacked fifty-two times, captured forty-four times, and destroyed at least twice. The oldest part of the city dates from the fourth millennium BC, making it one of the oldest in the world. Ceramic finds point to human occupation as far back as the Copper Age, and there is evidence of a permanent settlement during the early Bronze Age.

The city has been the spiritual center of the Jewish people since about 1000 BC, when King David established it as the capital of the Jewish nation, and his son Solomon commissioned the building of the first temple on Mount Moriah. During the First Temple Period, Jerusalem was the capital of the Kingdom of Israel and the temple was the religious and political center of the nation. The period ended around 586 BC, when the Babylonian ruler Nebuchadnezzar II destroyed the temple and took the able-bodied Jews captive. In 538 BC, after years of Babylonian captivity, the Persian King Cyrus the Great defeated Babylon and allowed the Jews to return to rebuild their city. Construction of the second temple was completed in 516 BC, seventy years after the destruction of the first.

When Alexander the Great conquered the Persian Empire, Jerusalem fell into Macedonian control. Then in 198 BC, Ptolemy V lost the region to the Seleucids under Antiochus III. The Seleucids attempted to turn Jerusalem into a Hellenized city, but that failed in 168 BC with the Maccabean revolt led by High Priest Mattathias.

In 63 BC Rome reconquered the region and installed Herod as a Jewish client king. Herod the Great, as he became known, devoted himself to developing and beautifying the city. He built walls, towers, and palaces, and expanded the Temple Mount, buttressing the court areas with blocks of stone weighing up to one hundred tons. After Herod's death, the city, as well as much of the surrounding area, came under direct Roman rule with Herod's descendants as client kings.

Peter seemed tense as they approached the city.

"What are you thinking?" Clement asked.

"Oh, many things," he answered. "There has been so much death here—

Jesus, Stephen, my fishing friend James. Many others too."

"I thought it might be the council."

"That too."

"When will it begin?"

"When we are all here," he muttered. "I've been thinking. I'd like to go directly to the home of some friends in the lower city and send word that I have arrived. We will do our sightseeing afterward."

"That's all right with me. It sounds like you want to deal with the important things first."

Word came back that Paul, Barnabas, and some others already had arrived and were welcomed by the community, but some former Pharisees were demanding that they order their converts to be circumcised and observe the Mosaic law.

"So the debate has already started," Peter fretted. "Let's join them and stir things up."

When the two travelers entered the room, the conversation came to an abrupt halt. James stepped forward and greeted Peter, "It is good that you are here. I hope you have been well." The Jerusalem leader was tall and lean with a long greying beard that failed to hide a constant solemn scowl. Clement thought he looked arrogant.

"I've been very well. We had a fine voyage."

"And who did you bring with you?"

Peter introduced Clement to James and the presbyters who were present, most of whom he knew by name. When he came to a stocky bearded man with a high forehead, he paused and reached out his hand. "Hello, Paul. I hear that you have been very successful in your mission to the Gentiles. That is such fine news."

The balding apostle took Peter's hand and pulled it to embrace him, but both men were stiff, and the kiss was clumsy. "I owe much to the good beginning you gave us, Peter," he declared.

Clement sensed that both greetings seemed forced.

Then moving to the center of the room, Peter immediately addressed them, "My brothers, you are well aware that from early days God made his choice among you that through my mouth the Gentiles would hear the word of the gospel and believe. And God, who knows the heart, bore witness by granting them the Holy Spirit just as he did us. He made no distinction between us and them, for by faith he purified their hearts. Why then, are you now putting God to the test by placing on the shoulders of the disciples a yoke that neither our ancestors nor we have been able to bear? On the contrary, we believe that we are saved through the grace of the Lord Jesus, in the same way as they."

The room remained silent. Then Paul and Barnabas began describing some of the signs and wonders God had worked among the Gentiles through them.

James raised his arms for quiet, assumed an authoritative posture, and spoke, "My brothers, listen to me. Simon has described how God first concerned himself with acquiring from among the Gentiles a people for his name. It is my judgment, therefore, that we ought to stop troubling the Gentiles who turn to God, but tell them by letter to avoid pollution from idols, unlawful marriage, the meat of strangled animals, and blood. For Moses, for generations now, has had those who proclaim him in every town, as he has been read in the synagogues every Sabbath."

Then the apostles and presbyters decided to choose representatives and send them to Antioch with Paul and Barnabas. The ones chosen were Judas, who was called Barsabbas, and Silas, leaders among the brothers. Copies were made of the letter for distribution:

> *The apostles and the presbyters, your brothers, to the brothers in Antioch, Syria, and Cilicia of Gentile origin: greetings.*
> *Since we have heard that some of our number who went out without any mandate from us have upset you with their teachings and disturbed your peace of mind, we have with one accord decided to choose representatives and send them to you along with our beloved Barnabas and Paul, who have dedicated their lives to the name of our Lord Jesus Christ. So we are sending Judas and Silas who will also convey this same message by word of mouth: It is the decision of the Holy Spirit and of us not to place on you any burden beyond these necessities, namely, to abstain from meat sacrificed to idols, from blood, from meats of strangled animals, and from unlawful marriage. If you keep free of these, you will be doing what is right. Farewell.*

That was it. Peter and Clement left the house and never went back.

12

That evening Clement asked Peter, "Was that easier than you expected?"

"The matter was agreed upon years ago. I don't know what caused it to come up again, so I didn't know how long the council might take. Paul was patient, which is unusual for him, and James was reasonable. Thank God that they were not their usual selves. Anyway, I'm glad it's over."

"You really don't like them, do you?" the young man asserted.

"It's not a matter of liking them or not liking them. Leadership in the Church is like leadership in anything else. You have to do what you can to bring people together. That requires assessing their personalities and guiding them along. I don't think too much about whether or not I like them."

"You are good at it."

"When I was young, I let my emotions take control. Now I'm more practical."

"I wonder if I will ever be a leader. I still don't know my purpose."

Peter paused before responding. "I believe that you can be a great leader. I see the qualities in you. But whatever you endeavor, you need to begin with what you can handle—and in what you care deeply about. Then as time goes by and you learn more, that's when you may be able to offer leadership."

"I think I understand."

Peter continued, "It was natural for our new Church to adopt a structure of deacons, presbyters, and bishops. A young man like you begins by serving, then moves to take care of a flock, and then goes on to become a leader, if the people elect you."

"Is there also an order among bishops?"

"The Church's understanding is that each bishop is the leader in his own city, but some cities are more important than others. Alexandria, Antioch, and Rome are the largest in the empire, and Jerusalem is very important to Christians. So these cities have more influence. That's why I left Antioch to go to Rome. I liked living in Antioch, but I could see that Rome was where I needed to be."

"I sure am glad that you came."

"Well, I'm glad too...So, shall we make plans for what we will see in

Jerusalem?"

"Yes!" the young man shouted. "What do you think?"

"I'm sure that you want to see the temple. We can do that tomorrow. And tomorrow night I'll take you to the garden where Jesus prayed at the time he was betrayed. There's much more beyond that. It will take us a few days."

"That sounds perfect. I'd like to see everything."

"Yes. And the council was so brief that we have plenty of time now. I'm up for going on to Galilee, if you'd like. There is much to see there too."

"That sounds wonderful. You lead, and I will follow."

That night both men slept peacefully. Clement thought of Sati and wondered how she was. For a long while he held her close and ran his fingers through her beautiful hair. Then he dropped into a deep slumber.

"This sure is a noisy place—so many people," the young traveler exclaimed in the morning.

"This is nothing compared to the crowds at the festivals," Peter commented.

Everyone was heading in the same direction—to the Temple Mount. It loomed over the lower city like a giant buttress of stone and marble. Roman engineers helped King Herod construct huge granite walls that held an enormous platform, over of a quarter mile long and nearly half as wide, with sides soaring up to ten stories above the ground. It took eighteen months using an estimated ten thousand laborers. On the plaza above were roofed colonnades all along the perimeter, housing vendors, and other activities that supported the temple operation.

"Is that the entrance?" asked the youth, pointing to a graceful set of steps arching over a street.

"Those are for the priests," Peter answered, as he led his friend to a lower set of broad steps leading to a pair of arches. "Pilgrims go in here." Inside, they ascended through semi-dark passageways until they arrived at the upper court, where the sun again was blinding. "This is the way Jesus entered each time he came to the temple."

"Did he come here often?" the youth asked.

"Joseph and Mary would have brought him here shortly after he was born to present him to the Lord and to make the necessary sin-offering as prescribed in the Law of Moses."

"How could a little baby have committed a sin?"

"He hadn't, and he never did. The sin-offering was required for the first child that opens the womb."

"Did every couple have to pay it?"

"Yes. That was the law. The next time he came here was when he was about twelve years old. I'm told that his parents came every year at Passover, but the first time they brought him for the festival, he got lost."

"Lost!"

"Not actually lost. When they headed back to Nazareth, he just stayed here."

"Didn't they miss him?"

"Not until they had journeyed for a day. It was a large caravan. They thought he was with relatives."

"What did they do?"

"They hurried back and searched for him diligently for three days, finally finding him in the temple, talking with the priests and asking them questions. All who heard him were amazed at his wisdom and understanding."

"Were his parents angry?"

"Mary and Joseph? Certainly. They had been very worried. His mother asked him, 'Son, why have you done this to us?' and he gave kind of a sharp reply."

"What did he say?"

"He said, 'Do you not know, woman, that I must be at work in my Father's house!' The first time I heard that, I thought, 'I would have slapped the boy.'"

"Did they?"

"No. Jesus was very attracted to the temple. He wanted to stay longer, but he went back to Nazareth with them and was subject to them."

Satisfied with the older man's answer, Clement headed toward the temple building. "Let's go see it."

"You can't go in!" Peter cautioned. "Only Jews are allowed past this court."

"I can't go in? Why not?"

"Well, that is the law. It's the most sacred place for the Jewish people, and only the priests can go inside."

"That's not very welcoming."

"It's not about being welcoming. Jews, as you know, maintain strict boundaries between themselves and Gentiles. You are lucky that you get to come this far. Let's look around."

The two spent the next half hour studying the beautiful details of the temple exterior. Then Peter explained another custom, "Over here are the money-changers and the booths where they sell doves and sheep for sacrifice. Pilgrims from Galilee can't carry their animals all the way, so they buy them here."

"It seems so—close."

"They used to sell them down below, but by the time we came with Jesus, they had moved their booths up here."

"What did he think of that?"

"He didn't like it one bit. He made a whip out of cords and drove out the animals and upset the tables of the money-changers. We were shocked."

"So were the money-changers, I bet."

"Ha! Them too…Jesus quoted the prophet Isaiah where it is written, 'My house shall be a house of prayer, but you are making it a den of thieves.' That stopped them short because they knew it was true."

"But they are back."

"Yes. They were back the next day. Jesus had made a point, though, and the people were getting it. The whole system was a burden on the poor that only enriched the wealthy."

"I see."

"When the original temple was founded, its purpose was to worship God and to provide food for the poor. But by our time there was little redistribution. It was all going to support the priestly class in lavish comfort. You see, Christ was never against proper worship. It was the drain on the poor that he tried to stop."

"So he failed to stop it?"

"Stopping it for one day blew the cover off of the system. The people were getting the message. That's when the conspiracy against him got serious."

"Tell me more about that."

"I will. I'll do that tonight when we go to the garden. Now I'm getting hungry. Are you?"

The silver moon over the Garden of Gethsemane gave plenty of light for Peter to find the way.

"The night was like this one," he explained. "There were a few clouds, and a partial moon was casting an eerie glow over the olive trees. When we finished dinner, we came here by crossing the Kidron Valley—the way we just came. Jesus liked this place. When he was in the city, he came here to pray. The chief priests and the scribes were seeking a way to arrest him and put him to death. They didn't want to do it during the festival for fear that it might cause a riot. Then Judas Iscariot went off to them, and when they heard him they offered him thirty pieces of silver. Judas led them here that night."

"Right while Jesus was praying."

"Yes. Judas left the dinner early."

"What did you do?"

"When we got here, Jesus said, 'Sit here while I pray.' Then taking James, John, and me a little farther with him, he began to be troubled and distressed. Then he said to us, 'My soul is sorrowful even to death. Remain here and keep watch.' We stayed while he advanced a bit farther. Then he dropped to the ground—by that rock right there—and prayed that if it were possible, the cup might pass him by. He prayed for a long time. The three of us fell asleep."

"How could you sleep at a time like that?"

"We didn't know the guards were coming. We wouldn't have stayed. I'm sure we wouldn't have."

"But Jesus knew, and he remained here."

"Yes. He may have been tempted to leave. That would have given him more time. He was quite forlorn. I saw him sweating—at night!"

"Was he afraid?" Clement asked.

"Looking back—I believe that he suffered every possible emotion: fear, disillusionment, abandonment, grief. But then his mood changed to utter determination. He prayed, 'Father, not what I will, but what you will.'"

"He made his decision?"

"Yes. He chose to stay. It was an unselfish act of sheer love."

"It certainly was."

"He simply submitted to his destiny."

"What an exceptional man."

"Then suddenly they came—guards and a crowd with swords and clubs! Judas stepped forward and gave Jesus a kiss, the prearranged signal, and they seized him! We all fled into the night."

"Judas betrayed him with a kiss?"

"Yes, a kiss. He probably thought that it wouldn't arouse his suspicion, but Jesus foresaw it all."

"And you just ran away."

"As fast as we could—in all directions. I'm still ashamed of what I did."

"Where did they take him?"

"I'll show you that tomorrow. I wanted you to first experience what it was like here at night."

"I'm glad that you did," Clement said. "Will you wait here while I go over to the rock and pray for a little while?"

"Of course."

Clement went to the rock. A small cloud had dimmed the moonlight, but he could see the outline of the temple across the valley. Dropping to the ground he lifted his eyes to the sparkling stars and poured out his heart, "Jesus, I know

I am not worthy to pray by the rock where you prayed. Forgive my boldness, but I wish to tell you how I feel. You continue to amaze me and inspire me. I am so grateful that Peter brought me to this holy place. I am beginning to understand your beautiful teachings and your awesome love, and I'm sure I will learn more in the coming days. Help me to have the faith that I see in Peter. Help me to submit to my destiny. Show me what you want of me, and I will do my best to do it…And please watch over my Sati, my lovely sunbeam. Keep her safe. Help her to know that I am thinking of her this very night. You know how I love her. I am very grateful for all the ways you have blessed my life."

13

In Alexandria the next morning, Sati decided that it was time to tell her parents about Clement. She chose to tell her mother first, while her father was out. Sati felt close to her mother and was not afraid to bring things up with her. "Mother, can I tell you something?"

"What is it, dear?"

"It's about Clement."

"Who?"

"Clement, the young man who was here with Anianus and Peter."

"Oh. Clement. He didn't say much that evening."

This made Sati a little nervous, but she kept talking, "On the balcony, we had a long talk. He is a remarkable young man."

"Oh. He seemed younger. How old is he—about seventeen, perhaps?"

"I think so. Anyway, we had a long talk about what is important to us in life and things like that."

"What does he find important?"

"Well…he's searching for that. He wants to find a worthy purpose, perhaps in the Church. That's why he is traveling with his bishop."

"When he grows up he will find his way."

"Yes. His father has a good business. They provide eggs to the household of the emperor."

"Eggs! How quaint."

"They make plenty of money."

"That's good."

The conversation didn't seem to be going well, so Sati just blurted out, "We are in love, Mother."

"What? In love! You only had one conversation."

"I know. But we talked about important things, and we kissed, and…"

"You kissed!?" complained her mother. "Why would you kiss him, when you don't even know him?"

"It's just happened. It was only one kiss."

"Kisses don't just happen. Someone initiates it. Did he force himself on you?"

"No! Of course not. Clement is not like that. He looked at me and drew me close. Then we kissed—twice actually—and we laughed because we knew we were in love. Then we came in."

"I hardly feel this is something to laugh about."

"It was a joyful laugh. We were happy that we both felt the same way."

"Well—he's gone now. Didn't they say they were going to Jerusalem?"

"Yes. And then back to Rome. He will explain this to his parents and then come back for me."

"You are not leaving for a foreign country with a boy you hardly know! And we know nothing about his family."

"Clement will be responsible. And I won't run away."

"No, you won't! So, when does he plan to come back?"

"That's the problem. It can't be right away. He needs to get established first—I said he is very responsible. It could take years."

"Years? You know, dear, you are getting to the age when you should be betrothed. Your father and I were talking about that. You can't just wait forever."

"I know this is complicated. I wanted to begin by simply confiding in you. He wrote me a letter, and I sent one to him in Rome. I have no choice but to just wait and see."

"How did you write a letter?"

"I know quite a few words," she lied.

"So, you feel you are in love, you sent a letter, and you plan to wait and see what develops?"

"Yes. That's all I can do right now."

"Are you planning to tell your father?"

"Of course. But I wanted to speak with you first."

"I want you to be happy, Sati. You should be allowed to choose your own love, but there are so many unknowns in this."

"Yes. That's the difficulty. But I love him, Mother. I love him with all my heart."

Hearing a sound, they turned toward the doorway. Kenamon stormed in looking very upset.

"You are home sooner than we expected, dear."

"I'm too angry to do anything else today!" he exclaimed. "Do you know what that Marcus told me?"

Neither answered. They just stared at his scowling his eyes.

"Those Christians are idiots! They want me to give my money away to the poor. They want me to bow to people who are beneath me. They told me I have to love my enemies. And I think they still want to cut off my foreskin! I can't stand them. I told that so-called holy man that I'm through, and I stormed out of his house."

Sati and her mother looked at one another in shock. They were speechless, and this certainly was not the time to bring up the topic of Clement.

14

Peter took Clement to the house of the high priest to explain what happened after Jesus was arrested, "They brought him here, to Caiaphas, and he called a meeting of the high council. I followed at a distance and watched from the outer courtyard."

"This building is enormous—a palace."

"Yes. A lot goes on here. It's the center of the Jewish government."

"Where did you stand?"

"The guards had built a fire right there," Peter pointed to an inner court, "and were warming themselves, so I just joined them for a while. We heard from people going in and out that the priests were trying to obtain testimony against Jesus, so they could put him to death. Many gave false witness against him, but their testimony did not agree."

"What happened then?"

"The high priest rose and questioned Jesus, saying, 'Have you no answer? What are these men testifying against you?' But Jesus was silent. So the high priest asked him bluntly, 'Are you the Messiah, the son of the Blessed One?' Then Jesus answered, 'I am,' and with that the high priest tore his garments, saying, 'What further need have we of witnesses? You have heard the blasphemy. What do you think?' They all condemned him as deserving to die.'"

"What did they do next?"

"They blindfolded him and struck him, saying, 'Prophesy!' That's when I failed him."

"You failed him! How?"

"While that was going on, I was here in the courtyard, like I told you, warming myself. One of the high priest's maids came along. Seeing me, she looked at me and said, 'You too were with Jesus the Nazarene,' but I denied it and went out to the outer court. The maid saw me again and said to the bystanders, 'This man is one of them.' Again, I denied it. A little later the bystanders said once more, 'Surely you are one of them; for you too are a Galilean.' I began to curse and swear, 'I do not know the man you are talking about.' That's when I heard the cock crow, as Jesus had predicted." Peter began to sob. "I remembered the words that he said to me at the supper, 'Before the cock crows twice you will deny me three times.' Then I broke down and wept bitterly."

Clement put his arms around the older man and comforted him.

"I've regretted it my whole life," he said through his sobs.

Clement answered, "Any man who feared for his life would have done the same."

"He forgave me later, but it haunts me to this day. I betrayed my Lord."

Clement noted how seriously Peter had taken the incident. "You loved him."

"I loved him, and I betrayed him."

The sobbing continued for quite a while, but the bishop wanted to continue walking. "Shall we go on?"

"When you are ready."

"Then they took Jesus to Pilate. Let's go see the fortress."

Herod the Great had built the Antonia fortress near the Temple Mount in honor of his patron, Mark Antony. It had towers at the corners, one of which was seventy cubits high, where guards could keep an eye on what was happening in the temple area. Pontius Pilate, the Roman prefect, lived in Caesarea but was in the Holy City at that time because of the festival.

"This is where they handed him over," Peter waved his arm. "They told the prefect that Jesus claimed to be the king of the Jews, and that he would destroy the temple and rebuild it in three days. Pilate questioned him, 'Are you king of the Jews?' Jesus didn't say much, so the chief priests accused him of many things. Again Pilate questioned him, 'Have you no answer? See how many things they accuse you of.' But Jesus gave no further answer."

"Why not?"

"Jesus was submitting. He had made his choice and was simply letting the events play out."

"I see."

"Now, there was a custom. On the occasion of the feast, the prefect customarily released one prisoner that the people wanted. A man called Barabbas was in prison, along with some rebels who had committed murder. When the crowd came forward and asked him to release a prisoner, Pilate asked, 'Do you want me to release to you the king of the Jews?' But the chief priests stirred up the crowd to have him release Barabbas instead. Then the prefect asked them, 'Then what do you want me to do with the man you call the king of the Jews?' They shouted, 'Crucify him!' And Pilate asked, 'Why? What evil has he done?' They only shouted all the louder, 'Crucify him! Crucify him!' So fearing a riot and wishing to satisfy the crowd, he released Barabbas to them, and after he had Jesus scourged, handed him over to be crucified."

"How terrible! Didn't the prefect even try to do justice?"

"No. Not at all. The governor didn't want to overrule the council, and it served Pilate's purposes to have Jesus out of the way."

"So they scourged him?"

"Yes. It was very brutal. The guards used whips with sharp weights on the ends that cut into his flesh with each blow. Those who saw him later said he was cut and bruised all over his back and chest—his arms and legs—even his face. They beat him for an unbearably long time, and when they finished he was half dead."

"How awful."

"Then they mocked him. The soldiers assembled the whole cohort and, weaving a crown of thorns, placed it on his head. They began to salute him saying, 'Hail, king of the Jews!' and they spit on him. Then they led him out to crucify him."

"And he tolerated all that?"

"He accepted it. Like I said, he could have used his power at any time to escape, but he stayed there and took it."

Peter showed Clement the route they followed: out of the fortress, through the city streets, out the city gate, and up the hill of Calvary. "They made him carry the heavy cross, and when he fell, they whipped him until he got up and continued on. About here," Peter pointed, "when he fell again, that's when they pressed Simon, the Cyrenian, to carry the cross the rest of the way."

"It is so much more vivid standing here. I can almost see it happening."

Walking farther up the hill, they came to a place with posts set securely in the ground. Four corpses were hanging on crosses there, and crows were pecking at their flesh. Roman soldiers were guarding the place to keep people from taking the bodies or damaging the crosses. Peter cringed. "This is where they crucified him. It is called Golgotha, the place of the skull."

Clement turned his eyes away. "Crucifixion is so cruel. Some people in Rome like to watch it—but I hate it. I feel so sorry for the poor victims."

"I know," replied the Galilean. "Christ was always concerned about those who were victimized. I've never understood why some people are so thirsty for the sight of blood."

"It's just too gory for me."

"Yes—for me too. The inscription of the charge against him read, 'The King of the Jews.' With him they crucified two revolutionaries, one on his right and one on his left. Those passing by reviled him, shaking their heads and shouting, 'Aha! You who would destroy the temple and rebuild it in three days, save yourself.' The chief priests and the scribes also mocked him, saying, 'He saved others; he cannot save himself.' Everyone was abusing him."

"He must have felt terrible."

"And in pain. They drove heavy nails through his hands and feet to fasten him. He had to lift himself with his legs to keep from choking. It was a long ordeal with waves of suffering. When he pushed himself up with his legs to take a breath, the pain in his feet was excruciating, and when he let himself down to rest, he'd choke for lack of air. All these things, the women told me."

"The women?"

"His mother was there, along with some of the other women from Galilee. I don't know how she stood it, watching her son suffer and die."

"It must have been horrible for her."

"She never left. At noon darkness came over the whole land until three in the afternoon. Then Jesus cried out in a loud voice, 'My God, my God, why have you forsaken me?'"

"He must have felt totally abandoned."

"I'm sure he did. He was quoting Psalm twenty-two, the cry of a man totally in despair, but who never lost faith in his God."

"It impresses me just to picture it."

"Yes. And when the centurion saw how Jesus had breathed his last, he said, 'Truly this man was the Son of God!' The way Jesus accepted the ordeal inspired him too."

"Did the centurion become a believer?"

"I don't know. If he did, he probably kept it a secret. Roman soldiers are totally locked in to the system, you know."

"Yes. My friends in Rome and I talked about it." Clement noted, "The army is appealing to boys from both the city and the countryside. They get three gold coins when they enlist, which is a huge sum of money for them. But then they have to serve for twenty-five years on low pay, if they last that long, and they have to swear an oath to obey every order, no matter how disgusting it is. I hate the thought of such a life."

"It is terrible. But there are always plenty of boys who take the bargain."

"That's how Rome keeps order. They rule with ruthless terror by recruiting youths who see it as a way out of poverty. They promise them a plot of land to retire on, but it's often in a swamp or on a rocky hillside. That's not for me."

"I'm glad you feel that way," the bishop remarked. "I'm sure our Lord has something better in mind for you."

Clement was silent, deep in his thoughts. Only when he looked up did Peter continue.

"When it was evening, since it was the day of preparation, the day before the Sabbath, Joseph of Arimathea went to Pilate and asked for the body of Jesus. Pilate summoned the centurion and asked him if Jesus had already died, and when he confirmed it, he gave the body to Joseph."

"Where did they lay him?" Clement was ready to leave the crucifixion site.

"His mother and the other women also went there. It's only a little way. They later showed us which tomb it was."

Arriving at the burial area, Peter said, "Here it is—the place where they laid him. Mary got to briefly hold the lifeless body of the son she bore, but the hour of the Sabbath was drawing near. Joseph had brought a linen cloth, so they hurriedly wrapped him in the cloth and laid him in the tomb. Then they rolled a stone against the entrance and went home. His mother and the others watched where he was laid."

"I'd like to pray here," said the youth.

"Let's both do that," Peter replied as he walked around to the other side and kneeled, facing away from Clement.

Clement knelt down where he was and stared at the many tombs all around him. "Jesus, my Lord. So many have died through senseless violence. You truly tasted the human condition when you accepted the same fate. I thank you and praise you for keeping me away from that life. I am beginning to understand why you submitted—it is how you show us the way. I am beginning to understand, and it makes me want to serve you all the more. Bless Peter. Bless his work. And bless my Sati, my wonderful love. Keep her safe and free from fear as she awaits my return. I love her from the depths of my heart—and I love you, my Savior and my Lord."

15

By the next morning both Sati and her mother had come to the same conclusion. "This isn't the time to talk to your father about Clement," Redji warned.

"I know, Mother, but it's hard to wait. I love him so."

"I've thought about that too," her mother added. "I will try support you, dear. I want you to be happy in your life. I don't want to force you into something you don't want."

"Thank you, Mother."

"The biggest issue, it seems to me, are your ages. Clement is so far from being ready to marry, and you have reached the time to become betrothed. Many girls your age are already betrothed. If you wait too long, you may be sorry."

"I know."

"You should consider other men…"

"I don't want to consider another man!" Sati interrupted.

"As I said—you should consider other men. I did when I was your age. I didn't know your father very well, but my guardian recommended him, and in time I grew to love him—and I'm glad that I listened to him."

"You were not in love with another at the time?"

"No. I wasn't. But I still believe that a girl your age—soon to be a woman— should pay attention to what her parents suggest."

"That makes sense, Mother. I will pay attention. But I don't think it will change how I feel about Clement."

"All I'm saying is that you should remain open-minded."

"I will try, Mother."

"That's good. Now, let's neither of us say a word to your father until he calms down."

"Yes, Mother."

Kenamon did not calm down. When he came home, he ranted on and on about how impractical Christians are. He said, "They don't try to get along with our Egyptian practices and customs. They are even more antisocial than the Jews!"

When Sati heard that, she went to her room and cried.

Peter spent the day finding a caravan that was going to Galilee. "It's too dangerous to go out on the roads alone, especially at night," he told Clement.

The next day they headed east, down to Jericho. The road was winding, and at one place of rest they beheld a panoramic view of the great valley below. "It's so different than I imagined," Clement shared.

"That's foreign territory over there," Peter explained. "Do you see that mountain on the other side? That's Mount Nebo. Moses got that far when he led his people here. He saw the Promised Land, but he died on the mountain."

"Did he fulfill his purpose?" Clement asked.

"Yes. He led them to the border and then gave Joshua the task of bringing them over here. Do you see the Jordan River?"

"Yes, but it's smaller than I had imagined."

"All of the twelve tribes were able to cross it and come into this land. They first had to take Jericho, where we will spend the night. But there's one more place I want you to see from here—across the wilderness."

"It's so barren."

"Quite barren—and very hot. Can you see that group of trees, where the river bends?"

"No...oh, yes! I see them."

"That's where John was baptizing. Remind me to tell you about it sometime. Our caravan won't go over there, but it's important. Everyone from Jerusalem and the whole region were coming out to see him. My brother and I went there too. We thought that John might be the Savior, but he said clearly that he wasn't."

"Did Jesus go there?"

"Yes. And he went into the water. John protested, saying, 'It is you who should be baptizing me,' but Jesus reasoned with him, and John baptized him. Then coming up out of the water, he saw the Holy Spirit come down upon him like a dove and remain upon him. And a voice from the heavens said, 'This is my beloved Son, in whom I am well pleased.' It was a wonderful day."

"You were there!"

"Andrew and I were there, and we saw it. But we had to get back to work in Capernaum. We didn't see Jesus again until he came to Galilee. I'll tell you about that when we get there."

The caravan was stirring, and people were picking up their bags. "Before we leave, I want to point out one more important place. Do you see that big barren area on this side of the river?"

"Yes."

"I'll tell you about it as we walk." After shouldering their packs and getting into line, Peter continued, "When Jesus left the Baptist, he came over to that stark region. He stayed there forty days and forty nights, and was tempted by the devil."

"By the devil!"

"Yes. He later told us what happened. He said the Holy Spirit led him there, I think to sort out if his time had come to begin his public years. He didn't bring any food, and afterward he was hungry. He told us that the devil tempted him three times."

"Three times?"

Peter explained what the tempter had said and how Jesus responded.

Clement was deep in thought about how even the Son of God was tempted. Then he asked, "Does this apply to us too?"

"Everything Jesus did applies to us, at least in some way. Temptation is something we all experience."

"I was tempted to avoid responsibility for as long as I could," the youth admitted. "I mean, I liked learning to read and write, and getting an education is important, but it also was a way of avoiding work."

"You are no longer a child. You are a man now."

"Yes. Falling in love with Sati has pushed me into it. I have to think like a man now. And I'm ready. I don't want to remain a youth any longer."

"That's good. I'm proud of you, my son."

16

The caravan continued up the Jordan River valley, a rift created by tectonic forces over many million years. The lowest point is the Dead Sea—the lowest place on earth, with shores a quarter of a mile below sea level. As they traveled north, they entered lush agricultural areas nourished by the fresh waters of the Jordan River, a welcome sight after the dry, barren slopes coming down from Jerusalem.

"In a little way, we will see the Sea of Galilee," Peter shared. "It's not far now."

Clement replied, "I hope it's as beautiful as you said. You certainly love it."

"The water is very beautiful, and the higher up you go on the hills, the more deeply blue it becomes. This end is shallow and marshy."

After another hour, following the road upstream, they came to the site the native Galilean had predicted. "This end is for growing crops. We fish to the north."

"The air is cool and clean. How big is the lake?" Clement asked.

"They say it's thirteen miles long and eight miles wide. The road is longer."

"Will we reach your city tonight?"

"I'd like to. The caravan will stop in Tiberias. But Capernaum is only a little past that, and I know some families who will take us in. It will still be light."

"Are you homesick?"

"Oh, yes. I love this place. It's been almost eight years."

"Is that Tiberias?" Clement asked pointing to a village ahead.

"No! Tiberias is a Roman city—much richer. It seems out of place up here."

"How do you mean?"

"Well, the Galilean villages are poor. Herod, that's Herod Antipas—King Herod's son—he built Tiberias to be his capital. He wasn't a king, only a tetrarch, ruling over Galilee and Peraea, but he acted like a king and liked to be thought of as one."

"Did he ever become a king?"

"No. Even though he named his city after the emperor, they knew he wasn't capable of ruling too big of an area. He was not great like his father. It was just a little village until he rebuilt it. There are hot springs there. Herod liked that."

"Was he rich?"

"Are you asking how he paid for it all? No. He taxed the whole region to get the funds. That's the main reason people hated him. He taxed and taxed and taxed. Can you imagine paying a tax to Jerusalem and one to Rome, and then having Herod come along and add another tax on top of that?"

"I'd say ouch!"

"That's what we all said—worse than that. Herod was a tyrant. The city of Tiberias is a monument to his pride."

In a little over an hour they came to the city. There was no mistaking it for a Galilean town—it bore all the marks of Roman engineering with strong walls and an impressive gate guarded by twin towers. The main street had shaded walks and upscale shops with expensive wares. Most of the buildings were stone with red tile roofs that gleamed in the afternoon sun. It had a theater and extensive docks and warehouses, and stately temples for Mithras and Isis as well as a small synagogue. Peter and Clement were among the few who hurried through as soon as the caravan disbanded. They still had two more hours to walk.

As they passed through the next Galilean town, Magdala, Clement asked, "Were any of the disciples from here?"

"No," the older man answered.

"Wasn't there a woman named Mary? I've heard you mention someone called Magdalene."

"Oh, her? I thought you were asking about the men."

"I am interested in knowing about all of them."

"Well, there isn't much to say. Mary Magdalene followed us, along with some other women."

"They said that Jesus liked her very much."

"Oh? That is what they say. I never paid much attention to her. Some people like to talk about women."

"Wasn't she at the cross and then went to the tomb with his mother?"

"Uh-huh," he verified.

Clement could tell that he wouldn't learn much about Mary Magdalene from Peter. *Perhaps someone else will tell me*, he supposed.

The sun was sinking into the hills to their left as they came to Capernaum. Clement was tired, but Peter was energized. Clement noticed that the town was not very big, and the houses were all mud brick.

They saw one impressive structure. "That's our synagogue," Peter exclaimed as he pointed with pride to a tall, stone building that dwarfed the humble homes. "I'll show you tomorrow. Let's find a place to stay."

The travelers received a warm welcome at the first house they called at—the home of Ezra, a fisherman, who was about the same age as Peter. Ezra was overjoyed to see his old friend and immediately got his whole family involved in preparing a hearty meal.

Clement felt out of place as he listened to the two friends swap stories, speaking mostly Aramaic. At one point he let his thoughts drift back to Alexandria and Sati. He wondered how she was feeling. There wasn't enough privacy to daydream and the room was too noisy to pray. So he quickly muttered, "Take care of her, Lord," and endeavored to return to the conversation.

After dinner Ezra and Peter wandered outside, leaving Clement with Ezra's wife and two youngest daughters. He asked her, "Did you know Mary Magdalene?"

"A little bit," answered the matron of the house, Ruth, who spoke only the most simple Greek. "I only saw her when they came here. Why do you ask?"

"Oh, I'm just trying to find out as much as I can about the people who knew Jesus."

"She was a pretty woman. They say she had been through a great torment before she joined the group—but she seemed happy when I saw her."

"Was she the same age as Jesus?"

"A few years older. They were close."

"In what way?"

"In a good way. She seemed very intelligent—a leader among the women. Her faith was very strong. She was devoted to Jesus."

"Was Jesus closer to Mary than to any of the other women?"

"I would say that. But he treated everyone the same way—you know what I mean?"

"I think I understand. They were good friends."

"Yes. Good friends. But with a special kind of bond. He was very fond of her."

"But they never married?"

"Oh my. No, no! It was not like that. He was too busy, anyway, to seek a wife. I don't think he even wanted a wife. He loved everyone—you know? But with some, he was more close than with others."

"It probably was that way among the men too."

"That's right. Yes. Some were more close in his life—both men and women, and Mary was one of those he felt closest to."

"Well, thank you for sharing that with me. Now I think I'll go join the men."

The next morning Ezra told the travelers, "I'll be with you in an hour, after I see how the boys did last night." His three sons, who fished with him, were married with homes of their own. "We have to make sure that the wealthy in Tiberias have something to eat. I'll catch up with you at the synagogue."

Peter waved in agreement and then asked his companion, "What would you like to see?"

"You are the guide. I'll just follow you."

"Let's go down to the docks first."

At a small cove along the rocky shore they came to a few small stone piers with steps down into the water. Waves lapping against the piers splashed in rhythm, and Clement noticed one boat, not tied well, that was banging against the hard mooring with loud thumps. He picked up a smooth stone and skipped it across the water. Seven boats were bobbing up and down about a mile out with men busily trailing nets behind them.

"This is where we fished," Peter said proudly.

"It looks like you had everything you needed," Clement replied.

"Yes. It was long, hard work, but we made a living. Sometimes we had to fish all night and then mend the nets in the morning."

"Did Jesus come here?"

"Yes. To this very place. My brother Andrew and I were casting our nets from the shore, and James and John were mending their nets just up from this dock. We looked up, and there he was!"

"What did he say?"

"I think he remembered us from the day with John the Baptist. When our eyes met, he just said, 'Come after me,' and we left our nets and followed."

"And then?"

"And then—that day—he healed many people. One was a leper—that might have been the next day. He cured my wife's mother, who was sick with a fever. He just grasped her hand and helped her up. Then the fever left her."

"How did she feel?"

"Perfect! As soon as the fever left she began to wait on us, as usual. And, oh! First he cast a demon out of the synagogue. Let's go over there. I'll tell you while we walk."

"Why was there a demon in the synagogue?"

"There was a man there with an unclean spirit. He cried out, 'What have you to do with us, Jesus of Nazareth? Have you come to destroy us? I know who you are—the Holy One of God!' Then Jesus rebuked him and said, 'Quiet! Come out of him!' and the unclean spirit convulsed him and with a loud cry came out of him. Everyone was amazed."

"That is amazing."

"Yes. He had such authority. And later he told us to be mindful that even some of those in the synagogue could have unclean spirits."

"But the synagogue is a holy place."

"That's true, but not everyone who was in there was holy. The scribes and the Pharisees didn't act with the authority that Jesus had."

"I see."

"They liked to pretend they were holy. The rest of us, of course, knew we were sinners, but the leaders, even in a little town like this, had roles in the system that held us down. Jesus knew it better than we did, but he showed us the truth."

"So he taught you by pointing things out to you."

"Exactly. Now—here we are," Peter said as they approached the stone building. "This is where we prayed and listened to the scriptures."

Clement studied the interior—two rooms, the larger of which had stone benches along both sides. At the far end he saw the customary niche where the sacred scrolls were kept. "Why are there two rooms?" he asked.

"For the men and the women!" Peter answered, looking like he was replying to a very odd question.

Before Clement could ask anything else, they heard a shout from the doorway, "Hello!" It was Ezra.

"I am telling this young man about our customs," Peter declared. "But he is asking more about Jesus, than about the Jewish faith."

"I want to know the background," the young man pleaded.

"Well, we are Christians now," said Ezra, who finished giving Clement a detailed tour of the building. "You know, I was thinking while I was down at the water about the time Jesus taught such a large crowd that he had to get into my boat. The whole crowd was beside us on the land. Do you remember that day, my friend?"

"I will never forget it. He told us the story of the sower and the seed."

"Tell me," demanded Clement.

Ezra related the story about how only the seed that fell on good soil grew and produced a harvest, and Peter explained the parable. "From that day, we knew we must be good soil—we must not just hear the word, but we had to accept it and embrace it and live it. He sowed the word anew in us, and we followed him."

That evening Peter told Clement, "I want us to move on tomorrow. There are two places farther north that I want to go to. They both are important for you to see."

Clement prayed again that night, in gratitude for all that he was learning about Christ, "Lord Jesus, I am seeing how good you are and how what you teach is the truth. Your seed is planted deep in my heart. Help me to be good soil. I want so much to bear fruit for you—if possible, one hundredfold. Watch over my mother and brothers and my father. And take care of my Sati, my love. And thank you for Peter. He is such a faith-filled man."

Then he closed his eyes, rolled to his side and held Sati tenderly until he fell fast asleep.

17

The next day as they said good-bye to Ezra and set out to travel farther up the lake, Peter muttered, "I wonder if I'll ever come back here." Clement heard, but allowed the older man to remain alone with his thoughts.

Bethsaida was a very small village when Andrew and Simon Peter were born there. Like many of the towns on the north end of the lake, it held a mixed population, some speaking Aramaic and some speaking Greek. When Assyria conquered the region in 721 BC, this brought in an influx of settlers who were pagan. There was plenty of fresh water, a grassy plain, and pools of bottom fish called *muscht*, which the brothers caught daily to live on. There was no commercial fishing like in Capernaum, which was closer to the markets in Tiberias.

Andrew and Peter learned from an early age to use cast nets to catch muscht. They didn't have a boat to go out into the deep water where the better fish were. They waded out in the mud until the water was up to their waist and cast a small circular net, which had weights around it that made it settle to the bottom. Then they pulled on a cord that closed the net and drew it in to see if they'd caught anything. If they kept at this long enough, they'd bring home a few fish.

The boys had no education. They grew up Jewish but spoke both languages used in the town. When their parents died, they had to fend for themselves.

A few minutes after crossing to the east side of the river, the travelers saw a few boys casting nets in the sea.

"This is where we grew up," Peter said as he and Clement entered the town a little farther up the hill. "We didn't have much of a house, if you could call it that, but we caught fish to eat."

"When did you move to Capernaum?"

"It's not far away, as you just saw, and as we grew older we began spending more time there. After we began working for Zebedee, who had six boats,

Andrew struck up a relationship with a girl, whose father consented to their marriage. A little later I did the same."

As the two looked around the town, Clement thought about how different his life was from Peter's. *I should consider myself lucky*, he mused. *My parents got me a good Roman education, and the egg business doesn't involve wading out in a muddy lake bottom.*

After an hour, Peter seemed finished. "Have you seen enough? I just wanted to come back here one more time."

Clement nodded, and the two headed up the river.

On the way, Peter explained that Caesarea Philippi was a pagan city with a temple to the god Pan, set into a grotto that had been considered a holy place from ancient times. Water gushing from springs at the foot of snowcapped Mount Hermon formed the beginning of the northern Jordan River, the principle source of the lake. Herod the Great erected a temple of white marble there in honor of his patron Caesar Augustus, and in 3 BC the tetrarch Philip II founded a city that became his capital. Upon Philip's death, the year after Christ died, the region was incorporated into the province of Syria.

Clement was impressed with the beauty of the place. "The cave is huge, and the temples are so stately. I can see why Jesus wanted to come here."

"I don't know why he led us up here," Peter answered. "It's all pagan—Jews had no reason to come here. He did a little teaching in the villages along the way. And as we were walking, he asked us, 'Who do people say that I am?' The disciples answered, 'John the Baptist, others say Elijah, and still others say one of the prophets.' Then he stopped and asked us, 'But who do you say that I am?' He stared at us for a long time. Then I spoke up and said, 'You are the Messiah, the Son of the Living God.' It was the first time that I had uttered such words."

"What did he say to you?"

"I don't usually tell people."

"Why not?"

"Because it may sound like I am proud."

"Will you tell me?"

Peter paused for a moment, considering his young companion's request. "He said to me, 'Blessed are you, Simon, son of Jonah. For flesh and blood has not revealed this to you, but my heavenly Father.' I was humbled."

"Did he say anything else?"

"He said, 'I say to you, you are Peter, and upon this rock I will build my church, and the gates of the netherworld shall not prevail against it. I will give you the keys to the kingdom of heaven. Whatever you bind on earth shall be bound in heaven, and whatever you loose on earth shall be loosed in heaven.' Then he strictly ordered us to tell no one that he was the Savior."

"So he commissioned you to lead the Church?"

"Yes. But that wasn't all."

"What else happened?"

"From that time on he began to tell us that he must go to Jerusalem and suffer greatly and be killed, and on the third day be raised."

"He knew it then?"

"He knew it. It was like he had a premonition."

"What did you say?"

"The others said nothing. None of us understood. Then I made my mistake."

"What mistake?"

"I took him aside and said, 'God forbid, Lord! No such thing shall ever happen to you.' He turned and shouted, 'Get behind me, Satan! You are an obstacle to me. You are thinking not as God does, but as human beings do.' I hung my head. He was so angry with me."

"What did he do then?"

"What he said to us then is what I brought you here to hear: 'Whoever wishes to come after me must deny himself, take up his cross, and follow me. For whoever wishes to save his life will lose it, but whoever loses his life for my sake will find it.' Can you understand what that means?"

"That I have to make a sacrifice?"

"That you have to be willing to make a sacrifice. We don't pick our own sacrifices—they just come."

"I would say that you've made a great number of sacrifices."

"Yes. And I'm not finished. But I'd do it all again, if I had to, and I'd make less mistakes."

"What kind of sacrifices do you think I will have to make?" the younger man asked.

"There is no way to know. We all make some sacrifices, but when we choose to follow the Lord, we choose a life that carries with it many challenges. It's up to you."

"It's up to me to do what?"

"It's up to you to decide that Jesus is the Savior, the Son of the Living God. After that it's up to him."

"What do you mean?"

"After that he will lead you. You only need to surrender, to follow where he leads you."

"I want to make that decision, Peter. I have to think about it for a while, though. Can I talk with you more about it, if I need to?"

"Of course."

"Where do we go from here?"

"We need to retrace our steps before nightfall."

The two travelers walked back to a small village just north of Capernaum. Peter didn't want to go back to Ezra's. He told Clement that he knew a trail through the hills toward the coast that was shorter and more scenic than going all the way back to the main road at Magdala. They were welcomed by friends of Peter, and after downing their tasty fish dinner, he fell deep asleep. Clement lay awake, studying the patterns of the stars.

"Lord, Jesus, I want to make the decision to accept you," his lips voiced quietly. "I want to follow you like Peter did. No one else inspires me like you do. No other prophet or hero attracts me. I believe that there is no other God except your Father, and I believe that you are his only Son. I thank Peter, and I thank my mother, for showing me the way to you. I now realize that if I want to have a purpose in my life, then my purpose must be you and serving your kingdom. So I declare this to you tonight: I believe that you are the Savior of the world, the Son of the Living God, and I surrender to you." Then after a few peaceful moments, he added, "But help me with this—I need to find a way to bring my lovely Sati to Rome. I don't know how to do it at this time. I trust you, though. Help me to trust in you the way that Peter does. Help me to maintain my resolve. Please also watch over Sati, my true love, and help her to grow in the faith as she waits for my return."

18

The next morning Sati complained to her mother, "I don't know what to do with Father ranting on about the Christians. I want to learn more and be baptized."

"That's out of the question," Redji replied. "You and I must be of the same mind as your father; he is the head of this house."

"I thought at the dinner with Peter that you were impressed with the faith."

"I was. Peter made Jesus and his mother sound like very fine people, but that doesn't mean that I would go against your father's wishes."

Sati hung her head and thought about her next words. "I know what I want, Mother. I want to become a Christian, and I want to marry Clement."

"You are only sixteen years old. You can't make decisions like that."

"But you said I am old enough to become betrothed. If I am old enough to accept a man, then I am old enough to choose my faith."

"Choosing a cult is up to the men to decide. In a modern city like Alexandria, there are a great number of cults. But no household is divided."

"Christianity is not a cult. It is a way of life. It is following the true God. Father was making that very point until he got angry."

Now the matron searched for words. "Your father explored that faith, but now he has made the judgement that it is not for us. So the matter is settled."

"It is not settled for me. If I have to, I will go on my own."

"You will not!" shouted the matron. "If you sneak over there, your father will sue them for interfering with our family."

"You may stop me now, but you can't stop me forever!"

Redji tried to take her daughter's hands, but she jerked them away. Then raising herself up and looking down toward her, she said, "We love you, Sati. Your father loves you, and I love you. We want only the best for you—and for you to be happy. If Clement comes back for you, your father and I may accept him. But you could compromise that possibility by doing something rash and angering him more."

Sati looked up through the tears that were welling up in her eyes and saw her mother's sincere smile. "I will not do anything rash."

"Good."

Then rising to her feet, Sati fell into her mother's arms. "I won't do anything rash, but I won't change my mind."

"I know, dear. Just be patient," Redji whispered.

"I will try, Mother," she wept. But going to her room, she dropped onto her bed and smothered her grief in wet sobs.

After thanking their hosts and lifting their packs, Peter and Clement set out on the trail up into the hills above Capernaum. The higher they went, the deeper blue the sea became.

"Do you like the view? It keeps getting better," the leader explained.

"It's already beautiful."

"Can you keep going? There's a nice spot to rest about a mile farther."

"I can do it."

Both men were puffing hard when they came to the place Peter was seeking—a gently sloping meadow with a rounded cliff rising above one side. Near the cliff, they refilled their water jugs from a sparkling spring.

"There," Peter said, sitting down in the grass. "Let's rest a few minutes."

Clement sat beside the older man, resting his legs and studying the view.

"A great crowd came here, not just from Capernaum, but from cities farther north as well."

"When was that?"

"Early on—not long after he called us to follow him. They were bringing their sick to be healed, and then—on a beautiful day like this—he just headed up here, and everyone who could climb came too."

"There's a lot of room here."

"Yes. He went over by the cliff, so it would reflect his voice, and he taught for about an hour without stopping."

"What did he say?"

"Oh, many things. I can't remember them all, but his words challenged us to the core. He called us blessed and said we were the salt of the earth and the light of the world. We didn't see ourselves that way. We were not from Jerusalem. But he showed that he trusted us more than the priests and the scribes. He said, 'Do not think that I have come to abolish the law. I have come not to abolish, but to fulfill.' And then he began to set a higher standard for us than Moses did. He put it this way: 'You have heard that it was said to your ancestors, 'You shall not kill,' but I say to you, whoever is angry with his brother will be liable to judgment, and whoever says to his brother, 'Raqa!' will be liable to the Sanhedrin, and whoever says, 'You fool,' will be liable to fiery Gehenna.' He went on and on like that, lifting our sights to a vision where every man lives in peace and harmony with everyone else."

"You still are moved when you talk about it."

"Oh, yes. He taught many things, but they all fit together into a beautiful vision. He could see the new kingdom so clearly, and he could make us picture it."

"What sort of things did he teach?"

"Against adultery and divorce, about prayer and fasting—and money! He summed it up saying, 'Do unto others what you would have them do to you.' He told us how to be true disciples."

"You loved it."

"I was weeping with joy. But parts of what he said were hard. Loving your enemies was the hardest."

"What did he say about that?"

"Let me think…I remember, 'You have heard that it was said, 'You shall love your neighbor and hate your enemy.' But I say to you, love your enemies, and pray for those who persecute you, that you may be children of your heavenly Father, for he makes his sun rise on the bad and the good, and causes rain to fall on the just and the unjust.' Then he said, 'For if you love those who love you, what recompense will you have? Do not the tax collectors do the same? And if you greet your brothers only, what is unusual about that? Do not the pagans do the same? So be perfect, just as your heavenly Father is perfect.' I'm sure that's what he said."

"That's beautiful."

"Some people find it too hard."

"I can see why."

"They are looking for laws they can follow to feel good about themselves. But Jesus called us to try to be as good as his heavenly Father. That's raising the bar pretty high."

"It certainly is."

"But, do you know what?" Peter added. "It's not just the high standard that keeps people away. It's that they don't want anyone to tell them what to do and what not to do. They don't want anyone to be their Lord, even the Son of God!"

"But if the Son of God asks it of us, then we must take it seriously."

"That's the way I see it. Only the Son of God can ask of us, what Jesus asks of us."

They both stopped speaking and pondered the words Peter had just uttered. He had never said it so clearly: Only the Son of God can ask of us, what Jesus asks of us.

After a few moments, Clement broke the silence. "So, if I believe that Jesus is the Son of God, then I am compelled to follow his teaching."

"You *want* to follow his teaching! You can't bear to not follow it. Only those who don't fully accept him can refuse him."

"I guess that's what separates real disciples from the rest."

Both men sat and pondered how Jesus taught so much on the mountain. Then, picking up their packs, they continued up the trail in silence.

As they went higher, the trail turned to the west. "We will lose sight of the lake now," Peter said. "Let's take one last look."

Clement studied the rustic Galilean, who was gazing at the sea, and remembered the words Peter had muttered as he left Capernaum, "I wonder if I'll ever come back here." Seeing a single big tear roll down the older man's cheek, he chose to remain quiet as they continued on their way.

About midday the two travelers came to a well-constructed road, obviously laid out by Roman engineers. Peter explained, "This is the main road, now, from Galilee to the coast. We need to get to the inn by nightfall, but it's not as hilly—we'll have easier walking. We'll head for Ptolemais and catch a boat to Antioch. Then we'll have an easy voyage back to Rome."

Rome! Hearing the word gave Clement a jolt of reality. He almost panicked, realizing they were on their way home. *I've got to plan how I will tell my parents. Telling them about the council and the places we saw in Jerusalem and Galilee will be easy. Mother will like how I finally accepted Christ—Father, too, if I don't make too big of a deal out of it. I've got to emphasize to him how I want to work in the business and save up some money. The last topic I'll bring up is Sati. I'll get everything else in place before I even mention her name.*

Over and over again, Clement rehearsed his speeches. He needed to get the points down and not make any mistakes.

Kenamon came home in a good mood, humming a little song. "Hello dear—hello princess, giving them each a kiss.

"What puts you in such a good frame of mind?" Redji asked.

"Oh, I'll tell you soon…actually, I can't wait to share the news. Sati, do you remember Lumeri?"

"Who?"

"Lumeri! He's a fine man, and very successful, if I may say so."

"I remember," interjected Redji. "Isn't he the good-looking man with three daughters, whose wife passed away?"

"That's him! It's been almost two years. He wants to get better acquainted with Sati."

Redji smiled widely. Sati looked shocked.

"I invited him to dinner on Tuesday. Is that a good day?"

His wife thought for a moment. "It should be."

"Good! This may lead to something wonderful," he sang.

Sati figured out what they were talking about and turned red. "No one asked me if I wanted to meet a man!"

"Oh, princess," her happy father exclaimed. "It's time for you to be getting acquainted with men, and a fine one like this doesn't come along every day."

"Why would I want to meet a man who has children?"

"They are lovely girls, and Lumeri is very rich. He needs an heir, you know."

Kenamon couldn't have done a worse job of introducing the potential suitor to his daughter. Sati grew even more red and anxious. Seeing her expression, he added, "He's a young man, darling—only thirty-four. And he's quite generous and respectful. Everyone loves him."

"You are the one who needs to be generous and respectful. You never even talked with me about it!"

"Hush, dear," her mother cautioned.

Kenamon gulped and assumed a dignified posture. "Well, I'm telling you now."

"It's too late!" Sati shouted, and ran out of the room.

"What happened?" Kenamon asked his wife.

"It's difficult," she answered.

"How difficult can it be just to have dinner with a man?"

"The difficult part is that Sati has already met someone. She has wanted to tell you for several days, but you've been in a bad mood."

"She's met someone? For the god's sake, who? I haven't given my permission for her to meet anyone."

"He came to dinner here. It's Clement."

"Who?"

"Clement. The young man you invited to dinner with Anianus and Peter."

"That kid! He's hardly a year older than Sati. And he barely spoke a word the whole evening."

"She says she's in love with him."

"Love. What does a girl her age know about love?"

"She's old enough to fall in love, dear."

"Well, not with a wimpy Christian, who can't even join in a conversation. I won't have it!"

19

As the ship approached the docks of Rome, Clement and Peter gazed at familiar sights. They had been gone nearly two months, and the young man was anxious to see his friends and family.

"I will need to stay close to home for a few days," Clement told his companion. "There is so much to share with them. Then I'll come and see you."

"That sounds fine, my son. Take your time. And don't forget to pray as you put your plans into place."

Clement headed for the Capitoline Hill, wondering who he would see first. When he walked in the gate, both of his parents were seated in the courtyard.

"So the traveler has returned!" greeted his father.

Cordula jumped up and ran to embrace her son. With tears in his eyes, Clement tenderly hugged her, then his father, then both.

"You are darker!" observed Urbanus.

"We were in the sun a lot."

"And you need a haircut."

"Yes. I will need a day or two to get back to normal."

"Well, tell us some things about your trip," he urged.

"I saw many things." Clement felt there was no better time than the present to begin the speech he had rehearsed. "I have grown up a great deal during these two months, Father. I would like to begin working in the business. It is time for me to apply myself to the work men do."

Urbanus leaned back in surprise. This was not what he was expecting to hear.

Then, before he could reply, Clement turned to his mother and shared, "And you will be pleased to know, Mother, that as I went to the holy sites and listened to Peter tell me about them, I have grown in my appreciation of Jesus. I understand him better now and have become a more devout Christian."

Also surprised at such unexpected news, Cordula managed to say, "That's wonderful, Clement."

"So, Father, when can I begin helping in the egg business?"

"Any time!" Urbanus exclaimed with both shock and joy. "Any time. I will discuss it with Cassius and Horus in the morning, and when you are rested from your voyage, you may begin."

"That sounds good, Father. I need to wash up and put on some clean clothes."

"You do that. You do that, and we'll have some wine and hear about the adventures that brought you to these conclusions."

A half hour later Clement rejoined his parents, who had been discussing the sudden changes in their youngest son. He picked up a cup of wine and took a sip. "This certainly is better than we drank in Jerusalem."

"Do they not have good wine there?" Urbanus asked.

"Everything tastes so different. It was excellent the two nights we were in Alexandria, but that all changed as soon as we docked in Caesarea. Peter loves the Jewish food, but I never got used to it. I am glad to be back."

Reaching for his hand, his mother admitted, "And we are glad to have you back, son."

Cassius and his wife joined them for dinner, but Horus said he was busy.

Clement told them, "Caesarea is like most imperial cities. They have both Roman and Jewish inns, but as we traveled into the interior, it was all Kosher." He shared how the council in Jerusalem had reached a conclusion in only one day and described the sights they saw in the Holy City and Galilee, but he avoided saying anything more about Alexandria. After dinner he said he was tired and withdrew to his room. "It will feel good to be in my own bed."

The next morning, Urbanus discussed with his sons how their brother could join in the family business. "Why don't we just have Clement follow you around for a few days and then we can find a job for him."

"He may as well start with me," offered Cassius. "That way he'll see how we get the eggs. Then Horus can show him how we deliver them."

"That sounds good. What do you think, Horus?"

"That will be fine," he muttered. Horus, as usual, didn't say much. The two brothers looked alike, but their personalities were quite different. Cassius was amiable and talkative, but Horus was serious and withdrawn.

"Good. Plan on showing Clement everything. I want him to know how we do things."

A little later that morning, while Clement ate breakfast, his mother asked him to explain how he came to fully embrace Jesus. He clearly was showing more interest than either of his brothers. "Does this mean that you might pursue a vocation in the Church?" she asked.

He answered curtly, "Peter taught me that when we follow Christ, we never know how things may develop. But my immediate plans are to apply myself to the work Father needs me to do."

"That's fine, dear, but I want you to know that I would love it if one of my sons became a presbyter or something."

"We'll just have to wait and see, Mother."

That afternoon, after going to the *tonsor* shop for a haircut and shave, Clement stopped by the home of his friend, Fidelis. The two had been pals since they were boys. Fidelis had a round face, curly brown hair, and still was spending his mornings with tutors. "You've got to pledge not to tell anyone, but I've got to share something," Clement admitted.

"What is it? You can count on me to keep a secret."

"Well—on the trip—I met the most wonderful girl, and I am in love with her."

"A Jewish girl?"

"No. No. She's Egyptian! We stopped for two nights in Alexandria, and that's where I met her."

"Is she beautiful?" his wide-eyed friend asked.

"Oh, very beautiful—a goddess. Her grandmother was European, and while she has many Egyptian features, her hair is brown and wavy with streaks of gold. When we kissed…"

"You kissed!"

"Of course we kissed," Clement said, raising up to his full height. "After dinner, as she was showing me the view from their balcony, we were just drawn together as if by some irresistible force."

"You sly fox. Have you told your parents?"

"No! Not yet. You are the only one, and you'd better not say anything to anyone!"

"I pledged didn't I? So what are you going to do?"

"What I have to do. I'm going to work in my father's business and save some money and go back to Alexandria to get her."

"That's going to take a lot of money."

"I know. But it's the only option I have. I won't be able to loaf around as much, but you and I will always be friends."

"Always!" Fidelis said, as he jumped up and embraced his buddy.

In the evening, when Clement was with his father, he asked, "Did you speak with Cassius and Horus?"

"Yes, we did. Yes, we did." Urbanus explained the plan he had discussed with Clement's brothers. "Take some time to see your friends. You can start with Cassius on Monday morning."

Clement expected his older brother to be agreeable. He always was. So he asked, "How does Horus feel about it?"

"Horus? He didn't say much. He was his usual self. But he'll be fine with it. He's always known that we'd make a place for you."

Early Monday morning the four came together at the family warehouse in a swampy area near the Tiber River. "I've looked forward to this day," Urbanus exclaimed with a big grin. "My sons—all my sons—working together as one family. A father's dream come true." Cassius smiled, but Horus scowled and muttered something under his breath.

"Today we'll visit a couple of farms," his older brother shared, "and tomorrow you can go with one of the carts." Then taking a sack of coins from the strongbox and motioning toward a cart, he said, "Let's go."

They headed north, along the Tiber, and about four miles outside of the walls, they approached a well-kept farm. "I try to see each grower at least once a month and pay them a little early. That keeps us on good terms. Otherwise, they get paid each Wednesday when they open their crates."

"How do you do that?" the younger brother asked.

"I invented the system. When I came into the business, I saw Father carrying around a large sack all the time. He could have been robbed, but of course they would have had quite a fight. Now the eggs come to us in locked boxes. We open the boxes and take out the crates. Then each Wednesday I lock their payment in with their empty crates—except for the ones I pay early. Using matching keys keeps the whole operation safe."

"That seems very efficient."

"Oh, very efficient. I told Father, 'We pay the growers one quarter denarius per crate. So we need to hone the system, making it efficient for both the growers and for ourselves. That's where the profit will be.' He understood that for us to expand beyond a small operation, efficiency would be the key."

"I get the idea. You have been very creative."

"Yes. And I treat the growers well. Father always was outstanding at keeping the emperor's top people happy, but I felt that there could be a similar advantage with the growers. And it's worked out well."

The farmer greeted his guests with a warm smile. "Who do you have with you today?"

"Alphaeus, this is my brother, Clement. He will be helping us with the business. Can I show him how you pack the crates?"

"Yes. Bring him in," he said, motioning to a low, mud-brick barn with a thick roof. "We keep it as cool as we can in here."

Inside, Clement saw a long workbench with a pile of crates on one end. "I refined the crates, too," Cassius explained. "Each egg has its own little compartment, do you see? The straw at the bottom cushions it, and the slats at the side keeps them from touching. And the crates can be stacked with all the weight on the four sides. There's no weight at all on the eggs."

"Ingenious. And what are these for?" Clement said, motioning to a crate partially filled with eggs.

"Those will be put on the cart tomorrow, along with the others they gather. Each layer has to be a full crate."

"I see," Clement revealed as he counted the compartments. "Twelve rows of twelve eggs, and they look so clean."

"Alphaeus's daughters clean the eggs before they put them in the crate. He knows that we inspect each crate and that every egg must be undamaged and presentable."

"You want to see the hens?" asked the farmer.

When he opened the door to a coop, the strong stench caught Clement by surprise. It was more than he could tolerate, but he tried not to let it show. "You have a fine operation here, Alphaeus. Thank you for showing us."

After visiting two other growers, the brothers returned to the warehouse. "I think I'll stop and see Peter on the way home," Clement shared. "See you in the morning. And thanks for showing me so much today."

"Sure. But get here early. The carts leave before dawn."

"Clement! Good to see you," Peter crowed. "Come in. Will you have some wine? And there is something I have to give you."

"I'll take a cup. I've been out in the heat with Cassius all day. What do you have?"

"First sit down. This will come as a great surprise."

"What is it?"

"I received a letter from Anianus."

"Oh, Anianus. What did he say?"

"First take a sip of wine. No. Take two big sips."

Clement did as instructed.

"He delivered your letter to Sati…and she sent a reply."

"My God! Let me see it," the young man gasped. His hands were shaking.

"Here it is. I only read what Anianus said—that he gave your letter to Sati and was forwarding her reply."

Clement's hands were trembling as he read the letter the first time. Then, with a huge smile on his face, he took another sip of wine and read it again. "Oh, Peter. What wonderful news."

"What did she say?"

"She said she was very moved that I spoke so boldly of my feelings, and that she loves me too. She treasures the bronze ichthys that I gave her. She says it will remind her of me as she continues to progress toward baptism and waits for my return. She says that it will be hard to wait until I come for her, but that she believes we can overcome all obstacles. Here, you can read it."

Peter took the letter and offered the gift that Sati had enclosed. "This is what she gave you. It looks exquisite."

"A locket. An ivory locket! Oh, how beautiful," he said as he brought it to his lips.

"Does it remind you of how she kissed you on the balcony?"

"Oh, yes. Oh, yes."

When Peter finished scanning the letter, he asked, "Are you going to open the locket?"

"Oh! I forgot. She said I should look inside. Does it twist? There. It's open." The young man's eyes bulged wide as he gazed into the locket. It was a lock of Sati's hair, the color of cinnamon with strands of gold.

20

Even though Clement knew that he had to be at the warehouse before dawn, he found it impossible to sleep. He kept caressing the locket, rereading Sati's letter, and dreaming of holding her in his arms. Remembering Peter's advice, he tried to pray, but he was just too excited to put prayer into words. The best he could do was say, "Lord Jesus, take care of her—take care of my love." His mind was whirling.

He kept opening the locket, staring at the strands of hair, and pressing it to his face, where he could detect the faint scent of Sati's perfume. Then he closed it tight and clutched it near his heart as he pictured their evening on the balcony and the day he would return to Alexandria to ask for his bride.

Giving up all hope for sleep, he got dressed and went to the kitchen, where he picked up some bread and cheese. Then, slipping quietly out of the house, he headed in the moonlight for the warehouse. The air was chilly, but the faint glow in the eastern sky offered reassurance that his life was heading in the right direction.

The building was empty, but within minutes a team arrived, and soon after that he saw Cassius. "Good morning," he shouted.

"Oh, Clement—you are here. Good. The carts are beginning to make their rounds. Go with this one that is hitching up. You'll see what they do."

"Where do you keep the teams?"

"They belong to the cartage company run by Sergius. His barn is close by. The carts are ours."

"Why do you use a separate company to make the rounds?"

"It's…more efficient. We don't have to feed the animals, and Sergius runs it with an iron hand."

As two more teams arrived, Clement noticed, "Are those slaves? Father said we don't employ any slaves."

"We don't. Sergius owns them."

"What difference does that make?"

"You'll see. Now get going. We have to get the eggs while it's cool."

As soon as Clement climbed onto the cart, the driver flipped the reins and the team jerked forward. Clement said hello, but the driver was silent, staring straight ahead. The only sounds he made were to control the mules.

For the first hour they headed up the Tiber, passing the farms he and Cassius had visited the day before. Then they pulled into one where the grower was standing beside a low barn with a thick roof. Without saying a word, the man unlocked a large box on the cart and his two sons quickly removed about six empty crates, while he carefully placed seven full crates into it. Then he locked the box and nodded to the driver. Not a word was exchanged.

The process was repeated at each farm as they headed back to the city. Clement's back was getting sore from sitting on the hard bench, but the driver seemed to be used to the discomfort. At Alphaeus's farm Clement hopped off the cart and greeted the grower, "Good morning, Alphaeus. Nice day."

"Should be nice," the farmer replied, looking at the sky.

"How do you know which box is yours?" the young man asked.

"By the color," he answered, pointing to a bright green stripe on the box he was unlocking.

"Oh. I see."

"Cassius likes to give each of us on the route a different color. He says…"

"It's efficient!" Clement interrupted.

Both men laughed. "You are learning much," the grower observed, as he finished loading his crates. "See you again."

"See you again." Clement waved as the driver pulled away and headed straight back to the warehouse.

Two carts had already returned when they pulled in. Cassius was unlocking the boxes, one at a time, and the drivers where stacking crates on the loading dock under his watchful eye as he noted the number from each farm. If all was well, Cassius signaled the driver to park his cart and unhitch his team.

One of the drivers had several broken eggs in two of his boxes. Cassius made a note and showed Sergius, who promptly snapped his driving whip across the slave's face, making a large red welt.

"He's not beating him in our warehouse, is he?" asked a shocked Clement.

"Of course not," his brother replied. "He only marked him here. He'll beat the slave in his own barn."

"What did he do wrong?"

"He didn't keep his cart out of the deep ruts, and as you could see, it took a couple of hard hits."

"And for that he gets a beating?"

"A beating and no dinner—that's the system. I deduct the cost of the broken eggs from the cartage company's payment, and Sergius establishes the necessary discipline. We've been handling it that way for years, and the operation is all the better for it."

Clement turned away, not liking what he had seen.

When all of the carts were unloaded, he assisted his brother with putting the correct number of empty crates in the boxes and watched as he carefully noted the amounts of the Wednesday morning payments.

On his way home, Clement decided to stop by the home of his friend, Fidelis. The youth was sitting in the courtyard, sipping a drink. "Hello, Clement. Would you like some cool wine?"

"That sounds good," replied the weary egg man.

"What did you do today?"

"I rode with one of the cart drivers and saw how we bring in the eggs."

"Was it interesting?"

"I wouldn't call it interesting, and I think that after doing it for a while, it would become very boring."

"What else is happening?"

"Oh! I have wonderful news. I got a letter from my love in Alexandria. She sent me an ivory locket and said she loves me and will wait for me. I didn't sleep a wink last night."

"So what are you going to do now?"

"I don't know. It will be two more weeks before my father assigns me a job and says how much I'll get paid. I guess I'll just have to wait and see."

"Yea. I guess so."

"I wish I knew how to handle this better. It's so new to me. I've never sought the love of a woman before, and I don't know what to do next."

"Maybe we should ask Bella! Now that my sister is betrothed, she could explain how a woman feels."

"What a great idea! When can I speak with her?"

"She's not home now. Stop by again tomorrow. I'll ask her to be here."

When Clement stopped the next day at Fidelis's house, his sister again was out. "But she said she will be here tomorrow," his friend explained.

On Thursday afternoon, the meeting occurred. Clement was anxious as he walked up the hill, but Bella set him at ease. She was a pleasant maiden with a full figure and a sincere smile. Everyone liked her. Fidelis already had explained the basics of his friend's situation, and after asking a few questions, she offered her advice.

"You have two problems, Clement. The first is that you need to come up with a time frame as to when you can return for her. It will be very difficult for her to stand the pressure until she knows this."

"What pressure?"

"That's the second problem. She is at the age when she should become betrothed. Everyone will be putting pressure on her—her parents, her family, her friends—especially her parents."

"Sati said in her letter that this was her fear."

"It's much more than a fear. When all that pressure engulfs a girl, it's hard to cope with it. Believe me; I know."

"Is that how you felt?"

"Of course. First I wondered when my hips would widen. Then I worried about my breasts. Everyone said I was becoming so beautiful, but I didn't know for sure—you know? I wanted some say in who I married, but my father kept bringing up names of men I didn't even know. Some nights I went to bed terrified."

"And then you found Franko."

"Franko found me! He and his father met with my father even before I knew what was going on. It was right before they came to dinner here that he told me it was happening. I was horrified, but Franko was nice, and after a few more dinners, I began to see what my father saw in him. I think it will be fine, but there is no way I can know for sure."

"You look so happy when you are with him."

"I am happy. I want to be a bride and have children. But still, I don't know *him*—do you know what I mean? A girl takes a big risk, but we have to take it.

There is no other option."

"It really helps me to get this perspective," Clement admitted. "I'll send her another letter as soon as I can figure out how long we will have to wait."

"No. Don't put it off until then. A young virgin needs a lot of reassurance. Write again as soon as you can. Your letters will help her to remain calm."

After thanking Bella and Fidelis, Clement raced to Peter's house. "I need to send another letter to Sati," he exclaimed. "Can you get one to her?"

The bishop thought for a moment and replied, "To Anianus in Alexandria? That won't be easy. I'll ask and see who may be going there. Write your letter, and I'll see what I can do."

That evening the young lover went straight to his room muttering, "This may be more important than my first letter." Then he took a reed pen and carefully wrote:

From Clement, your adoring lover in Rome—to Sati, the joy of my life and my love forever: greetings.

When I got your letter, my heart leaped with delight. It is so wonderful to hear that you share my feelings of love and you choose to wait for my return. Words cannot describe how happy you have made me. I am sure that I am the happiest man in Rome, and I will remain so as long as I know that you love me too.

I treasure the gift that you sent me. Each night as I press it to my lips, I feel like I am kissing you, and when I press it to my chest, I feel that we are entwined in each other's arms. I open the locket and brush your beautiful hair against my cheek and breathe in the sweet scent of your perfume. It makes me feel like we are close together as I kiss you and kiss you and caress you in my dreams.

I have begun to work in our family business so that I can save some money and come for you. It is too early for me to know how long that will take, but I will make it as short of a time as I can. If you feel pressure to turn to another man, please know that I am doing everything in my power to become the one who makes you happy. Every day I focus only on you and being in a position to come back to you and to your fine parents.

Send another letter when you can. I so much appreciate having your words echoing in my ears and knowing how you feel. I love you, my dearest Sati. I love you with all of my heart. I believe that our dreams will become reality.

21

Sati did not speak with her father, nor did he say a word to her. The efforts that her mother made to bring them together were to no avail. She knew how stubborn her husband could be and was learning that her daughter could be just as determined. Reluctantly, Kenamon went to see Lumeri and postponed the dinner.

"Maybe we should try a different approach, dear," Redji told her husband. When he only grunted in reply she added, "We've always been a happy family. Perhaps if we were nicer about this, she might soften up."

"Our daughter does not run this house. If she were in love with a suitable man, I could—soften. But this wimpy Christian is out of the question. I can't stand that cult, and the boy can't even hold his head up in a conversation."

"I will speak with her again, dear. But it would help if you would at least smile and say hello. Just show her that you love her."

"I have said that many times."

"I know you have, but try to show it rather than say it. Just let her see how you care for her. That may clear the way for more reasonable conversations."

Kenamon paused, obviously thinking about his wife's recommendation. "I'll...I'll try."

"Try your best, dear. We need a breakthrough."

Clement read his new letter to Bella and Fidelis. She said it was beautiful, and he thought it sounded very adult. With their encouragement, he raced to see Peter to send it.

"I'll see what I can do," the apostle replied. "I haven't heard anyone say they were going to Alexandria."

"Please try," the young man pleaded.

"I will ask around. It may take a few days, though."

"That will be fine, as long as it gets there safely."

While Clement watched, Peter wrote a short note to Anianus. Then he folded the letter with it and put his seal on the outside. Clement was quite relieved.

The following Monday, Clement began working with Horus. His brother seemed annoyed, but cooperated when his father insisted.

"It's quite simple," Horus explained, talking down to his younger brother. "We have five delivery points to the emperor's household. We just have to get the eggs there without breaking."

"Who transports them?"

"I don't use Alphaeus. I think it's better to keep the two operations separate."

"Do you use locked boxes?"

"The whole cart locks—to prevent theft."

It seemed to Clement that he had to pry out each bit of information. "Do you bill the emperor?"

"I send a tally tag with each shipment and give the paymaster a summary each Saturday. Then I pick up our payment on Tuesday."

"That's quite fast."

"Yes. Father convinced Claudius how important it is that we pay our growers each Wednesday. After that, it's been almost automatic. I have few issues, as long as the eggs keep arriving without breaking."

"So what will we do today?" Clement asked.

"You can watch me sort them. After the carts are unloaded, I examine the crates and separate them according to quality."

"How do you do that?"

"It takes experience. I sort the crates into five categories. The finest go to the emperor's quarters, while the lesser grades go to the staff and the lowest to the slaves. You will see."

"Do you charge more for the better eggs?"

"Of course."

When the carts began arriving, the two brothers watched as the crates were placed on the loading dock. Horus inspected the eggs and told Clement where to stack them. In two hours the crates were neatly arranged into five groups. Then Horus counted the crates and placed a tag showing the number on each section.

Shortly after they finished, other carts started arriving. Each driver seemed to know which section he was to load, and as soon as Horus unlocked the enclosure, the driver carefully began placing crates in his cart.

"These are slaves, I presume."

"Of course. But only the most trusted ones go to the emperor's quarters. Rufus knows what each can handle."

"Rufus? Does he run this transport company?"

"Yes."

When all the carts were loaded and locked, Horus asked Clement, "Will you be coming back tomorrow?"

"Yes. All week."

The older brother waved and said, "You go on ahead. I have a few more things to do here."

"I have good news," Peter told Clement. "I found a man who knows someone who is going to Egypt. The traveler is not of our community, but my friend says he is reliable."

"That is good news. When is he leaving?"

"In just two days."

"Wonderful."

"You are off early," noted the apostle. "Will you have some wine with me?"

"That will be a pleasure."

Handing him a cup, Peter asked, "So, are you learning the egg business?"

"It seems fairly simple, really. Cassius uses a transport company to bring in the eggs, and Horus sends them on to the palace. A couple of things trouble me, though."

"What things?"

"Well, both transport operators use slaves to drive the carts. One got a beating last week and no food because a few of his eggs got broken."

"That is not untypical."

"I know, but father told me that we don't employ slaves. It seems like splitting hairs, though, when they work in a system that we control."

"You would prefer not to use slaves?"

"If we are not going to use them, they shouldn't be in any part of the operation."

"That's true."

"And another thing—we pay the growers all the same, a quarter denarius per crate, but Horus separates the crates into grades and charges more for what he calls the highest quality."

"Better eggs deserve a higher price."

"Yes, but I don't see any difference in the eggs. Horus says it takes experience to tell the difference. He's so secretive, though. I can't communicate with him very well."

"Hmm." The apostle stroked his beard. "Judas was like that."

The next several days were similar. As soon as the shipments were loaded, Horus sent Clement home.

On Friday the bachelor told Bella, "Peter found someone going to Egypt. My letter is on the way."

"Sati will be so happy to get it," Bella replied. "You really do love her, don't you?"

"Yes! With all my heart. How can you tell?"

"Because she is all you think about, from morning to night."

"I couldn't get her out of my mind if I wanted to. On Monday I'll find out what job my father wants me to do. After that I'll have a better idea of how long it will be before I can return to Alexandria. I'm very nervous about it."

"I'm sure that she is nervous too, waiting to hear from you."

"What do you suppose she is thinking right now, Bella? You understand the female mind."

The girl laughed, "She's thinking of you and pining her heart out."

Sati noticed the difference in her father's demeanor—an entire week where he was pleasant to her. *I know that he loves me*, she admitted. *I'll have to at least appear to cooperate.* She decided to bargain.

"Father, perhaps I was not fair to you. If you agree to not put pressure on me, I should be open to meeting anyone you suggest."

Kenamon was delighted. "That's my princess. Your mother and I want only what is best for you."

"I know, Father. And I respect that. But can you do it without trying to persuade me against my will?"

"I must! And I will," vowed the skilled businessman, who was accustomed to making deals. "I must, and I will."

With that, Sati went over to him and gave him a sweet kiss. As he gave her a warm hug, he sniffed his nose and wiped moisture from his eyes.

"Does this mean we can invite Lumeri to dinner?"

"Yes, Father, you may—as long as you keep your promise."

That night Clement lay in his bed with his eyes wide open. *Everything is so difficult*, he thought. *I wish a boy and girl could fall in love and get married, and that would be it. But adults have to conform to so many expectations. I have to get along with my father and my brothers, and who knows what problems Sati is facing. It's so complicated.*

"Did you pray about it," he heard Peter ask, like he did on the ship in Cyrene.

He realized, he hadn't been praying hardly at all. *I must pray more, rather than worry so much. I must put this in the hands of Christ.* When the words did not form on his lips, he got out of bed and knelt on the floor, but his mind was not in a prayerful place. "Tomorrow I've got to settle down and pray to Jesus," he muttered. "I must, and I will."

Out on the great sea, a stormy wind was howling. The captain told his passenger to tie down his belongings, so they wouldn't be swept away. Nodding, the man pushed his things into his bag so he could bring them below deck. But in his haste, two papers slipped from his fingers, including a letter addressed to a presbyter in Egypt.

22

On Monday morning Urbanus met with his three sons at the warehouse. "My sons, my sons—all working together. This is a beautiful sight."

"We want to make you proud of us, Father," replied Horus.

"So…what job shall we give to your brother?"

When Cassius was silent, Horus spoke up, "I've been thinking about this. If we can expand our supply, we can make more profit. The number of people working in the emperor's household is always increasing a little, but we could take on another major customer, if we had the eggs to sell."

"Who would that be?"

"It could be a big food seller. Magnus has five or six locations now. If we had more eggs, finding a customer would be easy."

"Hmm. How could we do that, Cassius?"

"Some of our growers could add more coops, and I could work with some of the smaller farmers who are right along our routes, if I had the time."

Horus added, "Sure. If Clement helped you with your operation, I bet you could double our volume.

"I don't know about doubling it."

"Not right away. But if we could increase our intake by—say, a quarter, I'm sure I can find someone who will want the eggs."

"Yes. With Clement's help, I probably can do that."

"And Cassius, now that you soon will be a father, maybe you could take a day off each week."

"That would be very nice. Bringing in eggs seven days every week certainly keeps me away from home."

"Would you like a day off, as well, Horus?" asked his father.

"Maybe later. For right now I am fine with just Cassius taking one."

"Well, then it's settled. Cassius and Clement, you work out how you will split up the tasks, and Horus, start looking for another customer. But keep it quiet until I speak with Claudius. I want him to know that keeping him satisfied will always be our top priority."

Redji and Kenamon did their best to make the dinner with Lumeri as perfect as possible. He asked the wine merchant what variety the suitor preferred, and even though it was expensive, he brought home four bottles. She ordered five stately lilies to dress up the atrium and went with Sati to select a new gown.

"You look beautiful, dear," she said, admiring how grown-up her daughter looked in semitransparent linen. "I'll ask the dressmaker to take it in a little through the waist. Then it will fit you just right."

Sati tried to scowl, but couldn't help smiling as she saw her reflection in the polished mirror. It felt good to see herself dressed as a woman. She blushed as she observed her own smile, but then straightened her shoulders and tipped her head back, revealing a bit of pride and confidence. "Yes. Thank you, Mother."

Lumeri arrived carrying gifts. "For the lady," he said, handing Redji an exquisite arrangement of flowers. "And for her lovely daughter." Bowing graciously from the waist, he opened a small box and showed a delicate golden bracelet to Sati.

"Take it, dear," her mother whispered.

"Allow me," the gentleman replied, carefully opening the clasp and laying the bracelet across her wrist. "Do you like it?"

"It's beautiful."

"Then it is yours," he assured her, snapping the clasp closed.

"Sit here, Lumeri," gestured the host, who had previously arranged to sit at the suitor's right, with his wife and daughter directly across from his guest.

Sati was surprised at how handsome Lumeri appeared, tall and erect, with wavy black hair and smooth skin, a little lighter than most Egyptian men. It made him look younger than his age. He spoke with assurance like a man accustomed to being in control. His eyes seldom blinked as he gave his full attention to each person, leaning toward them as he listened—a bit closer as he addressed Sati. A gracious smile never left his face, and words swept off his tongue like butterflies. The man obviously was at ease in polite conversation.

"This wine is excellent—one of my favorite varieties. You have fine taste, Kenamon."

"Thank you."

"And Redji, this duck is outstanding. Do I detect an apricot sauce?"

"Our cook continually outdoes herself."

"Treat her well. You have a rare gem in your household." Then turning to Sati, he asked, "Do you like dates?" When she nodded, he added, "I am experimenting with a small orchard just south of the city. It is just a hobby, for now."

When she smiled, he asked her, "What do you like to do—in terms of hobbies, if I may ask?"

"My hobbies? I am learning to play the lyre."

"She's getting quite adept," interjected her mother.

"The lyre! Such an amazing instrument for soothing the soul. I would love to hear you play some time—but not this evening. I don't wish to ever put a woman on the spot, nor make her feel ill at ease. Sometime, perhaps."

"Yes. Perhaps."

Through the meal, Lumeri continued to control the conversation with questions, putting each in a way that it would tend to be answered with a yes. Kenamon and Redji were delighted, and Sati was enjoying herself more than she thought she would. She realized that her father had arranged for her to meet a very nice man, who seemed quite considerate and respectful.

"I must check on our sweets," the hostess noted, rising and going inside. Her husband trailed along.

Sati felt awkward. Lumeri simply smiled. Then she asked a question she had rehearsed, "What do you think of Christians? I am very impressed with the one they call Jesus and would like to become baptized."

The guest was not prepared for such a frank expression from a maiden, but he took it in stride. "I am an open-minded man. I try to see what is good in all things."

"My father was inquiring about the faith, but he changed his mind. My mother is following him, but I see no reason why a wife needs to be of the same faith as her husband. What do you think?"

"I am in total agreement. As I said, I am open-minded. And I see that you have a mind of your own."

Sati blushed. She had planned for the question to be a test that might turn away Lumeri's interest, but this did not happen. "In some ways, I am a conventional Alexandrian, but in other ways, I am quite different."

"I find all of your ways fascinating," he instantly replied, flashing a broad smile.

At a loss for words, Sati was relieved when her parents returned with trays of sweets. Lumeri took a plate of sugared berries and offered them to Sati, "Something sweet—for the sweetest of this house." She took one and blushed as she put it between her lips.

The next day, more gifts were delivered, along with an invitation to dine at Lumeri's. Sati's plan to turn away the suitor's interest apparently had not succeeded.

On Wednesday as Cassius watched, Clement placed the correct number of coins in each grower's box, being careful to deduct the amounts some already had been paid. "That was perfect," Cassius observed. "Now lock up the boxes."

Clement did as directed and turned with a smile, "This is not difficult. A person just has to count carefully."

"Correct."

"You have made this a very efficient process, Brother. It should be easy for us to expand."

Cassius gloated and thanked his new partner for his diligence.

On his way home, the young egg merchant stopped in to see Peter. "Are they keeping you busy?" the older man asked.

Clement explained how he had begun working with Cassius in hopes of expanding the supply sources. "Horus gave me fourteen denarii. I don't know, but I assume that was for the two weeks I was in training."

"Not bad pay for an apprentice living at home."

"I suppose. I thanked him, but I don't know what to expect in the future, and it's too early to press my father for a commitment."

"That's true."

"I've been thinking about telling him about Sati. That way he will know what I will be needing."

"Have the two of you been getting along well since you got back?"

"Yes—quite well—and he is treating me like a part...a junior partner."

"This might be a good time to reveal your feelings."

"Thanks, Peter. I think I will.

That evening during dinner, Clement cleared his throat and put the additional information on the table. "I told you about my trip through Palestine, but I neglected to say much about Alexandria."

"You were only there two nights," his mother remembered.

"That's true, but something very important happened the first night. When Peter and I got to Bishop Marcus's house, a man was leaving who was overjoyed to meet Peter. He is a catechumen, and he invited us to dinner where he could ask more questions about Christ."

"That's nice."

"Yes. Well, I've been meaning to share with you…they have this magnificent view from their balcony."

"Yes—and…"

"Their beautiful daughter showed me the view, and I have fallen in love with her."

Urbanus was quick to respond, "That's pretty fast for one trip to a balcony."

"I know. I still can't believe it, but it happened. We have exchanged letters. She says she loves me too."

"How old is this girl?"

"About a year younger than me."

"Well, she's at the age to become betrothed, but you are much too young to fall in love."

Clement took a deep breath and poured out the whole narrative, beginning with the vision on the ship with the two white birds and concluding with his recent second letter. He left nothing out.

"This certainly explains why you have taken such an interest in the business," his father blurted.

"Yes, Father. But it is time for me to begin to work like a man—you said so yourself—and if I ever hope to have Sati for my wife, then I must put myself in a position to support her."

"Most boys don't seek a wife until they are in their mid-twenties."

"I wasn't planning for this to happen. It just did! So I am approaching it with the most mature choices I can think of."

"Hmm. I have to agree with you on that. And I am not against your becoming more mature. How soon do you plan to go back to Alexandria?"

"I told her how it could be a long while. She said she would wait, but for how long, I don't know. I don't even know how much a man needs to have when he seeks a wife."

"He needs more than you have, and how can we know if you will even want to stay in the egg business?"

Clement hung his head and mumbled, "I am not trying to have you make a premature commitment, Father. I don't expect that. I simply said that I don't know how much a man needs."

"Well, enough to get your own house, and the travel costs, and so forth. Cassius and Horus reached that point by the time they were about twenty-five."

"Twenty-five! I can't go that long without seeing Sati."

"Maybe we should just see how things go for a while," his mother offered.

"No, I can calculate it right now," Urbanus blurted. "Clement, if you live here and dedicate yourself to the business until your twentieth birthday, you'll have several hundred denarii, and I will make you a gift of a trip to Alexandria, if that is what you want. By then you also should be carrying a full load in the business and earning more money. Does that make sense to you?"

"Yes, sir. It makes very good sense. That's the kind of information that I need."

"But won't it be difficult for them to wait that long?" asked his mother.

"Clement says he wants to be an adult. Well, I have made a very generous offer. If their romance endures for that long, then they certainly are in love. If it doesn't, then..."

"Don't worry, Mother. Father has, as usual, come up with a sound approach. In fact, now that I hear it, the wait doesn't seem as bad. I think this is a very satisfactory proposal, Father. I appreciate it."

Fidelis thought the plan sounded good, but Bella had concerns.

"That is a very long time for a maiden to wait," she cautioned. "As soon as you get a letter from Sati, let's review this and take steps to let her know."

23

Sati didn't want to go to Lumeri's house, but she felt trapped. She had attempted to make him want to turn away, but that failed. Now she had to keep her promise to her father.

Kenamon had insisted on purchasing another new gown for his daughter, one even more becoming than the first, and her mother brushed an extra dash of color onto her cheeks.

Lumeri's house was enormous, on a level plot in an elegant district. Just inside the main gate a stable boy ran up and took charge of their rented carriage. Sati had never seen an estate so impressive.

"They say he owns three hundred farms," Kenamon whispered. "He gets a third of the rice, and overseers handle all of the details."

Several servants emerged from the giant doorway, followed by their host. "Good evening! Good evening! I have so much looked forward to this day. Come in. Come in."

Lumeri led them past a long curving stairway to a large atrium, which was shaded at the upper level by a movable curtain. Seeing Sati look up, he remarked, "We keep the curtain in place until the sun sets. It is just about time to remove it. Do you like to look at the stars?"

"Yes. Of course."

"Another hobby of mine is studying the stars. An advisor told me that this will be a very fortunate year. I believe he will prove to be correct."

After they sat down and accepted cool drinks, Sati looked up just in time to see the curtain finish rolling away, revealing the blue evening sky. Their host added, "After dinner I will read the stars for each of you."

Sati sipped her wine and noted as she set it on the table that a servant promptly refilled each person's goblet.

Lumeri asked Kenamon to confirm what he heard about the ivory business flourishing and graciously complimented Redji on her youthful appearance. Then turning to Sati he asked, "Have you been playing the lyre?"

"The lyre? Oh yes. I practice a little each day."

"Now don't forget. One of these days I want to hear you play. The music of the lyre is such a treat to the ears and a gift to the heart."

Sati was at a loss for words and, smiling, took a sip of her wine.

"Ah! Here are my darling daughters," Lumeri exclaimed as three girls entered the room. "This is Bunefer, who excellently recites poetry." The girl of about eleven years looked alert and intelligent. "And Sitamun, who knows all the delights of the table." The nine-year-old, though shorter than her sister, appeared to weigh a bit more. "And my sweet Nefrusheri, who we call Sheri." The smiling girl, a little younger than the others, blushed and gave the guests a low bow. "My darling girls bring such joy to me."

"You never had a son?" Kenamon asked, realizing that he had crudely stated the obvious.

"No. We were not blessed with a boy. But I am happy with my lovely girls."

Two servants brought in a table and more chairs. "Let us gather for dinner. Redji: you and Sati sit here by me. I love to be surrounded by beauty. Is that all right with you, Kenamon?"

"Certainly," he replied as he took a seat opposite the girls.

Sati didn't say much as the dinner was served. Even though Lumeri was a pleasant man, she was unaccustomed to his style of conversation and hoped that if she kept quiet, he might lose interest in her. Lumeri, as usual, controlled the dialogue and used his charm to keep everyone at ease. His daughters were quite polite and spoke only when asked a question by their father.

At the end of the meal when the girls were excused, Kenamon asked, "May I see your stable?"

"Certainly," Lumeri said, summoning a servant to show him. Redji followed her husband, giving Lumeri and Sati a few minutes alone together, as they had done at the first dinner.

"Did you like the food?" he asked.

"It was very good."

"You have not said much this evening."

"I am trying to figure you out. Are you looking for a maid to take care of your daughters?"

Surprised at her boldness, he answered, "They already have a very fine governess, and I bring in tutors for their lessons."

"Are you looking for someone who will bear you a son?"

"My, my. You are full of questions. My dear, I am a young man, who unfortunately lost his lovely wife to a tragic illness. I have many years to live and much love and generosity to offer. I cannot just become a hermit."

"I didn't mean to imply that you are not a man of good intentions."

"I am only dining with you with good intentions. And I am hoping that you will come with me to see my dates. We could get to know each other better. May I ask your father if we could go on such an outing?"

"If you want to."

"Good. Oh. Here they come now. Good. Sit here. I want to read the stars for each of you."

Everyone laughed as Lumeri pointed out their stars and explained how each was destined for much happiness. On their way out to their carriage, he whispered something in Kenamon's ear and smiled when his guest nodded.

Clement lay on his bed with feelings of anxiety. The day had presented a greater degree of certainty for him, but he couldn't stop worrying about Sati. "I hope she replies soon to my letter," he muttered through his breath. Then he opened her ivory locket and brushed her hair across his cheek, noticing that it didn't give him the usual satisfaction. There was an ominous knot at the top of his stomach that didn't go away, even when he fell into a fitful sleep.

The next day Cassius stayed home from work, and Clement handled the intake of eggs with confidence. He was relieved to see that none of the crates contained any broken ones—he didn't want to be the source of any further slave beatings. Horus didn't say a word to him all day, which seemed odd. *I guess he just likes to be alone*, he mused.

Kenamon explained to his wife and daughter how he had given permission for Lumeri to take Sati to his date farm, and on Saturday the landowner arrived in a carriage. She saw that the conveyance was covered but was glad that she had worn a substantial dress that would protect her from the burning sun.

"Good morning, Sati. You look lovely today. Isn't this a beautiful day to see the dates?"

"Yes," she said, giving him her usual reply.

"And Kenamon, Redji, I will take good care of your charming daughter and return by midafternoon."

"Very good, Lumeri. Have a good time."

Sati was uncomfortable since it was her first outing with a potential suitor. Assuming this, Lumeri did everything possible to put her at ease. "The farm is not far, just a few miles up the river. It will take only an hour. Are you comfortable?"

"Yes," she lied. The ride was smooth, but she did not want to be in the carriage.

Lumeri pointed out the sites, many of which were farms that he owned. "My grandfather and father put the estates together," he noted. "But I add a few more holdings each year. The share of the crops adds up to more than I require, so I have my overseers negotiate the purchases."

If he has everything he wants, why does he need me? Sati wondered.

The date farm was beautiful, lying along a bend in the slow-flowing river. "The rich, moist delta soil is perfect for dates, and I arrange the varieties into groups, so they will not become lonely."

"Does that not help them pollinate?" she asked.

"Very perceptive, my dear. I like to express things in the best possible way."

"Then express to me what your intentions are."

"Again, you are quite frank and to the point. You are extremely enchanting, and I believe quite charming. You will make someone a very fine wife."

"I wonder who that might be."

"Only the gods know. But in my humble way, I hope to be included among those that you consider."

"Haven't you already discussed that with my father?"

"Of course not. I told Kenamon that it was time for me to put away the garments of mourning and look to the future. That's all. I would never put a proposal to a woman's father, unless I knew that she wanted me to."

"What if a woman were to say that she didn't want you to?"

"Then I would honor her decision—heartbroken, of course. But helpless, under the circumstances."

Sati considered her next words carefully. "If a man were to imply that he wanted to speak with my father, I would say that I needed a month or two to get better acquainted and ponder the matter. That is reasonable; do you not think so?"

"Yes, my dear. Such a response would be quite reasonable. Now come. I want to show you my favorite grove of dates."

24

Three months later, to the day, the family gathered to celebrate Clement's eighteenth birthday. Even Horus and his wife attended. Clement invited Fidelis and Peter.

Toward the end of the evening he spoke with the bishop quite resolutely, "I have not heard from Sati, so I am going to send another letter to her. Can you find someone who can personally deliver it to Anianus?"

"Give me the letter and I will do my best to get it to him."

That night before going to sleep, he penned the following:

From Clement in Rome, who loves you dearly—to Sati, the sunbeam of Egypt, who owns my restless heart: greetings.

Today was my eighteenth birthday, a day of both joy and sadness. My soul leaped with joy when I received your letter, but has been in despair since it has not heard further word. How I long to hear those three little words again from you, which echo my continuing song—I love you, I love you, I love you.

As I said in my last letter, I have joined in our family business, which is expanding. I have saved some money, and my father told me that he will send me to your city upon my twentieth birthday. Now that the time frame is established, that doesn't seem like too long of a wait. I hope that you feel the same way.

It is my assumption that you and your family are now baptized. This bridges the

*distance for us in that we both now are of the One Body of Christ. Each Sunday
I pray for you during the breaking of the bread.*

*I think of you day and night. I open your locket and gaze upon the golden strands
of your hair. It makes me feel close to you, even though we are separated by many
miles of open sea. I treasure the memories of the night we met, and I dream of the
day when we shall be united.*

*Please send another letter as soon as you can. I love you with all of my heart, and
you shall possess my love always.*

Within the week, Peter located a man traveling to Alexandria, and after explaining how he could find Anianus, he placed Clement's letter along with his own brief note in his care.

Redji did her best to reason with her daughter. "It has been three months now, and you should be giving Lumeri some sense of your feelings."

"I know, Mother. I was hoping to receive word from Clement."

"If he had sent even one more letter, then you might have grounds for waiting."

"I know."

"He obviously was enchanted with you when you first met—you said that his letter was filled with words of love. But when nothing more comes of it, then it appears to be just a young boy's fantasy. One kiss in the moonlight hardly outweighs all that Lumeri is promising you."

"Lumeri has been very kind, and I have not returned his kindness."

"That's right! And it has been a month since he spoke with your father. Can you not see that you are jeopardizing the opportunity of a lifetime?"

"I see that clearly, Mother. Perhaps it is foolish of me to wait for Clement."

"You are not a fool. You fell in love with a fine young man. But nothing has come of it."

"I wish I loved Lumeri like I love Clement."

"Love will come as you share your life with your husband. You will have the joy of motherhood and many moments of mutual happiness. That is the way love grows for couples. You may not feel it intensely now, like you did with Clement, but in time you and Lumeri will have an enduring love that greatly surpasses your earlier memories."

"I suppose you are right, Mother. Perhaps I have had just a young girl's fantasy."

Egyptians did not have formal ceremonies for marriage like those in other parts of the empire. When a couple decided to wed, a simple contract was drawn up and the wife moved in to her husband's house.

"I am the happiest man in the world," Lumeri expounded as he signed the document.

"Now, Sati…" He handed her the reed pen.

After a moment of hesitancy, she uttered, "You are a kind man, my husband," and carefully inscribed her name.

"And the parents…"

Kennamon quickly scrawled his name.

Cheers rang out and bubbling wine was poured. Kenamon beamed and Redji smiled with both delight and relief. Lumeri and Sati were legally married.

"And now, my dear. Will you please get your lyre? My joy will be complete, if on this momentous day, you play me a delightful song."

25

For Clement, Thursdays were the most difficult. Cassius was off, and Horus lurked around the warehouse like an overprotective hen. The gulf between them seemed to have widened since his birthday.

Clement kept his distance and focused on his duties, but when he needed to ask a question, Horus barked the answer like an angry schoolmaster. On those days, the young man looked forward to stopping by Peter's house for a cup of wine and some moral support.

"His behavior certainly seems odd," Peter shared. "Have you tried giving him more compliments?"

"I don't feel like being nice to him when he treats me that way. He acts like he is in charge, when Father specifically tells us that we are to work as a team."

"You have good reason to be suspicious. If I were you, I'd keep an eye on him for a while."

"Yes; the whole situation makes me uneasy." Taking a sip of wine, he brought up another matter, "Any word from Alexandria?"

"Not yet, but the man who took your letter should be returning any day now."

The following Tuesday, Horus told Clement, "I need to leave early today. Can you lock up?"

"Yes, Brother. I too will leave in a few minutes."

When they arrived Wednesday morning, Cassius was screaming, "Someone broke in last night and stole the strongbox!"

"How did they get in? I locked the door," Clement protested.

"The door was forced open. You can see the marks. And here, where the strongbox was attached—they pried it loose. See, the pins are broken. They must have used an iron bar."

"We'll get to the bottom of this," Horus predicted.

"But I need the coins for today's payments."

Horus took charge. "Let's not panic. Clement, you run home and tell Father. He has a strongbox in his bedroom and probably can give you a sack for today. In the meantime, Cassius and I will look around for more clues."

Clement raced home.

Urbanus was shocked. "We've never suffered this kind of loss. How much was in the strongbox?"

"Horus didn't say."

"Well—I'll go get a sack of coins. Then we'll go down there."

At the warehouse Horus told his father, "It must be someone who knows our operation. He knew that on Tuesday night the strongbox would be full."

"I'm afraid you are right," Urbanus said as he handed the sack to Cassius. "Here are one hundred denarii. Get busy with today's payments."

"Who would do such a thing?" Clement pleaded.

Horus offered several possibilities. "It was someone we trust. Alphaeus, or one of his men. I don't think Rufus would have done it. Or it could have been one of us."

"One of us!" three voices exclaimed.

"Well, somebody took the strongbox, and he pried it loose quickly. He knew just where to look for it."

"We need a more efficient system," Cassius asserted. "There is too much risk in leaving that much money here."

Horus had a suggestion. "It would be just as easy for me to bring the money from the palace home on Tuesday afternoons. Then I can bring what we need here early each Wednesday."

"That's a good idea, son." Urbanus concurred. "When you have time, figure out how much we lost. And I want all of us to keep our eyes open for anyone who looks suspicious."

"Should I confront Alphaeus?" asked Cassius.

"No! Don't let anyone know that anything even happened. The culprit may get careless, and then we'll catch him."

Thursday afternoon, Clement wanted to share the news of the theft with Peter, but when he entered the house, the bishop was displaying a sad frown. "Is something the matter?" he asked.

"Sit down, son. I'm afraid there is bad news."

"What is it?"

"Here. Read this."

Clement took the paper in his hands and gasped as soon as he read the greeting.

Anianus, a presbyter of Alexandria—to Peter, bishop of Rome: greetings.
I received the letter from Clement addressed to Sati of the household of Kenamon, and I regret to inform you that the young woman is now married to a prominent landowner in our city. Under the circumstances, I thought it best to return the letter to the sender. We would not wish to interfere in the harmony of the new couple.

He held his breath as he stared at the parchment, which was becoming a blur in his shaking hands. While the events portrayed were a known possibility all along, the young lover was totally unprepared for the message. Wet tears welled in his eyes, and he had to wipe them clumsily on his sleeve. He might have read the words again, but both papers fell silently to the floor. Speechless, he let his head drop heavily into his hands.

The fisherman sat down and put his arms around the youth, who turned and sobbed on his chest. He tenderly caressed the lad's back with his calloused hands but was unable to utter any words of comfort.

For a long time, the two men just sat in silence. Peter poured two cups of wine. Clement took a sip and spit out his feelings. "I don't know what I'll do— I love her so. I still love her, even if she is married to a prominent landowner. I gave my heart to Sati. She has been my sunbeam for all this time, since the day we met. I don't think anyone will ever replace her in my broken heart."

"Things do not always go the way we hope, my son."

"They certainly don't."

"Take some time with this, Clement. Don't make any hasty judgments. Such a loss cannot heal quickly."

"This loss will never heal," he predicted angrily.

"No. It may be a scar that you bear all of your life."

"If I have a life."

"You already have a very blessed life. I carry scars, too, but I do not carry them alone."

"If you are saying that Jesus will bring something good out of all of this, I don't want to hear it. Right now, I just want to lick my wounds."

"That's fine, my son. I can't take away your pain, nor can Christ. All we can do is love you."

26

To Redji of the house of Kenamon—from Sati, your loving daughter: greetings. Please come and see me. I think I may have some news.

Redji smiled wide when she read the note and hurried to her daughter's side. "Are you…?"

"I think so."

"Have you told Lumeri?"

"I wanted to talk to you first."

Sati explained the signs, which her mother confirmed. Then they both squealed with delight.

Lumeri, of course, was overjoyed. He danced around the house for an hour, thanking the gods for his good fortune. Then he gathered his daughters around him and told them, "We have such fine news. Sati is going to have a baby. Isn't that exciting?"

His words were met with three blank stares.

"We will have a new baby in our house, and we will have such fun!"

Still the stares—no response.

Finally, Bunefer, the oldest asked, "Will he be a boy or a girl?"

"We do not know, of course," her father answered. "We must wait and find out."

"When will we know?"

"We will know when the baby is born. That will be in a few months."

Sitamun began to shout, "I don't want a boy! Can't we have a sister?"

"No, darling. The baby already is a boy or a girl, but we can't see it, so we are not able to tell. But with either a girl or a boy, I will be very happy, and you should be too."

Finally, Sheri, the youngest said, "I will be happy, Father," not quite knowing what to make of her sisters' reticence in light of her father's joy.

"Can we go play now?" Bunefer asked.

Lumeri sat down and looked at his wife in shock. "I thought they would be happy, as you and I are."

"They may need a little time, dear. They were not expecting this news."

"You may be right. I will try to calm down and let them adjust slowly."

Kenamon also was happy to hear the news. Something else was occurring in his life, however, that was very troubling. Two other ivory dealers had suddenly met their deaths.

"They both were murdered!" he told his wife. "That bothers me. It's too big of a coincidence."

"Did you know them well?"

"Not very well. But why would two dealers suffer the same fate in such a short time?"

In his grief over losing Sati, Clement at first did not notice that Horus was watching him in the warehouse. His brother was acting as though he suspected him as the thief who took the strongbox.

"What can I do?" he asked Peter later that day. "I know that I didn't take the money, but I can't prove it."

"An innocent man can't prove that he is trustworthy. All he can do is be trustworthy. Jesus showed us that."

"But Jesus was crucified, even though he was innocent."

"Yes. That's my point. He didn't try to state evidence in his defense. If he had, they would have come up with another charge against him. No—he loved even his accusers."

"Horus has always been difficult to love. He is my brother, but even when we were boys, he acted like he hated me."

"Boys can be like that. When you came along, you took his place as his mother's favorite."

"I remember a time when he and I ate a berry cake that Mama had baked for dinner. He ate more than I did, but he put the blame on me. I got punished the worst."

"That story could have been a parable in Jesus's teaching. He said we should not resist evil, but do good to those who harm us."

"I've been doing that, but it hasn't gotten me very far."

"We do it not because it gets us far, but because we are followers of Christ."

"Oh, Peter. You can be so difficult."

"It is difficult, at times, to follow Jesus. But each time that you live up to his expectations, you grow more in your faith."

"I'm learning that, my good friend. I know you are right, but it is hard."

Kenamon and Redji came unannounced to Lumeri's house with frantic looks on their faces. "We must see Sati at once!" Kenamon shouted.

The four gathered in the atrium. "A third ivory dealer has been murdered!" he gasped. "They cut his throat right in his storage depot. Some of us have been talking, and we think Baufre is behind it."

"But isn't Baufre already the largest dealer?" Lumeri asked.

"Yes. And he wants it all. He didn't try to buy anyone out. He just got rid of them!"

"Are you sure?"

"The two dealers who were killed earlier—Baufre already has taken over their supply and latched onto their customers. And yesterday when the third was murdered, he threw a feast for his friends."

"What will you do?" shrieked Sati.

"We sold our house and put as much as we could in the carriage. We have to flee for our lives. There is no other choice!"

"But you can't just leave."

"We have to, dear. Don't you see?" her mother explained. "Leaving is the last thing we want, but we have to go."

"But I will miss you so!" she screamed, throwing her arms around her mother.

"You will be safe with Lumeri. And you need to take care of the baby," she cautioned.

"But I am afraid for you."

Her father answered, "We will be safe, as long as we leave today. From here, we are going straight to the harbor."

"Where will you go?"

"We don't know yet. We likely will go north—to Europe. We'll get on the first ship heading that way."

Lumeri asked, "Do you need money?"

"Thank you for asking, but the man who bought our house gave us enough to get a new start."

"I will give you some more."

"That is kind of you, Lumeri. But we must hurry."

While Lumeri rushed to his strongbox, Sati pleaded, "Don't leave me here alone!"

"When this has subsided, we will come back or send word to you as to where we are," her father assured. "You will be fine, and we will be too. But we must leave today."

"Take care of yourself, dear, and take good care of the baby," urged her mother. "I want to hold my first grandchild."

Lumeri returned and handed a sack to Kenamon. "Thank you," Kenamon sobbed.

Amid Sati's tears and screams, they rushed out the door to their carriage.

Over the next several days, Lumeri did everything possible to comfort his wife. Two more ivory dealers were found dead, which, despite the horror, at least added credibility to Kenamon's decision to leave the city.

"They got away in time, darling. I'm sure they are fine and on their way to safety."

"I believe they are safe," she admitted. "But it is so sad. The ruthless always get away with what they do."

"Not always, dear. Baufre may yet be caught and brought to punishment."

"But that won't bring my mother and father back to me. I need my mother now."

"You will have the best of nurses, my dear."

"Thank you, Lumeri. You are so good to me. But a nurse is not a substitute for a mother."

Her husband heard her point and felt it would be best to reply with a caress, rather than words.

Sati thought of Clement, *I wonder how it is in his life. Everything could have been so different. I at least loved Clement.* Then she looked up at Lumeri and said, "I don't have anyone that I am close to."

"You have me."

"I didn't mean it that way. You are a fine husband. It's just that I have no close friends now. The girls I knew either have families or seem so childish. We don't get together anymore."

"After the baby is born you will have something in common with your old friends or make new ones."

"I want to become a Christian."

"You said that before we were wed."

"This might be a good time for me to get involved with the Church."

"This hardly seems like a good time to begin anything new. After the baby is born would be better."

"I suppose you are right. I will wait until then."

Clement applied himself to the egg business. He was handling the warehouse with competency, which his father and older brother appreciated. Cassius shared whenever he added another grower to their routes, but all the youngest brother ever got from Horus were frowns.

"Tell me the truth," Horus demanded one afternoon when they were alone. "You stole the strongbox. Didn't you?"

Shocked at the unprovoked accusation, he pleaded, "No, Brother. I did not. Why do you think it was me?"

"You need money, and you knew where the strongbox was kept."

Remembering Peter's advice, Clement calmly answered, "I was as shocked as you when the theft occurred. I still am."

"Anyone can act shocked."

"I was totally shocked. I didn't need to act."

"I still think you did it."

Very calmly, Clement replied, "I can't prove to you that I didn't do it, but I hope that in time you will come to trust me."

Horus gave out a low grunt and walked away.

Clement hung his head. He did not expect this to be the last of such confrontations.

As the presence of the expected baby became more pronounced, Lumeri was disturbed that his daughters didn't show much interest.

"You girls should stay close to Sati now," he told them privately. "You will learn much that you will need to know when you are older."

They just frowned.

"Becoming a mother is a wonderful experience. You will know the joy someday, and you can begin to learn about it now."

"Sati doesn't seem happy," Bunefer declared.

"Oh, don't confuse her sadness over her parents having to move away with the joy of giving birth to a child. Be kind to her. She needs your friendship at this time."

Sitamun objected, "She's not our mother. She shouldn't be having a baby here."

"My princess, don't talk that way. We all were sad when Mama died, but we have a new mother in the house now."

"She's not my mother, and he won't be my brother," the middle daughter said coldly.

"Please, Sitamun. You must learn to treat Sati as your friend."

"All of my friends are someone I chose. I will never ask your wife to be my friend."

Bunefer tried to reason with her father, "You have to understand our point of view. We were happy with our mama, and we adjusted after she died. We had to. But whether or not we like Sati is up to us to decide."

"Yes," Sitamun added, "and whether or not we like the new brother is up to us to decide too."

The girls had never spoken to him like this. Sheri, the youngest, seemed afraid to say a word. Lumeri was not accustomed to being disagreed with by anyone, especially his children. He was speechless, perhaps for the first time in his life.

It was as though a spell hung over the house of Lumeri. His wife was grieving, his daughters were obstinate, and he, himself, was feeling anxious. Regardless of how hard he tried, he couldn't bring the situation under his control.

Sati was bored and lonely. She picked up her lyre a few times, but no music came from its strings. Occasionally, while Lumeri was out, she walked to the stable and talked to the steeds. They seemed to listen but didn't offer any words of hope. It was something to do to pass the time, and she went there nearly every day.

"Why do the children hate me?" she asked her favorite mare, whom she called Rosa for the light red cast across her mane. "You have had children; you should know."

The animal looked at her and returned to eating her hay.

"Did you love your husbands, Rosa? They wanted you because you are beautiful, but did you love any of them? I wished that I loved mine. It would make this so much easier."

The mare shook her shoulders, but Sati didn't know if that was a yes or a no.

"I still love Clement. I wish this was his baby and I lived in his house. He has no daughters to disdain me. But I probably will never see him again. He has lost interest in me. My mother said it was just a boyish fantasy. I don't know…I was so sure that he loved me."

The animal nodded.

"I believe that I shall always love him. Come what may, I will love him until I die."

"Wheeee!" came a sound from the stall behind her. Turning, she saw the enormous black stallion snorting.

"Do you want to be my friend too?" she asked the steed. "Here, let me pet your nose." Opening the gate, Sati reached up toward it, but the giant animal lunged forward toward the mare, nearly choking on the rope that secured his neck. He kicked his legs in an attempt to regain his balance, and Sati felt a sharp pain across her left side. Hearing the noise, a stable boy ran to the stall and attempted to calm the stallion, but before he could drag Sati out, she felt another heavy hoof hit her right hip, and she fell unconscious.

When she awoke, Lumeri was standing over her. She blinked her eyes and noticed that he was crying. "I will survive," she promised.

Lumeri, however, through his tears, gasped, "You lost the baby. It was a boy."

27

Clement put down the egg crate he was carrying, suddenly feeling the impulse to pray for Sati. He dropped to his knees on the warehouse floor and poured out his heart to Christ:

"Jesus, my Lord. I hope you are watching over Sati, whom I love, even though she is now married to another. Protect her from all harm. Keep her safe from all evil influences that may surround her. Help her to become closer to you and grow to know you better as she pursues the Christian life.

"You know how much I love her—how I still love her. Even when she is in the arms of the prominent landowner in her city to whom she is wed, I still love her and remain devoted to her. I pray always for what is best for her, and I hope that she is happy.

"Oh, Jesus. You are the only one to whom I can turn—both in my sorrow and in my hope. I don't know what led me to drop to my knees at this moment, but I trust that you know and that you care enough to intercede, if she needs your loving kindness.

"If she is in pain, soothe her. If she is distraught, comfort her. If she is in danger, protect her. If she has any reason to worry, please, please, bring her to a place of safety and security.

"If she is lonely—let her know that she is not alone—as I am praying for her, just as I would be if I was at her side. Sati will always be my love—my sunbeam—for as long as I am alive—and for all time.

"And Lord Jesus, if I may once again pray in the way you prayed to your heavenly Father on the night you were beset by evil—whatever is best for Sati, make that prevail—not my will, but thine be done."

"What are you doing!" barked the voice of Horus, who was standing over Clement on the dock, glaring down at him. "What in hell are you doing?"

Clement lifted his head and muttered, "I'm praying."

"It's the middle of the day! This is no time to pray!"

"I...I...felt the need to pray."

"So you felt the need to pray. This is not Sunday. This is a work day."

"I just had to pray for my love, Sati. So I..."

"Sati! That fickle girl, who stole your heart and broke it—she doesn't belong in here. She has no business in this warehouse."

Restraining the impulse to strike out at his brother, Clement whimpered, "I love her. Don't you know?"

"How can you love someone who tossed you aside? You are more of a fool than I thought."

Clement didn't say another word but went back to stacking crates. Horus, however, spoke with his father and made a big case out of the incident.

"That's the way it is when you take the Lord's commands seriously," Peter told Clement. "You feel persecuted."

"That's exactly how I feel," Clement exclaimed. "First Horus blamed me for the theft, and now he ridicules me for praying. I wouldn't have used the word persecuted—this is not that severe. But now that you say it, it is how I feel."

"Get used to it. You will feel it for the rest of your life."

"It's a terrible feeling."

"Sometimes people tease you for small things—sometimes they take away what you treasure most. You want to hit back, but you don't. They get away with it, but you don't. They get ahead, and you get set back. It happens over and over again when you follow Jesus."

"I don't know if I'll ever get used to it."

"The feeling won't go away, but it won't hurt as much when you realize that the person persecuting you simply hasn't progressed. In a way, Horus is still a little boy. He may grow up someday, though. Maybe after he has children."

"You are so positive about people. How can you remain hopeful for someone who chastises a person at prayer?"

"Jesus was chastised, and more. I have been chastised, and more. But Jesus didn't give up on people. He didn't give up even on his executioners. He prayed for them. So I figure that I need to do the same. It's the same for you too now."

"I will keep trying to do as you say. It's not easy, but I'll keep trying."

"You don't do these things because I say so. You are following the ways of Christ. It's becoming a habit with you, and that is a beautiful thing to see."

Clement blushed. Peter was right. He liked the changes that he was experiencing in himself.

"I shouldn't blame Sati," Lumeri muttered through his breath a few days later. "It's not her fault that the stallion kicked her.

"It is her fault that she opened the gate to the big stall without someone to help control the steed—that's a fact. That is a fact, and there is no getting around it. Yet, it would be a mistake to allow this incident to come between us—we can have another son.

"We can have another son, but this son was my oldest, my heir, and now he is lost. If she had not gone to the stable, he would have grown into a fine man. Oh, I am so confused. I hate to blame Sati. Yet she is the one who failed."

"I shouldn't blame myself," Sati told Rosa the mare, still feeling the pain from her wounds. "I was just trying to pet the stallion's nose. I didn't know that he would lunge for you when I opened the gate. Yet, I am the one who opened it. None of this would have happened if I had left it closed.

"I hope that this does not create a breach between Lumeri and me. We can have another son. I want him to have a son. I will try to make it up to him in every way I can. I will give myself to him again as soon as I feel well enough.

"If he would have let me make new friends, I wouldn't even have come to this stable. I told him I wanted to become a Christian, and he held me back. Now I can't bring the subject up at all, at least until I am pregnant again.

"I shouldn't have been thinking of Clement. He never wrote back to me. It was when I was pining for him that all this happened. I shouldn't blame myself. I shouldn't."

28

Three years later, when the family gathered to celebrate Clement's birthday, his father invited everyone to lift their cups, "To Clement, who is becoming a man and who we all hold in pride."

"To Clement!" voices cheered.

"And let me add this: because of Clement's dedication to the warehouse, Cassius is bringing in more new growers and Horus is adding to our customer base. The operation is prospering as never before. It now is possible for us to increase Clement's status to that of warehouse manager, and very likely in the not-too-distant future to full partner. You are doing well, my son. We all are very grateful."

As Urbanus embraced his youngest son, everyone applauded. Clement noticed out of the corner of his eye that Horus, however, was neither smiling nor cheering. After thanking his father, he approached first Cassius and then Horus, giving both warm embraces. Cassius, with a big grin, kissed his brother on both cheeks. Horus seemed embarrassed, but awkwardly kissed the new manager as well.

"All you need now is a wife!" shouted Cassius.

"In due time," Clement replied. "That's a big step. I have not yet begun to consider it."

"It won't be long, I bet," added Cassius's wife, Lucilia. I can introduce you to some very nice maidens."

"Now don't push him," interjected Cordula. Clement is only twenty-two."

"But he is maturing rapidly," Urbanus boasted. "My bet is that he will wed before his twenty-fifth birthday."

One afternoon when Clement was with Peter, the bishop revealed a serious matter weighing on his mind.

"Do you remember Paul?"

"Of course. I was in the room in Jerusalem."

"Yes. Yes. That's not what I meant. I received a copy of a letter that he sent to the Thessalonians. I'm not sure what to make of it."

"What does it say?"

"It's kind of long. I asked the presbyters to read it and give me their thoughts. You can read it too, if you like."

"Sure. Is there something in it that troubles you?"

"Not specifically. After he left Jerusalem, Paul went on a second missionary journey, this time to Thrace and Macedonia—then down the Greek peninsula to Corinth. He took Silvanus and Timothy with him, making converts in Philippi and Thessalonica and Beroea, although there was hostility there as well. From what I hear, he sent Timothy back to Thessalonica to strengthen the community, and when he reported back to him, he decided to write them a letter."

"It sounds like his journeys were fruitful."

"Oh, yes, yes. Paul is accomplishing what he set out to do. I thank God for him."

"Then what bothers you?"

"It's the tone, and I don't really care for putting preaching in writing. The written word can be misinterpreted too easily."

"Verbal teaching can be misinterpreted too."

"Yes, but when a man is speaking, he can tell if his listeners are hearing him correctly. They can ask him questions, and he can ask them some too, if he thinks they are not understanding."

"There is something to be said for both ways of communicating."

"Maybe I'm old-fashioned, but I like to keep things face-to-face."

"And you are very accomplished at that."

"Yes, I am confident with the personal approach. Would you like to read the letter?"

"Certainly," Clement replied, accepting the document from the bishop's hands and scanning the first page. "He's thanking the Thessalonians for their dedication to the faith…and reviewing how he began working among them—that part may have been a bit pompous or self-serving."

"Oh, that's Paul," Peter said with a big grin.

"He is praising them for 'imitating the churches in Judea' and telling them of his travel plans. That's fine."

"Yes."

"He's exhorting them to good conduct and mutual charity."

"That should be common sense for followers of the Way. Don't you think?"

"I don't understand this part about those who have fallen asleep. Is he talking about those in the faith who have died?"

"Yes. I didn't like how he put that."

"It sounds like he is encouraging those who have had loved ones pass away to keep up their hope for them. He says, 'If we believe that Jesus died and rose, so too will God, through Jesus, bring with him those who have fallen asleep.' That's a very hope-filled point."

"Oh, yes. I agree."

"And now he talks about we who are alive, who are left until the coming of the Lord. He says, 'For the Lord himself, with a word of command, with the voice of an archangel, and with the trumpet of God, will come down from heaven, and the dead in Christ will rise first. Then we who are alive, who are left, will be caught up together with them in the clouds to meet the Lord in the air. Thus we shall always be with the Lord.' That certainly is a consoling message."

"It's consoling, but it kind of paints a different picture from what Jesus said to us."

"What did Jesus say?"

"He also said that a time of tribulation would come. Paul makes it sound like it will happen quite soon, while Jesus said, 'only the Father knows the day and the hour, not even the Son.' And Jesus was talking about these things in Jerusalem. Paul is writing to Greeks, far away. The point of view isn't the same. Jesus said he would return suddenly, but I've listened to these sentences several times. Paul makes it sound like the living will be snatched up into the clouds. That's what makes me uneasy. His written words can give some people a different impression than what we heard Jesus say. We asked Jesus questions. Paul never had the opportunity to do that."

"Hmm. I can see why you are concerned."

"I'm glad that you do. I don't want to criticize Paul, but I want what the Church says to be right."

"Do you think he will write more letters?"

"I don't know."

The following Tuesday, while Horus was obtaining the weekly payment from the palace treasurer, Clement was alone in the warehouse and noticed a glow over the loading dock and felt a tingling sensation in his body. He approached the dock with a little fear, but with a sense of joy as well. Stepping up onto the dock, he detected a warmth there that he had never before experienced, and all traces of the fear left him.

"Who is there?" he called out. No one answered, but the feeling of joy grew stronger. "Are you Jesus?" he asked quietly. Again, he heard no answer. "Are you an angel?" Again, all was quiet. *This can't be a demon*, he concluded. *I feel too much love.*

"Do you have a message for me?" he asked, hoping that it was from a divine source. But as he listened for a response, the sensations gently diminished, and eventually subsided. He had no idea how long he had stood there, but he guessed it was no more than a couple of minutes. He still felt filled with joy, but that was all.

"What happened?" he muttered. "I have never before felt this way. It was like I was given a taste of divine joy." He dropped to his knees and lifted his heart to Christ, trying to express his gratitude in prayer, but no words formed in his mind. He just knelt there in the big empty building, feeling filled with blessings from above.

After about a quarter of an hour on his knees, he stood up and quickly finished his duties. Then after locking the building securely, he raced to share the experience with Peter.

"You are puffing. What's wrong?" the bishop asked.

Clement threw his arms around his friend, exclaiming, "Nothing is wrong. Everything is wonderful!" Then stepping back, he hurriedly recounted what had happened and asked, "Have you ever felt anything like that?"

After getting in touch with his memories Peter shared, "That's the way I felt when I was with Jesus—surrounded by joy and love. One time, while he was standing in my boat, teaching the crowds on the shore, he finished and said, 'Put out into the deep and lower your nets for a catch.' I protested, 'Master, we have worked hard all night and have caught nothing, but at your command I will lower the nets.' We caught more fish than we could hold in one boat and had to signal for another."

"What did you do then?"

"I felt filled with joy and love, just like you said, but I fell to my knees and cried, 'Depart from me, Lord, for I am a sinful man.' I was astonished at the catch of fish. So were James and John. But I became afraid. I felt so unworthy to be in his presence."

"I don't know if I was in his presence or not, but I felt love all around me. Since you were with him so often, it probably is hard to compare."

"Yes…probably…you might want to speak with Linus about this. He has talked about such feelings and, like you, he also came to the faith after just hearing about Jesus."

"I might do that."

Linus was a presbyter in Rome, a little younger than Peter and very devout in his faith. The following afternoon Clement went to his home, a small flat up a steep flight of steps over some shops. The presbyter was a balding man, but his straight grey hair and long beard gave him an appearance of wisdom and dignity. His children were grown and his wife had passed away four years earlier.

"Hello, Linus," Clement greeted.

"Ah, Clement. Peter told me that you might come to see me. Come in. Come in."

"Am I interrupting anything?"

"No. I was just sitting here praying. I will continue later. So, you had an unusual experience."

Clement described what happened, as he had done for Peter. Linus listened attentively, at times stroking his beard.

"I'm trying to think of when I first felt that way," the older man began. "Did it feel like someone was there?"

"I can't say yes or no. I saw a faint glow and felt the warmth, and I called out, 'Who is there?' and waited for an answer. But there was no reply."

"You don't hear anything in these cases. Well, a few people have said they heard something, but usually there is only silence."

"I didn't hear a thing."

"That's normal. In these cases, it is something that we sense, more so than something we hear or see. I am surprised that you saw the glow and felt the warmth."

"The glow was quite faint, but the warmth was distinct. We keep the building as cool as we can—for the eggs."

"Of course. Well, Clement, you are a fortunate young man. The Holy Spirit may we working in your life."

"The Holy Spirit—in my life! I have never done anything to make me worthy to receive a visit from the Holy Spirit."

"It's not about being worthy. Didn't Peter tell you that?"

"No."

"No one ever feels worthy when they are granted special favors. The Holy Spirit chooses whose life he comes into based on things only he knows. He may have something in mind for you that you don't yet imagine."

"Like what?"

"I don't know. I just said the Spirit may have something in mind for you. You will just have to wait and see."

"Wait for what?"

"You must wait until there are more signs. Come and visit me once in a while, and we will talk about what is going on in your life."

"How often?"

"You be the judge of that. The important thing is that you pray—pray often. Pray when you are happy and pray when you are discouraged. Just pray."

"I will do that, Linus. Thank you."

Clement couldn't tell his father or brothers—not even Fidelis. He was afraid that they might tease him or say he was crazy. A few days later, when they were alone in the house, he summoned the courage to share the experience with his mother.

"How are things with you, Clement?"

"Fine, Mother…can I tell you something?"

"Of course you can."

"A few days ago, I had an unusual experience while I was alone in the warehouse. I saw a faint glow over the loading dock and when I climbed up there, I sensed a warmth and felt filled with love and joy."

"My goodness. Were you frightened?"

"A little at first, but that went away. The feeling only lasted a few minutes. I spoke with Peter about it—and later with Linus."

"Did they offer any explanation?"

"Both were helpful, but Linus said something I don't fully understand."

"What was that?"

"He said that the Holy Spirit may be working in my life. I asked, 'In what way?' but he said he didn't know. Then he suggested that we meet together from time to time and discuss any further signs. I asked what the signs might be like, but he said we just have to wait and see…Oh! He also told me to pray, to pray often. I said I would."

Cordula gave her son a warm hug. "I will pray too, my son. We both will pray. You know, I have hoped that one of my sons would become a presbyter."

Clement drew back and looked into his mother's eyes. "I think about that too, now and then. I will pray for guidance."

The young man did pray more, and he did visit with Linus, but he didn't report any more unusual experiences.

29

About a year later, Peter suddenly was in a rage. He received a copy of another letter written by Paul, this one to the Christians in Corinth. Paul had left the Greek city and gone on to Ephesus, where he was supporting the Church in the region and attracting converts. Reports of division within the Corinthian community had provoked the missionary to compose the letter. Clement was with Peter and Linus when they discussed it.

"This is the way I felt when we saw that man preaching in Jesus's name," Peter ranted.

"But didn't Jesus say to let him continue?" noted Linus, who held the letter in his hands.

"Yes, he did. And I wouldn't mind Paul doing what he does, as long as he gets it right."

"Do you feel that Paul oversteps his authority?"

"Paul is not a bishop, yet he puts himself above the bishops."

"But it sounds like he is trying to settle some issues that are dividing the assembly. Isn't that important?"

"That is important. The letter starts out fine. He heard about the divisions, and he urges them to stay united. He even tells them to avoid saying, 'I belong to Paul' or 'I belong to Cephas'—that's all fine, but he should have stopped there. The letter is way too long."

Linus added, "I didn't care for how he set himself up as the standard that everyone should follow."

"Yes. That's another thing. He makes a lot of points about how humble he is, but when I first heard the letter, it sounded like a lot of boasting. Did it sound that way to you?"

"He says that no one should boast. He says, 'God chose the foolish to shame the wise'—but he certainly sees himself as an authority."

Peter added, "An authority on faith, an authority on church order, and an authority on morality. That part about a man living with his father's wife—everyone knows that's wrong. He didn't need to go on and on about it. Much of what he wrote is just common sense."

Clement cut in, "I kind of liked how he worded the part about 'a little yeast leavens all the dough. Clear out the old yeast, so that you become a fresh batch.' That's a powerful way of communicating. Paul is good at that."

Peter frowned, knowing that Clement was right, but still preferring his own style of face-to-face communication over the written word. "And all those things he said about marriage and virginity—I don't see why that was necessary. Jesus didn't address all those minute points."

"The letter says that the Corinthians had questions in this area," noted Linus.

"So what if they did? Paul could have sent a representative back to Corinth to talk about their questions. Now that he put it in writing and so many copies are being made, his answers could become rigid, like the views of the Pharisees—which Paul was one of and Jesus was against!"

Clement added, "I need some guidance on marriage, since I have not yet made a decision."

"Fine!" Peter insisted. "So, you come and talk to me, or to Linus, or to someone else, who can advise you on the particularities in your case. When Paul puts these things in writing, it sounds like there are general rules, and he is the expert on those rules. He wrote three pages on that topic alone!"

Linus got back in the conversation, "On personal topics I prefer face-to-face conversation as much as you. But here toward the end, where he teaches about spiritual gifts and the resurrection of the dead, the Church needs some norms to follow, and putting them in writing can make them consistent."

"They already are consistent."

"How do you know? You've been to several cities, but this is a vast empire. There probably are regions where no one is sure of the answers. Someone has to put something in writing, and Paul shows great skill in doing it. Do you not like Paul?"

"This is not about whether or not I like Paul. It's about who has the firsthand knowledge of what Jesus said. Those of us who were there with him are the only ones who know for sure the gospel that Jesus taught." Linus started to say something, but Peter continued, "Paul had a remarkable experience on the road to Damascus. He told me about it, and I believe that the Lord called him to his special mission. That's why I gave him as much instruction as I could and let him go. We must never forget, though, that Paul was not an eyewitness."

"He says that he is following the Holy Spirit."

"Linus, my friend, I believe that Paul is inspired by the Holy Spirit as much as or more than anyone. That's why I give him so much latitude. Can I help it, though, if I am cautious about the fact that he never walked with Jesus through

Galilee? The gospel message must stay central, more so than these other points."

"You could restrain Paul."

"I don't want to restrain him. Paul is doing great things for the faith. I just hope he stays focused on what is most important."

"I hear what you are saying, and I feel your concerns are fair. Do you think Paul will write more letters?"

"He probably will."

Another source of anxiety for Urbanus's family that year was the demise of Emperor Claudius. He died in the early hours of October 13, and his ashes were interred eleven days later in the Mausoleum of Augustus, after an elaborate funeral. The senate deified him immediately, praising his nearly fourteen years of imperial service.

All of Rome was whispering the word "poison." While some said Claudius simply succumbed to the effects of his illnesses, most of the gossip put the blame on Agrippina, his current wife, who had talked the emperor into adopting her son Nero just four years earlier. Claudius had recently changed his will, recommending both Nero and young Britannicus for the role of emperor. The boy would have been considered an adult under Roman law in just a few months, but when Agrippina had Claudius's secretary executed and his correspondence burned, his supporters turned to Nero, one of the last male descendants of the great Augustus.

Nero was only seventeen years old and began receiving advice on his new duties from his mother, the Praetorian Prefect, Sextus Burrus, and Lucius Seneca, his tutor. Urbanus was acquainted with Seneca, and made it a point to immediately inform the respected scholar of the terms of his egg contract and share how his operation was now in its third generation of loyal service to the entire line of emperors.

"How did your meeting go with Seneca?" Horus asked in front of his brothers.

"Quite well," Urbanus answered. "I don't think we will have any problems. I told him that I'd like to meet the new emperor personally, as soon as that can be arranged."

"What about his mother?"

"You raise a good point. She's the one I fear the most in this situation. Agrippina could go in any direction at any time. My hope is that she'll focus on the larger matters, not on our mundane egg deliveries."

"She's a seeker of power."

"Yes. That makes her both predictable and unpredictable."

"What can Clement and I do?" asked Cassius.

"This won't affect your end of the operation. But Horus, you should spend more time at the palace. Try to get to know as many people as you can, just in case we need to call upon some friends."

"I understand, Father. I'm already bellying up to them."

"Good. That's part of business, you know."

Cassius seemed pleased, but Clement was uneasy.

Nero, guided by the advice of Seneca, began excluding his mother from his personal affairs, much to her dismay. In anger, Agrippina switched her allegiance to Britannicus. Then during dinner on February 12, the night before the youth would have turned fourteen and become an adult, he took a sip of wine and died within minutes. Nero said the death was from an epileptic seizure, but all of Rome concluded it was the work of the notorious poisoner Locusta that took the youth. Then within days, the emperor had his mother expelled from the imperial palace.

There were anxious hours in Alexandria, as well. Four years had gone by without any signs of another pregnancy. Lumeri was displaying less of his optimistic confidence, and Sati was feeling more lonely and isolated. They tried with earnest to conceive another child, even calling upon the aid of conjurers and astrologers.

Sati tried several ancient Egyptian potions, but when all they did was make her sick, she became discouraged. The two spent less and less time together, and when Sati asked for a room of her own, her husband agreed. Occasionally she took out the bronze ichthys and pressed it to her lips. It brought back long-lost memories, but it didn't make her happy.

30

Clement occasionally thought about his faraway love, opening the ivory locket and gazing at the golden contents with which she had expressed a young girl's feelings. He was not a happy man either. He did pray for her, though, and continued to pray often, not forgetting Linus's advice after the experience of the warm glow in the warehouse.

Clement continued to participate weekly in the Sunday morning breaking of the bread, and he realized he was getting a growing benefit from attending. As the feast of Passover approached, he noticed that he was thinking about Christ all the more and feeling grateful for his life as a Christian.

On the Sunday morning commemorating the Lord's resurrection, he walked with his mother and father to the liturgy. Cassius and his wife were there as well. Although Peter was presiding, Linus was selected to preach, and when the presbyter read from the book of the prophet Isaiah, Clement felt the hair on his neck tingle.

Thus says the Lord:
All you who are thirsty,
  come to the water!
You who have no money,
  come, receive grain and eat;
come, without paying and without cost,
  drink wine and milk!
Why spend your money for what is not bread,
  your wages for what fails to satisfy?

That is so true, Clement sensed. *That is ultimate truth! Why have I been laboring these years just to make money and put eggs on the emperor's table? It hasn't made me satisfied. It hasn't made me feel like I felt when Peter took me to Jerusalem or when I gave my heart to Sati.*

Realizing that he had stopped listening, he brought his attention back to the reading.

Seek the Lord when he may be found,
  call to him while he is near.

Jesus: it is me, Clement. Are you near? Come to me. Come to me, if you are for real. I do seek you. I do want you. Come to me. He felt surrounded by love, and his heartbeat quickened.

Again, he had to force his attention back, just as Linus finished reading.

My word shall not return to me void,
  but shall do my will,
  achieving the end for which I sent it.

119

Your word has come to me, he breathed. *You have come to me in your word. I feel your presence. I feel you near. Oh, Jesus, I shall not let your word return void. I will do your will—I will achieve the end for which you sent your word to me. I will achieve the purpose for which you gave me faith. I am passionate to do it.* He began to suck in deep gasps of air.

Linus began to preach, but Clement didn't hear a word he said. He was caught up in the feeling—caught up in knowing that Christ was there with him. It was like nothing he had ever felt before—joyful—intense—peaceful—surrounded by love. And it stayed—the feeling didn't diminish during the entire time the presbyter spoke. He knew it was Jesus. It felt like it was Jesus. He had no question this time about who was encircling him. It was Christ: Christ teaching, Christ healing, Christ forgiving, Christ suffering, Christ dying, Christ rising, Christ alive!

"Halleluia!" he shouted. "Halleluia!" All eyes turned toward him.

His father looked at him like he was crazy. His brother dropped his head and looked the other way. Linus stopped speaking, and everyone searched for the source of shouting. "Who said that?" they whispered.

When Linus began speaking again, Clement looked around. The eyes were moving back toward the presbyter, but two people were staring at him with big, wide grins on their faces—his mother and his bishop.

He put his head down during the rest of the liturgy and studied the feeling he was experiencing. It still was intense. It still was joyful. He still felt surrounded by love. When the time came to approach the altar for the bread, blessed and broken, he got to his feet and shuffled forward, following his mother.

Accepting the bread, he felt nourished by divine love, and receiving the wine, he felt close to the suffering Christ—unusually grateful for the sacrifices his Lord had gone through—unusually grateful for the gift his Lord had bestowed—absolutely unworthy to be standing in his presence, but fully confident that doing so was what Jesus wanted for him at that moment.

When they returned to their places and his mother closed her eyes for a prayer of thanksgiving, Clement looked around the room. He looked first at the people and then at Linus and Peter, all of them happy and filled with peace. He pictured himself a little older, sitting in Linus's place and feeling satisfied that he had done his best to bring his flock closer to the Lord. This was another first for the young Christian. He had previously given some thought to becoming a presbyter, but this was the first time he had ever visualized himself doing what presbyters do. *I could do that,* he thought. *I actually could do it!*

As they left the gathering, Clement was aware that his father was scowling at him, but he simply ignored it. For the first time in his life he was ignoring his father's feelings, and he sensed a new power inside.

Then he saw his bishop rushing toward him. "Come see me, son. Come see me this afternoon, if you can."

"Yes. I will."

Cordula had prepared a feast for her family, but when Clement told her, "I must go and see Peter," she nodded approval. When her husband objected, she said to him, "We must let him go. Something important is happening. I don't know what it is, but I am certain that the right thing for us to do is to let him go."

Clement ran to Peter's house. Hearing that the bishop was with Linus, he ran on to the presbyter's flat. After climbing the steep steps, he entered the room panting. The two had just poured some wine.

"Ah! The halleluiah man," Linus greeted. "Come in. Come in and sit down. I will pour you a cup."

"What happened today?" asked Peter. "It must have been something remarkable."

Clement took a sip of wine and shared how he felt during the liturgy. He told the story with such enthusiasm and passion that when he finished he was puffing again.

Peter spoke first, "That's the way I felt many times when I was with Jesus. My heart raced and my skin tingled. I felt surrounded by love."

"Were you filled with joy and gratitude?"

"Yes. Exactly."

Linus asked, "Did you feel like you were in Christ's presence?"

"Absolutely. It was wonderful."

"You have had a remarkable spiritual experience—a great gift."

"I was not expecting anything like this. And I haven't done anything to make me worthy of it. In fact, for a moment I felt unworthy, but then—that went away. It felt like Christ was accepting me the way I am."

Peter laughed, "Ha-ha!"

Linus added, "Christ does accept us the way we are. He wants us to grow from that point, but when he works in our lives, he begins with what we actually are."

"Are you sure? Do others say that?"

"That's my experience, and others have told me the same. You are being led, son, by Jesus."

"Where is he leading me?"

"Like I told you earlier, there is no way to tell. You just have to follow and find out."

Peter added, "Jesus said, 'Come, follow me.' He didn't say where we were going. We just went."

"You followed."

"We followed. I don't know if Jesus had a precise plan. We went from village to village and circled and backtracked. He sent us out and received us back."

"What Peter is saying is that where Jesus takes us is dependent upon how willing we are to go. He doesn't force us. He calls us, and we take a step. That repeats, and where we end up depends upon how faithfully we follow."

"That's amazing."

"When you think about it, it's not that amazing. How else could he lead us? He can only guide us to the degree that we say yes. He can only move us to the extent that we follow."

When you put it that way, it all makes sense. I want to go. I want to say yes. Is there anything else?"

"Pray. Pray more. If you are at a loss for words, don't let that stop you from praying. Just sit there with your heart open to him. He will take care of the rest."

"I will do that…Can I ask you this: After I received the bread and wine—his Body and Blood—I pictured myself older, in the role of a presbyter. Does that mean that he is leading me to become a presbyter?"

Linus answered, "Maybe he is. The image that entered your mind could have come from Christ, or it could have come from your imagination. Again, the only way to tell is to wait—to pray and to wait. In time, we will know."

"I'm ready to start now," the young visionary exclaimed.

Both of the older men laughed, and Peter added, "You are, what, twenty-four years old?"

"Almost twenty-four."

"You have plenty of time. I think you should make your meetings with Linus more regular, say—twice a month. You come to him and tell him what is happening with you, and he will guide you along. Can you do that?"

"Of course."

"Linus, do you have any more advice, before we eat, for our budding branch of the vine of the Lord?"

"Only this: Don't make any changes in your life right now. It's too early. Stay where you are living. Keep on working where you are working. Be open to something new, but don't act on anything new. Allow things to just happen. We'll talk every two weeks, but be patient. And pray more. Pray every morning and every evening. Will you do that?"

"Yes. I will."

"Good," Peter added. "Do you still feel the presence of Christ now?"

Clement paused and looked down, then answered, "Yes."

"Ha-ha!" both men waved their arms in the air and applauded. Then they poured more wine.

31

Urbanus liked to praise his sons, and the occasion of Clement's birthday was no exception.

"Does everyone have enough wine? Good. Now gather around."

He lifted his wine and crowed, "To Clement, who is helping our business grow and flourish."

"To Clement," multiple voices joined.

After taking a sip and encouraging the others, he continued, "Cassius, Horus, you along with Clement are my heirs. It has always been my dream that you would work together and prosper together because no bonds are more enduring than those of a family. You share my blood, and that makes me proud.

"Each of you has always been a partner, although Clement, since you were the youngest and began helping most recently, have not—until this day—been recognized as such. You have learned the business quite well, and are carrying a vital portion of the load. So, from this day forward, you also shall be known as a full partner. I am exceedingly grateful that you three are working in harmony for the sake of the whole. I love you, my sons, and I pray that the unity we share this day shall prevail for all of your lives."

"I'll drink to that," shouted Cordula. Everyone lifted their cups and joined in the praise, including Horus, although the middle son's eyes could not fully hide his selfish desires.

"Now one more thing," Urbanus added. "A couple of years ago, when we gathered for Clement's birthday, I predicted that he would be married by the time he was twenty-five. Now, Clement, as you know, your father has the reputation of being an honest man. Will you be making my prediction come true?"

The birthday boy blushed bright red, and he set his wine down and embraced his father tenderly. "Thank you. Thank you. I will continue to make you proud of me, Father." Then he shouted, "There is only one thing missing. I need to meet a maiden!"

That evening in Alexandria, as the daylight was fading, Sati was pacing the floor. It was not like her husband to stay out so late. The cook told her that their dinner was ready, and the girls were getting restless.

Then she heard the sound of hoofbeats and carriage wheels on the stone driveway. But when the door opened, the one who entered was not Lumeri, but the driver.

The man's face was white like bleached parchment, and he was shaking.

"What is it?" Sati asked.

"The master…the master has been involved in an…accident."

"What kind of accident!"

"We were at the date farm. He was bit by a viper."

Sati screamed. Hearing her, the girls came running. "What's wrong?"

"We were at the date farm. Your father was down by the water. There was a viper, and your father didn't see it and stepped on it."

"How is he?" Sati asked, anxiously.

"He's…he's dead, mam."

"Dead!" they shrieked.

"I rushed him to the physician. But it's a long way in from the date farm. I whipped the horses as hard I could, but it was too late."

Sati dropped to the floor. Her head was spinning.

"Was anyone else with him?" Bunefer asked.

"He had a—a friend with him. We loaded him into the carriage and rushed back as fast as we could."

"How terrible," screamed Sheri.

Sati pulled herself back onto her feet. "I am so confused. He can't be dead."

"I tried to save him, mam."

"Who was the friend?" Sitamun asked, coldly. "Was it a man or a woman?"

"Sitamun!" Sati scolded. "This is not the time…"

The driver looked down at the floor.

"Tell me!" Sitamun demanded. "Tell me, was it a man or a woman?"

"It was a woman, miss."

"So, he brought a woman to the date farm," the plump daughter concluded.

"Why do you suppose he did that?"

No one answered.

"He brought a woman to the date farm because his wife was not making him happy." Swinging her arm in a broad arc and pointing at Sati she screamed, "It's your fault! It's your fault that our father is dead. He wouldn't have been with another woman, if it was not your fault!"

Clement, alone in his room, felt strange. "I must pray," he muttered. Dropping to his knees, he lifted up all of his loved ones. "Take care of them, Jesus," he breathed.

Then he realized it might be Sati, and getting out the ivory locket, he held her in prayer as well. *Is something wrong with Sati?* Panic overcame him. He didn't usually feel this way when he thought of her. He was shivering.

Getting into bed, he whispered intercessions for his love—over and over and over. It was a long and restless night.

A few days later, Horus came down with a fever. His wife told Urbanus that he was sweating and his head was throbbing.

The next day, Horus was worse. His face was burning red and his whole body was hot.

Cassius asked, "What are we going to do about the weekly statement for the palace. It's Saturday, and they'll be expecting it."

"I think I can make it out," Clement replied. "When Horus wasn't here yesterday, I put the tags on the crates. I found the tallies from the previous days and the papers that he uses for the weekly statement. I can add up today's counts and write them down. I've seen Horus do it."

"Good," his father agreed.

"I don't know the prices, though, for each grade of eggs."

"I'll tell you those."

After Clement tallied the week's shipment, and his father told him the prices for each grade, he completed the statement and double-checked it. "That's it," he advised.

"Fine. I'll deliver it. Hopefully Horus will get better by next week."

The fever subsided a bit but was replaced with urgent cramps and diarrhea.

On Tuesday, Horus was improved, but still bedridden and occasionally fainting. Urbanus wanted to be with his son and asked Clement to go to the palace and pick up the payment.

When he arrived at the window, the paymaster told him that he needed to see Pallas, the Secretary of the Treasury. This made Clement nervous, but when he found him, Pallas was smiling.

"Tell your father that we appreciate the discount."

"What? I don't understand."

Pallas laughed. "Is something wrong with Horus?"

"He is sick. It's a fever," Clement advised.

"I'm sorry to hear that. I hope he gets better soon."

"Thank you. He's improving, but he still is weak today."

"It's been quite a while since Urbanus made out a statement."

"I made it out. Is there a problem?"

"It has the old prices on it. Eggs haven't been that low for years. We appreciate discounts, but I knew Urbanus had made a mistake. I've known him for a long time. Look here, I corrected your statement. See the differences?"

Clement scanned the statement. The differences were substantial. "Thank you for fixing it," he replied.

"Sure. And here is your payment. Next time be sure to submit it correctly."

Rushing home, Clement handed the sack of coins to his father and told him what happened. Urbanus put down the sack and studied the corrected statement, staring at the numbers. He began to shake and his face turned red.

"My son…"

"What, Father?"

"My own son…"

"Yes, Father."

"My trusted son…is a thief."

With that, Urbanus dropped the paper and clutched his chest. He moaned from what appeared to be pain in his arms, and his face grimaced as he sucked in air. Then he lost his balance and slumped to the floor.

"Mother!" Clement called as he straightened his father's body and loosened his clothing.

When Cordula saw her husband lying on the floor, she screamed.

"I must go get a physician," Clement sobbed.

"Yes. Go quickly."

While his mother was leaning over her husband, crying and pleading for him to regain consciousness, Clement hurriedly picked up the statement from the floor and rushed out the door.

The general manager of Lumeri's estate quickly held the necessary meeting with Sati and Lumeri's daughters.

"Lumeri reviewed his wishes with me just two months ago," he told them. "We are fortunate that he liked to keep his affairs in order. There is no uncertainty in this matter."

"What did he tell you?" asked Bunefer.

"The estate is now owned by you and your sisters. You may not divide it before Nefrusheri, the youngest, has reached the age of thirty. You will have plenty of money. There has been a surplus every year, which has been used to acquire more land. I am at your service to continue to manage the estate for as long as you wish."

The girls smiled with delight. It was everything they hoped to hear.

"Did he say anything about me?" Sati inquired.

"The girls are to give you a satisfactory sum with which you can make a transition, mam."

The room was as silent as a cave while the four pondered what they had heard. Lumeri's manager sat facing them with a stone face. He had nothing more to say, and no one asked any more questions.

Sati didn't want Lumeri's wealth, and she didn't want a continuing relationship with his spiteful daughters. Realizing that she was free to go her own way, she felt her heart lift and did her best to conceal her secret joy. "Thank you," she said to the manager, as she stood up to go to her room.

I'm free! she sang to herself as she ascended the stairs.

When Sati got to her room and closed the door, she began dancing in circles, waving her arms like a child. "I'm free," she breathed in. "I'm free," she breathed out. "I can leave this prison. I can meet new people. I can become a Christian. I can even go to Clement!"

Her movements stopped, though, as soon as his name formed in her mind. *He must be married by now, or betrothed—he's twenty-four.* Sitting on her bed, she picked up the bronze ichthys and studied the familiar details. *I will have to think this through. I must do things step by step. I'll have to find out if he's single or married, or if he even has feelings for me. And if he wants to see me, I'll need to be honest and say that I can't give him children...Anianus can find out. I'll go to him first. I will have enough money to get by while he sends a letter to Rome.*

While there was no way of foretelling her future, the pathway seemed clear. *It will be lonely for a while*, she thought, *but I have been isolated here. I will be all right. I will begin a new life.*

An hour later, while Sati was pondering her possibilities, there came a knock at her door. It was Merti, the girls' governess. "They want to see us in the atrium," she said.

I wonder what this is about? Sati asked herself as they descended the stairs.

Bunefer motioned for them to take seats. "We called you in because we felt that we may as well get this over with as quickly as possible," she said with a wry smile. "Merti, you have been of great service to this household for many years, but your services are no longer needed. You are to seek employment elsewhere. We will give you the highest recommendation, should your prospective employer ask, and we are giving you twenty denarii to carry you over."

"But Sheri is so young, and…"

"Sheri is fourteen. She is no longer a minor. And I am eighteen. We are fully capable of handling our own affairs. Your services are no longer needed."

While Merti was accustomed to giving direction to the girls and having them comply, all she could utter was, "Yes, Miss."

"And Sati, our father indicated that you are to receive some money for your transition. Here it is."

Bunefer handed her stepmother a small sack of coins. Peeking inside, she saw that they were neither silver nor gold. "There are twenty denarii in there," Bunefer indicated, "the same as Merti."

"But that is hardly enough," Sati pleaded. "Your father wished for me to receive a satisfactory sum for my transition."

"You will have to make do with that. Under the circumstances, you should expect no more."

"What do you mean? I loved your father and have been with him since you were children."

Sitamun cut in and spoke bluntly, "Our father would be alive if you had been a good wife. You weren't. Those are the circumstances, so you shouldn't complain."

"But all I am asking for is enough to get by for a few months."

"A few months is out of the question," Sitamun said coldly. "We want you both out of this house by noon tomorrow."

"Tomorrow!" Sati and Merti exclaimed.

"Yes. Tomorrow, and if you are not gone by then, we'll have the magistrate throw you out."

32

Clement faced a dilemma. His father was dead, and he knew that Horus had systematically been taking money from both his family and the emperor, which is what killed Urbanus. Yet, if he revealed his brother's secret, it could further devastate his mother and turn Horus against him even more. He held the evidence, of course, in the marked-up statement, which he carefully hid out of sight in his room. Not knowing what to do, he turned to Peter.

"I've got to decide how to handle this before Horus returns to work tomorrow. I'm the only one who knows his secret."

Peter listened to the tale of deceit and asked a number of questions. The whole thing was hard to believe. "Are you telling me that Horus slowly raised the price of eggs to the emperor without telling his father, and that he pocketed the difference? A son cheating his father is bad enough, but also the emperor? That's unheard of."

"I know. I couldn't imagine it. Father figured it out, though. When he saw the statement, it was such a shock that it killed him."

"This is horrible. If you expose Horus, your whole family could get in trouble with the palace, and if you don't, then your brother can go on getting away with it."

"Yes. And it isn't just the overpricing and stealing. Horus also has been upgrading some of the eggs and charging more for them when there's no actual difference. Father knew this was going on, but not the degree to which Horus was doing it. I knew it too, but neither of us suspected that he kept raising the prices for the higher grades and putting the difference in his own strongbox. It's been happening for years. That's why he never wanted to take a full day off. He kept it all hidden."

Peter rubbed his beard. "I always said he reminded me of Judas."

"That's not all," Clement added. "At this point I don't want to work with Horus. I am a third owner of a business that I don't want to have anything to do with. I was moving away from the notion anyway because I want to devote my life to serving Christ. Now I don't want to even touch the money, or the business, or my brother. Yet I have to think about my mother and, of course, Cassius."

"Is there any way that you can stall for time?"

"Possibly. I may be able to pretend that I don't know until after the funeral. That will give me more time to think. I could tell Horus that I misplaced the statement. The payment from the palace was based on the prices he would have charged. I could keep this a secret until everything calms down."

"Why don't you do that? And speak with Linus. He may have additional ways of looking at this."

Clement couldn't see Linus until after the funeral. Horus was not happy to hear that his younger brother had lost the statement, but he was relieved that his own secret had not come out while he was sick. Cordula and Cassius were in too much grief to notice how restless and anxious Clement was. He was not his usual self, but under the circumstances, neither were they.

The day after the funeral, Clement met with Linus and shared the whole sad tale. Then the presbyter asked, "How do you feel now about continuing in the family business?"

"I hate the idea! Like I said, I don't want to touch the money, or the business, or my brother."

"And what would you rather do?"

"I would rather serve Christ. I want to help people come closer to Jesus."

"Are you sure?"

"Like I told you before this happened," Clement explained, "after I had the second spiritual experience, I knew that this is my purpose. I get no satisfaction out of putting eggs on the emperor's table."

Linus smoothed the beard protruding from his chin while he formulated his next question. Then nodding he asked, "Have you been praying, like I advised you?"

"Every day, except since I uncovered the secret and my father died."

"And do you still feel the presence of Jesus around you, like you first did?"

"Before Horus came down with the fever, I'd say yes. Since then I haven't really checked."

"All right, Clement. I believe that you are sincere, and it definitely looks like you are being led into something new. My advice is that you get your affairs in order and start preparing to become a presbyter. You won't be making a commitment right away, and neither will we. You'll just move in that direction and see how it goes."

"That sounds great! What do you mean by getting my affairs in order?"

"Well, that would include things like parting from the business, finding a way to earn some part-time income, and learning to get along on less."

"I can do that."

"Yes, but don't rush. Take your time. Make sure each step is the right one. And pray. Pray like your whole life depended upon it."

Urbanus had put very little about his estate in writing. He had not expected to pass away so young. Two days after the funeral, Cordula, Cassius, Horus, and Clement met in the home of the family lawyer to hear what the head of the house had instructed.

"There is very little to go over," the lawyer told them. "Urbanus wished for the business to go to his three sons in equal shares and for his wife to have the use of the house for the rest of her life along with the weekly funds she has been accustomed to receiving. Here are the notes. You will see where he signed in his own hand."

They all scanned the document.

"That is what I expected it to say," Cordula revealed. "Thank you."

"Do any of you have any questions?"

"No," Cassius said.

"None," Clement added.

Horus looked like he wanted to say something, but then he closed his lips and shook his head.

"Fine then," the lawyer concluded. "You may call upon me for any further needs at any time."

At the warehouse during the next few days, Horus acted like he was in charge. Cassius was still in a grieving daze, and Clement was careful not to raise his brother's suspicions. It was Horus who made the first move.

"Brother, I want you to know that I am grateful for how well you handled things while I was sick."

"Well, I just did what had to be done," Clement answered. "I wasn't sure how to handle things at the palace, but it seemed to work out all right."

"Yes. You did well."

"Thank you."

"Clement, I've been wondering about something. From time to time you've talked about not staying in the egg business. Are you still thinking that way?"

"How do you mean?"

"Well, you like to do things with Peter and Linus—for the Church, you know—and your interest seems to be growing. I was just wondering if you were planning to permanently be a part of the operation, or if you had other ideas."

Clement was surprised by his brother's frankness, but he responded honestly, saying, "I have thought about becoming a presbyter."

"You would be a fine presbyter."

"Do you think so? Why do you say that?"

"You are very devoted to Jesus and the Church, and you have the qualities."

Clement was getting suspicious. Horus had never indicated that he even noticed such things. "Why are you asking?"

"Oh, I was just thinking. If you ever wanted to get out of the business, I would buy your share."

"You are very blunt."

"Well, there's no reason not to be. We are brothers, and if you don't want to continue in the operation, I'll do the right thing."

"Wouldn't the right thing be for both you and Cassius to buy me out?"

"It would be, if Cassius had any money, but he doesn't. He spends it all on his family. I am a saver. I'm the only one who could do it."

"But then you and Cassius wouldn't be equal partners."

"That's true, but we get along well. I don't think things would change very much."

"Well—Brother—I certainly wasn't expecting to hear this from you today."

"No. I didn't expect you to. I just brought it up for you to think about."

"I will think about it," Clement assured him, "and I'll get back to you."

Peter was not as surprised to hear Horus's proposal as Clement was.

"Horus moves fast. He's a schemer," the bishop observed.

"You sure understand people."

"Well, don't forget, I spent three years with Judas."

"Hmm. What do you think I should do? I don't want to stay in the egg business, but if he buys me out, he will do it with money he stole from our family."

"Horus probably doesn't look at it that way," Peter suggested. "He probably feels that he earned the extra profit by dealing more cleverly with the palace than his father did. So, from his point of view, it is his money to do with as he wants."

"But he did it so deceitfully. Father never would have allowed such overcharging if he'd known."

"You are looking at this like a serious follower of Christ. Horus sees it in his own way."

"I am a serious follower of Jesus, but I can't understand how Horus can be so different. He's baptized, and he goes to the breaking of the bread every Sunday."

"You have much to learn about people, my son. Just because a man gathers with us each week, that doesn't mean he holds Jesus in his heart."

"I pray for my brother."

"That may be all that you can do at this point. So keep praying—and wait. Let Horus make the next move."

Only a week went by before Horus confronted Clement again. "Have you given any more thought to what we talked about?"

"I've thought about it some. I'm not sure, though. I don't want to rush things."

"Yes, you should take your time. Another idea came into my mind, though. Would you like to hear it?"

"I guess."

"Well, it's about the house. You live there with Mother, and Cassius and I have our own houses. You will need a house, if you want to get married. Perhaps that could be a part of our arrangement."

"In what way?"

"The business has value and the house has value. I could pay Cassius for his share of the house and give it to you along with my share. That way you'd own a house. You and Mother are close anyway. It could be a good deal all around."

"Isn't the business worth more than the house?"

"Yes, of course. So, as well as giving you the house, I'd also have to pay you an additional fair sum."

"You certainly have been thinking about this."

"I'm looking at what can be best for our family. So think about the options."

"I will, Brother. I will."

Clement hesitantly shared the proposals with his mother, and from that point changes happened very rapidly. She was delighted that her youngest son wanted to become a presbyter and she would continue living with him in the house. Cassius's wife was again pregnant, and he needed the extra money. Horus was gloating, and Clement brought home a shiny strongbox, which he had never imagined needing.

A few days later, they met with the lawyer to sign the papers and came back to the house for a celebration.

"To our family!" Horus cheered as he raised his wine.

"To our family!" voices echoed.

They still felt the loss of Urbanus, but they enjoyed a sense of unity that, while different from prior times, gave them new optimism. Clement continued to pray for his brother in hope that he would mend his ways.

Feeling that he needed to relax, the new homeowner went to see Fidelis, whom he had not seen since the funeral. He found him just inside the gate. "Hello, good friend."

"Clement! It's good to see you. How have you been?"

"Well, it's difficult to say good-bye to one's father, but we are managing."

"Will you have some wine?"

"Certainly."

"I will ask Bella to bring some out. She's inside with Rosina. You remember Rosina, don't you?"

"Oh, yes." Rosina and her older sister were members of the Christian community and friends of Bella. The three girls each had become betrothed at about the same time.

"It was terrible how it happened."

"How what happened?"

"How the man she was going to marry was killed."

"Oh? I didn't know."

"He was in the palace guards, and one day while he was training, he took a nasty slice through his left side. The blade didn't touch his heart, but the wound got inflamed. Within a week, he was gone."

"How terrible!"

"Yes. And Rosina was devastated."

"That must have been quite a shock."

"A horrible shock. Bella is spending time with her. But she's young. She'll find another man in due time."

"You make that sound so easy."

"I didn't mean it that way. It's just that Rosina has a resilient character. She's not only beautiful, but also able to spring back from adversity. Don't let either of them know I said this, but someone will take an interest in her very soon."

"You sound like a male pig," Clement laughed. "Go get the wine."

As the three emerged from the interior of the house, Clement realized that Rosina had matured since he last noticed. Her form had become full and round, and the pleasant smile that she habitually displayed was bright, even after losing her lover. One thing that he hadn't noticed before, though, was that her light-brown hair had faint highlights—not as pronounced as Sati or her mother had, but certainly distinguishable. She was pretty.

"Hello, Rosina," he greeted. "I was so sorry to hear about your loss."

"Thank you," she said. Then smiling sincerely she added, "And your father. I hope he didn't suffer long."

"It was very fast. Intense, but not lengthy."

"That's good."

Bella waved, "We were just going out. Good to see you, Clement."

"Good to see you. And Rosina, it is good to see you again."

Rosina waved with a glint in her eyes. Her quiet smile spoke all that needed to be said.

The two men sat down and sipped their wine. Both seemed to be thinking.

"You know," Fidelis commented, "Rosina may be just right for you."

Swinging his arm and slapping his friend's shoulder, he barked back, "Swine! Pig! Hog!" and they embraced like schoolboys.

33

Meanwhile, Sati and the governess walked out the driveway before the sun got high, each carrying small bags. Their hearts were heavy, but both were hopeful.

"I know a woman who places servants," Merti told her. "Would you like to come with me?"

"I may as well. I have nowhere else to go."

"It's not very far. We can get there before it gets hot."

The walk was at least two miles. When they reached the house, they were perspiring. Merti greeted the woman and explained their circumstances.

She told them, "You will have no problem, Merti. You have plenty of experience and a good recommendation from a respected household. I don't know about your friend, though. Sati, what experience have you had?"

"I have not ever worked—I've just been Lumeri's wife. I have no family here. They had to emigrate while I was with child. Then I lost our baby."

"Hmm. I don't know what to tell you…no experience…but you have lived in a fine home. I can tell by your speech that you are cultured."

"Two fine homes. My father was an ivory dealer, and Lumeri, of course, was a prominent landowner."

"Yes…" The woman frowned, but then brightened. "Wait! I have one idea. There is a government official who has a daughter with partial paralysis. That might be a possibility. Are you willing to inquire about it?"

"Yes. I am willing to try anything."

"The job may not pay much beyond your room and board, and with no experience, you may have to indenture for a while."

"Indenture? For how long?"

"That will be up to the head of the house and the matron. You can interview and see what they say."

"All right. I will do that."

The woman gave Merti and Sati directions, and they departed for their destinations. Sati only had to walk a little over a mile, and when she reached the house she was nervous. She said a prayer, like Anianus had taught her, and went in the gate.

A servant greeted her, and when she explained her purpose, the servant had her sit and wait for the matron.

The wait was not long, and the matron was cordial, "I am Kasmut. Are you Sati?"

"Yes. I was sent because you may have an opening."

"We do. Our daughter Maia has a partial paralysis. She needs someone to assist her—and to offer her companionship."

"I can do that."

The two women chatted for quite a while. Kasmut seemed reserved, but likeable. Sati guessed that she was about forty. She was short and carried a bit of extra weight, but her hair had very little grey. The matron wore heavy cosmetics on her cheeks and around her eyes.

"Would you like to meet Maia?" she asked.

"Yes. Of course."

"Let's go to her room." Kasmut led Sati to a spacious room on the main floor that served both as their daughter's bedroom and living area. "Maia, dear. I brought someone to meet you."

The girl appeared to be a little younger than Sati with some of her mother's features. When she waved her right arm, Sati guessed that it was her left side that was paralyzed. The girl's head was tilted up and turned to the right.

"Hello, Maia. My name is Sati."

"Sati?"

"That's right. Sati. My name means sunbeam. I am pleased to meet you."

"Can I call you Sunbeam? It's easier for me to say."

"Yes, if you wish. What have you been doing?"

"Me? Looking at the birds." Several birds were pecking just outside of the window.

"They are very pretty."

"I've been feeding them." Maia had a small sack of rice on a table near the window. The birds were having a feast.

"May I throw them a little food?"

"Sure. It's fun."

Sati picked up a small handful of rice and tossed it out to the birds, causing them to scurry for it. Then turning to the girl's mother, she smiled and said, "I like Maia. I think I can do this."

"I think you can too. Let's discuss it with my husband when he gets home."

Paser also was a likeable man, a little pompous, but that is to be expected in a government official. He was portly and greying. Sati guessed he was about fifty. He listened while his wife pointed out the benefits of hiring Sati, nodding affirmatively from time to time. "Does Maia like her?"

"Yes," his wife answered.

"Fine. Well, Sati, the usual rate would be your room and board plus one denarius per week. However, you have no experience, so we will need to take that into account. Do you know how that is done?"

"No."

"You would agree to serve for five years. We will hold your weekly payments for that time and, after you have performed your duties faithfully, we will increase the amount by a third. However, we would reserve the right to end your service at any time, in which case we would pay you the amount owed to date. Is that clear?"

"Do you mean I couldn't leave during that period?"

"That's the usual practice."

Sati had not considered tying herself down again, but under the circumstances she had little choice. "May I see my room and think about it until dinner time?"

"Yes, my dear," Kasmut offered. "It's right next to Maia's. Bring your bag."

The room was smaller than Maia's and not as bright, but it seemed adequate. The biggest issue was the five-year commitment. When Kasmut left, Sati muttered to herself, "Do I dare accept these terms? I will be imprisoned again with no way out. I'll be approaching thirty when my time is up. I can't have children, and I don't know if any man will want me, but I will receive about three hundred denarii. That's enough for a new beginning. In the meantime, I can make some new friends and become a Christian. And what choice do I have? I can't go very far on the twenty coins those horrible girls handed me."

"We're having a party," Fidelis announced. "Plan to come and bring whoever you like."

"I'd love to come," Clement assured him, "but I don't know whom I'd bring."

Bella had the answer, "Rosina said the same thing. You can be her escort."

Clement suddenly felt odd—odd and old. He hadn't been close to a girl since the evening on the balcony in Alexandria, more than seven years earlier.

When the date of the party arrived, he put on his best toga and spent quite a bit of time combing his hair. He knew Rosina's parents, who were members of the Church, and easily found their home, which was nice, but more modest than his own. They greeted Clement warmly, noting that they heard that he might become a presbyter.

Rosina also had primped. His heart skipped ahead several beats as he noticed the attractive gown she wore. "You look radiant!" he exclaimed.

"Thank you." She might have added a compliment as well, but her soft smile sent the message as she took his arm.

Clement was at a loss for words as they walked to the party. He cleared his throat once, and Rosina looked up, but nothing further came of it. Then, just before they walked in the door, he asked her, "Do you feel as awkward as I do?"

"Maybe more," she answered. "Let's just relax and have fun."

That put Clement at ease, and he told her so. She gave him her usual smile, but it was genuine, from the heart of one who had lost a love to another who had suffered the same fate.

They actually did have a good time at the party. There were a few good-natured remarks from people seeing the two together for the first time, which made them blush, but gave them feelings to remember.

When they arrived back at her home, he took her hand and their eyes met in a breathless moment of hope. Then she kissed him on one cheek and ran into the house.

Peter joked, "They're talking about you and Rosina in the assembly."

"We've only been to one party together," the bachelor protested.

"Well, you know how people talk."

"I wish it would stop."

"Now that you have a house and are preparing to become a presbyter, there's bound to be gossip. Anyway, I wanted to ask how you are—losing your father and all."

"It's hard," Clement admitted, "but we're dealing with it. Actually, I've been quite busy with all the new things going on and haven't had much time to think."

"And how is your mother?"

"She's getting along. Some days are harder for her than others. I'm spending as much time with her as I can."

"Good…and how about Horus?"

"In what way?"

"Well, how is he acting? Does he suspect that you know?"

"He's acting very nice. Exceptionally nice. Maybe he's afraid that I know—I can't tell."

Peter said, "I'm thinking that he came very close to getting caught. That must have scared him. Men like Horus sometimes shape up after they've had a close scrape."

"I hope so," Clement agreed. "I hate what he did, but I've been praying for him every day."

"Good. Keep it up. And how is Cassius?"

"Cassius is always happy, no matter what."

"I know. Well, it looks like your family will get through this loss."

The first weeks in Paser's household went fine for Sati. Maia needed quite a bit of assistance getting ready in the mornings and into bed at night. For the rest of the day, Sati mostly provided companionship. The girl had begun to call her Sunbeam or "my Sunbeam friend," and Kasmut was pleasant and considerate. Paser was out of the house most of the day and showed her respect in the evenings. Even though Sati had been retained as a servant, they had her dine with the family because Maia liked having her at the table. All in all, she felt blessed. It certainly was better than being alone in the house with Bunefer, Sitamun, and Nefrusheri.

One evening Kasmut asked, "Are you enjoying it here?"

"Yes, mam." Sati answered. "Maia is my friend, and you both are very nice to me."

"Is there anything else that you need?" asked Paser.

"If there were some books at Maia's level, I could read to her. I can only read simple sentences, but I could improve—and Maia could learn too. She likes stories."

"I will get some. But I was asking about you, personally. Is there anything you would like?"

"Hmm. My room is fine. I can't think of anything."

"That's good. If something comes up, don't be afraid to let us know."

"I appreciate that—very much….there is one thing."

"What is that?"

"I wasn't going to bring it up until I had served here longer."

"You can bring it up now," he assured her.

"If I could have an hour or two off now and then, I would like to prepare to become a Christian."

Paser furled his brow and carefully worded his response, "As you know, I am an Egyptian official. In my party, discussions are ongoing about how much latitude to allow foreign sects. Let's put that off for a while. Perhaps something may yield in the future."

Sati lamented, *What does he mean by that? How long in the future? Why can't there ever be a way for me to become a Christian?* Her heart ached with the refusal.

34

The next time Clement came to see Fidelis, Bella also was at home. Seeing him, she squealed with delight, "Did you have a nice time with Rosina?"

"It was a nice party. Thank you for inviting me," Clement replied.

"Hey! You can't dodge the question that easily. Did you enjoy being with her?"

"Oh, yes. Rosina is a very nice maiden."

"Are you going to see her again?" she asked with a grin.

"I might. I don't know if she likes me."

"What do you mean? Of course, she likes you."

"She does?"

"Clement, you're such an oaf. I know that she likes you."

"How do you know?"

"Because she told me so, you imbecile! We girls talk about everything," she laughed.

"Well, I might…"

"Would you like to see her again?"

"Yes, of course. But how?"

"You really don't have much experience with women, do you? Just do this: Sunday morning, after the breaking of the bread, invite her to *passeggiata* with you that evening. You walk together through the plazas, and then take it from there."

"Is it that easy? I've never done it before."

"I'm not surprised. You're going to be a bachelor all of your life until you learn a few things."

Clement blushed bright red, like a ripe apple. "I think I would like to do as you say."

"Well, good. But don't put it off, or someone else might ask her before you."

Sunday morning after the liturgy, Clement approached Rosina, exactly as Bella had suggested. She quickly accepted his invitation to walk together, as if she knew he was going to ask.

That evening he went to her home, took her arm, and they strolled through the neighboring plazas. They talked in short sentences with long pauses in between, but he enjoyed being with her, and she seemed to like it too.

When they got back to her home she invited him in. Once inside, she said, "My parents have gone to bed. Let's sit here," she suggested, pointing to a small couch. "Would you like some wine?"

"Yes. Thank you," he replied.

Rosina brought two cups and sat next to him on the couch. He was conscious of how close it brought them, feeling her warm arm press against his.

"Do your parents mind, if I come inside with you?" he asked, immediately realizing how stupid it must have sounded.

Rosina smiled. "It's fine. I was betrothed for almost a year, you know."

Clement wondered what she meant by that, but guessed she was saying that being close to a man was not new for her. As he was thinking about what to say next, he felt her cuddle closer to him and lay her head on his shoulder. Clement realized how much he yearned to have the soft presence of a woman close to him. He put his arm around her and pulled her closer, thinking, *I wasn't expecting this. I thought we were just going to walk.*

Rosina seemed to be waiting for him to do something, but he wasn't sure what. After a few minutes, she turned toward him and reached her arm around his side, giving him gentle caresses. When he wrapped his free arm around her, he looked and saw that she had lifted her head and closed her eyes. He leaned closer in to her and closed his. Then before he knew it, he was being kissed, and to his surprise, the kisses continued.

The inexperienced bachelor let down his reticence and pulled her body against his. With that, she clung to him, increasing the duration of her kisses. He was getting aroused and noticed that her breathing had become deeper.

With a little giggle and a big grin, she jumped up—turned—and leaped onto his lap. They kissed intensely for several minutes. He briefly wondered how far they could go without his having to repent, but realized that Rosina would not venture beyond what is considered appropriate for virgins in Rome. Waves of excitement overwhelmed his conscience.

His heart thumped like a drum as her kittenish purrs became louder. Clinging to one another seemed to contain their loneliness, and he became oblivious to the passage of time. Then Rosina gave a big sigh, pulled back, and laid her head on his chest. Everything felt so, so sweet.

Rosina giggled and caressed his neck. Neither wanted to let go—they simply savored the moment they had shared and let their minds slowly drift back to reality.

Clement chuckled and said, "I'm sweaty," and Rosina laughed. Then as he released his arms, she stood up and fanned her neck with her hand.

"May we walk together again?" he asked.

"Why don't you come here for dinner?"

The next afternoon Clement thought about seeing his friend Fidelis, but when he remembered that all secrets reached that household, he decided to visit Peter instead. He found him with Linus in a heated discussion.

"It's actually a valuable contribution to the Church," the presbyter pleaded.

Peter replied, "I still don't like it. And he sent it with a woman!"

"Phoebe is a holy woman and a leader who has served the Church in Corinth with faithful dedication."

"It's an affront. That's what it is."

"What are you two arguing about?" Clement asked.

When Peter groaned, Linus explained, "We received another letter from Paul. This one is addressed to those he calls 'the beloved of God in Rome.' It's a long and detailed exposition of the faith, very well composed, I would say."

"Flowery speech, that's what it is," Peter interjected. "He's showing off his education like a philosopher. I'd like to wring his neck."

Turning to Clement, Linus advised, "Paul wants to come here. I think that is the core of our bishop's concern."

"There is no need for him to come here!" Peter snorted.

"If he wants to go to Spain, he will pass this way."

"We are doing just fine without him. I don't want him here. He can go west to Spain and out in the ocean, if he wants to."

Linus explained to Clement, "Paul wants to come here to enlist support for a mission to Spain. Such a journey has long been on his mind. Now, with his missionary teaching successfully accomplished in the east, he is seeking new opportunities in the west. I admire his courage for wanting to spread the faith to all nations as Jesus commanded. He's a brave and dedicated man."

"When is he coming?" Clement asked.

"Not right away. He says he first needs to travel to Jerusalem. He has a sizeable collection to bring to the saints who are suffering in the Holy City."

Peter held out the letter and snapped, "Look at this list of those here who he sends greetings to: Prisca! Aquila! Epaenetus! Mary! Andronicus! Junia! And more! Do you see all the names?"

"Yes."

"Is my name on the list?"

"No."

"Why didn't he even mention me. Does he think I'm dead, or gone north to Britain?"

Both men were quiet. Linus had thought about the question but hadn't come up with a reasonable explanation.

"I'm going to Antioch," Peter growled. "I trust Evodius. I want to ask him face-to-face what is going on in that region. I'm leaving as soon as I can get the money."

Clement went to dinner at Rosina's. Her parents welcomed him, almost treating him like one of the family. Then he invited her to his house, where she and his mother became instant friends. The following week, Rosina prepared a special pasta with anchovies and clams for Clement. They spent a lot of time together and ended most evenings in her home on the now-familiar couch. The two never strayed beyond the limits of propriety, but alone in his room he visualized their lying together in an intimate embrace. He had long conversations with his mother, asking questions about family life that had never before entered his mind. He continued to pray in the mornings but allowed his practice of evening prayer to lapse. Once he forgot his biweekly meeting with Linus and didn't even miss it.

While Peter was away, Clement studied the lengthy letter from Paul. He was amazed at how vividly Paul could use words to inspire people's faith and encourage their dedication. The missionary clearly believed that humanity would be lost without the gospel. The letter answered a number of questions that Peter thought could be settled with common sense, but Paul laid them out with clarity and step-by-step precision. Clement hoped that when Peter returned, he would understand how the literate missionary's epistles added greatly to the bishop's pastoral instincts and talents. He and Linus concluded that the differences between the two great men were matters of background and communication style, rather than doctrine or Christian practice.

Linus observed, "The Church needs both Peter and Paul. I wish they both could see that."

"Do you think you will marry Rosina?" Clement's mother asked one day.

"I'm thinking about it. She is a sweet person. We seem to get along well, and I like her family. How do you feel about her?"

"Oh, I love Rosina. She's kind and considerate, and she doesn't put on pretenses like some girls."

"Yes. I appreciate that. And I like how she doesn't talk too much; you know how too much talk can get on a man's nerves."

"She communicates with her eyes."

"Exactly! I guess she's the ideal woman."

"Do you have any reservations?" his mother asked.

"Not really. Rosina is dedicated to the faith, and she seems pleased with my plans to become a presbyter. I told her that it will cut into my time and I won't be earning as much money as some men, but that doesn't seem to bother her."

"She is accustomed to not having much money."

"Yes. Coming from a home of modest means, her expectations are not beyond what I will be able to provide."

"Are you sure you can earn enough?"

"Fairly sure. I've talked to Linus about it. While I never will be able to have a full-time career, I'm already beginning to make a few denarii each week reading correspondence to merchants and helping them with their accounts."

"Your education should enable you to get by."

"I think so, as long as I keep my tastes simple…and Rosina seems to understand."

"Do you pray about this decision?"

"Linus says I should, and I'm beginning to address it. I'll continue to ask the Lord to guide me."

"Then there's nothing standing in your way."

"Probably not, but I'm not rushing into it."

35

A few weeks later, Kasmut praised Sati for her compassion and dedication to her daughter.

"Maia loves you, and we are most grateful," she gushed.

"I am grateful too, mam. I needed a place to go, and you took a chance with me."

Paser admitted, "It was a risk, but it is working out well all around. We are very happy with you."

"Thank you," Sati told them as she went to her room for the night.

"I'm lonely," she whispered to herself in the silence. "I'm grateful that they took me in, but I have no life of my own. I need love. I need a man who loves me and friends who care for me. But that is at least five years away."

With that, she got out the bronze ichthys and fingered its curved lines. "If only it had worked out with Clement," she muttered. "Clement loved me—I'm sure that he did. And I loved him. I still do."

Then closing her eyes, she called upon her only salvation. "Jesus. It's me, Sati. Do you hear me? I hope that you do. Do I have to spend my whole life feeling so lost and lonely? They say you are the Lord of Life. I need life. I need love. I need hope. Do not leave me forsaken in this pagan household. I want to become a Christian, but Paser won't let me. He says that something may yield in the future, but I have no idea what he means by that.

"Help me in whatever way you can. I have no one else to turn to. I want to pray with your followers. I want to pray with a husband. I want to receive your Body and Blood in the company of those who believe in you. Come to my aid. Do not leave me alone.

"I pray also for Clement. I have no idea what is going on in his life, but I pray for him—for whatever he may need at this moment. Look upon Clement with kindness and bless him with your love. Keep him safe from all harm and lead him in your ways. I wish I knew how to pray better, but I believe that you hear me. Take care of Clement...I love him.”

Linus sensed that something was not quite right with Clement. The enthusiasm with which he approached his preparation to become a presbyter seemed to have waned. Clement had not yet mentioned Rosina, and Linus had not yet heard. At their biweekly meeting, he bluntly brought up what he had observed.

“Has anything changed, Clement?”

“I can’t think of anything. Why do you ask?”

“You are not your usual self. You used to have such passion for the Lord. I don’t hear you expressing that in the same way.”

“There’s been a lot going on—with my father’s passing and everything.”

“Clement, tell me. Have you been praying?”

“Somewhat. I pray most mornings.”

“And what about the evenings?”

“I’m...I’m tired in the evenings. I will try to get back into my old habits.”

“That probably will help,” the presbyter shared. “How do you feel during the breaking of the bread?”

“How do I feel? All right. I attend every Sunday—with Mother.”

“And how about your ministries? Do you approach them with enthusiasm?”

“I...I have not fallen down in my work.”

“I asked if you feel enthusiastic—like you used to tell me you did.”

“Enthusiastic? Well, I’m growing accustomed to those things now. I have not missed an assignment.”

“Clement, has anything changed in your life?”

“No, except for what I said—about my family. What are you saying?”

The experienced presbyter drew a deep breath before answering. “I’m sensing an obstacle to grace.”

Clement was jolted. “An obstacle to grace! What’s that?”

“It could be anything that has come between you and Christ. It may not be so severe that it severs your relationship with him, but it is big enough that it’s getting in the way. It sounds like something is distracting you from your dedication to him. That’s why I’m asking if anything has changed.”

“I understand your point, but I can’t think of anything right now.”

“Well, keep what I said in mind. Every night, before you fall asleep, ask yourself, ‘Have I done anything today that could put a barrier between me and Jesus?’ Do this every evening, without fail. That is the only way we will get to the root of this dilemma.”

Clement assured Linus that he would pray more and examine his conscience every night, and on many evenings, after returning from Rosina's, he did what Linus suggested. The presbyter had painted a vivid image—an obstacle creating a separation between him and Jesus. The picture haunted the young aspirant. He kept thinking about it day and night.

Peter returned, and when Clement heard he rushed to his house. Linus was with him, along with another young man that he didn't know.

"Hello, Clement," the bishop greeted. "Do you know what I learned in Antioch? I was just telling Linus. They are reading Paul's letters in the liturgy, just like Isaiah and Jeremiah. It's going on all over the eastern region. At first I was disturbed to hear of it, but Evodius assured me that the practice is aiding the faith. On Sunday morning when I joined in the breaking of the bread, I watched the people listen to the passage from Paul's letter to the Corinthians about divisions in the Church."

"What did you make of it?" Clement asked.

"It was good. I mean, I never would have thought of doing such a thing, but the people really listened. I could see them listening with their eyes and ears and minds. It helped them get the point that division is our worst enemy."

"So, you liked the practice?"

"Well—I told Evodius that I didn't object. I'm going to give it time and see how it turns out."

"That is wise," Linus added. "The faith is growing. Now that it has spread beyond the reach of those who were eyewitnesses, we need to be open to new practices."

"Exactly!"

"So, do you feel better now about Paul?"

"Oh, that rascal is going to be a thorn in my side for a long time. I'll have to live with that, if I want the Church to reap the benefit of his efforts. Do you know what I mean?"

Both of his assistants knew exactly what he meant. They had been praying that their leader would see it.

"Oh!" Peter snickered. "I haven't introduced this fine young man. Meet Mark. He will be assisting me for a while."

The two extended their hands to the newcomer.

"Mark just finished his apprenticeship in Antioch. He can read and write in several languages and is from a fine family that I knew while I lived there. I told him I needed a man with his talents, and he packed a bag and came along. Mark can craft the alphabet with such precision, it's amazing."

Linus asked, "Does this mean that you plan to do more in writing?"

Peter answered, "Certainly. We have to keep up with the times, you know!"

It had been three days since Clement had seen Rosina when his mother mentioned her name.

"How is Rosina doing?"

"All right, I guess."

"What do you mean, you guess?"

"I need to talk with you about Rosina. I've been thinking about her a lot. I don't think I'm in love with her."

"But you seemed so happy together," she protested.

"I like being with Rosina. But I'm beginning to feel that it's because I need a woman in my life. I'm just not sure that Rosina is the right one."

"You get along."

"We get along, but we don't talk. We hardly speak to one another.

"You've only been seeing her for a short time."

"That's the point. We've only been seeing each other for a short time, but everyone is beginning to assume we are going to get married, including Rosina."

"Do you not like her?"

"I like her. Rosina is an ideal maiden in every way. It's just…I don't feel that I love her."

"That may take more time. You both are young."

"I'm almost twenty-five," he asserted. "I wish I could just take a break for a couple of weeks and see how I feel."

"Clement, she will get angry with you if you don't see her. It's already been three days."

"I know. That's the dilemma."

"And even if you could go away for a couple of weeks, what difference would that make? No marriage is perfect, Clement. Two people grow in love as they live their lives together. If you think you can wait until you find the ideal woman, you may grow old and lonely."

"That might work!" he shouted. "Thank you, Mother," he gushed, giving her an affectionate kiss.

"What?"

"I could go away for a couple of weeks. Rosina can wait that long. That will give me time to think."

"You really are serious about this, aren't you?"

Clement ran out of the house and straight to Linus. At the top of the steps, he was puffing.

"Clement, why are you running?"

"The obstacle in my life. I think it may be Rosina."

"Who is Rosina?"

Clement related the whole story of how he was seeing Rosina and how he had come to realize that their relationship may be a mistake. "I long for the love of a woman," he said. "I don't think she loves me either. She just wants a man!"

Linus was not judgmental. He simply asked questions and suggested options. "You may find it helpful to make a retreat. Spending some time by yourself, alone with the Lord, will help you discern if you have a true calling to the presbyterate."

"I want to do that. Where should I go?"

Linus suggested the house of a hermit in Tuscany. "Go there. Stay for two weeks and pray for as much of the time as you can. Be open to what Christ may choose for you. Then come back, and we'll see how you feel."

Clement ran home and packed a bag. After saying good-bye to his mother and Rosina, he headed up into the hills of Tuscany. Each day he told the Lord how he needed certainty, and each evening he listened for answers.

Throughout the stay he grew more certain that he should continue on his pathway in the Church. By the end of the two weeks he regained his former passion for his work and felt sure that he should let Rosina marry another man.

When he saw Linus he told him, "More than anything else, I feel the presence of Christ with me again. I missed the feeling, but it's back."

Linus was overjoyed.

Cordula was disappointed about Rosina, but pleased that her son was his old self again.

Rosina was angry, but when word got out about the breakup, three men asked her to *passeggiata*.

Peter was elated. "I want you to be happy, my son. God will bring you the right wife."

"I hope you are right," Clement replied. "I have to have faith that he will. It's going to be very lonely again."

36

Even though Clement was lonely, the next four years flew by. He worried, at first, how Mark would fit in to the organization of the Church in Rome. Peter kept Mark close by his side, but assured Clement that the two were not in competition. "You will be bishop someday," Peter predicted. "Mark is just a writer." After hearing this several times, Clement put his trust in Peter's pronouncement and made friends with Mark. He even taught the young scribe how to earn spending money by helping merchants with their correspondence and accounts.

Under Nero, limits were placed on fines, fees for lawyers were restricted, and he overruled the senate's attempt to give former owners the right to revoke freedoms granted to slaves. When tax collectors were accused of being too harsh on the poor, he transferred the authority to lower commissioners. He called for a number of impeachments of governmental officials and arrested others for corruption and extortion.

Nero became personally more powerful as he removed Marcus Pallas from the treasury and Burrus and Seneca from their advisory posts. He got involved with Poppaea Sabina, the wife of the statesman Otho, and soon after arranged the murder of his mother, Agrippina. Nero had a loyal freedman stage a shipwreck, but the hearty lady swam to shore and the assassin had to stab her and frame the death as a suicide.

Linus gave Clement one final examination before allowing him to be ordained.

"Do you love the Lord, your God, with your whole heart and with your whole soul and with your whole mind and with your whole strength?"

"Yes."

"Do you love your neighbor as yourself?"

"Yes, I do."

"Do you love your enemies?"

"I no longer have any enemies. I love all people."

"You speak well, Clement. I have watched with joy as you have grown in the faith. Are you ready to make a lifetime commitment to Christ and his

Church?"

"I am."

"Will you serve his people with love, defend the faith with honor, and always set a good example by your own righteous life?"

"I will."

"Will you pray the prayers of the Church with dedication and preside at the liturgy with integrity?"

"Yes, I will."

"And will you obey your bishop in all things, treating him as you would treat your Lord, Jesus?"

"I will with the grace of God."

"Clement, you have studied the faith and put what you learned into pastoral practice. I believe you are ready to be ordained. I will tell our bishop."

"Thank you, Linus. You have been safe harbor for me, a beacon of hope, even in my times of failure and trouble."

"Everyone has those times, my son, but you recovered very well. I'm sure that Jesus is pleased with you."

After the two churchmen embraced, Clement hurried home to share the news with his mother. He told her not with a boyish shout, but with a mature and humble pronouncement. "Linus said today that I am ready for ordination."

"Oh, Clement. I am so pleased. I've prayed for this moment ever since you were a little boy."

Giving her a warm hug, he added, "I haven't spoken with the bishop yet. He will set the date."

"Any date will be fine. Then we'll have a celebration. We'll invite the whole family and all of our friends."

"It will be a wonderful day, Mother."

"But tell me, my son. Are you certain? Do you have any reservations?"

"No reservations, Mother. I know in my heart that this is the purpose for which I was born. All of the twists and turns of my life and all of the peaks and valleys have brought me to this point. I am as certain as any man can be."

"You seem very happy."

"I am. I will undertake the work with passion."

"It's just..." She paused, but he waited until she found the words she was seeking. "It's just that everything would be perfect, if you had a wife."

Clement laughed. "Things can't always be perfect. I still hope to have a wife, but I think you know that Sati is my true love. I doubt that I will ever get beyond that."

"I know, son. And I will keep praying for you."

Peter set the date of ordination for the Sunday after the Paschal Feast, two weeks before Clement's twenty-ninth birthday. In addition to the usual readings and prayers, the bishop called upon all the saints in heaven to come to his aid and dressed him in the distinctive stole of a presbyter. Then, while the whole community watched in silence, he placed his hands on Clement's head and prayed that the Lord would grant to him the charism to lead worship *in persona Christi*—in the person of Christ.

Clement had wondered how he would feel at that moment. Would there be a particular sensation? Would he be filled with joy? Would he see angels? Actually, he felt none of those things—just humility. He felt totally humble before the awesome trust that was being shown to him and the immense responsibility he was accepting. *Thank you, Jesus*, he prayed in silence. *Thank you for all you have given me. I am your servant. To you I surrender all that I have and all that I am, forever.*

At the house, just about everyone gathered to celebrate, including Fidelis and his wife, Bella and Rosina and their husbands, and many friends and business associates. The place was crowded, and both Cordula and her youngest son drank more wine than usual.

Horus proposed the first toast, "To Clement, who God has called from our midst and who has fulfilled one of the dreams of our family. We are proud of you, Brother. May our Lord always guide you and help you to new peaks of achievement."

"To Clement," voices cheered.

Peter thought the toast was odd, given all the deceit of previous years. Was Horus sincere, or was he just putting on a show? The bishop couldn't tell, but he knew that the middle brother needed more time in which to progress in the Christian life.

Clement was congratulated until his hands were sore, and his mother got hoarse from saying thank you so many times. By the end of the evening, they dropped into their beds, exhausted.

Sati couldn't stand it any longer. That same afternoon she snuck away from her responsibilities and ran to the home of Anianus, who now was the bishop of the city. "I don't know if he will even remember me," she muttered as she rang the bell at the gate. To her surprise, he answered the bell himself.

"I want to become a Christian!" she pleaded. "I have been waiting thirteen years. I probably will get into trouble coming here, but I can't wait any longer. Will you help me?"

The bishop asked, "Do I know you? Your face is familiar."

"My name is Sati. We met long ago when you were visited by Peter and Clement."

"Oh my God, yes! You are Sati! I remember your hair. How can I help you?"

"I want to become a Christian. I want to follow the faith of Clement. My employer won't allow me to, but it is my only hope," she cried.

"Were you not married to a prominent landowner?"

"He died, and his children kicked me out. Now I am indentured. Tell me what I must do to become a Christian."

"Well, the normal way is to attend instruction, and at the next celebration of the Paschal Feast you can be baptized. Can you come here on Tuesday evenings?"

"Maybe Paser will let me. I don't know. I will ask him again."

"Do you live with Paser, the government official?"

"Yes. I help his daughter, who is partially paralyzed. I will try to come here Tuesday evening, but I must go back now before I get in trouble. Thank you. Good-bye."

Anianus tried to ask more questions, but the frightened woman turned and ran out of sight. "Perhaps she will return Tuesday evening," he murmured.

37

The new presbyter settled into his work—his pastoral ministries, presiding at the breaking of the bread, instructing catechumens—all the things he had looked forward to doing. He found the work truly satisfying, like he had hoped it would be. Every day he was helping someone grow closer to Christ.

Clement also was spending more time with Mark and was pleased that their friendship was deepening. Mark knew that his assistance to Peter would evolve, but he was disappointed that so far, the bishop asked him only to help with reading correspondence and drafting replies, rather than undertaking any serious new writing.

"I told Peter that he shouldn't try to imitate Paul," the young scribe shared. "Do you know what I'd like to do? I'd like to put the whole gospel teaching in writing. Just think of that! Then copies could be sent all around the empire, and people could hear stories about Jesus just like they were hearing them from an apostle."

Clement replied, "That's a great idea! I see the benefit, and I really encourage you. What does Peter think?"

"He hasn't said yes or no. He just says I first should spend time listening to him teach, and then later think of setting it to writing."

"If you waited, you would become more familiar with how he words things."

"Yes. I understand that. I don't feel I'm ready quite yet, so I'm willing to wait for a while."

No one in Rome yet knew it, but at that moment a ship was docking near Napoli, and Paul was preparing to disembark. The missionary apostle's situation had changed greatly since he wrote the letter to the Romans. He was not coming to enlist support for a mission to Spain. Instead he was being escorted in chains by troops as a prisoner seeking to have his case heard by the emperor.

Paul had gone to Jerusalem with a collection of money for the beleaguered Christians in the Holy City. He initially was warmly received but also warned that he was gaining a reputation for being against the Law of Moses. James told him, "Those who observe the law have been informed that you are teaching all the Jews who live among the Gentiles to abandon Moses and that you are telling them not to circumcise their children or to observe the customary practices."

The warning turned out to be necessary, for after only one week, some Jews from the Province of Asia noticed Paul in the temple and stirred up a crowd there with bitter accusations. He was seized and dragged out by the angry mob, but he escaped by surrendering to a group of Roman centurions, who arrested him and took him to the tribune. Paul constantly pleaded in his own defense, saying he had been a law-abiding Pharisee.

The tribune secretly transported Paul by night to Caesarea to avoid a vicious plot by zealous Jews to kill him, but the governor, Felix, held him in custody for two years until a new governor, Porcius Festus, reopened his case. Festus even got the Jewish king Agrippa involved, but fearing that he would be killed if he appeared again in public, Paul appealed for his case to be forwarded to Rome. Being a Roman citizen, Paul was entitled to have his case heard by the emperor. Festus replied, "You have appealed to Caesar, and to Caesar you will go."

So Paul and his companions sailed for Rome where he was to stand trial for his accused crimes. However, as they passed Cyprus, strong winds blew the ship off course, and they ended up shipwrecked on the island of Malta, where they spent the winter. When the skies again were clear, they sailed on to Syracuse and Rhegium, then landed in Puteoli, near Napoli.

A few days later, unaware of Paul's arrival, Peter hurried to find Clement. "Clement! My son! You must read this!"

The new presbyter looked over a letter, which read:

> *To Peter, most holy bishop of Rome—from Anianus, the Lord's humble servant in Alexandria: greetings.*
> *My hope is that all is well with you and that the Church in Rome is thriving. I am writing, however, to share a most unusual experience that may be of interest to your young friend Clement. Two weeks ago, a frightened woman rang at my gate, pleading that she be trained in our faith. The woman was Sati, the one whom Clement wrote of his love to, but I returned the letter because the young woman already was married. Now it seems that the husband has died, and Sati is indentured in the house of Paser, a government official. I told Sati which days we hold instruction, but two Tuesdays have passed without her returning. I do not know what to make of this, but I thought that Clement may wish to know.*

Clement sank to the ground in disbelief, almost fainting, but clinging to consciousness in order to glean every possible bit of information that the letter contained. Sitting on the floor, he studied every detail, amazed at what he was seeing.

"I must go at once," he muttered. Then rising, he told Peter, "I must go. I must go. I will resume my duties faithfully when I return."

"I understand, my son. Go with God."

Running out the door, he shouted, "Tell Linus, I'll be back!" and off he rushed.

"Mother! Mother, where are you?" he shrieked as he came in the door.

"Here, Clement. What's wrong?"

"Nothing is wrong! At least not that I know of." Then catching his breath, he explained, "Peter got a letter from Alexandria. Sati is no longer married! Anianus knows where she is!"

"Oh, Clement," his mother sighed. "What are you going to do?"

"I'm going! I'm going to her as fast as I can."

"But you don't know if she even wants to see you."

"That's true, but I can't pass up this opportunity. I have to take the risk. Oh, Mother—this is such wonderful news."

She reached to embrace him, but he bounded up the stairs. Returning quickly with a small sack, he kissed his mother, gasping, "Got to book a ship!" Then out the door he ran.

Cordula sat down. "Thank God it's spring," she whispered. "The winds will be good." Then she prayed for her son, "Lord Jesus, you who are the Lord of Life and the Savior who led my son into your service, please, please guide him and assist him at this juncture in his life. Help him to do the right thing. If it is that he should go, then help him find a good ship. If it is to stay, then raise a great obstacle that will keep him here.

"I am afraid for Clement. During this moment that he perceives to be a time of hope, he may make a huge mistake. He hardly knows this woman, and she hasn't communicated with him very well. Is it true love for my son, or is it just an act of desperation? Don't leave his side until he knows."

Clement returned wearing a big grin. "I found a ship. It leaves the day after tomorrow."

38

The day that Clement sailed, Paul arrived in Rome, coming by land along the Via Appia from Puteoli, where he had stayed seven days. When some of the brothers heard that he was nearing Rome, they went to the city of Three Taverns to meet him. The Roman officials allowed Paul to remain in his lodgings while he awaited trial, and there he met with all who came to him.

"Are you going to go to him?" Linus asked Peter.

"It's up to Paul to come to me."

"But he is under house arrest; he cannot come here."

"I know, but he can send for me. When he sends for me, then I will go to his house."

"That's hardly a welcoming gesture," the presbyter complained.

"It was hardly a welcoming gesture when he sent a letter to my people without even mentioning my name."

"But you can't harbor a grudge. You have to forgive him."

"I have forgiven him!" the bishop of Rome shouted. Then very quietly and methodically he emphasized, "When he asks for me to come to him, I will go."

Upon arriving in Alexandria, Clement went immediately to the house of the bishop. It was morning.

"Clement! You came so quickly," Anianus said in greeting.

"I want to go to Sati today. Have you heard any more from her?"

"Not a word. You may stay here with me. Put your things down."

"I'm very grateful, my friend. I must hurry."

"Well, freshen up a little and put on a clean tunic. You are going to the house of a government official."

"All right."

"Are you hungry? I will fix something, and then you can go."

Clement hurriedly washed and put on a clean tunic while the bishop set out some bread and oil. Anianus was pleased to hear that his guest had become a presbyter.

"And you are the bishop now," the traveler replied.

"Yes. We all were sad when Marcus passed on. He founded the community here, and he is now enjoying his reward."

Clement stuffed the food in his mouth, took a long gulp of wine, and said, "Thank you. We will talk later. Now I must go."

Following the bishop's directions, he arrived at the house of Paser shortly after noon and boldly rang the bell, not knowing what he would do when it was answered. Kasmut, Maia, and Sati were dining in the courtyard, and when she saw him, she shrieked.

Clement gave them a low bow and introduced himself to the matron. Then going to where Sati was seated, he knelt down before her and quietly stated, "I have waited thirteen years for this moment."

Sati was frozen in her chair and began to sob.

"I said I would come back, and I am here."

She was speechless.

"I love you. I have loved you from the moment we met on your balcony."

Sati jumped up and fell into his arms, still too shocked to say a word or even kiss him. Clement cradled her against his chest and sobbed tears of joy.

Kasmut didn't know what to make of the intrusion, but Maia waved her right arm with glee. She had never seen her Sunbeam friend so happy.

"Perhaps you could explain what this is about," the lady requested.

Clement began the account, but Sati interrupted, wanting to frame the story in her own words. When she finished, she was out of breath.

"Well, this is totally unexpected," Kasmut exclaimed.

"May we have some time to speak alone?" he asked.

"All right. I can see that you must. Sati, let's bring Maia back inside. Then you can sit out here."

Clement's heart beat in loud thumps as he watched the two women move the partially paralyzed girl inside. *She is still beautiful,* he noticed. *She is even now, after all these years, the woman of my dreams. And her hair still radiates—she is without doubt the girl with the golden hair. Oh, I love her so!*

When Sati returned, she sat down and with great composure took his hand and cleared her throat. "I must tell you a few things," she admitted, looking sorrowfully into his eyes. "I am no longer a virgin."

"I know," he gushed. "You were married to a prominent landowner."

"I lost our child, and it does not appear that I can have another."

"Oh. I am so sorry. That must have caused you great pain."

"Do those things not bother you?"

"Of course not. I love you."

"And I am penniless. My parents had to leave, and I have nothing to offer you."

"I want nothing but you," he pleaded for her to understand.

She added, "I am not yet a Christian. I kept your ichthys. I wanted to become baptized, but the men wouldn't let me."

"I am very pleased that you want to join the faith. Anianus told me in his letter that you came to his house."

"Is that how you found out where I was? Why didn't you write to me?"

"I did write to you," he groaned. "I wrote two letters. When you didn't answer the first letter, I sent you another. But Anianus returned the second one because you were married!"

"I sent a letter to you, through Peter."

"Yes. I got that letter, and the ivory locket. See! I still have it. I kiss it and brush your hair across my cheek."

"But you didn't write back."

"I did write back. Like I told you, I wrote two more letters, but Anianus sent the second one back."

"Your first letter from Rome didn't reach me. It must have gotten lost."

"That explains why I didn't hear from you again. You never got my first letter. Oh my God! All these years I thought that you didn't want me or love me."

"I thought that you didn't love me! When I didn't get another letter, everyone pressured me to marry Lumeri. I wouldn't have married him, if I had known."

They stared at one another in disbelief. One lost letter, blown away by the maritime wind, was all that had come between them for thirteen years.

"We are together now," he chuckled.

Sati brightened. "We are together now. Let me touch your face. Is this real?"

"This is real," he assured her as he took her into his arms.

When Paser came home, they had to explain the whole story again. At first he was reticent to let Sati go, but when his daughter spoke up to him like she had never done before, he acquiesced. Not being able to withstand his daughter and wife's frowns, he promptly gave Sati the denarii she was owed along with the five-year bonus. Sati kissed Maia goodbye, and the happy couple left the house carrying Sati's small bag and wearing hopeful smiles.

39

On the voyage to Rome, Clement and Sati stayed as close together as they could—cuddling, whispering, caressing, giggling, kissing, gazing at the wonder of the other, and talking about all the details of their lives that each wanted to know. Each day affirmed their commitment and drew tighter the bond that circled them with love. Clement drew her soft body close to his, again getting in touch with his need for intimacy but not allowing his desire to grow too great. They were not married, and both accepted the limitations of their transitional state.

They considered themselves betrothed, even though there was no one to whom they could ask permission. Clement looked forward to introducing Sati to his mother, and Sati felt sad that her parents could not share her joy. The bright blue sky over Rome filled their hearts with hope as they walked along the busy streets to his home on the Capitoline Hill.

His greeting was simple, "Hello, Mother. I'd like you to meet Sati."

Cordula took one long look at the Egyptian beauty and opened her arms with a smile. She had already decided to accept the unknown woman if her son brought her home, but her warm embrace revealed a fresh choice of motherly satisfaction. "Welcome, my dear. I am so glad to finally meet you."

Sati had been nervous, even though her lover had assured her of his mother's generous spirit. Now in the cradle of her arms, she relaxed and drew a deep breath of relief. "I am glad to be here. I knew that you would be very nice."

Clement watched in glee as the two women spoke little nothings to make the other comfortable. He expected them to like one another but had not thought it would occur so instantly. "Let's sit down. I'll get some wine. I know you two have much to talk about."

The introductions to Cassius and Horus, Peter and Linus, and Fidelis and Bella also were joyful. Parties were held to celebrate the couple's betrothal, which now became official. Bright smiles greeted them wherever they went. Peter agreed that Sati should be given accelerated instruction so that she could be baptized before the wedding, which was scheduled for September.

Sati took a separate room in Clement's house until the wedding, but each evening they cuddled in the living area.

One evening she asked, "What are you thinking?"

He replied with a smile, "How nice it will be when we can go to bed together."

Squeezing him gently she whispered, "Me too."

"I want so much to become one with you, with nothing separating us."

"I long for that too." Then she added, "I want you to know that I didn't love Lumeri like I love you."

"You didn't have to say that."

"I know. You are so kind and understanding. But I have no secrets from you. I have had sex, and I enjoyed it until after I lost the baby. I expect that I will enjoy it even more with you."

"You can teach me what I don't know."

She laughed, "You didn't need to say that!" Then she noted with a smile, "There isn't much to learn. You just do what comes naturally."

"That seems easy enough. I'm ready right now."

"Now don't say that!" she giggled, slapping his hand. "It will be all the more fun after we are married."

When Clement resumed his ministries, Linus brought him up to date on the arrival of Paul.

"Are you telling me that Peter hasn't been to see him even once?"

"That's right. I told him he should go to Paul, but he is stubborn. He keeps saying, 'It's up to Paul to ask for me.' And after all, Peter is the bishop of this city."

"Yes, but if Paul can't leave his house, and people are going there to see him, then Peter could do as much."

"That's what I kept saying. He won't budge on it though. And Paul knows what Peter wants. He's hardheaded too."

"Have you been to see Paul?"

"No. I figured that our bishop set the precedent. I don't feel that I should go before he does."

"I guess you're right. I won't go either. I'll wait," Clement affirmed. "I don't know Paul, actually. I don't know what I'd say to him if I did see him."

"Paul is at his best when he's on the road. I'm sure he's terribly uncomfortable cooped up here in Rome like a caged rooster, even though the guards are treating him well. He likes to be out where he can make conversions in numbers. I expect him to go on to Spain as soon as the emperor hears his case."

"Do you think he will be acquitted?"

"I expect so. There isn't much of a case against him."

"When do you think Nero will hear his case?"

"I don't know."

Sati was happy to learn the Christian ways. It seemed so reasonable that if there is only one God who sent his Son to redeem us, that we should do our best to follow his teachings. She was glad that she had prayed so often over the years of waiting and that her husband would be a leader in the faith.

"This is a day I have looked forward to for so long," she told Clement the morning of her baptism. "I am ready to embrace Christ."

"Are you also ready to embrace his cross?" he soberly replied.

"Don't speak to me today like a presbyter. Just be my husband."

"I'm sorry. I don't want to dampen the joy of this day. The two go together, though, the joy and the cross, the hope and the suffering."

"I know. I learned it over the last thirteen years—nearly fourteen now. I have suffered greatly."

"After today your suffering will be joined with his, you will become a part of his redeeming life."

"I want that."

"I'm glad that you do. I've learned too that there can be no resurrection without death. Our sufferings are small compared to his. Our pains are little in relation to what he did for us out of great love."

"I am still learning that."

"That's what energizes me to work as a presbyter."

"And I admire you for it. I love how you devote yourself to such a worthy purpose."

Sati got quite soaked in the baptismal pool as Peter submerged her three times, in the name of the Father, and of the Son, and of the Holy Spirit. Helpless in his strong arms, she marveled, "I've died from my past, and now I live for Christ—I and my husband."

After they wrapped her in a white garment, Peter anointed her with blessed oil. "You are a Christian now," he said, "and ready to become a Christian bride." Everyone applauded as the new follower of Christ beamed with delight.

The day before the wedding, Clement gave his bride a golden ring.

"It's beautiful. Oh, Clement. I feel almost married."

"We are almost married. Our day is tomorrow."

"I have a gift for you also. I will get it for you."

As Sati turned to go to her room, Clement admired her movements. "How lovely she is," he marveled. "She was beautiful when we first met, but now—now she is a mature woman. I am so privileged to have her as my wife."

Sati returned with a wide smile, carrying a gift wrapped in linen folds. "I hope you like it," she cooed, handing him the parcel.

"What is it?" he exclaimed as he carefully removed the wrapping. "Oh, my goodness. What a handsome silver box."

"It's for your office, where you will meet with people. See—it has an ichthys surrounded by symbols of the four winds, which will help carry the faith to all nations."

"I love it!" he expressed as he gave her a kiss. "I shall be proud to display it to all who come to me."

"I wish I could have spent more."

"But this must have cost a great deal. You had it custom made."

"It took most of what I received from Paser. I don't want his money any more. All I want is you."

They kissed with passion, anticipating the joy they would feel, entwined together the following night.

The next morning Sati got up early and quietly snuck out of the house to meet her bridesmaids at Bella's. This was to observe the Roman custom of the bride's family walking in procession to her husband's home. Linus, who was assuming the role of her father, joined her there as well. They also followed the ancient

Roman tradition for fooling evil spirits by the bride and bridesmaids dressing alike and the men wearing garments like the groom's.

When the procession arrived, Linus extended his hand to Clement in the timeless gesture of the father giving his daughter in marriage. Then with a cheer, the wedding party carried Sati across the threshold. Little girls watched every detail in awesome wonder while the young boys squirmed and made faces. In most Roman households, the wedding feast would begin at this point, but Peter added a long prayer of blessing over the new couple, which consecrated their marriage before God.

Everyone had good words to say as they lifted their wine to the newlyweds. Horus deferred to Cassius to make the first speech, which was long and rambling, but he followed up with several short toasts of his own. Before long everyone was celebrating—shouting and cheering and telling stories of love.

Bella laughed, "I taught him everything he knows."

Fidelis blurted, "He's more of a man than I thought."

Rosina toasted the groom, happy for Clement, but pleased that she had ended up with a man more suited to her disposition.

No one was happier than Cordula, who had prayed many years for this wonderful day. According to her plan, she left with the last guests and stayed overnight with a friend.

Alone in the house, Clement took his bride's hands and asked, "Are you happy?"

"Exceedingly happy," she replied. "I missed not having my parents here to share my joy, but other than that, everything was perfect."

Having no words to comfort his bride, Clement cradled her in his arms and brushed away her one big tear.

"I'm sorry," she said.

"There's nothing to be sorry about. You spoke reality. We carry some pain, you and me. I thought about my father today too. We both have had losses."

Then taking the tips of her fingers, he led his bride to their bedroom.

The light of the moon coming in the window cast a spell of magic around them. She asked him to loosen the tie at the back of her neck, and as he watched the folds of her gown drop past her supple back, drape momentarily on her hips, and then glide silently to the floor, he felt every nerve in his body quiver. After tenderly kissing each shoulder, he extended his arms and drew her near, caressing her sweet neck with his lips, which made her arch her neck and tremble. They remained in this position treasuring the beauty of the moment while time left the room.

Turning quickly, Sati circled her arms around her husband's neck and smothered his face with kisses. Then he lifted her gently in his strong arms and carried her tenderly to the bed.

At first they just gazed deeply into each other's eyes, savoring the moment. Then they drew closer, until their bodies were fully together. Clement was overwhelmed by the sensation. "This is so good," he whispered, after which no further words were spoken. Having her soft, responsive body close against his was more exciting than he had ever imagined.

She melted into his embrace as, for the first time in her life, she experienced the erotic power of true love. Their kisses became more passionate and determined.

The months of waiting had reached their limit, and their bodies yearned for the pleasure for which men and women were created. Together they discovered erotic heights and savored their union of love.

There was no reason to hurry, but arousal turning to passion brings on its own urgency. They would have a lifetime to love slowly, but this night moved on its own momentum. They joined in the union of delight and entered into the motion that God granted to ensure the continuation of life. Neither had ever known such joy.

40

The lovers settled in and happily enjoyed each day, pleased with the choices they made. Sati made more friends in the Christian community and cherished her life with Clement. He spent his days devoted to his ministries and his nights with his wife, treasuring the hours in their bedroom.

Cordula let Sati take charge of the house, and the two grew even closer as time went by. Horus and Cassius kept the egg business humming so well that Horus had to buy a larger strongbox.

It was odd that the emperor never heard Paul's case, and the unusual fact that neither Peter nor Paul ever contacted the other became so commonplace that no one bothered to talk about it anymore.

Almost three years after the wedding, tragedy struck the city of Rome. On the night of July 18, fire broke out near the Circus Maximus adjoining the Palatine and Caelian Hills. Starting in shops selling flammable goods and fanned by summer winds, the conflagration instantly grew and swept the whole area. There were no walled mansions or temples there, or other obstructions, that could arrest the blaze. It swept violently over level spaces and climbed hills, but returned to ravage the lower ground again, outstripping every counter-measure. The city's narrow winding streets and irregular lots aided the fire's progression as it jumped from block to block.

People were terrified—young and old—helpless before the advancing flames. Some died in their homes, and others tried to flee, but when they looked back, menacing flames sprang up around them. In the confusion of speeding carts, mothers carrying crying children and fathers helping elderly loved-ones, no one knew which way to run. By morning a large section of the city had burned and the fire was still raging.

Clement and Sati could see the smoke rising, but accurate news was impossible to obtain. "I must see if the flames reached my people," the presbyter cried as his wife and mother tried to dissuade him from leaving the house. Reaching a vantage point higher up on the hill, he surveyed the awesome scene. The flames had not come to the Capitoline district—they were eating their way north, and much of the Palatine and Caelian Hills along with the valley between were consumed. "This is horrible! Much worse than we thought," he muttered as he hurried back to inform his household.

"Most of the areas where our people are living are away from the blaze," he revealed. "The Trastevere is, of course, untouched. It's across the river. I want to go over there and see what Peter and Linus are thinking of doing."

"Be careful," Sati pleaded.

"Don't worry," he answered. "I won't go near the flames."

Some of the other presbyters and deacons already were with the bishop when Clement arrived. He corroborated what they had heard, as to which districts were burning.

"Our first duty is to help our people," Peter ordered. "Go through your districts and see who has needs. Find out where the missing may have fled. Then come back here and we'll decide how to focus our efforts."

"Will we stage a humanitarian effort?" a deacon asked.

"That will be our mission tomorrow. Tell people to start making bread. The homeless can't bake for themselves. We'll help all who need it—Christians, Jews, and Gentiles. But today we must assess the situation."

As the men dispersed, Peter confided to Linus and Clement, "I fear for the worst. We have fires every year, but it is so dry now, and the *vigili* firefighters are already exhausted."

Clement agreed, "I'm afraid you are right. If they can't get it under control by tomorrow, all hell could break loose."

On his way to his next destination, Clement stopped by the warehouse and found Horus, busily moving crates. "Hello, Brother. What are you hearing?"

"Oh, Clement. Hello. The palace wants all the eggs they can get. They want us to keep making deliveries."

"Do they think they can get the fire under control soon?"

"They are trying, but no one is making predictions as to when."

"If you need any help, I may be able to give you a few hours later this week. Tomorrow we likely will begin humanitarian efforts."

"Thank you, Brother. Stop by any day you are free."

Clement went next to the house of Pamphilus, where his flock met on Sundays for the breaking of the bread. The owner of the large stone dwelling was worried, but he had not yet heard of any members needing assistance. Clement promised to stop by the next morning to get an updated report.

When he reached his own home, the women were relieved. Their anxiety increased, however, when he shared what he had learned.

That night the fire raged anew, and fresh winds blew some of the flames straight toward the palace on the remaining area of the Palatine Hill. Nero watched the inferno from a tower in the gardens of Maecenas on the Esquiline Hill, where witnesses saw him singing and playing the lyre. The emperor had previously admitted that he was disgusted with the old dwelling and had envisioned a new grand Golden Palace with expansive grounds, if only he could acquire the land. Now the fire was yielding the acreage he wished for, but at a terrible price.

The next day the emperor opened up the Campus of Mars and some of his own gardens to accommodate the homeless. Food was brought in from Ostia and neighboring towns, and the price of grain was cut in half. He had emergency accommodations set up for the destitute and was seen personally in the streets directing efforts to handle the crisis.

The Christian communities in Trastevere gave generously to the humanitarian effort. With his own district so far untouched, Clement helped deliver food to the thousands of homeless huddled on the Campus of Mars. There were few facilities for cooking, and those reclining in the field hungrily devoured the fresh-baked bread he carried in.

One woman took only a half loaf and pointed to a group huddled near her. "Feed them," she said. "They need it worse than I do." They were a family of six, and the father was groaning in pain from the impact of jumping from their second-floor flat as flames engulfed their building. After he reached the ground, he stood and caught his five children, but his wife would not jump. She perished in the blaze.

"How did you get here?" Clement asked the boy of about eleven, while handing loaves to the younger children.

"I stole a hand cart," the lad admitted, "and wheeled him here. The younger ones followed."

"You did well, son. May I see your father?"

The boy nodded, and Clement lifted the father's tunic revealing the twisted stump of his badly broken left leg and a gash growing red from infection. "My God. He will never walk again," he whispered.

"I know," the boy answered, apparently overhearing. "I don't even know how long he will live, he's in such agony."

The presbyter was amazed at the lad's courage in the face of such tragedy. "You will be the father now," he stated.

"I know," he replied again.

Turning to the tallest girl, he asked, "How old are you?"

"Nine," she answered, staring at him in a somber daze.

"What is your name?"

"Dulcia."

"Well, sweet Dulcia, take good care of your children. You are all they have."

Clement knelt and prayed to heaven that the bedraggled family might get more aid. He was sure that his prayers were heard but left with more hope than confidence that enough would arrive. When he got a few steps away, he broke down in tears.

By late afternoon the flames seemed to subside, but that night the inferno raged anew as the heat drew strong winds up the hills and blew hot embers onto tinderbox roofs across the city. Men were seen with torches, attempting to rekindle the blaze and direct it toward the Esquiline Hill. Rumors were spreading that the emperor had given orders to initiate the fire, and his staff was continuing to carry them out.

Cordula, Clement, and Sati huddled at home and prayed that the conflagration would die from its own appetite. As they quivered in bed, Sati asked, "Will the flames reach our home?"

"I don't know, dear," he answered. "It's in God's hands." He did his best to comfort his wife, but her fear reemerged and took control—the first time in their marriage that her fear overcame the security of their warm bed and his loving arms.

Two days later, with the fire still raging and nearly half of the city destroyed, the emperor's *vigili* intentionally torched a large area of older homes, creating a barrier to block the blaze from reaching the Esquiline district. Angry residents attempted to hamper the efforts, but when that failed they took out their disdain through looting.

The Christians, most of whose homes were untouched, continued to give aid to the victims. By the end of the sixth day, the hungry flames had consumed their fill and the panic in Rome began to subside. Of the city's fourteen districts, only four remained intact. Three were leveled to the ground, and the other seven were reduced to scorched and smoldering ruins. Nearly three quarters of the city was destroyed.

41

Rumors have a life of their own, and the public—rich and poor—concluded that Nero had instigated the fire.

His people cited the evidence to the contrary: the emperor was out of the city the night the fire began, he initiated monumental efforts to help the dispossessed, his fire crews fought valiantly to save the city, and the vandalism and looting obviously were acts of a deranged minority. All this was to no avail, however, as an angry population clamored for answers.

That's when Nero blamed the Christians. The strange cult had reached Rome as an obscure offshoot of Judaism, popular among the city's poor and destitute. Members spoke of a new kingdom and a new king. The Jewish authorities rejected the Christians, and Roman citizens considered them a most troublesome minority. The public had heard that the group's infant god grew up and was eaten, body and blood, in a cannibalistic ritual, which believers continued to reenact. They were worse than the Carthaginians, who burned their babies but at least didn't eat them.

The emperor ordered the arrest of a few known Christians and put them to torture until they confessed their crimes. These first martyrs were burned at the stake in a public display of retribution.

Then Nero paid for reconstruction of the city's public buildings, enacted stricter planning and building laws, ordered wider, straighter streets, better firefighting facilities and water distribution systems, and paid bonuses to families who rapidly rebuilt their own houses. Yet all this beneficence did little to repair his public image.

Desirous of restoring his popularity, he ordered another, much larger round of Christian arrests. These were charged not just with setting the fire but also with hating the human race, and they were executed in bloody spectacles so dramatic in violence that they swayed the public's attention. Seeing the pleasure the citizens took in the slaughters, the emperor kept them going. The historian Tacitus later wrote of the brutal exhibitions:

> *In their very deaths, the victims were made the subjects of sport: for they were covered with hides of wild beasts and torn to death by dogs, or nailed to crosses, or set fire to, and when the day waned, burned to serve for the evening lights.*

"This is going to take a totally different response," Peter told the presbyters and deacons. "Tell your people to stay off of the streets and out of the plazas, where somebody might identify them. We must lay low until this situation calms down. They shouldn't hide their faith, but neither should they unnecessarily expose it nor, above all, put others at risk."

A deacon asked, "What should we advise them to do, if they are arrested?"

Peter answered, "There is no more glorious way to die than to suffer in the passion of Christ. We all must be steadfast with the Lord, regardless of the cost. How we handle this local persecution will set an example for generations to come. We should be proud to die for our faith! Yet, people should not seek martyrdom, nor should they antagonize the guards. Make that clear. Some of us must survive this trial in order to pass on the faith to the next believers."

Clement's first concern was with Pamphilus, the owner of the large house in which they met on Sundays. Realizing how he had put himself and his family at the pinnacle of exposure, he pleaded for Clement to move the gatherings. "Give me one last Sunday," the young presbyter protested. "I have a vital message for all to hear. After that, we can meet in smaller groups."

As they gathered on Sunday morning, Clement could feel the anxiety rising like the heat on an August day. He felt so young and inexperienced as he prepared to face them and prayed that the Lord would assist him with the delicate challenge he faced. Then he began speaking from his heart, quoting parts and paraphrasing parts of Paul's letter to the Romans:

"My friends, my brothers and sisters, we all have good reason to be afraid. Many of those we know have been taken to the arena, where they met bloody deaths. And there is no sign that the persecutions are about to cease. There is no end in sight. So, what are we to do?

"The great apostle Paul, who has been living for some time just south of the city, told us in his letter, 'I urge you brothers, by the mercies of God, to offer your bodies as a living sacrifice, holy and pleasing to God, your spiritual worship. Do not conform to this age but be transformed by the renewal of your mind, that you may discern the will of God, what is good and pleasing and perfect.' There has never been a time since he wrote these words that they have been more applicable to us than today.

"We have been baptized into Christ and we have died with him. We have received his presence into our bodies and into our hearts. We have lived our days with joy, and we hope to rise with him and be lifted into his eternal kingdom. So, do not conform to this age! Be transformed, and be prepared to accept whatever comes to you! Live without fear because your resurrection is with the Lord.

"We, like Paul, consider the sufferings of this present time as nothing compared with the glory to be revealed to us. All creation is groaning in labor pains even until now, and we ourselves, who have the first fruits of the Spirit also groan as we wait for redemption. For in hope we are saved, and if we hope for what we do not yet see, we wait with endurance.

"None of us should seek martyrdom. And none of us should take unnecessary risks that might expose ourselves or our neighbors to Nero's tortures. Some of us will be martyred. Some of us will be spared, but those who are spared may face further suffering and more pain than those who are killed. Those who are burned may rejoice in sharing in the sufferings of Jesus. Those who are spared will rejoice also, but soberly because theirs will be the task of passing on the faith, which must never die.

"Do not be afraid. Now is the time for courage. Now is the time to live in the grace of Christ Jesus.

"Pamphilus and I feel we should take steps to limit our exposure to Nero's troops, so we no longer will be meeting in his house. We are simply too big of a gathering to pass by the emperor's spies. Thank you, Pamphilus, for so graciously offering us your home. May God bless you for your generosity.

"From now on we will meet at my house, which will require us to be in smaller groups, but we will arouse less suspicion. Don't come if you think you are being followed. Enter only if you know you are safe. I will offer the prayers of thanksgiving several times each Sunday. That will make us less conspicuous and will allow me to know what each family is facing.

"Above all, do not be afraid. Paul asked, 'What will separate us from the love of Christ? Will anguish, or distress, or persecution, or famine, or nakedness, or peril, or the sword?' He answered, 'No, in all these things we conquer overwhelmingly through him who loved us. For I am convinced that neither death, nor life, nor angels, nor principalities, nor present things, nor future things, nor powers, nor height, nor depth, nor any other creature will be able to separate us from the love of God in Christ Jesus, our Lord.'

"Take these words to heart. Ponder them and live them. Christ will not abandon us, if we do not abandon Christ! Take heart, and help one another. Together we will persevere. Together we will keep the faith."

The room was silent. Everyone had their head down, pondering the trials to come. Then Clement motioned for the gifts to be brought forward, and he offered them to God on the altar. Each soul rededicated their life to Jesus, and as each received the consecrated Body and Blood of the Lord, they entered into the profound experience of unity that characterized his followers since he instituted the sacrifice at the Last Supper.

As each family quietly left, Clement thanked them and gave them God's blessing. They had never needed it more.

In the coming days, several families were taken to slaughter. They crucified Pamphilus with flames searing his legs. They fed his wife to the dogs. Paul was beheaded, and many others were burned at the stake. The onlookers thought it was great fun.

Linus and Clement urged Peter to leave the city, and he reluctantly agreed to go. "Now don't come back," Linus advised, "unless you hear Jesus, himself, order you to return." Peter loaded his wife and daughter onto a cart and waved as he headed away, but after traveling only a few miles he turned around and returned to face his destiny.

Cassius and his family continued to attend the gathering at Clement's house, but Horus was not to be seen.

Clement spoke with Mark, encouraging the writer to begin putting Peter's stories about Jesus to paper. "I am ready to do it," the young scribe vowed, "but Peter hasn't told me to go ahead."

"Don't wait for Peter," Clement advised. "He could be taken at any time. You are the one who sees the purpose of the written gospel. Follow your passion. Don't let anything get in your way."

These turned out to be prophetic words. The next day the bishop was arrested and taken to the Mamertine Prison, a dungeon just downhill from the

Forum. He was lowered by rope through a hole in the floor into the dark, damp depths of the cramped cavern, where he languished with little food or water. In the stinking quarters, he met other prisoners and shared with them the truth of Christ.

42

Sati was adamant, "I lost you for thirteen years. I don't want to lose you again."

"I'll be careful, dear."

"You say you will be careful, but you take risks every day."

"I have to see to the needs of my people."

"Please, Clement. Think also of me—and your mother. We love you—I love you. I can't live without you."

"I am taking precautions."

"You may be taking precautions, but you are not listening to what I am saying. I can't live without you. I have no one else but you."

Clement took his wife in his arms and held her close. He didn't know how to respond. He had responsibilities to her and duties to his people.

"Do you not have anything to say, when I am pleading with you?" she bawled.

"The Lord will protect us for as long as he wants us on this earth," he whispered.

Pushing him away, she yelled, "What if Nero wants you dead, and I am left here alone?"

Clement sat down and looked up at her. "Everyone is tense at this time. We will get through it."

"There is no guarantee of that!" she shouted even louder.

Cordula came in from her room. "I heard shouting. Is anything wrong?"

Clement was silent. Sati was looking down at the floor.

"Pardon me," Cordula said. "Perhaps I shouldn't have intruded."

"No! Come in!" Sati demanded. "Your son doesn't seem to understand that a wife needs her husband to stay alive. Don't you think Jesus wants him to stay alive for me?"

Now her mother-in-law was speechless.

Clement tried to reason, "Most of the time they take whole families." He couldn't have said anything worse.

Sati screamed, "Peter's wife and daughter are home alone, right now!"

When her son had no reply, Cordula admitted, "We are all afraid. I am afraid too. But we must have faith."

With that, Sati broke into tears. "I want to have faith, but I am so terrified." Both Clement and Cordula put their arms around the sobbing woman, caressing her lovingly. "I love you both," she wept. "Just hold me tight."

Two weeks later, Linus broke the news to Clement, "They took Peter out this morning."

"They took Peter! Where?"

"It wasn't to the arena. I heard they took him and a few others to Vatican Hill, probably to the circus there."

"My God! Is there nothing we can do!"

"We knew this might happen."

Clement hurried down the steps and ran toward Vatican Hill, sobbing much of the way. "Oh, Lord. Don't let him die," he pleaded.

As he neared the racetrack, he spotted Albus, one of the deacons, who motioned for him to come to where he was hiding. "Rest here, Clement. Catch your breath."

"What happened? Is Peter in there?"

"Yes, he is—along with some others. The guards are crucifying them."

"Crucifying them! No!"

"I was close enough to overhear," Albus confided. "Peter said he wasn't worthy to die like his master and asked to be crucified upside down."

"Upside down! How could they do that?"

"They made sport of it. They laughed and tied him and nailed him—I heard him scream. Then they just hoisted him up, and he's hanging there now. Those brutes!"

"How long has he been hanging like that?"

"At least two hours."

"How can he stand it?"

"I don't know. I was thinking of sneaking over to the entrance and looking in. Do you want to go?"

Clement glanced across the street toward the entrance. No one was in the area. Everyone ran away when they saw the guards and prisoners. He replied, "I'm with you."

Together the two men strolled across to the racetrack's entrance.

Looking through the gate, their eyes spotted the big man hanging upside down, beet red and grimacing in agony. "Can he last much longer?" Clement asked.

Albus shook his head.

The elderly leader did hang there, suffering, for several more minutes. Then his movements became more violent. Blood and foam drooled from his mouth. The red in his face became ungodly bright. Then all motion stopped and he hung there lifeless.

Both Albus and Clement felt sick. One of the guards walked over to where the victim was hanging and stared at him. Then picking up his spear, he shoved it into his side. A gush of red blood poured out.

"God have mercy on him," Clement prayed.

"What should we do now?" Albus asked.

"I don't know. Do you think they will burn him?"

"I hope not. This execution is different from the others. It's not in the arena."

"I wonder if they would give us his body, if they don't have orders to burn him."

"Are you thinking of asking them for it?"

"I wasn't really thinking. But maybe we should," Clement suggested.

"Do you mean go in there and just ask them?"

"I'd like to try. Peter has done so much for me. I've known him ever since I was a boy. He ordained me. I can't just leave him."

"All right," Albus assented. "You can't get him alone. I'll go with you."

The two men shook hands and then walked through the gate, doing their best to hide their fear. Walking straight to the centurion, Clement asked him, "Can we bury his body?"

The officer took one hard look at the two insane visitors and whispered a question to the guard that had stabbed the victim. When the guard nodded, the officer turned back and said, "Take him!" and walked away.

Clement and Albus went immediately to work, untying the ropes and ripping Peter's hands out of the nails. Then they half carried and half dragged the heavy, lifeless body out the gate.

"There is a garden not far away;" Albus suggested, "let's try to get him there."

Grunting and struggling, the two men found the strength to move the heavy man toward the garden. A third man joined them, who helped them carry Peter.

Then just as they reached the garden, they spotted another brother, Antonius, running toward them. "What are you doing?" he asked.

After briefly relating what had transpired, the four dug a deep hole and slid the bishop's body into it. Antonius, who was a stonemason suggested, "We should put a marker down with him. I have my tools."

"Good idea!" Clement exclaimed. "That way our people always will know where he was laid."

Antonius found a smooth stone and brought it to the hole. "What shall I write?" he asked.

"Just write, 'Peter is here.' That's enough. We must hurry."

"Tell me letter by letter, so I can do it right."

"I will," Clement agreed. "Π- έ- τ- ϱ- ο- ς- Ε- ή- ι. Peter is here."

"There. Is that good?" Stephanos asked.

"Perfect. Now bury it with Peter; we need to move quickly."

After they filled the hole and smoothed the ground, the four hurried to report back to Linus.

When they arrived at his flat, most of the presbyters were there too. Clement hurriedly explained how they had buried Peter's body, and while they all grieved for the apostle, they also were relieved that the great leader had been spared the long agony of a typical crucifixion.

"We must elect a new bishop," Linus soberly stated, although all eyes already were looking at him for direction.

"The obvious choice is you," Clement replied, and all the others agreed.

"I am humbled. But there is little time. What matters must we attend to this very day?"

While the others thought about the question, Clement blurted, "We've got to get Mark out of the city. He's the only one who can preserve Peter's memories. When Peter was arrested, I encouraged him to start writing, but now I think he should go somewhere else to do it."

Linus agreed. "Antonius, Mark lives with you. Go and tell him to get ready to leave. Albus, go and book a ship. Get him out of town by early tomorrow. Send him to the east. Send him to Philippi—I'll get word to Bishop Alexios. He'll be safe there."

As the deacon and stonemason rushed out the door, Linus sat down and put his head in his hands. "I don't know how to handle this," he admitted.

"We will help you," Clement asserted, and the rest agreed. "We'll stay in close contact and assist you in every way."

By the time Clement got home, it was getting dark. Most of his neighbors had closed their doors, and his wife and mother were worried.

"Sorry I'm late."

His mother rushed to embrace him, but Sati remained in her chair.

"Have you eaten?" the older woman asked.

"Not since morning."

"You must be starved."

"Yes. I'd like something, please."

"I will dish you some pasta."

"Thank you."

Sati stood up and shouted, "Where have you been? We've been waiting for hours!"

"It's been a long day, dear. They crucified Peter."

Cordula listened in horror as Clement related how the head of the Church was taken to Vatican Hill and was crucified upside down. Sati just stared at him with a cold glare.

"You make it sound like you were an eyewitness," she blurted.

"Yes, dear. I was. Albus and I watched through the gate."

"You went up to the gate!"

"The streets were deserted. We had to see."

"You didn't have to see."

"We had to, dear. After he succumbed, a guard stuck a spear in his side, and blood poured out. We asked for his body and…"

"You asked the Roman guards for his body! Are you crazy?"

"No, dear. The centurion said, 'Take him,' and we drug him out to a nearby garden. Two other brothers came and helped us bury him."

Sati dropped to her chair. "My God, Clement. I can't believe it. I can't believe you would expose yourself to such danger."

"We needed to. They would have burned his body if we hadn't taken it."

Sati began to sob. Clement stood there for a moment, dumbfounded. Then he went to embrace her, but she screamed, "Don't touch me!" and rushed out of the room. Clement sat down and put his head in his hands.

Cordula put a plate of pasta in front of her son and rubbed his shoulders. "Sati was very worried."

"I know, Mother. I'm doing the best I can. I probably shouldn't have gone, but Peter was my friend, the one who helped me to embrace Christ and to become a presbyter. I couldn't just stay away."

"You did very well, Clement. Very well. Sati loves you, you know."

"It doesn't sound like it when she shouts at me."

"The shouts are from her fear. She will calm down. Then you can reassure her."

"We have never argued before."

"All couples argue once in a while. You need to show her that you understand her point of view."

"I can't not do my duties."

"Of course, dear," she agreed, "but you have duties to both the Church and your wife. At times like these, it can be difficult to balance them."

"It's impossible to balance them."

"Nothing is impossible where there is love."

"I do love Sati. She is my whole life," he gushed, as he turned and sobbed on his mother's bosom.

Cordula held her son while he grieved and then whispered, "Both of you need to cry now. Then you can think clearly and promise to meet her needs. That's the way to make up. You will kiss and make up."

Clement took a few small bites of the pasta as he pondered his mother's advice. When he seemed to be getting back in control of his emotions, she said goodnight and went to her room. He sat there for a long time in the dark.

Clement formed his first words and crept into the moonlit bedroom. "I'm sorry, Sati. I shouldn't have taken such a risk. I wasn't thinking straight. I am very sorry."

Rolling toward him and looking at him in the dim light, she opened her arms and beckoned him to come. "I'm sorry too. I shouldn't have shouted."

"You were afraid, and rightly so," he whispered as he slid beside her. "I should have been more considerate."

"When you didn't come home, I got so afraid. I thought of the worst."

"I am home now."

"Will you promise me that you will think twice before you take any more risks?"

"I've been thinking about that. I will promise that to you. You deserve as much."

"Oh, Clement. I love you so much."

"I love you, darling. I don't want you ever to be afraid."

"I feel so good in your arms. Don't ever leave me a widow."

"I won't," he vowed. "I won't."

43

As winter passed and spring flowers burst into bloom, tensions eased in the city of Rome and calm came again to the house of Clement. Cordula heard no more shouting, and Sati found security in the arms of her husband. When the persecutions ended, another family offered their large house for the Sunday gatherings of Capitoline Hill Christians, which permitted them all to again join in one liturgy.

Nero had a new interest. With the Palatine and Caelian Hills in ashes and part of the Esquiline as well, he appropriated a vast acreage for his next project. He had dreamed of an immense *Domus Aurea*, a Golden House worthy of his personal magnificence, and he poured massive imperial resources into its construction. The project included groves of trees, pastures with flocks, vineyards, pavilions, and palaces, covering more than three hundred acres. Other Roman aristocrats had built villas outside of Rome in rural settings, but Nero brought the countryside in and clustered a number of structures around an artificial lake. To shape an appropriate entrance for his narcissistic endeavor, the emperor straightened out the winding Via Sacra to create an axial view from the Forum into an enormous arched entrance and placed there a twelve-story high bronze, nude statue of himself modeled on the Colossus of Rhodes.

The Esquiline wing alone of Nero's new complex contained 140 rooms, cut along a terrace in the hill, facing the lake. Beyond that, a great *nymphaeum*, or fountain-and-pool feature, cut into the as-yet-unfinished Temple of the Divine Claudius, which Nero suspended to concentrate efforts on his own monument. Then to water the vast project, the grandiose emperor redirected the *Aqua Claudius* aqueduct into his personal garden paradise. All this was done to provide a suitable setting in which he staged lavish theatrical and artistic productions and entertained his noble guests in splendor.

That he had enemies, no one doubted, but since he controlled the elite Praetorian Guards and was the last living heir of the divine Augustus, all that his subjects could do was bide their time until his excesses, brought on by his enormous ego, became his own undoing.

Linus asked Clement to accept another assignment in addition to continuing to pastor the Capitoline Hill community: overseeing those interested in becoming presbyters and deacons. Clement complained that he was too young for the job, but Linus insisted that his age was an advantage—the memories of his own formation period would be fresh in his mind.

As he began meeting with the men, he found the experience inspiring. They were solid in their faith and totally determined to help people know Jesus and grow closer to him.

One man in particular impressed Clement. Darius was a handsome Roman with broad shoulders and wavy black hair, whose eyes never left those of the person he was speaking with. Darius was intelligent, well versed in Latin and Greek, and seemed to always accomplish what he set out to do. While only twenty-eight, he already operated a thriving business, advising wealthy aristocrats on how to get the most from those they employed.

At their second meeting Darius asked Clement, "What must I do to be especially favored by Jesus?"

Clement didn't know how to answer the odd question. He replied, "What is it that you hope for?"

The young man without hesitation said, "I want to head a flourishing community, have a beautiful wife, dutiful children, riches beyond most people's imagination, and hold the respect and admiration of everyone."

Clement was taken aback. "Do you want to take the place of Nero?"

Darius looked shocked.

"I was only joking," Clement apologized. "Most presbyters don't get those things. Serving Christ well is its own reward."

"I want to serve Christ well," Darius avowed, "but I believe that I can accomplish that and also grow rich at the same time."

"Darius, Darius. We are led by Jesus to do what he wants. It's not about what we want."

"How can you say that? You haven't tried to do both; have you?"

"No, my dear man. I have not tried to grow rich by the world's standards. All I've tried to do is serve the Lord. Sometimes worldly rewards follow, but believe me when I say that is not the objective."

"Then why should I not want for both?"

Clement paused and took a deep breath, then told the young man, "I believe there is an obstacle between you and Christ. Do you know what it is?"

"I am not aware of any obstacle. I have followed his teachings perfectly ever since I was a little boy."

"Darius, I'm going to give you my best possible advice. Close your business, take the money you have and give it to the poor, pray to God for guidance, and come back and tell me how you feel. If you still want to become a presbyter, I will help you in every way I can."

The man looked at Clement long and hard, forcing himself to keep smiling. Clement looked on him with love—the man was greatly gifted. But the perpetual smile slowly faded from Darius's lips. He got up and without comment left the room. Clement sat there quietly, sad about what had transpired. He did not know that the one who went away with even greater sadness was Darius.

During the next two years, Nero began singing in public in an attempt to improve his popularity. Although some in his inner circle encouraged him to act and sing, others considered it shameful. Craving the attention, the maniacal ruler accepted every possible opportunity to perform and was rewarded with enthusiastic applause.

The young emperor also was persuaded to compete in the Olympic Games in order to improve relations with Greece and display Roman dominance. Nero raced a ten-horse chariot and nearly died after being thrown from it on a sharp curve. He usually also faltered when acting or singing, but was awarded the crowns anyway and wore them proudly when he paraded in Rome.

At the same time, unrest began brewing in the province of Palestine. The tensions and frustrations of decades of Roman oppression were fomenting into demands for freedom and justice. Stabbings and banditry were plaguing the ruling class, and they were appealing to the Roman governor to take action. In Jerusalem, tax payments were withheld, and construction work slowed for lack of funding. The populace hated the temple authorities for their collaboration, and on top of that, the Zealot party was pressing for an independent Jewish state.

Rebellion against Rome would have been considered insane, except that most of the Jews believed in the righteousness of their cause and felt that God would come to their aid if they fought in faith and did their best to defend the Promised Land that God had granted them.

In July news came that Menahem ben Judas had captured the mountain fortress of Masada. How he managed to trick the Roman soldiers stationed there to open the gates was anybody's guess, but in the process he garnered vast stores of weapons, which he distributed to those Jews who would use them. In addition, Eleazar ben Hananiah, the son of a former high priest, was convincing the *Sanhedrin* council to not accept any more sacrifices from foreigners. This bit of intrigue would mean that the temple could no longer accept payment and perform the twice-daily sacrifices for Nero. In August the council approved the measure, and Rome considered it an open act of rebellion.

In Rome, the presbyters were concerned not only for the Jews in the Holy City, but they also worried about the Christians. "What will happen to them?" a deacon asked Clement who was presiding at the monthly meeting while Linus was away.

Clement answered, "They are not likely to join in the fighting, so people like Eleazar and Menahem will call them traitors. The Romans see them as Jews, so this puts the brothers there in a very tight spot."

"What options do they have?"

"Their best option probably is to leave their homes and flee while they can get away. At some point the Romans will cut off that pathway as well. If they stay where they are, they will get caught in the middle of a conflagration."

Another said, "If the Christians could get out, I wouldn't care if the whole city was destroyed. Those stubborn dogs never did us any favors."

"Don't talk that way," Clement scolded. "Jesus would hardly want his own people killed. Even if the Jews persecuted us many times over, that's no reason for us to wish them harm."

The man fell silent.

"We have to be clear about one thing," Clement demanded. "Our job is to pray for both the Romans and the Jews. We should not take sides in this. No one will win, regardless of the outcome. The only winner will be death itself.

"What would Jesus say, if he were in this room right now?...'Love your enemies, do good to those who harm you, pray for those who have persecuted you.'

"Both sides are in the wrong, you know. Neither is giving heed to the commandment, 'Thou shall not kill.' Neither is giving any credence to the teaching, 'Love your neighbor as yourself.' If there is any legacy that Jesus left us, it is to not try to overcome evil with evil. Violence doesn't redeem; only Christ redeems. Retaliation is so ingrained in the human psyche that neither side can even imagine laying down their swords. The only people who can imagine doing that is us—it's us because Jesus showed us the way.

"The posture we take on this matter is very important, and we need to be unified. Our people need to know that we are united in opposition to this war— to all wars. Do you want to live in a world without war?...Then you should want to live in a world where all people are brought into the faith. And all people will only want to come into the faith if we keep it pure. We, who lead the people, need to demand that it be kept free of hate, free of violence, free of oppression, free of domination, free of greed, and free of disunity. There is no more important time for those of us who are entrusted with leadership to stand up for the truth of Christ than times like now, when armies are poised and ready to clash.

"When this war is over and people look back, what will they say?...Will they say that Christians are no different than pagans or Jews? We can't let that happen. We must be different so that people will say, 'Look at the Christians. They are different. They have something different that the world does not have. They have something different that the world needs. They have something different, and I want it too! They have something different, and I want to be one of them!'"

Clement took a deep breath and added, "I'm sorry if I get carried away. Please pardon me if I have spoken too strongly. I'm only trying to affirm the truth of Christ as it applies to our situation in this time and in this place. That's our role, and we must help our people to see it."

The room was silent. No one even moved. The presbyters and deacons simply sat where they were, pondering and absorbing the vision that Clement had posed. Then one by one they came to him, embraced him, and pledged to stand with him. Some whispered their gratitude. Some simply looked into his eyes and held him. None of them would forget the day, and none of them left the room without affirming their faith and praying to God for the courageous leader that the Lord had placed in their midst.

In the fall, Roman forces reached the outskirts of Jerusalem, but then suddenly stopped. The governor didn't want to subject his troops to a wintertime siege of the walled city, so he ordered his armies to withdraw to Caesarea. Many Jews considered this sign of weakness to be an omen from God that victory soon would be theirs.

In Rome, however, the senate assessed the situation and concluded that they needed to increase the forces in Palestine to ensure a decisive and speedy victory. They called upon the experienced general Vespasian to sail to Antioch, reconstitute the forces, and prepare for a springtime assault. He planned to march south to Galilee and join his son Titus, who would come north from Alexandria. Together they would have the massive force of three legions, more than sixty-five thousand men.

In March, while Vespasian's forces began moving in unseasonably good weather, the Roman governors of the Provinces of Gaul, Spain, and Portugal decided to rebel against Nero's tax policies. Nero took the news of the revolt with remarkable calm, not letting it interrupt his enjoyment of an athletic competition in Napoli. When his advisors finally got him to see the seriousness of the situation, the emperor reacted with paranoia, suggesting that all governors in the empire be executed and every member of the senate be poisoned at a banquet. Fortunately these fanatical ideas went unused as loyal forces in Germany defeated the Gauls, but the whole matter left Nero unnerved.

In June an advisor convinced the emperor to flee for his own safety. He talked of sailing east to Egypt, but the Praetorian prefect turned on him, and the senate declared Nero a public enemy and sentenced him to be flogged naked with rods by his peers.

Running through the suburbs of Rome, without even a bodyguard, he stopped to rest the evening of June 9 at the villa of one of his secretaries, where he muttered, "How ugly and vulgar my life has become." Then hearing the sound of hoofbeats from troops coming to arrest him, he sobbed, "What a loss I shall be to the arts," and attempted to stab himself in the throat. The deed had to be finished by his secretary, but the once-powerful Nero lay on the floor, dead.

44

All of Rome was gossiping about Nero's demise, which was generally welcomed by senators and the upper class. The lower populace, slaves, and those who made a living off of the emperor's excesses were upset by the news. Members of the military initially had mixed feelings, particularly those who had allegiance to imperial authority but were promised bonuses to overthrow Nero. The senate acted quickly to avert possible riots or civil war by naming Servius Sulpicius Galba the new emperor.

The presbyters of the city also were caught up in the clamor, shouting and arguing as they gathered for the monthly meeting with their bishop, who was late arriving.

"I'm not a bit sad to see him gone!" said one, whose members had suffered greatly in Nero's violence.

"But the new emperor could be worse," answered another.

Then the bishop came in the door, out of breath from running. "I have news of even greater importance!" he shouted, motioning for silence. "Listen brothers. In my right hand, I have a copy of a document prepared by our brother Mark, who we sent away from the persecution and haven't heard from since. He introduces it as 'The beginning of the gospel of Jesus Christ, the Son of God' and it traces the story of Jesus from the time of John the Baptist to the crucifixion and the empty tomb."

All the presbyters sat stunned in silence, staring at the parchment booklet.

Linus continued, "With this, we can teach the life of our Savior to the entire city and surrounding environs, in fact to the whole world! I read it hurriedly, and let me tell you, it's wonderful. It reads just like Peter, himself, is talking.

"Mark finished the text in Antioch, but Bishop Evodius said he persevered through many trials and hardships on the way. In fact, Mark nearly died of fever, but by a miracle of God he survived and handed the gospel over to the Church. I am brought to my knees in gladness at how the Holy Spirit led Mark to safety and helped him compile this masterpiece. The bishop said Mark now is trying to gather more information to add to the gospel by seeking people who may remember more details about Christ, while they are still alive."

"Are we going to make copies?" Clement asked.

"Certainly. I've already asked five of our scribes to get busy on that as soon as I return with it. My hope is that by the end of the month each of you will have a copy to use when you gather."

"Do you mean we can read the text in our liturgies, like the letters of Paul?" another presbyter asked.

"Of course! The accounts that Peter told about Jesus are the most important things we should read. It will be just like when we heard Peter tell us the stories, but now they will be heard by the whole Church!"

"Is that what they are doing in Antioch?"

"Yes, in Antioch and throughout the east. They actually are ahead of us on this, but we will catch up and surpass them. Once you read it, you will agree. The accounts are short, and you will be able to read a passage and preach on it, every Sunday."

The room filled with murmurs of excitement. Clement bubbled with joy, delighted that he had encouraged Mark to get started on the writing at the time Peter was put in prison.

At home, Clement shared the news with his wife and mother. Cordula, who had heard Peter preach often, instantly understood the value of the new document. Sati, who was more accustomed to hearing her husband preach, was less aware of its potential but shared their excitement.

"When will you begin using it?" she asked.

"Linus said he hopes to give each of us a copy by the end of the month. I'm hoping to get a piece of it before that, maybe by this Sunday."

At the Sunday gathering of the community, Clement introduced the gift of the new written gospel, "Most of us knew Peter, and some of us met Mark. Peter was a great leader and teacher, and Mark was a gifted scribe. Between them they have preserved a lengthy narrative of the words and deeds of Jesus. I can't express how happy I am to have it.

"After the Great Fire we suffered a violent persecution, and Peter was put to death. But we survived. We survived as a community, and our leader's memories have survived in the written gospel. I have only one page today, but Bishop Linus has scribes working to get us a complete copy by the end of this month. So, we will begin today by listening to the opening lines of the gospel, which contain an important message for our time.

"It reads as follows:

> *The beginning of the gospel of Jesus Christ, the Son of God.*
> *As it is written in Isaiah the prophet:*
> *Behold, I am sending my messenger ahead of you;*
> *he will prepare your way.*
> *A voice of one crying out in the desert:*
> *'Prepare the way of the Lord,*
> *make straight his paths.'*
> *John the Baptist appeared in the desert proclaiming a baptism of repentance for the forgiveness of sins. People of the whole Judean countryside and all the inhabitants of Jerusalem were going out to see him and were being baptized by him in the Jordan River as they acknowledged their sins. John was clothed in camel's hair, with a leather belt around his waist. He fed on locusts and wild honey. And this is what he proclaimed: 'One mightier than I is coming after me. I am not worthy to stoop and loosen the thongs of his sandals. I have baptized you with water; he will baptize you with the Holy Spirit.'*
> *It happened in those days that Jesus came from Nazareth of Galilee and was baptized in the Jordan by John. On coming up out of the water, he saw the heavens being torn open and the Spirit, like a dove, descending upon him. And*

a voice came from the heavens, 'You are my beloved Son; with you I am well pleased.'

"It's amazing, when you think about it, how a chain of witnesses brought the faith to us. The prophet Isaiah foretold how a voice would appear in the desert to prepare the way of the Lord. Then John the Baptist suddenly came on the scene, baptizing thousands as they acknowledged their sins. This prepared the way for Jesus, who showed us the face of the Father like never before. Peter followed Christ and told stories about him, right here in Rome. Mark put the stories in writing, and this morning we are hearing a passage in our gathering. A chain of witnesses brought the faith to us—a chain of witnesses guided by the Holy Spirit.

"Some of us heard about Jesus from Prisca and Aquila. Others heard it from Peter. I had the great fortune when I was a youth to travel with Peter to Jerusalem and Galilee—that's when my faith blossomed. On a day like today, it behooves us to ponder how we received our faith: who first told us about Christ and who were the chain of witnesses that made it possible. It makes us lift up our arms in joy, and it makes us bend down on our knees in gratitude.

"I owe a lot to my mother. She taught me the faith and encouraged me to become a presbyter. She is here today. Mother, I owe so much to you—I love you.

"Do you remember who that key person was for you? That person, whoever it was, who also was part of the chain of witnesses? That key person who opened the clouds for you and proclaimed, 'Jesus is the beloved Son of the Father, and in him *I* am well pleased'? That person showed you how fervently he or she believed by showing you how pleased he or she was to be a Christian. That person spoke in her own name, *I,* and you knew how devotedly she embraced the Lord. People like that are the iron that holds the links of the chain together. They are the tempered metal that the Holy Spirit uses to ensure the propagation of the faith. They are the present-day Baptists, who prepare the way for us to know Christ and to love him and serve him with all of our hearts.

"Each of us here also is a link in the chain. We are what make the chain unbroken. We are the disciples who will prepare the way for our children and others to come to know the Lord. We are the followers who can witness to the difference that Jesus has made in our lives.

"I've said it before, and I'm sure that I will say it again, that the first step in bringing others to Christ is to share how we have experienced him in our own lives and what a difference that has made for us. After that—after we have done that well—then we can tell them who Jesus is and what he did during his sojourn with us. The first step, always, is to let people know how pleased we are to know the Lord. That's what makes them want to know him too.

"We have so much today that the first followers didn't have. They were successful in spreading the faith, and we can be too. We know that Jesus died for us. We know that he was raised on the third day. We know that his Spirit has *miraculously* helped the faith to spread. We have baptism and the breaking of the bread, and we have an entire *ekklesia*, an entire Church—both here on this hill and throughout the world—that supports us and encourages us and aids us in our own personal mission of witness. We are so lucky. We should be filled with joy.

"So today, as we approach the altar to receive his precious Body and Blood, let us approach with hope. Let us come with determination. Let us receive him with humble gratitude, which will empower our works on his behalf. Come to the altar as a chain of witnesses, as an unbroken chain of all who have gone before us, all who are with us today, and all who will follow in this vital task after our days are done. Receive him into your bodies and into your lives. Receive him and go forth to share all that he has given us to all who have yet to hear.

"Join in the amazing chain. You will feel the power and the joy, and you will feel his presence in our midst."

As usual, Clement sat down and gave the gathered assembly a few moments to ponder his words. A still silence permeated the room as each got in touch with their place in the chain of faith and renewed their determination to give witness to the Lord.

Many had tears in their eyes, but one woman caught his eye as she wiped the drops from her cheeks, the girl with the golden hair—his beloved wife—who had waited thirteen years to become a Christian, and who was more grateful than any on this hope-filled day.

45

The next year was full of surprises—almost creepy, as if the gods were frowning on Rome. The new emperor, Galba, lost favor among the legions due to his overly strict discipline and miserly frugality. He refused to pay the customary bonus upon his accession to the throne, saying, "I select my troops; I don't buy them," which brought the reputation of the lackadaisical Nero into a quick recovery.

Galba soon lost favor in the senate as well, when his faction proved to have no constructive ideas and was not capable of governing the empire in an era of change. The calendar could not be turned back to the age of Augustus when the aristocracy ruled by divine right. He simply was the wrong man for the time, and with a circle of corrupt advisors around him, he became thoroughly unpopular in less than six months.

On January 1 of the fateful period, two of the three legions in upper Germany refused to swear the traditional new-year oath of allegiance to the emperor. Then on January 2, further down the Rhine, the troops of lower Germany proclaimed their own commander, Aulus Vitellius, as emperor of Rome.

Then the young general Marcus Salvius Otho, who had supported the elderly Galba in hopes of succeeding him to the throne, turned on him and began courting the allegiance of the army. On January 15, while Galba was offering a sacrifice at the temple of Apollo, Otho snuck into the Praetorian camp and persuaded the senior officers to salute him as emperor. Later that day as the old ruler was being carried through the city, he was cut down by Otho's mercenaries and left to rot in the streets. When Otho marched into the senate flanked by the ranking guards, the council formally granted the young general the imperial powers.

Otho might have become a reasonably good choice for the throne, except that the legions in Germany had already began to march toward the city with Vitellius at the head of their columns. Otho, who enjoyed the support of both the senate and the Praetorians, and who had added the name Nero to his own, began restoring some of the late emperor's appointees to his own administration. But as Vitellius's legions continued their march south, Otho gathered as many troops as he could muster and set up a defensive line along the Po River.

The confusion was not good for business, and with so many of the emperor's men leaving the city, the demand for eggs plummeted. This put Horus and Cassius in a double bind—a plentiful supply from the growers who expected to be paid, and falling demand from the palace, which was diverting much of its cash toward the eminent war. Crates of eggs went to rot every day.

"Our expenses are exceeding our receipts," explained Horus at a meeting of the family. "We can't continue to pay salaries to ourselves or any of our workers, or even your allowance, Mother. We have to tighten our belts and cut back."

Cordula sighed and murmured, "We've been through lean times before. Urbanus always got us through."

"But with the threat of civil war, there's no way to tell how long this will last. It could be months before we see any cash flow again."

"I will wait it out," his mother replied. "I see no reason to panic."

Cassius, however, was not as confident as his mother. "I can't wait even one month," he said. "There isn't enough in my strongbox to go two weeks, and I have my two sons' educations and a wedding feast to pay for."

Then Horus revealed, "I will not leave you in the lurch, Brother. If necessary, I will buy out your share of the operation."

"You will do no such thing!" his mother shouted. "Urbanus willed that the business would be shared by his sons, and we only agreed to let you buy Clement out when he chose to become a presbyter. Your kicking Cassius out at this time is out of the question!"

"But Mother, I'm only trying to help my brother, who has gotten himself into a pickle barrel."

"I won't listen to this, Horus. Don't speak of it anymore."

Then Clement added, "Horus, I'm having a difficult time following your reasoning. You are saying that there is no money to pay Cassius's salary, but you have the funds to buy out his share? Where is that money coming from?"

"I have some money saved. You know that I've always been a saver, while Cassius spends every coin he gets."

"So you have plenty of money, but the business is broke. And only you know which is which."

"Don't insult me, Clement. I have kept impeccable records. You can see them, if you wish."

"Enough of this clatter," shouted their mother. "There must be another

189

way."

Clement stood and suggested, "Cassius, what if you simply tell the growers that you can't accept all of their supply?"

"They have geared up for us," he protested, "to operate at the peak of efficiency. I can't just tell them not to ship eggs."

"Couldn't we just return to them only the number of crates that we will need the next day. Everyone will adjust, and we'll all get through it."

"I can't do that. I have made promises and…"

Clement interrupted, "Business agreements need to be modified when circumstances change. If you won't confront the growers, I'll do it for you. I'll start tomorrow morning, and go a day on each route. You ride with me because they know you, but I'll do the talking. They are reasonable men. We will give them a reasonable proposal, and most of them will accept it."

Cordula was smiling. "Good for you, Clement. You will make this work. Don't you think so, Cassius?"

"I guess so," he answered.

The conversation ended on a hopeful note. Horus, however, was frowning.

Clement explained the facts to each farmer with a smile on his face. They were quick to understand how the need for eggs had gone down and trusted the brothers of the house of Urbanus to do right by them under the circumstances. Only two growers swore that they would never do business with them again, but the next morning even they accepted the reduced number of empty crates and complied with the new system. Cassius was amazed at how easily the change was accomplished.

Horus quit speaking to Clement and was not seen again at the Sunday morning gatherings of Christians. Clement felt bad about it, but both his wife and his mother assured him that he did what was right and should allow time to heal the wounds. All three vowed to pray for Horus.

Otho realized that nothing could stop the German legions except superior force, which he did not possess. Vitellius crossed the Alps with about seventy thousand men, while Otho had at most twenty-five thousand. They met in a confusing battle where it was hard to tell who was who. Before long, with his nerves shattered, Otho withdrew and took his own life.

On April 19, the senate proclaimed Vitellius emperor, and business in Rome returned to normal. Horus and Cassius breathed a sigh of relief.

Every emperor had his vice, and Vitellius's was a voracious appetite. During his reign, all of Rome took to gastronomic excess like their ruler. His enthronement banquet featured seven thousand game birds and two thousand fish. Vitellius preferred delicacies like pheasant brains, pike livers, flamingo tongues, and the milt of eels. The emperor's inner circle not only had to pay for his feasts, but they also were required to keep up with him. Quintus Crispus once excused himself from a meal pleading illness and told a friend, "If I had not fallen ill, I would have died."

Despite this overindulgence, however, an uneasy feeling continued to hang over Rome like a cloud. In the early fall, Vitellius found himself in the same position as Otho did six months earlier, as the legions in Syria and Judea hailed their general, Vespasian, as emperor, and they were joined by the armies on the Danube. Vespasian had bided his time, pledging his loyalty to each succeeding emperor, while secretly building a power base of his own.

In December, forces supporting Vespasian clashed with those of Vitellius just outside of the city of Cremona in a confusing battle that continued all through the night. The rising sun exposed how scattered and vulnerable the emperor's armies had become, and the rebel legions went straight to Rome, where they placed a noose around Vitellius's neck and dragged him through the streets, then they tortured him with sword cuts until he died. Finally the gloating troops dragged him by a hook to the Tiber River and dumped him in. The senate found it distasteful to consider a man of only equestrian birth for emperor, but in the interests of preserving the empire, they gave Vespasian the throne.

46

The new emperor had two sons, Titus Flavius Vespasianus and Titus Flavius Domitianus, both ready-made heirs. Vespasian quickly restored order, first to the legions and then to the depleted imperial treasury. He held up grain shipments from Egypt until he was sure of his support in Rome and then released them with heroic bravado. A welcome calm finally came to the city, which again felt itself in strong hands.

At about the same time, another newcomer arrived in the Christian community of Rome, Anacletus of Athens, who had served in the Greek city as a presbyter. He was an intelligent, charming, wealthy widower and the owner of a large house in the Trastevere district, where the Christian population was growing. Linus held a reception where he and the other presbyters could get acquainted.

"What do you think of our new presbyter?" Linus asked Clement.

"He seems likeable. I have a good first impression."

"I'm glad that you do. I have good feelings about him too."

"What role do you plan to give him, if I may ask?"

"He simply wants to form a new community. We could use another location west of the river, and his large home seems to be in just the right place. Beyond that, time will tell. Anacletus is older than the rest of you and very learned. I want to see how he does first with one community and then think about the future."

"That sounds like a good plan. I think I'll invite him for dinner."

The following Sunday afternoon, Anacletus found his way to the house on the Capitoline Hill, carrying a jug of wine and two bouquets of early-blooming flowers. Both women were impressed by his courtesy and smiled to one another as they put the flowers in water.

"You are so thoughtful, Anacletus," Sati remarked. "Thank you. They will look lovely on our table."

"Your table already is lovely," he smiled, "adorned with two beautiful ladies. The blooms just add an extra touch of color."

The two women blushed, fully appreciating every word.

Clement suggested, "Sit down, new friend. Have some wine and tell us what brought you to Rome."

Taking a sip, the newcomer replied, "I was happy in Athens. It is a wonderful city, and I had many friends. But after my wife died, I felt led to move on to something new."

"I know the feeling," Clement concurred while the women listened.

"Do you? I prayed about it for a long time—about four years. The feeling never went away."

"Did something trigger you to think about coming to Rome?"

"That's exactly what did happen. You see, when I first read a copy of the gospel—Mark's written gospel—I thought, 'Rome is the center. Rome is at the heart of where things are happening in the Church.' And then one particular passage stood out to me, and the longer I focused on it, the more certain I was that I should come here."

"What passage was that, if I may ask?"

Anacletus thought for a moment and replied, "I am hesitant to mention it because I am new here. It may sound pompous or grandiose."

Clement added, "I won't push you, but I once felt led to act further on my faith when Peter told me stories about Jesus."

"You were so fortunate to know Peter. I never had the pleasure of meeting him."

"Oh! Peter was a great man—a bit rough around the edges. He was a fisherman, you know."

"Yes."

"But Peter was sincere about fulfilling his call to be a fisher of men. He kept at it to the very end. Do you know that even while he was awaiting execution in the Mamertine Prison, he evangelized some of the others down there?"

"I hadn't heard that."

Cordula spoke up, "Do tell us about the passage that inspired you. We won't think it is pompous."

"I can't refuse. It's very simple: Jesus cleansed the temple. He drove out those selling and buying there and overturned the tables of the money changers. That impressed me in a different way than it affects Jewish Christians. I am a Gentile, a proud Greek. And to me, the temple that needs cleansing is the empire centered now in Rome. The empire has become so corrupt, and these last choices for Caesar were so stupid that I believe the Church has a role in cleansing it from top to bottom."

Those listening were stunned. "Do you mean to overthrow the regime by force?" Clement asked.

"Of course not. Just the opposite. Christ taught us to not oppose evil with evil. He said we should love our enemies. No, I picture the role of the Church as cleansing the empire, reforming it and making it Christianized. The first step is converting individual hearts, which we are doing in every province. The next step will be to cleanse the social order, to make it more just and humane. There is no other institution that can do that except the Church."

"I never thought of that," Clement exclaimed. "You are quite a visionary."

"Oh, I wouldn't call myself that. Each of us has a limit, though, in how far we can see. Peter and the disciples saw to the initial spread of the good news. Perhaps people like us, who come along later, will see a bit farther. There is no limit to what can be achieved if we all follow the promptings of the Holy Spirit."

"Wow! That's amazing. Anacletus, I am so happy that you decided to come to Rome. You will enrich our ministry here. And I am pleased to have you as a friend."

Vespasian left his son Titus in charge of the siege of Jerusalem. The city was surrounded by thousands of Roman troops, and the war was won except for the final battle. The Jews should have surrendered, but their leaders still felt that God would intervene on their behalf, if they had sufficient faith.

Inside the walls there were at least three antagonistic factions—the Zealots, the displaced Galileans, and some freedom fighters from Idumea, south of the Holy City. Each sought to impose its own brand of revolution on the fight for independence. They all held the conviction that with God on their side, Jerusalem would be protected. Titus's repeated calls for surrender fell on deaf ears.

So in May the siege began. Titus built platforms for his artillery, and put his rams into action. The outer wall was breached on May 7, and the second fell four days later. Then the general concentrated on the Antonia fortress and the temple district.

As the shortage of food became critical, Titus had his men feast in full view of the rebels, but this led to few defections. Instead, vigilantes searched their neighbor's homes for hidden stores of food, and when they found any, they beat the hoarders. Bodies piled up in the streets, but the rebels shouted, "Death—not slavery!"

In July the Romans wrapped the city with a wall of their own, to protect their forces and cut off all chance of escape. Titus captured the Antonia fortress. Then as the Jews retreated into the temple, he chose this as his next target. When the rams could not penetrate the thick gates, he ordered them set afire. Soldiers tossed torches into the temple until the blaze became a conflagration. Thousands burned to death in the holocaust. After taking out all the valuable loot they could carry, the troops watched what remained of the magnificent structure crumble in sections to the ground.

The siege lasted for 131 days. Several hundred thousand Jews perished. The most able-bodied survivors were sent off as slaves, while the weaker ones were executed on crosses or ravaged by beasts as entertainment for the troops. Titus ordered the total destruction of Jerusalem—all that remained was a section of wall on the western side. Just as Jesus had predicted, not one stone was left upon another.

There was joy in the streets of Rome, but Christians in the city took little solace in the news. Linus declared a week of prayer for the victims, and Anacletus promoted a collection to assist the Christians who had fled during the lull before the siege and now wished to return.

Clement's heart was torn—he found it hard to believe that the loving God would use such brutal means to free the Holy City for Christianity. "Anacletus is right," he muttered. "This bedeviled empire needs to be totally cleansed from top to bottom."

47

Vespasian systematically promoted his public image by helping rebuild Rome. He added the Temple of Peace and finished the Temple of the Deified Claudius. He also began construction of the immense new Flavian Amphitheater, using funds from the spoils of the Jewish war. This enormous structure would serve the entertainment needs of bloodthirsty Rome for centuries.

Six years after the new emperor was enthroned, Bishop Linus became seriously ill, and the Christian population began to speculate on who might succeed him. When a group of presbyters and deacons showed support for Clement, he told them, "I am very honored, but too young. I'm only forty-five years old."

"But none of us are much older," they pleaded. "Who do you suggest?"

"Why, Anacletus, of course. He is intelligent and mature, and he has done a fine job building up the new community in Trastevere."

"But he is not from Rome," one deacon protested.

"That's true," Clement agreed, "but Anacletus has a far-reaching vision. The Church is becoming a worldwide institution, and we are going to need a leader who can steer the faith into a new era. Most of the original followers of Jesus are deceased. The age of eyewitness testimony is coming to an end, but a new era of truth and awakening lies before us. I thank God for bringing Anacletus here to the center of the world, and I believe he is the right person at the right time for the work ahead."

The next day Linus passed from this life, and Anacletus of Athens was elected bishop of Rome.

As the new Flavian Amphitheatre took shape and rose toward completion, all of Rome watched the construction. It was expected to hold up to 75,000 spectators for gladiatorial contests, theatrical performances, and other forms of amusement, making it the largest structure of its kind in the world. No one knows who first called it the Colosseum, but the name stuck. The huge project captured the imagination of the citizens, even more than Nero's gargantuan house or his giant nude statue.

One day Clement asked Sati, "Have you noticed how the boys are playing with swords?"

"Real swords?"

"No—sticks, pretend swords. They seem to be doing it more."

"Boys have always pretended they have swords."

"But they seem to be doing it more lately. I'm wondering why."

"I don't know," she answered.

"I think it may be because we have a new military emperor. Vespasian has made the army seem more attractive."

"That might be. The people like Vespasian."

"All the boys want to grow up to be like him. I hate how it diverts their minds away from the more important things."

"They want honor and glory."

"Honor and glory—the rewards of the brave. But we need to build a new society based on the values of Christ, the kingdom of God, for which he gave his life."

"Don't try to convince the neighborhood boys of that. You'll get us into trouble."

"I know," Clement replied. "But I want our Christian boys to stay out of the army. They have more important things to do with their lives."

"Be careful how you approach this. Think before you act."

The next day as Clement was walking past the vast amphitheater project, he noticed how many more boys than usual were playing there. Two caught his attention.

"I am Romus, the mighty gladiator," a boy of about eight shouted to his friend. "I killed you, and you are dead!"

"I got up and stabbed you back!" the younger boy screeched.

"No, you didn't! I cut your throat and stuck you through your heart. You are bleeding to death."

Clement stood between them. "Boys, boys. Don't say things like that. You don't want to kill each other."

The two looked at him like he was crazy. Then the taller one shouted, "Get out of my way, or I'll kill you too. I'll be honored for how many men I slaughter in one day."

"Yea!" the younger boy pronounced. "Let's stab this heathen now," as he lunged toward Clement with his stick.

The other boy came at the strange man from the other side, brandishing his sword. "Die! Die, heathen!"

Clement lowered his open hands and forced a smile. Then he backed up, turned, and began to walk away.

"Look at the coward! Look at the coward heathen!" they shouted. "He won't last long in the Colosseum."

Clement kept walking, pondering how caught up the boys were in the attraction of violence.

On Sunday morning, Clement stood before his people and read from the Gospel according to Mark:

> *"Jesus said to his disciples, 'Is a lamp brought in to be placed under a bushel basket or under a bed, and not to be placed on a lampstand? For there is nothing hidden except to be made visible; nothing in secret except to come to light. Anyone who has ears to hear, ought to hear.' He also told them, 'Take care what you hear. The measure with which you measure will be measured out to you, and still more will be given; from the one who has not, even what he has will be taken away.'*

"I try each week, to apply the gospel to what is happening in our lives, right here on the Capitoline Hill. Lately I've been noticing something that troubles me, which I also believe troubles you—or it should.

"You have seen how honored emperor Vespasian has become. He has again brought peace to the realm. You also have seen how the new Colosseum is gaining visible prominence in our city with each passing day. Vespasian encourages our boys to fight—to fight for the empire and to fight in athletic competitions. He is using his prestige to gain recruits for the army, and when the Colosseum is finished, he will use it to gain competitors for the arena. The attraction of fighting is growing, and the lure of violence is gaining in popularity. I see many more boys today imagining themselves as great heroes with swords, beaming before the crowds who cheer for them and give them honor and glory.

"We cannot control what goes on in the mind of the emperor, nor can we control what goes on in the minds of his subjects, young and old. What we can control is how we respond to what we see—how we respond in our homes, in the plazas, in our workplaces, and in the markets. We can control how we view these things. We can control how we talk about them within our families.

"Each of us has been given the light of faith. Each of us has been granted a measure of grace. I am asking us to consider how we plan to use these gifts in light of the developments around us. Will we buy in to the already over-militarization of the empire, or will we shine our light on how that demeans the teaching of Jesus? Will we go to the Colosseum and be entertained by the slaughter, or will we use the measure of grace we've received to say 'No!' and focus instead on helping build up the kingdom of God in our midst? Above all, will we allow our youth to be carried away by the attraction of honor and glory, or will we teach our boys what Jesus said about love and encourage them to seek lives of service and value?

"Now is the time to think about these questions. Now is the time, while we are celebrating the Eucharist and remembering how Christ gave up his life so that we might live in a loving world. There is no better time than now, here in our Sunday worship. We must stand for peace, not violence—justice, not oppression.

"I ask each of us to reflect. I ask each of us to consider. I ask each of us to decide where we stand. Do we stand with Vespasian and allow our boys to be drawn into ever-increasing violence? Or do we stand with Jesus and resist the pressure to conform to public attitudes? The choice is yours.

"The choice is yours, but remember this: Christ chose you to have the light of faith. Christ chose you to have a great measure of grace. Care for these gifts, my friends. Care for them and treasure them. Let your light shine for the truth of Jesus. Let God's grace overflow into your homes and into your neighborhoods. Let the vision of Christ permeate your lives, so that you and your families are the finest examples of Christian living the world has ever seen. Don't hide your faith under a bushel basket. Let it shine. Let your faith shine. Let it change our city. Let it change the world."

Clement sat down and bowed his head for the customary period of silence, feeling good about the words he had said. He didn't notice that five men got up and walked out, one leading his two sons by their hands.

On Wednesday, Bishop Anacletus paid Clement a visit.

"Good morning, Clement. How are you on this beautiful day?"

"Oh, fine. Fine. What brings you to my house today?"

"Well, some men from your district paid me a visit yesterday."

"Oh. Who?"

"The ones who got up and walked out after you preached."

"Oh? I didn't notice…What did they say?"

"They seemed angry. They said that they were just trying to be constructive, but I could tell that they were holding back their feelings. They accused you of being unpatriotic."

"Unpatriotic! Is that the word for it? I was suggesting that they consider their loyalty to Christ and his teachings more importantly than their allegiance to the emperor. I guess they didn't accept my message."

"Apparently they didn't."

"I don't know what to do. The boys are getting more and more enamored with fighting and the glamour of the army and arena. That isn't what we want our Christian boys to do."

"No. It isn't."

"I told them to let the light of their faith shine, to use the grace they have received to help build up the kingdom of God."

"That's what you should tell them."

"I told them to teach their boys and to encourage them to seek lives of service and value."

"That's what we want them to do."

"If you are here to reprimand me for what I said, I will obey you, but I feel very strongly about this."

"I am not here to reprimand you."

"Then why are you here?"

"I'm here to inform you of what some of your people are feeling. After that I'm here to encourage you to keep up your good work. You are challenging them to the core."

"I hope so. Someday there will be no need for armies because there will be no terror, no oppression, no slavery, and no war. When all Christians are firmly united against all forms of violence, it no longer will exist."

"You are doing well, Clement. Keep at it, but do it intelligently. Use all the skill that the Holy Spirit has given you."

"Thank you, bishop. Thank you for your support. I will do as you say."

"Don't stop. Don't be shy."

"I won't. I plan to come back to this point every two or three weeks. My job is to preach the gospel."

"Yes, it is."

Four years later another death rocked the Mediterranean world. Vespasian, who had kept the region in peace for nearly ten years became ill with a serious fever and diarrhea. At the end—almost fainting—he cried out, "An emperor ought to die standing upright," and while attempting to rise, died in the arms of those assisting him. The sixty-nine-year-old warrior was succeeded by his oldest son Titus, who had risen in popularity after crushing the rebellion of the Jews.

Then, one month to the day after Titus's enthronement, occurred one of the most catastrophic volcanic eruptions in European human experience. Mount Vesuvius, south of Napoli, spewed forth a deadly cloud of molten rock, hot ash, and gases to a height of more than twenty miles in an explosive shock felt all the way to Rome.

Pliny the Younger, who was about twenty miles away across the Bay of Naples, wrote an account of the eruption:

Broad sheets of flame were lighting up many parts of Vesuvius. Their light and brightness were the more vivid for the darkness of the night…it was daylight now elsewhere in the world, but there the darkness was darker and thicker than any night.

I cannot give you a more exact description of its appearance than by comparing to a pine tree; for it shot up to a great height in the form of a tall trunk, which spread out at the top as though into branches. Occasionally it was brighter, occasionally darker and spotted, as it was either more or less filled with earth and cinders.

The sea seemed to roll back upon itself, and to be driven from its banks by the convulsive motion of the earth; it is certain at least the shore was considerably enlarged, and several sea animals were left upon it. On the other side, a black and dreadful cloud, broken with rapid, zigzag flashes, revealed behind it variously shaped masses of flame: these last were like sheet-lightning, but much larger. Soon afterward, the cloud began to descend, and cover the sea.

The ashes now began to fall upon us, though in no great quantity. I looked back; a dense dark mist seemed to be following us, spreading itself over the country like a cloud. "Let us turn out of the high-road," I said, "while we can still see, for fear that, should we fall in the road, we should be pressed to death in the dark by the crowds that are following us." We had scarcely sat down when night came upon us, not such as we have when the sky is cloudy, or when there is no moon, but that of a room when it is shut up, and all the lights put out. You might hear the shrieks of women, the screams of children, and the shouts of men; some calling for their children, others for their parents, others for their husbands, and seeking to recognize each other by the voices that replied; one lamenting his own fate, another that of his family; some wishing to die from the very fear of dying; some lifting their hands to the gods; but the greater part convinced that there were now no gods at all, and that the final endless night of which we have heard had come upon the world.

The following Sunday morning, Clement stood before his people saying, "I haven't heard that any of us have relatives in the region of the eruption, but we all should pray for the victims and the survivors. I'm sure that our Lord would want us to do at least that."

Then clearing his throat, he added, "Each Sunday we have been hearing a passage from the Gospel according to Mark. The following short episode comes next:

> *Jesus withdrew toward the sea with his disciples. A large number of people followed from Galilee and from Judea. Hearing what he was doing, a large number of people came to him also from Jerusalem, from Idumea, from beyond the Jordan, and from the neighborhood of Tyre and Sidon. He told his disciples to have a boat ready for him because of the crowd, so that they would not crush him. He had cured many and, as a result, those who had diseases were pressing upon him to touch him. And whenever unclean spirits saw him they would fall down before him and shout, 'You are the Son of God.' He warned them sternly not to make him known.*

"I'm not sure which sea Jesus was near when this occurred because I never heard Peter tell this story. My guess is that it may be the great sea that links our cities around the empire, rather than the small Sea of Galilee, since the passage mentions people from all over the region. The important point is that people were going far out of their way in order to touch him, hoping that their diseases might be cured.

"Jesus is the Son of God! At every moment during his public years, people were healed and unclean spirits were cast away. He used a power that was his alone because he was divine. If we had only this one episode, our faith would be justified, but this is only one account among many that proves he was who he claimed to be.

"My friends, if you or a loved one is ill, pray to Jesus. Pray to him for healing, just like all those who came to him that day in Tyre and Sidon. They came in faith, and we come before him in faith—today and every day. If you or a loved one has experienced a loss, pray to Jesus. Pray to him in faith because he is the Son of God.

"Don't let anything stop you from putting your needs before him. Christ alone cares. Christ alone delivers. Christ alone heals every wound."

Clement sat down for a while, as was his custom, so people could think about what he had said. Then he led them in the breaking of the bread.

When the liturgy concluded, the people were not as enthusiastic as usual.

They smiled as they came past him, shaking his hand and saying, "That was nice." The exception was a group of women clustered around his wife. They were as animated as a flock of sparrows. He wondered what was going on.

Sati revealed the secret that afternoon at the dinner table. "Clement, a few of us were talking after the liturgy."

"I noticed. You all seemed so energized."

"Well, we have a wonderful idea. Nine of us want to go to Pompeii to look after the needs of the people there."

"Pompeii! But it's so dangerous there."

"Don't be silly. The major eruption has passed. There may be a few earthquakes, but nothing to worry about."

"I'm talking about the people. Some may be so desperate that they'll do most anything. And there may be diseases and roaming animals. You don't know what you might run into."

"Listen to you, Padre Bravery. I've never known you to worry about such things. And there will be nine of us. No one will mess with that many wily women. The others are planning to stay here and take care of the children."

"The emperor is sending food supplies and physicians. You don't need to go."

"Food and medicine are not all that they will need. We'll care for the injured and help people get messages to loved ones. We may find orphaned children. There are lots of things we can do to help."

"What gave you this crazy idea?"

"It's not a crazy idea. It's a good idea, and you gave it to us at the liturgy. Or I should say, you should have given it to us, instead of rambling on about how Jesus is divine. We already know that."

Then standing up in front of him, she continued, "Jesus helped real people in real ways. That's what we want to do, and that's what you should have preached. Pompeii is like the place where Jesus went—it's near the sea, there were people from all over, and they all were seeking help. That's what we plan to do. Don't you see?"

He did see, clearly, but he still didn't want her to go. "We've never been apart since we were married."

"Well, poor child, you've been lucky. Many men have to leave their families for work. You've been secure here for all these years. Anyway, your mother will make you your favorite dishes, and when we come back you'll be all the more pleased to see me."

Clement was getting desperate, but couldn't counter her arguments. "You usually are the one who is afraid. I remember the time I came home after burying Peter. You were shaking, and you made me promise not to take risks. I'm only asking you for the same consideration."

Seeing that she had won the battle, Sati bent down and kissed him on the forehead. "And I'm so glad that you made that promise. Going to Vatican Hill was a crazy thing to do, but I understood why you did it. Now you can understand why we want to do this. It's important to us as followers of Christ."

Out of breath and out of excuses, the anxious presbyter sighed and gave in. "How long do you expect to be gone?"

"Not more than two weeks. We can do a lot of good in that time, and we don't want to worry our husbands."

When the day came to leave, he helped his wife pack. One man provided two horse-drawn carts for their journey, and Clement attended the send-off, offering a blessing for their mission. He was proud of his wife—for her newfound courage, and for the faith-filled Christian she had become.

The women had a good time, working long days and enjoying their evenings together. There was one mishap: two of their number were stopped at knifepoint and robbed. The others shared their remaining coins, though, and all vowed to keep the whole matter a secret from the men in Rome.

On the Sunday after the women returned, Clement stood before his people and explained, "Today I want to do something different. As you know, some women from our community went to Pompeii and ministered for two weeks among the survivors who were so devastated by the eruption. This not only was a beautiful act of kindness, but also a perfect example of the kind of loving service that Jesus, himself, calls us to do. So before we proceed with the breaking of the bread, I want to ask those who went to Pompeii to share some stories of their experience. That is probably a better way to open up the gospel message for us than the homily I gave before they left.

"Ladies, please come forward and tell us some of the things that you did."

With a little further encouragement, the women stood as a group and shared some of their experiences. This took a much longer time than the usual preaching, but the people hardly noticed. They became totally engrossed in the fresh, heart-warming stories and at the end burst out with grateful applause. After the Eucharist as people left the house, they grabbed Clement's hands and exclaimed how pleased they were with the day's gathering. One told him, "I learned more today about loving my neighbor than in a whole year of your sermons." The man meant it as a compliment for his pastor, who blushed in delight at how beautifully the women had demonstrated the gospel.

48

Everyone expected Titus to have a long reign on the throne, but within two years the popular emperor came down with a fever and passed away. He was only forty-one. There were rumors of foul play, but no evidence. His last words were, "I have made but one mistake," but history has not revealed what that mistake was.

Domitian, Vespasian's other son who was then just thirty years old, left his brother's bedside even before he was dead to hurry back to Rome and assume control of the government. The new ruler had no friends in the senate, but they reluctantly awarded him the throne. He had a very disturbing way about him: cold, precise, and morbidly suspicious. He liked to impale flies with his stylus, a skill that sent chills through his enemies and kept potential friends at bay. The son of Vespasian was determined to make his mark on history. He trusted no one, nor did he permit anyone to stand in his way.

The intelligent young emperor knew he needed allies and did his best to get the military leaders on his side. He granted the entire army an ample pay raise, the first since the reign of Augustus, and balanced the extra cost with reductions in the number of legions, proving that he was a practical leader, even though this left the eastern frontier exposed.

The presbyters of Rome were worried about Domitian, who lacked the diplomatic personality of his father and brother. Fearful rumors arose among the city's minorities that a new round of persecutions could be eminent.

"He scares me," Clement told Anacletus.

The bishop replied, "We have to wait and see what he actually does. He may focus on other groups and leave us alone."

"I heard that he doesn't like Jews."

"Domitian has the reputation of not liking anyone. We can't hide from him—we have grown too great in numbers to do that. I think it is time that we distinguished ourselves even further from our Jewish brothers through our humanitarian efforts and peaceful ways."

"That may be a good strategy. I agree that it's impossible for us to hide."

"Let's discuss this in the next meeting of the presbyters."

Two topics of importance were on the agenda for the meeting of church leaders: what posture to take in light of the new emperor and what to make of a new written gospel that had just been received from the east. Bishop Anacletus had asked Clement to read the text and report his first impressions.

Clement told the men, "I must say that this document impresses me greatly. It should make it easier for new people to grasp the essence of Jesus because it presents him as one who speaks and teaches. Mark, as you know, liked to focus on the things Jesus did more so than on what he said. This text is more conversational."

"Can you give us an example?" a presbyter asked.

"There are many passages where we hear Christ speaking. In fact, near the beginning we hear a long teaching sermon that took place on a mountain in Galilee. It's very moving. I felt like I was right there in the crowd, listening to him. Here is just the beginning:

When Jesus saw the crowds, he went up the mountain, and after he had sat down, his disciples came to him. He began to teach them, saying:
'Blessed are the poor in spirit,
for theirs is the kingdom of heaven.
Blessed are they who mourn,
for they will be comforted.
Blessed are the meek,
for they will inherit the land.
Blessed are they who hunger and thirst for righteousness,
for they will be satisfied.
Blessed are the merciful,
for they will be shown mercy.
Blessed are the clean of heart,
for they will see God.
Blessed are the peacemakers,
for they will be called children of God.
Blessed are they who are persecuted for the sake of righteousness,
for theirs is the kingdom of heaven.
Blessed are you when they insult you and persecute you and utter every kind of
evil against you, falsely, because of me. Rejoice and be glad, for your reward will
be great in heaven.'"

The room was silent. "That's beautiful," someone said.

Clement gave them time to absorb what they heard, then added, "It is beautiful, isn't it? The author has a great gift, which I believe was inspired by the Holy Spirit."

"Who is the author?" another asked.

"His name is Matthew. That's all I know."

"Could that be Matthew the tax collector?"

"It could be," Clement answered, "but this Matthew doesn't identify himself that way, and there are a lot of Matthews in this world."

"How can we find out?"

Anacletus answered, "I have already sent letters to Antioch and Ephesus with that question. We'll have to wait until we get a reply."

Another presbyter asked, "The beatitudes you read to us sound similar to those we have in the sayings document."

"I noticed that," Clement replied. "Mark had a copy of the Sayings of Christ when he left here. I know he did. He had his notes that he made while he listened to Peter preach, a copy of the sayings, and the beginning of his own narrative. He left quickly during the persecution with all three. My guess is that Matthew may have used both Mark's gospel and the rest of the sayings in composing this new gospel. There are a lot of parallels with Mark."

"So you're saying that Mark didn't put as many of the sayings of Jesus in his gospel as Matthew did?"

"That's the way it sounds to me."

"Why not?"

"I don't know. I'm interested in hearing what you think when you read it. Two different authors with a great deal of material in front of them are not likely to put the same emphasis on the same things."

"Does anyone know what happened to Mark?" a deacon asked.

Anacletus answered, "No one has heard from him. Bishop Evodius said he was heading from Antioch to Galilee to search for eyewitnesses. That was many years ago."

"Do they think he is dead?"

"If he survived, someone would have heard from him by now."

Clement ended his report saying, "Like we have done in the past, we'll have scribes make you each a copy. That will take about a month. Then after you have studied this gospel, we will meet again and discuss how to put it to use."

The room instantly was filled with the buzz of conversation. In their enthusiasm for the new gospel, no one remembered to even bring up the topic of Domitian.

The new emperor had greater matters to deal with than worry about minority cults. Anacletus's strategy of emphasizing humanitarian works and peaceful ways, seemed to be effective. There were no threats from the palace, and the Christian communities of Rome were busy utilizing the new gospel. Their only disappointment was not knowing what happened to Mark or the certain identity of the gifted writer Matthew.

Then, only a little more than a year later, another gospel text arrived, again from the east—one written by the physician Luke, who had been a traveling companion of Paul. This codex included an additional narrative about the apostles, tracing the activities of the early Christian leaders from the day of Christ's ascension to the middle years of the reign of Nero when Paul arrived in Rome.

"We seem to be blessed with an abundance of gospels," Anacletus told the gathering.

"Why does Luke's differ so much from Matthew's?" a presbyter asked.

"The answer probably lies in what they considered most important in relating the story of Jesus to their communities. Matthew seemed to be addressing a Jewish-Christian audience, while Luke wrote for Greeks. Did you notice how even the words of Jesus differ from what we have in the sayings document? They certainly adapted what they got from their sources to fit the needs of those they wrote for."

"With these two gospels, we hardly even need the sayings collection anymore."

"You may be right. Time will determine what will be preserved and what will not."

"But in some cases, they tell the same stories, but in a differing sequence. Why is that?"

Clement replied, "We need to remember that the two writers were not eyewitnesses. They put on paper what they heard. Even Mark had that disadvantage. I remember him complaining that while he took plenty of notes when he heard Peter speak, he didn't know for sure which story followed another. I can see where he had to tie some of the accounts together like beads on a string."

Another presbyter said, "Overall, I like this gospel. It seems more up-to-date for our population here in Rome. As you said, it's more understandable for people who never were Jewish."

One of the deacons added, "I agree, and I liked the additional stories that aren't in either Mark's or Matthew's books. The parable of the man traveling from Jerusalem to Jericho who was beaten by robbers really touched my heart. The priest and the Levite passed him by, but the Samaritan—the foreigner— brought him to an inn and cared for him. That really puts Christ's point about 'who is my neighbor' across. I wonder where Luke got that story?"

Anacletus answered, "They certainly did their research. Each of these gospels makes an important contribution to the faith. I am grateful that the Holy Spirit guided each author to do his best. Together these documents give us a vivid portrait of Jesus."

"May we begin using this gospel in our liturgies?" another asked.

"Yes, of course. Luke has good credentials, being a companion of Paul. I say go ahead, as soon as you like."

After the meeting, Clement brought up another topic with the bishop. "I didn't want to say anything in front of the others about the Acts of the Apostles, but are you not bothered by it?"

"In what way?" the bishop asked. "It provides a great deal of information about the Church in the years after Christ ascended."

"That's well and good, but Luke presents it from the point of view of Paul. He makes it sound like Paul was more important than Peter."

"Well, Luke knew Paul personally. He didn't know anything about Peter except what Paul told him."

"That's my point. The story seems biased against Peter. That may not be the right choice of words, but it conveys how I feel."

"I understand how you feel," the bishop admitted. "You knew Peter—you loved him. He was like a father to you. Coming from Greece, I can tell you that Paul also was a great man, who fearlessly preached the gospel from city to city. This one text may give extra weight to Paul, but other documents tell us much about Peter. Together they give us a portrait of the earliest days of the Church."

"I just hope people don't end up placing more emphasis on the statements of Paul than on the words of Jesus," Clement replied. "There now are three gospels, but seven letters of Paul—the early letter to the Thessalonians, two to the Corinthians, that letter to the Galatians that made Peter sound so old-fashioned, the note to Philemon about his slave, the long letter to us in Rome, and his letter to the Christians in Philippi. If you add the Acts of the Apostles, that makes eight documents that present Paul's point of view and only three that tell the story of Jesus."

"Clement, Clement. Numbers aren't everything. Don't make such an issue about this. Over the years the Church will determine what is most important.

It is not up to you and me to decide."

"What if more documents turn up, some of which aren't even true about Christ?"

"Now that would be a different matter that we would have to deal with. In fact, what you are picturing certainly is possible, even likely. We may have to deal with those issues from right here in Rome. We are the Church at the center of the empire. Let's always keep the hazard of heretical books in mind as we look after our flocks, not just here but from east to west."

49

Sati broke the news to Clement, "Your brother is quite sick."
He replied, "Cassius was as strong as a horse when I saw him Sunday."

"It's not Cassius. Horus is the one who is ill."

"Horus? I haven't seen him in weeks. How bad is he?"

"It could be very bad. His wife said the heat rises and falls every two days. The physician thought it might be *ague* fever."

"Marsh fever! Horus doesn't go into the marshes. It is swampy, though, below the warehouse."

"That might be how he got it."

"My God! That's fatal in half the cases. I'd better go see him."

"I think you should."

Clement rushed to Horus's house, where his wife cautioned, "His fever is hot today. But it will be good for you to go in to him."

Going through the doorway, he saw his brother lying in his bed shivering, with beads of sweat covering his brow. "Hello, Horus," Clement greeted. "How are you feeling?"

"Oh, Clement. Is that you?"

"I'm here, Brother."

"That's good. My knees and elbows hurt."

The symptoms were obvious to Clement. The disease was so common in the city that people often called it Roman Fever. "You are strong, Horus. You will get better."

"I hope so. It's been more than a week now. I vomited this morning."

Clement recognized the additional signs, but so did Horus.

"I may not make it, Brother," he moaned.

"Yes, you will. You have a good physician."

"I feel so weak."

"Well, you must rest and do what the physician advises."

"I'm doing that, but I'm afraid."

"Hush. Don't talk that way."

"I'm very afraid, Clement."

"Would you like me to pray for you?"

"If you wish."

Clement paused and collected his thoughts. Then he prayed, "Jesus, Lord. You see how sick Horus is—he needs your loving care. His family needs him too. Help Horus to recover from this illness. Make the symptoms go away, and lead him to the fullness of life. He is a good man, Lord Jesus. His heart is full of goodness. Heal him, Lord. Make him whole again…"

Before Clement could finish the prayer, Horus began to sob.

"Don't cry, Brother."

"But, I am not worthy of that prayer."

"Yes, you are."

"I am not!" he blurted. "I have done bad things."

"We all do bad things from time to time."

"I have been bad all of my life. I've been a selfish man." Clement began to reply, but Horus interrupted, "I stole the money from the strongbox. Then I blamed you."

"I know, Horus. I forgave you."

"I cheated the emperor, and my own father."

"I know. I learned that back then, while you were ill."

Horus sobbed, "I killed my own father. It was the shock of finding out what I did that killed him, wasn't it?"

"Yes, Horus. It was."

"And you never told anyone?" he muttered.

"No, Horus. Peter advised me to keep your secret in confidence. I never told Mother, or anyone."

"You are a saint, Clement."

"I am just a man—like you—but I try to follow Jesus as best as I can."

Horus sobbed more. "I have been unfaithful to Jesus. I had the gift of faith, but I pushed it away with my selfishness. There is no hope for me."

"There always is hope. Where there is sorrow, there is hope. Are you sorry for the things you did?"

"I am filled with remorse. But there is no hope now."

"Nonsense," Clement blurted. "I believe our father Urbanus is with the Lord right now, praying for you with all of his might."

"How could Father still love me and forgive me?"

"On earth, he may not have been able to forgive. But in the kingdom of heaven, all things are possible. I believe he has forgiven you."

"Oh, Clement! That is my fondest hope. I want to make amends with Father. Will I be able to?"

"Do it now, Horus. Don't wait."

"What do you mean?"

"Tell our father you're sorry now. Do it now!"

Clement waited while his brother thought about the proposal. Then he heard him say weakly but sincerely, "Father. It's me, Horus—your son Horus. I am very sick now, as you may know. But I want to tell you that I am sorry for all of the stupid, selfish things I did. I have sinned against Jesus and against you. I don't deserve to be called your son. Can you forgive me? Please forgive me, if you will?"

"That was nice, Horus. Very nice…You remind me of a story in the new gospel that we received from Luke. Jesus told a parable about a son who had sinned against heaven and against his father. When the son came to his senses, he rehearsed his apology and went back to his father, but the father didn't even listen. The father was so happy to have his son back that he didn't even let him ask to be forgiven. He just threw his arms around his son and cooked the fatted calf for a feast."

Horus broke down in big, wet tears, and then he pulled his brother down to where they could embrace. Clement cradled him in his arms and said, "You are forgiven, Horus. You are forgiven."

The sick man let out a great sigh, as if the weight of the world had been removed from his shoulders. Then he smiled, closed his eyes, and fell into his final sleep.

"Those were his last words," Clement told the family. "He asked his father to forgive him, and then fell asleep smiling."

Horus's wife began to sob. Sati went to her and cradled her in her arms.

"I'm glad that you went to him," Cordula said. "I prayed for years that he would repent."

"Yes, Mother."

"I always knew that it was something Horus did that upset Urbanus so badly.

211

I didn't say anything because I didn't want to sully Horus's name."

"You loved him, Mother."

Cordula cried. Then wiping her eyes, she said, "I loved him. I loved him just as I love all of you. I couldn't not love him just because he went wrong. I always hoped that he would turn his life around."

Clement went over to his mother and put his arms around her. "He did turn his life around. He turned his life around, and Christ saw him do it."

After the funeral, Cassius made a surprise announcement to the family. "This is a sad day for us, but I have something positive I want to say, and it is this: I never expected to run the business by myself. I never even wanted to. But now I have to do it, and fortunately my sons are old enough now to help.

"None of you will ever have to beg for money," he stated. Then turning to Horus's wife, he said to her, "I will be giving you more than you were expecting."

"And Clement, I am especially grateful for all that you have done for our family. That time during the civil war, when the palace didn't want all the eggs, you saved our business, and you saved my place in the operation. I will always be grateful.

"So, Clement. Someday you will be bishop! You will not have time to earn a living, but your living will come from our family business. I want you to begin now to serve God's people all the time. You and Sati also will never want for funds, as I will be providing for your needs every week, just like I do for Mother.

"Now don't...don't say no. I am not doing this only for you. I'm doing it for the Church. Our Lord needs good people like you, Clement, laboring in his vineyard and doing his will. Supporting your work is how I will be supporting the Lord."

The two brothers embraced fondly, tears streaming from their eyes. But no one had more tears of joy than their mother. Even with all of her losses, she was the happiest woman in Rome.

50

Two years later, Anacletus came to Clement with a serious expression on his face and a booklet in his hand. "I received a codex of letters from Bishop Dionysius in Athens. They surprised me, but I feel they may be important."

"Who wrote the letters?"

"Well, that is an interesting question. Each letter indicates that it was from Paul. There is one to the community in Ephesus, one to the Colossians, a second letter to those in Thessalonica, and three letters to individuals, a Timothy and a Titus."

"But Paul was killed by Nero twenty years ago. How could these just be surfacing now?"

"That was my first question," the thoughtful bishop replied. "My guess is that they were composed more recently by people close to Paul. That's fairly common among philosophers in the secular world. A disciple can add to his master's writings things the great one may have wished to communicate when he suddenly died. That may be the case with these."

"Does that make them forgeries?"

"No. The letters are Pauline—they express Paul's thoughts, even if they were not written by him."

"I'm confused," Clement admitted.

"You have to take some time to let this congeal in your mind. Paul was executed twenty years ago, but his followers have been working all that time in the cities throughout the eastern provinces. They have been in communication, both personally and in writing, about matters and concerns that are important to them. Now someone has gathered some of those letters and made copies of them."

"Who did that?"

"Bishop Dionysius said he doesn't know."

"What are you going to do with them?"

"We will have to decide. I want you to read them and tell me what you think."

"Will you suppress them?"

"That's not my initial thought. Everything the letters say is orthodox. They don't contradict the faith, so there may be value in preserving them. Please study them. I am interested in hearing your opinion."

"Yes. Certainly. I'll do that right away."

Clement reported back to the bishop a week later. "The new letters, as you said, seem orthodox. I see nothing wrong in them."

"Good."

"They don't sound like they all are from the same author. The letter to the Ephesians has a distinctly different personality, and the man who wrote it certainly had less open views about women than Paul did."

"Yes," the bishop laughed. "Paul would not have used the words, 'Wives be subordinate to your husbands.' He makes a good point, though, that Christ is the head of the Church, and the Church is subordinate to Christ."

"I can't argue with that," Clement joked.

"So you saw nothing objectionable in the letters?"

"No."

"Neither did I. I think we'll just let them have their own lives. If the Church receives value from them, then they will be preserved."

Clement brought up another point, "I've also thought about the potential hazard that some new writings might pose. As we discussed earlier, it is likely that some people may compose documents that contradict the faith. Have we decided what we should do about them?"

Anacletus stroked his beard and replied, "There will need to be some principles to govern heretical writings. The bishops will have to develop those principles as time goes along. My view is this: recognized writings will need to bear the imprint of the Holy Spirit—they will need to display beauty, harmony, power, and efficacy that go beyond mere human authorship. They also will need to be received by the whole Church—that is to have universal acceptance. And certainly, they will have to have apostolic origins—be written by an eyewitness or a close follower of an apostle. Paul made this point in his letter to the Corinthians when he stated, 'I received from the Lord what I also delivered to you.' The gospel of Christ is being handed down in an apostolic succession from the first generation of Christians to those that follow. Any writings that don't meet these standards should not be considered apostolic."

"That's so logical," Clement replied. "I had never thought about this in such an intelligent way."

"Keep those principles in mind when you become bishop."

"Now, Anacletus. You have many years yet to serve the Lord."

"Not as many as you may think. I am feeling older every year."

A few weeks later, Anacletus told Clement, "My son, I have been thinking about putting in writing some recommendations for the Church, particularly in the east where persecutions are breaking out. Will you help me with that?"

"Of course, Bishop. I'll do anything you ask."

"Good. I will appreciate your assistance. You see, I am thinking of writing in Peter's name, and since you were close to our first bishop while I hardly knew him, your collaboration will be invaluable."

"I'm honored. But why should you write in Peter's name. You are the bishop of Rome."

"That is true, but I am not well known east of Athens. I got the idea after we talked about the latest Pauline letters. If I write in Peter's name like they did for Paul, the words will carry more weight."

"Hmm. I see. If the followers of Paul can do it, so can the followers of Peter. I probably am the best person to help you do that. What do you plan to say?"

"I am thinking of addressing the letter to the provinces in the east where our people are beginning to be persecuted by their pagan neighbors. I want to encourage them to live as God's people even as they feel separated from the society around them. Christ is their hope—they have experienced new birth in their faith. The suffering and death of Jesus can serve them as both a source of salvation and an example to follow. I will address some specific situations, such as issues within the family, those where they work, even slavery. Their suffering is likely to increase, and they need to be inspired to live faithfully, regardless of what is happening around them."

"That's quite a bit to put in one letter."

"It is a lot. I see this as a general letter, giving advice to the whole Church."

"Well, I certainly will help you in every way I can."

Over the next weeks, Anacletus brought sections of the proposed letter for Clement to evaluate. He made a number of helpful suggestions.

"My first reaction, Bishop, is that you are an intellectual Greek, while Peter was an uneducated fisherman. The writing sounds too polished to have been written by him."

"I will try to make the words more down-to-earth. If Peter had written the letter, he could have used an educated secretary."

"I'm sure that he would have, but please keep that in mind."

"I will."

"I like how your tone differs from the letters of Paul."

"Thank you."

"And the part should be very helpful where you said, 'Beloved, do not be surprised that a trial by fire is occurring among you, as if something strange were happening to you. But rejoice to the extent that you share in the sufferings of Christ, so that when his glory is revealed you may also rejoice exultantly.' That should inspire and encourage all who are feeling outcast or threatened with violence."

"Yes. Do you have any other ideas?"

"Well—I also thought about the conclusion. You could end the letter as though it is being conveyed by a companion of Paul and also include greetings from Mark. That would make it more realistic. You might consider these words: 'I write you this briefly through Silvanus, who I consider a faithful brother, exhorting you and testifying that this is the true grace of God. Remain firm in it. The chosen one at Babylon sends you greeting, as does Mark, my son. Greet one another with a loving kiss. Peace to all of you who are in Christ.'"

Anacletus laughed, "So Peter and I are the chosen ones of Babylon?"

"The letter is from the bishop of Rome. Everyone will know what the phrase means."

"I like it. I will have some copies made, and we can send them out."

51

During the seventh year of the reign of Domitian, Anacletus passed away peacefully in his sleep. Clement was quickly elected to succeed him as bishop, and the date of his installation was set for the sixth day of June, his mother's eightieth birthday. Clement was fifty-seven.

Several bishops came to Rome for the ordination, including two from great distances: Ignatius of Antioch and the aging Onesimus of Ephesus.

Everyone was happy. Clement had served the Church faithfully for most of his life in ever-growing ways. The presbyters and deacons had deep respect for Clement and pledged their loyalty. Cassius and his family were elated, Sati was beaming, and Cordula was as proud as any mother could be.

Ignatius presided at the liturgy. Accompanied by song, the bishop-elect came forward and lay prostrate before the altar, a sign of human unworthiness before the call of the Lord. Dionysius of Athens read the passage from the beginning of the Acts of the Apostles where the disciples asked, "Lord, are you at this time going to restore the kingdom to Israel?" and the risen Christ answered, "It is not for you to know the times or seasons that the Father has established by his own authority, but you will receive power when the Holy Spirit comes upon you." The white-haired bishop then spoke directly to Clement, emphasizing the unknown hazards that servants of Christ are called upon to face, but do face with the help and guidance of the Spirit. Then each bishop came to Clement and prayed over him with the traditional laying on of hands, the sign of the Holy Spirit conferring the graces of the office and the Christian community passing on the authority of succession. Then they dressed him in the bishop's garment and celebrated the Eucharist.

At the conclusion of the liturgy, the new bishop addressed the assembled crowd with words of humility: "Today I am honored to accept the mantle of *episkopos* and serve as your bishop. I also am deeply humbled. Never did I seek the presbyterate in order to rise up in office. I did so only to serve our Lord and Mighty King, Jesus Christ.

"On this day, I cannot help but reflect upon the great gifts possessed by my predecessors, Peter, Linus, and Anacletus. They taught me important lessons about what a bishop should be. Peter—who I loved like my own father—was so steadfast in his devotion to the Lord that even in the midst of tension and struggles, he always brought people together, to the center—to the key that is most important—to the unity that Jesus prayed for at the Last Supper. That's why our Lord entrusted him with the keys to the kingdom. And Linus—who was so steady and wise during the persecutions of Nero—what a great man he was. That's why we followed his leadership with confidence and trust. And, of course, Anacletus of Athens, who came to us with experience in the worldwide Church and the vision to see that great things are on the horizon for the followers of Christ. We accepted him and turned to him, even though he was new to us.

"I don't know what challenges we will face in the years ahead. I only know that we will face them with hope and with faith that Jesus—the Lord of the earth—will be present in our midst, guiding us, fueling our courage, and challenging us to build up the kingdom of God. We live in a sinful world, a world racked by violence and greed and the lust for power. But it is God's world—we must never forget that. This is God's world, and we are the servants that will assist the Lord in setting it right.

"Thank you for your confidence. Thank you for your support. Thank you for giving me the opportunity to serve you, whom I love. I pray that God will bless us all, and I call forth that blessing in the name of the Father, and of the Son, and of the Holy Spirit."

After a loud "Amen!" all those present followed the new bishop to a reception in his honor.

The next day Clement met with the assembled bishops for an informal discussion of the conditions facing the Church around the empire. "What new situations are you dealing with?" he asked.

Ignatius spoke first, "I don't know how many of us are experiencing the notion that Jesus didn't really die but only appeared to do so. This attitude stems from the ancient culture of Antioch, where gods are perceived only as immortal and do not suffer the pains of the flesh. My presbyters say that this hurdle is the biggest obstacle to evangelization."

"But Christ came to us in the flesh," Clement affirmed. "Peter taught that from the beginning, and Paul said, 'If Christ did not rise from the dead, then our faith is in vain.'"

"For us it is good news that God came to us in human form, but many Syrians find that incomprehensible. They say that Jesus only seemed to be human—that his human form was an illusion. They say it is nonsense for us to teach that a divine being would suffer and die."

Clement asked, "How many of us are experiencing this issue?"

Only Onesimus of Ephesus waved his hand.

"So, this matter seems to be confined to the east."

Ignatius added, "I believe so. It's an eastern view that is causing us trouble, but our churches are growing. We would be growing even faster, however, if this attitude was not so entrenched in the Syrian psyche."

"Well, keep us posted on any further developments."

"I will," the Antiochian avowed. "Actually, Onesimus is facing a much bigger threat."

"What is that?" Clement asked.

The aging bishop answered calmly, "Persecution."

"Persecution! Is it severe? We all thought that Domitian might strike out at the Church, but we haven't seen it so far."

"It's not from the emperor, at least not directly from him. What is happening seems to be confined to the Province of Asia at this point. Local officials are coming down on us for not worshiping the emperor. They hate us for refusing to continue the long-standing practice of worshiping our rulers. In Ephesus and in many of our cities the magistrates are arresting Christians and slaughtering them. The rise of Domitian has been good for business in our province, and most merchants are supporting the magistrates. At this point the officials seem to be trying to teach us a lesson by executing our well-known members."

"How are your people handling it?"

"That varies from household to household. Most have gone to their deaths with courage, but some have retracted their faith. The officials make much out of those cases."

"Peter and Linus taught us to put emphasis on our humanitarian works and peaceful ways. That got us through the terrible persecutions of Nero."

"We are doing that, of course, but Asians like to punish those who deviate from accepted norms. They say it preserves order and peace in our cities. I pray that this practice will calm down before much more damage is done."

"We will pray for you, Onesimus. Please keep us informed, and I will try to come to your city, if I can be of help."

The house of Clement on the Capitoline Hill continued to enjoy peace and joy. Sati loved her mother-in-law, who was showing definite signs of aging but still was bright and alert. Cordula became somewhat stooped over and frequently made use of a walking stick. Her hair became quite grey, but Sati also began to show strands of white among her beautiful brown and gold waves. The two often joked about their hair, but Clement said age made Sati look only lovelier. The couple treasured their intimate moments in each other's arms, although on many nights this led only to tender hugs and kisses, lacking the energy and urgent desire they used to feel.

Cassius's two oldest sons were helping in the egg business. When they gathered for dinner on Sunday afternoons, his mother often remarked how Cassius had become so much like Urbanus. He never seemed to grow tired of listening to her share the story. The balding merchant had become quite a businessman, delegating duties to his sons with the same sense of organization that characterized his earlier efforts to create efficiency. The weekly payments that he made to her and Clement were constant and founded on love.

Before long another new presbyter, who was from Bethlehem, arrived in the imperial city, but he said his family was more Greek than Jewish. Evaristus loved his homeland and carried deep sorrow for how brutally the Roman legions were treating his people. It had been two decades since Titus had crushed their rebellion, but Domitian insisted that the restrictions his predecessor made against Jews entering the Holy City be kept in place.

Evaristus wanted to give his family a fresh start.

"I think it's ideal that you chose to come to Rome," Clement told the newcomer. "You will bring a perspective that we have lacked."

"I do understand the Jewish people. I want to help in any way I can, although I can afford only a tiny house in Trastevere."

"Actually, one of our members purchased Anacletus's large dwelling. You can take over that community. They need a pastor, and I think you will be a good fit."

"I don't know if I can follow in the steps of such a great man," the Jewish-Christian admitted.

"You will do fine."

"Thank you. I appreciate your confidence."

"Now tell me, what is happening in the Holy City?"

"The Romans continue to maltreat the Jews, and of course they think that Christians are a sect of Judaism. Many of our people who escaped before the siege have returned, but they are having a very rough time."

"I had heard that. We sent a collection."

"That was very helpful. But now, Domitian keeps taking. He has expanded the *fiscus Judaicus*, the tax on Jews that replaced the former Temple Tax. Vespasian used the money to pay for the upkeep of the Temple of Jupiter in Rome. That was a terrible humiliation—only those Jews who renounced their faith were exempt. Now Domitian has extended the tax to all family members, not just the heads of households. What had been two denarii is now ten to twenty for large families. That's a big slice out of income that few can afford."

"How terrible."

"The resentments are extremely strong. It wouldn't surprise me if they mounted another revolt in the coming decades."

"Will they never learn not to fight power with violence?"

"Not in our lifetimes. Throughout their history they have fought enemies, and many times have succeeded. The scriptures tell the stories."

"I know. If only they would have listened to Jesus, by now their lives would be better."

"Yes. They would be."

"Tell me," the bishop asked. "Is it true that many rabbis now are advocating the removal of some of the sacred texts from their scriptures"

"They are not seeking to remove them so much as to downgrade the importance of all writings in Greek that were not first composed in Hebrew. They don't want to use them in their synagogue services any longer. This is a reactionary step backward. Some of those books, like Judith and Tobit, and of course the books about the Maccabees, are valuable. And the book of Sirach is endowed with much wisdom and beauty. It seems a shame to ignore them when they can fill people with the Holy Spirit."

"I agree. I see no reason for Christians to turn away from these books."

"That's correct. They are sacred writings. The leaders want to turn back the calendar to the time before Alexander brought new ways to their country."

"That's not possible, even if it were desirable. Most Jews in Rome today don't even speak Hebrew."

"They don't in Rome, nor throughout the diaspora. Without the temple in Jerusalem, there is no longer a central administration for the Jewish faith. Some rabbis are holding councils. They want to adopt an official canon of biblical books. Moves like that may unify the people. Only time will tell."

"Only time will tell, and it has been our policy not yet to attempt to create a cannon of Christian books. We want to wait and see how they are received in the various communities. Maybe someday we will adopt such a list."

"Waiting probably is a wise move."

"Is there anything else happening in Palestine that I should be aware of?"

The new presbyter thought for a moment and replied, "I might mention one more thing. The Jewish people have a great respect for wisdom and knowledge. A few who at first seemed attracted to Jesus, are focusing on knowledge as a source of salvation, rather than the grace of Christ."

"Why would anyone want to do that?"

"Well, they do. Why, I don't know. But then you and I understand our Savior. These people dip their toes into the faith and then run away like it was icy water. They want salvation without suffering."

"How odd. Are there many of them?"

"The numbers are small—just a few teachers gathering small numbers at this point. But if the trend continues, this could pose a problem for evangelization."

Clement asked, "Do you have contacts in Palestine? Can you keep me informed on any developments?"

"I do have friends who I hope to keep in touch with. I will do my best to keep you informed."

"Good." Then embracing the newcomer, he said, "Evaristus, my friend, welcome to Rome."

52

Sati adjusted quickly to the life of bishop's wife, even though Clement had to be away from home more often. She didn't complain a bit when he sailed to the Greek peninsula, but in less than two years, he began to plan a longer voyage and wondered how his wife would handle it.

"Dear," he whispered in bed, "I may have to make a longer trip."

"Where to?" she asked without a hint of anxiety.

"To the province of Asia. The persecutions are continuing, and I'd like to visit with John in Ephesus."

"That shouldn't take too long."

"Well, while I'm there, I would like to stop at each of the larger cities and encourage the bishops."

"That makes sense."

"It will take at least two months."

"That's what I guessed."

"Will you be all right?"

Sati rose up and looked intently at her husband. "I'm not a shrinking vine, you know. I can handle things here, and I have your mother for company."

Clement exhaled in relief and smiled. "I wasn't worried that you couldn't deal with it. I just wasn't sure if you'd like it."

"Well, of course I'd prefer that you were here always. I miss you when you travel, but I know it comes with your responsibilities."

"Good. Thank you."

Sati kissed him and laid her head on his chest. "What I love about you, Clement, is that you are considerate. You don't just run off like Peter did, not telling his wife until he was rushing out the door."

"I'd never do that."

"I know you wouldn't. And I appreciate it."

Then he shared, "You are much stronger now than when you first came to Rome."

"Yes. I am."

"And not as frightened."

"That's right. I'm not."

"I'm proud of you."

"Well…your courage…I've learned from your courage."

Clement moved his body closer and caressed her face. She studied his eyes in the moonlight and pulled him toward her. Then she smiled and whispered, "You always come back to me. That's all I need."

Their lips met and didn't part. Without further words, they expressed their love in tender unity.

Ten days later, Clement kissed his wife and mother good-bye, and rode with his brother to the docks. "Don't worry about Sati or Mother," Cassius assured him. "I'll look in on them every day."

"Thank you," Clement laughed, "but don't overdo it. They're confident they can get along by themselves, and you might offend their sensitivities."

A small boat carried the traveler with his bag and cushion to the Ostia harbor. As they drifted toward the port, he recalled how he loved the blue sky over Rome on clear spring days. Then, out on the sea in a sturdy ship, Clement saw two white birds fly along, watching the progress of the vessel. They appeared to see that he noticed them and called in greeting. "Hello, beautiful birds!" he shouted. "Will this be a safe and fruitful voyage?"

Their immediate reply confirmed his confidence.

Winds were favorable, and the ship made good time, stopping in Rhegium and Sparta and reaching Ephesus in only eight days. Clement walked past the large open market and admired the beautiful Library of Celsus before asking at a shop for directions. The house of Onesimus was a short walk back up the hill to the north.

The balding, white-haired bishop greeted him warmly. "Welcome, Clement, welcome. Thank God you have come. The situation has gotten more tense since we spoke at your installation."

"What is happening?"

"Put your things down and have some wine. Then I will tell you."

Clement put his bag in the room the bishop reserved for guests and made use of the basin and towel before returning to the main living area. "Thank you," he said. "It is good to freshen up after the voyage."

"Please have some wine and take some bread and cheese."

"Thank you, Bishop. Your hospitality is appreciated."

"That is the least I can do. Clement, things are very tense here. All over the area, the provincial officials and city magistrates are cracking down on Christians who will not worship the emperor."

"But Domitian has not given such an order, has he?"

"No. The local officials are acting on their own. They are hoping to impress the emperor with a show of loyalty. The region is prospering, and the merchants are insisting on punishing all nonconformists. Those who produce and sell the artifacts that are used in the emperor cults are the most insistent."

"Business has a way of influencing politics," Clement observed.

"Yes, and it has become a movement now. The various factions are unified in requiring that all Christians bow down and make a sacrifice to the divine Domitian."

"Can't they just pledge their loyalty? In the rest of the empire we accept the emperor's political rule without it becoming a religious issue."

"Not here. The leaders insist that there is no distinction. They say that any cult that gathers without worshiping the emperor is a conspiratorial threat to peace and order."

"Have you tried to reason with them?"

"There is no 'them' to reason with. The movement has no specific leaders, and the issue is too diffuse and pervasive. I thought things might settle down, but it has gotten only more stressful. And there is no end in sight."

"Hmm," Clement mused. "So we simply must live with this persecution for as long as it takes?"

"Yes. We see no other alternative."

"Hmm."

"Will you address our people on Sunday?"

"I can, but I don't know what I'll say."

"That's the day after tomorrow. Rest here and pray about it. Perhaps the Lord will give you the words."

Clement spent Saturday in prayer and read through a copy of the gospel according to Luke. He hoped to find something that could inspire the Ephesians, since Paul had written some of his letters while imprisoned in the city and they knew Luke had been a companion of Paul.

On Sunday, Onesimus warmly introduced the bishop of Rome. It was so quiet that you could hear a pin drop. All eyes were upon Clement as he went to the raised table where the scriptures were read.

Clement looked at the crowd. Their faces betrayed deep feelings of anxiety, but they gazed at him with hope that he might bring an answer to them that would quell their fears. Then he spoke from his heart.

"My friends, I come to you in the name of Christians all over the empire.

We have heard of your plight here and are praying that the persecutions that seem to be confined to your region will soon end. We know that Christ looks upon all of you with love and compassion. It tears his heart when even one follower is martyred, and he weeps when so many are persecuted.

"We are looking to God for advice. Let us listen for a moment to the words of the evangelist Luke:

> *And raising his eyes toward his disciples he said,*
> *'Blessed are you who are poor,*
> *for the kingdom of God is yours.*
> *Blessed are you who are now hungry,*
> *for you will be satisfied.*
> *Blessed are you who are now weeping,*
> *for you will laugh.*
> *Blessed are you when people hate you,*
> *and when they exclude and insult you,*
> *and denounce your name as evil*
> *on account of the Son of Man.*
> *Rejoice and leap for joy on that day!*
> *Behold your reward will be great in heaven,*
> *for their ancestors treated the prophets in the same way.*
>
> *But to you who hear I say, love your enemies,*
> *do good to those who hate you,*
> *bless those who curse you,*
> *pray for those who mistreat you.*
> *To the person who strikes you on one cheek,*
> *offer the other one as well,*
> *and from the person who takes your cloak,*
> *do not withhold even your tunic.*
> *Give to everyone who asks of you,*
> *and from the one who takes what is yours*
> *do not demand it back.*
> *Do to others as you would have them do to you.'*

"The people who heard these words of Jesus that day in Galilee were in a situation similar to yours—not identical, but similar. Their leaders had chosen to collaborate with the emperor, rather than support the people, hoping they would benefit from his continuing favors. Many were persecuted for their faith, and every single person listening felt powerless.

"Those who were crowded around Jesus had been oppressed for decades— longer than you. Christ didn't provide them with a method to overpower the oppression. He instead offered them a way to live in the midst of it—to soften its impact—while staying faithful to the commandments of God.

"I'm sure that some were disappointed with his solution—love your enemies. Human nature wants to strike back. But Jesus showed them how they were blessed. They could laugh and leap for joy, for their reward would be great in heaven, and—most important—they could live in the kingdom of God, that very day!

"We *can* bless those who curse us. We *can* turn the other cheek. We *can* offer even our tunics and not demand back what is rightfully ours. We *can* do all of these and more—because we have Christ in our hearts and in our lives.

"Never lose hope. Never doubt your decision to follow Jesus. Never turn your back on your fellow sojourners. Stay together. Stay together in faith. Stay together in Christ.

"You may have to suffer; you may have to carry your cross; you may have to die! But know this: Jesus did too. Yes, Jesus suffered and carried his cross—and Jesus died on it—for you! For you—because he loved you, and he wanted to be an example to you. He wanted to show you the way—the only way that works—the only way that fulfills the plan of God for making this world a better place. That will never happen if people always try to repay violence with violence.

"Remember the words of Jesus that the physician who accompanied Paul so poetically gathered from the tradition. They are living words that can sustain us through even the most difficult of times. Remember the words. Ponder them and pray with them. Keep them ever-present in your mind. Teach them to your children. Comfort one another with them. And if you have to—if there is no other way—carry those words to your grave.

"You are blessed people, here in the province of Asia. You are blessed with the mission of being a living example to the rest of the Church, to be a living example to the empire, to be an example of the living Lord in the midst of a world of hate and death.

"Do it well. Live your task well. Represent your Savior well, and the world will see. The world will be a better place because of you.

"God bless you for your goodness. God bless you for your faith. God bless you for your perseverance. May God bless you for following Jesus with your whole heart and with your whole soul and with your whole mind and with your whole strength. Do unto others as you would have them do unto you, and you will never regret it. You will never regret it, and your joy will be great in heaven."

Clement lowered his head and returned to his chair. Then he closed his eyes and thanked Christ for helping him speak to the people. He prayed that the message would sustain them through the difficult times ahead.

After the liturgy, Onesimus thanked Clement for his inspiring words. "People were listening intensely. I never would have thought of saying what you told them."

"I wouldn't have thought of it either. It felt as though Christ was telling the people what he wanted them to hear."

"Well, we all greatly appreciate your coming here to share it with us."

"Thank you. I'm glad that I came."

"Will you visit some more of our cities?"

"That is my plan. What do you suggest?" Clement asked.

"Well, that depends upon how much time you have. South of us is the city of Melitus, where you can go up the Meander River to Heirapolis, Laodicia, and Colossae. Paul founded the communities in those cities. Then you can continue by cart around to Philadelphia, Sardis, and Smyrna. And if you can stay longer, you might consider stopping at the coastal towns from Pergamum to Troas."

"I will try to do that. Are some of the cities close enough that I could visit two in one week?"

"You might be able to do the three cities east of Melitus in two weeks. They are close together."

"Hmm. It would take six weeks before I would get to Pergamum. I'll try to visit as many as I can."

"That will be most appreciated."

"I'd like to see John while I am here. Can I do that and still get to Melitus before Saturday."

"Certainly, if you want to. I can send a message to John for you to see him tomorrow and arrange for a ship south on Tuesday."

"That sounds ideal. I would hate to be this close to John and not see him."

"Have you never met?"

"No. I am intrigued by his reputation, and he is one of the last living eyewitnesses."

"Yes, most of the others have passed on. You will enjoy John. He is a fine man, very intelligent and well-educated. We all love him."

53

John lived farther out from the center of Ephesus than the bishop, who accompanied Clement to his humble, mud-brick abode. John was expecting them.

"Aha, friend Onesimus," the white-haired elder exclaimed. "So, you brought the bishop of Rome. To what do I owe this honor?"

"This is Clement. He asked to meet you."

Clement was impressed with the old man's vitality. Even though he appeared to be at least eighty years of age, John's face was slender, and his long white beard came to a point, projecting a distinguishing image of wisdom and intelligence. "It is a pleasure to meet you, sir. I had hoped to speak with the last remaining eyewitness."

"I am an eyewitness—that is for sure. And there are not many of us left who knew Jesus."

"I only know what Peter told me about him."

"Oh, so you knew Peter. Was he still an impulsive rascal in his old age?"

"He had matured when I met him. That was during the reign of Claudius. He still retained some of the attributes that people tell about when he was a young man, but in Rome he became a paragon of patience and strength, always bringing people together, focusing on unity."

"It sounds like you were close to Peter."

"I loved the man—I loved him like my own father."

"I thought he was bullheaded, but Jesus had faith in him," the elder revealed.

"Were you not friends when you fished in Capernaum?" Clement asked.

"Oh! So, in Rome they think I am one of the Zebedee brothers. Everyone makes that mistake."

"Are you not the apostle from Capernaum?"

"Never was. I was a disciple from Jerusalem. I met Jesus when he stayed with Lazarus and Martha and Mary. I didn't travel everywhere with the Galilee group; I was too young. But I was there when he went to the Baptist at the Jordan, and I was in the upper room the night he was betrayed. I saw everything he did in and around the city. Jesus loved me as much as any."

"I'm confused. I thought you were the apostle John."

"Everyone thinks that. I gave up trying to straighten it out years ago. John is a common name."

"I know."

"Anyway. Those brave and strong fishermen all ran away when the guards came with Judas. I was the only man who stayed with his mother at the cross."

"And he entrusted her to you."

"Yes. Mary was such a dear lady. I cared for her like she was my own mother all of her life. That was easy—she was such a saintly person. And we got along well, even after we moved here to Ephesus."

"Is it true what they say, that when she died she was carried straight to heaven?" Clement inquired.

"Totally true. At the moment of her death, she just disappeared. There is no grave or marker here. When I looked into her empty bed, I could detect the sweet scent of roses."

"My God. How beautiful."

"That's what I said at the time. I still shiver when I think about that day."

Clement paused for a moment and asked, "John—you undoubtedly remember many, many things. Have you ever thought of putting them in writing?"

"Do you mean like Matthew and Luke did?"

"Yes."

"They copied Mark, you know."

"I know. They utilized Mark's gospel and the collection of Christ's sayings, and they added some precious accounts that Mark may not have been aware of."

"I can tell you other things that none of them knew—things that happened in Jerusalem and some in Galilee that Mark left out."

"That will be wonderful."

"Do you know that Jesus cured a man who was born blind? That was unheard of. And he raised our friend Lazarus from the dead. He had been in the tomb for four days, but Jesus shouted, 'Lazarus, come out!' And the dead man come out, still bound with the burial cloths. I was standing there, totally astonished."

"That's amazing. I wish I could stay in Ephesus long enough to hear all of your stories."

"Did Peter tell you that on the night of the last Passover, Jesus washed our feet?"

"No!"

"He lowered himself like a slave and showed us the importance of serving one another."

"Can you write these accounts?" Clement asked.

"I was schooled in the Greek language and can use it well. I've thought about writing from time to time, but my hands are getting old."

Onesimus, who had been listening blurted, "I can provide you with an excellent secretary, and our scribes will make copies. I agree with Clement. You can make a valuable contribution to the faith."

"I remember many things," the elder replied. "Maybe I *should* write them down."

Clement couldn't contain himself. "Please do it, sir. Every bit of knowledge about Jesus will be treasured in the years ahead. Do it while you can."

"There won't be much longer that I can."

"So please do it."

"I can have a secretary come to your home this week," Onesimus offered.

"All right. You two are so insistent. I will write some memories, if it will help the Church."

"It will help the faith immensely," Clement asserted. "Thank you, sir. Thank you for making what may be a priceless contribution to the faith."

54

Clement hardly slept all night after the surprising conversation with John, but he had to get up early Tuesday morning to catch the ship to Miletus. Bishop Onesimus gratefully embraced the traveler and wished him a safe journey.

In the port city of Miletus, Clement offered a message similar to what he had given to the Christians in Ephesus. Then he rode in a cart pulled by two mules along a bumpy road up the Meander and Lycus valleys to Hierapolis. He didn't like how the driver whipped the mules, but was in no position to offer advice.

The bishop of Miletus had told Clement about the limestone cliffs of Hierapolis, but he was unprepared for the dramatic impact the ancient formations made as the cart approached from the river. Created by centuries of flowing water from the hot springs above, the cliffs appeared to be covered with white snow on the warm summer day. The traveler guessed that they were about a mile wide and loomed several hundred feet high. As the cart passed the ponds below and circled up around the formations to the plateau, the city atop the cliffs came more fully into view.

Clement was further surprised to see a modern and beautiful Greek city with colonnaded streets out in the middle of nowhere. Bishop Papius later explained that Hierapolis was the hub of a vast region, with two theaters, several temples, and a huge market square to serve the population. The hot springs had attracted both tourists and religious pilgrims for as long as anyone could remember.

"Come in and rest," Papius greeted. "That is a long ride, isn't it?"

"It was even longer for the mules," the sweaty traveler shared.

"Try our wine. We are very proud of it."

Taking a sip, Clement said, "Hmm. This is excellent. And it certainly is refreshing."

"Hierapolis is known for many things, including good wine."

Papius was grateful that the western bishop had made the journey to his region, and when Clement mentioned that he had visited John, Papius said, "John is a remarkable man—so educated and intelligent. He did a great deal of teaching here with a witness unsurpassed in credibility. I call him 'John the Elder' to avoid any confusion. He sometimes refers to himself as 'the disciple Jesus loved.' There is no reason for people to mistake him for a fisherman."

"I am excited that he finally is putting his memories in writing."

"Yes. I also hesitated to write what I know. In a way, I also am a witness to Christ from the many travelers who have passed by these cliffs. I made enquiries about the words of the elders—what Andrew or Peter said, or Philip or Thomas or James or John or Levi or any other of the Lord's disciples knew, and whatever Aristion and John the Elder were saying. I did not think that information from books would profit me as much as information from a living and surviving voice."

"Then you should write too. We are entering a new era where the only surviving voice will be in the form of the written word."

"You make a good point. I also hold much truth that should be preserved. I've been wondering what I should do with it, and with John beginning to write, I possibly shall as well."

"Please share with me some of the things that you know," Clement requested.

"John the Elder used to say, 'Mark, in his capacity as Peter's interpreter, wrote down accurately as many things as he recalled from memory—though not in an ordered form—of the things either said or done by the Lord. For he neither heard the Lord nor accompanied him, but later listened to Peter, who used to give his teachings in the form of accounts, but without providing an ordered arrangement of the words of the Lord. Consequently, Mark did nothing wrong when he wrote down some individual items just as he related them from memory. For he made it his one concern not to omit anything he had heard or to falsify anything.' I know those things."

"Papius, I knew Mark personally. I can vouch that everything you just said about him is true."

"Thank you."

"You seem to have memorized the statement you just made."

"That is how I retain facts. It is a gift from God. I was told that 'after Mark wrote, Matthew put the words in an ordered arrangement in the Hebrew language, but each person interpreted them as best he could.'"

"That is exactly how we view it in Rome! The written gospel has emerged from the best of testimony, even though the writers were acquaintances of the eyewitnesses."

"People need to know that."

"They do. So please, do your best to put what you know in writing."

"I will. You have given me the motivation to do it."

After visiting the communities along the Lycan, Clement took another journey by cart over the pass to Philadelphia with a driver who was more considerate to the mules. Then he traveled down the Hermus Valley to Sardis, Smyrna, and Pergamum, encouraging the people and preaching his message of hope.

Pergamum, once an influential city, had been in decline, and local leaders were particularly harsh in attacking Christians in hopes of gaining the favor of the emperor. The town had no bishop, but the single presbyter, Erhan, whose name meant 'brave leader,' had diligently kept together the fragile community of believers.

On Sunday afternoon, after Clement had addressed the people, he and Erhan enjoyed a relaxing dinner and talked about the days ahead. "You are doing good work here, Erhan."

"I do the best that I can, but we never know when the next attack will come."

"Are there ever any warnings?"

"Seldom. When things seem calm, that's when the pagans strike."

"This practice of requiring the entire population to bow down and worship the emperor seems so senseless. Don't you tell the leaders that you pledge to obey all the civil ordinances and decrees?"

"We do, but they want more. They want every household to fit into one homogenous whole, and worshiping the emperor provides that single identifying sign. When they arrest a person, he has to either worship the emperor or face death."

"That is so unfair."

As Erhan refilled their cups, both men pondered the irony of the situation. The demands were similar to those the Sanhedrin had placed on Jesus, and on Peter and James—conform and keep silent, or die.

Then, just as Clement took another sip, three men rushed through the door brandishing sharp swords. "Come with us," the leader snapped.

Erhan protested, "This man is a visitor. Let him go."

One of the men came up to Clement and put the edge of his sword against his face. Clement instinctively ducked back, which caused the man to flinch and the sharp edge sliced his left cheek.

"Stop!" the leader shouted, as the outsider winced in pain. Then picking up a cloth, he tossed it to Clement. "My brother was only going to ask you where you are from."

Clement pressed the cloth against his bloody cheek and answered, "I am from Rome."

"Oh my—a Roman. Well, come with us. The magistrate will decide what to do with you."

The party marched solemnly to the office of the magistrate, where the leader whispered in his ear. An angry crowd was gathering.

The magistrate asked Clement, "Is it true that you are a Roman?"

"Yes, I am a citizen born in Rome, and I live there," Clement replied, still holding the cloth to his cheek.

"When do you plan to leave Pergamum?"

"Tomorrow morning. I have a ship booked."

"You will leave today! These men will go with you to pick up your bag and escort you to the harbor."

"Yes, sir."

Then turning to the other prisoner, he snapped, "Presber Erhan, I hear that you do not bow down and worship the divine Domitian, which is a crime punishable by death. You will remain here in custody until you do. We will give you a maximum of two days. Is that clear?"

Erhan nodded.

"Now go, people. Go home, all of you. Nothing more will happen today. And take this Roman to the harbor."

Clement wanted to protest, but his eyes met those of the presbyter, who clearly wished him to comply. "Go with God," Erhan said silently with his lips. Clement did the same and followed the guards, but after a few paces he broke down and wept.

At the harbor a ship was leaving for Rome, and Clement took it without visiting the remaining cities to the north. The captain dressed his wound as best as he could, but he said it probably would leave a scar.

Sati shrieked when she saw the wound. Even though she was glad to have her husband home early, no amount of reasoning by Clement could convince her that he had not exposed himself to danger. The two were as close as ever, and Sati clung to him tightly out of both love and anxiety. However, within days it became clear that her pervading fears had returned.

55

Even though Rome was calm during the next year and Clement didn't even mention any traveling, Sati grew more anxious. It was similar to the cloud that had hung over her after the miscarriage in Egypt, and the skies seldom cleared. Cordula was eighty-three and getting feeble. Sati knew that she would not have her mother-in-law's companionship for much longer.

Clement was happy in his work with the growing Christian population of Rome, but he was frustrated with constantly having to tell how he got the red scar on his left cheek. After a year of explanations, people quit asking, but it made him self-conscious when they stared at the wound.

Then in early August, just as the weather in Rome was getting unbearably hot, a package came from Athens. The bishop there simply mentioned that the contents had come to him, and he wondered if the Church in Rome had seen it. The single codex contained a gospel written by 'the disciple Jesus loved,' three letters from John sent to churches in his province, and a lengthy book that began with the words, 'the Revelation of Jesus Christ.' Clement was so excited that he stayed up all night reading the documents by the light of a candle.

At dawn, he slipped quietly out of the house and rushed down the hill and across the bridge to see Evaristus. When the presbyter heard what Clement held in his hand, he couldn't wait to begin reading.

"This prologue is so theological," Evaristus exclaimed. "You can tell that it is founded on decades of reflection. And the use of symbols is so vivid: Word—life—light, 'this life was the light of the human race; the light shines in the darkness, and the darkness has not overcome it.' What an excellent way to describe Christ!"

"That's only the beginning."

"This John certainly was an eyewitness. It shows on every page."

"John told me he was there when Jesus came to the Baptist at the Jordan and when Jesus cleansed the temple."

"He says in the gospel that Christ drove out the money changers, right after he went to that wedding feast where he turned water into wine."

"Wasn't that a precious story? This is personal testimony. And apparently John knew the sequence of events better than Mark."

"Does he correct all of Mark?" Evasistus asked.

"You will see as you read further. It's like John knows that everyone has heard Mark, Matthew, and Luke, and he wants to supplement those accounts, not replace them."

Scanning ahead, the presbyter noted, "Each story is described in such depth and detail."

"Please study the entire text, and come to my house tomorrow."

"I will do that.…What are these other writings?"

"There are three letters to Christian communities in his area. The last book is quite different—an apocalyptic witness."

"Really!"

"The writer said he was exiled to the island of Patmos. He had the vision there."

"Oh, I want to read that. Apocalyptic expectations have become quite prominent in the Jewish homeland. Can we talk about these tomorrow?"

"Yes. Please come to my house."

"You were up all night and out early," Sati fretted. "Is something wrong?"

"Not at all, dear," Clement exclaimed. "I received a package of documents written by John in Ephesus, which I am very excited to have. Evaristus is reading them today and will come here tomorrow. You can sit with us, if you like."

"I was afraid there might be a problem."

"No, dear."

"That's a relief. I might listen in for a while. Will he be here for the midday meal?"

"He probably will be, and you are welcome to join us. Mother too."

"Your mother is not feeling well. Why don't you bring some food to her room."

"I will." Taking the tray Sati had prepared, Clement went to his mother's room. She was sleeping. Clement put the tray on the table, and on hearing the sound, Cordula opened her eyes. "Clement? Is that you?"

"Yes, Mother. I brought you some bread and oil."

"That's too hard to eat. I'll just have some water."

As Clement lifted the cup to his mother's lips, he noticed how pale they had turned and how deep the wrinkles around her eyes had become. He vowed to be more attentive at this time of her life and whispered, "There. Is that better?"

"Thank you, son. You are kind to me."

"You are most welcome, Mother."

"What were you and Sati arguing about?"

"We were not arguing, Mother. I stayed up all night reading some exciting documents from the east and took them out early for Evaristus to read. Sati thought that something bad might have happened."

Cordula smiled with the wisdom of age. "Sati is worrying more these days. Have you noticed?"

"I have noticed, Mother. I wish I could do something for her—these could be our best years, at this time of life."

"Just be with her, Clement. She needs you now, perhaps more than ever. She seems to be getting more afraid, even when there is nothing happening."

"I will, Mother. I will do exactly as you say." Then, kissing her forehead, he asked, "Shall I leave the tray?"

"No. I'm not very hungry. Maybe I will eat this evening."

The next morning Evaristus appeared through the door with a smile on his face and the booklet in his hand. "These are marvelous!" he gushed. "There are such beautiful accounts on every page. I especially liked the vivid stories and the testimony. You can tell that John was present in the upper room by how clearly he described the washing of the feet and the long final prayer of Jesus to his Father. Why didn't Mark have any of that?"

"Mark only knew the things that Peter talked about. Peter was probably not with Jesus every day of the public years, and even on the days he was, he may not have noted the importance of the things John tells us."

"This gospel is such a valuable contribution."

"It's priceless."

"Why do you suppose John refers to himself as the 'beloved disciple?'"

"When I was in Ephesus, he told me that he was a disciple from Jerusalem who knew Jesus intimately, but he was not one of the Galilean apostles."

"He's not a Galilean fisherman—that's for sure. This John is very well educated and erudite. I wonder why he waited so long to write."

"He didn't say. But the gospel certainly displays the years of thought and prayer that the old man mulled over. I, for one, am glad that he waited. Did you look at the letters?"

"Yes. The first one is more of a theological treatise than a letter."

"That's what I thought," Clement agreed.

"He speaks of many antichrists—not one, but many."

"He uses the term to refer to all who spread false teaching. Some in his region are saying that Jesus was not actually born in the flesh nor died for our sins."

"I didn't know that," Evaristus admitted.

"Apparently, those in the east find it difficult to imagine that a divine being could come to earth as a human. They say he only appeared to live in the flesh and only appeared to die."

"How could anyone think that?"

"Well, you are from Judea, and they are from Asia. Their history and culture are vastly different from yours."

"I know. But still, if he didn't die and rise, our faith is in vain."

"Paul said that."

"I was quoting him," Evaristus explained.

"I thought so."

"Getting back to the letter, John refers again to 'the new commandment' that we love one another. What he said is so true: people only know that we believe in Jesus when they see us love one another—and love them."

"I liked how he worded that. We won't gain converts if they see us taking revenge and resorting to violence."

"Our God is the God of Love."

"Amen."

"In the third letter, he calls himself a presbyter. Why is that?" Evaristus asked.

"John may have been a presbyter—he didn't tell that to me, though. He was highly respected throughout the region—people saw him as a leader. Bishop Papias of Hierapolis called him John the Elder. Or—and this is only a guess—the third letter may have been written by a presbyter friend of John."

"I see the possibilities."

At that point, Sati came into the room. "Please join us, dear. We are talking about the documents from John."

Sati took a chair and listened.

"What did you think of the apocalyptic vision?" Clement asked.

"It's chilling."

"It frightened me a bit to read it."

"Apocalyptic literature has been popular in Judea for the last two hundred years. It borrows from the words of Ezekiel, Zechariah, and Daniel. The language is highly symbolic and is not meant to be taken only literally. In Jerusalem we learned to ponder the symbols and take meaning from the emotional power of the vivid descriptions."

"I didn't understand all of the references," Clement admitted, "but I saw how the author comes down hard on the 'beasts' of empire. He leaves no doubt that God is not pleased with Rome, the 'harlot Babylon,' and plans its destruction."

"He makes that totally clear. I notice that you refer to him as 'the author.' Do you question that it was John?"

"It doesn't sound like the same John that wrote the gospel and letters. He doesn't sound like the John I spoke with in Ephesus."

"I had the same impression," Evaristus agreed. "This last writer is of Jewish descent too, but is very different in his interests and perspective. Like the book of Daniel, it is 'resistance literature.' It is meant to encourage people in a time of crisis."

"The Christians in the province of Asia are in a crisis right now," Clement stated. "Local officials are demanding that they either bow down and offer worship to Domitian or face the sword. When I read the book I immediately recalled how afraid they are there. The presbyter of Pergamum was arrested right before my eyes and given two days to conform or die."

"How terrible!"

Sati sat up in her chair and scowled, but kept her lips pursed.

Clement didn't notice her. "They expect the violence to get worse. The visions in the letter speak to their fears."

Evaristus hadn't seen her either. "The violence is so vivid at the breaking of the fifth and sixth seals," he said before reading:

When the Lamb broke open the fifth seal, I saw underneath the altar the souls of those who had been slaughtered because of the witness they bore to the word of God. They cried out in a loud voice, 'How long will it be, holy and true master, before you sit in judgment and avenge our blood on the inhabitants of the earth?' Each of them was given a white robe, and they were told to be patient a little while longer until the number was filled of their fellow servants and brothers who were going to be killed as they had been.

Then I watched while he broke open the sixth seal, and there was a great earthquake; the sun turned as black as dark sackcloth and the whole moon became like blood. The stars in the sky fell to earth like unripe figs shaken loose from the tree in a strong wind. Then the sky was divided like a torn scroll curling up, and every mountain and island was moved from its place. The kings of the earth, the nobles, the military officers, the rich, the powerful, and every slave and free person hid themselves in caves and among mountain crags. They cried out to the mountains and the rocks, 'Fall on us and hide us from the face of the one who sits on the throne and from the wrath of the Lamb, because the great day of their wrath has come and who can withstand it.'

"My God, that is compelling."

Sati got up and left the room. Clement noticed, but was so caught up in the discussion of the visions that it didn't fully gain his attention.

Evaristus continued, "The book ends on a positive note. Babylon is thrown down, Christ is victorious and the New Jerusalem comes down from heaven. What could be more hopeful?"

"That's right," Clement agreed. "But this text can put fear in the hearts of even the most brave. I don't know how useful it will be."

"Only time will tell."

"You are wise to say that, Evaristus. My first thought was to suppress this book, but it might be best to wait and see how it is received throughout the Church. I don't think we should place emphasis on it, though."

"I agree with you on that. And the whole document can so easily be misinterpreted."

After Evaristus left, Sati confronted her husband. "You never told me that the presbyter in Pergamum was killed."

"I left right away. I can only assume that he was killed. It is not likely that he would have renounced his faith."

"But you purposely withheld that from me!" she fumed.

"I didn't do anything on purpose, dear. I was tired when I got back, and I only told you the high points."

"And you withheld the low points. You always do that. Do you see why I worry?"

"I am sorry, dear. I'll try to keep you better informed."

"Can't you see how terrified that I am? You expose yourself to danger, Cordula is declining, and books like these scare the life out of me."

"I have noticed, my love, that ever since I got back from the east you have been upset."

"Upset! That's too weak of a word to describe how I feel. The scar on your face reminds me that I could lose you any day and be left here without anyone!"

"I won't leave you, dear. I won't leave you."

Sati fell into his arms and sobbed. "Promise me that you won't die before I do. I couldn't live without you. Promise me that you will outlive me!"

Clement kissed her hair and caressed her neck. "I promise, my love. I promise."

56

Clement made it a point to spend more time with both his mother and his wife. Within a few weeks, Cordula passed away peacefully in her sleep. Clement and Sati had sat with her during the evening, talking about earlier times, and praying with her. The last words she heard before falling asleep were "I love you" from her youngest son, who tucked her blanket around her frail body and kissed her tenderly.

Cassius and Clement were shaken by the loss of their mother, but no one was more grieved than Sati.

"She was my best friend," said Sati after the funeral.

"I feel so lost now," Cassius cried. "It's hard to believe that I am the oldest now living."

Clement had few words—he was deep in grief, yet highly grateful for all that his mother had done for him.

The bishop of Rome began to spend long evenings in his chair, saying little, just pondering the events of his life. He often noticed long, blank spaces in his thoughts, where he simply sat in emptiness and felt the divine presence wrap around him with love. He and Sati continued to express their devotion in their bedroom—embracing, holding hands, whispering endearing phrases, and longing for the energy and passion that had punctuated the early years of their marriage.

Sati clung more tightly to her husband. The fear of losing him never went away. She spent time with her woman friends, particularly those who had gone with her to Pompeii after the eruption. They had formed a study group, focused on the newly received books. The one in the group who could read fairly well said the words out loud while the others followed along. This enabled them to discuss the connection between the sacred words and their own lives, and they picked up more reading skills than most of the women of Rome. After one of their number got a copy of the Book of Revelation, their discussions became more animated, however many of the women went home after their meeting feeling tense and frightened.

"Do you think the events are coming soon?" Sati asked her husband.

"I don't know, dear. Evaristus thinks the writing was intended to encourage those in Asia who are facing persecution. It's not to be taken as a precise prediction of events to come."

"It frightens me just to think about horrors like those."

"There are more important things to think about in the books—like how God loves us and how Christ wants us to love one another and make this world a better place for his kingdom."

"I don't want to suffer through tribulations like those described in that book."

"No one wants to, and few will have to. God loves his children too much for that."

"But it sounds so—imminent!"

"Jesus said there would be an end to the age of power and domination, but he did not know when it would happen—only the Father knows. And I'm sure that oppression will not die without a struggle. But Jesus never said that we can escape without any moments of hardship. He showed that to us when he went to the cross. He did promise that he had prepared a place for us and would come and take us to himself. We should be consoled by those words."

"Now you're sounding like a bishop, but I know you are right. Just hold me close. I need that more than I need a lesson. Just hold me close."

In the fourteenth year of the reign of Domitian, Clement began to feel led to make another journey to the east. He wanted to make sure that the communities in Macedonia and Thrace were staying consistent with the teachings of the Church and encourage the missionary work in Bithynia and Pontus along the shores of the Black Sea. He heard that traveling preachers had gone as far as the Crimea at the far tip of the region.

He didn't know how to explain the need to Sati. She had entered a new time of calm, but the anxieties had not completely gone away. Finally, one evening, he just blurted it out, "I think I should be making a journey."

"So that's what has been on your mind. I could tell that something was brewing."

"I wanted to be sure that it was needed before I explained it to you."

"Have you prayed about it?"

"Of course. And the feeling just keeps growing. I've not heard of any crises in the regions, but I still feel I should go. It's more about supporting opportunities to further spread the faith than about dealing with problems like on my last voyage."

"You would have been smart not to have mentioned that."

"The scar on my cheek reminds you. Doesn't it?"

"That and the stories about violence and persecution."

"If I go, I won't take any chances."

"You said that last time, and you've already decided to go."

"I'm sorry, dear. Maybe I should wait a year."

"You won't, and you shouldn't. If it has to be done, then you should go now. You are not getting any younger, you know."

"You are right about that," he laughed. "But I won't rush away. The weather will be better later."

"Just hold me. Just hold me close until you leave."

The night before Clement sailed, he and Sati had another intimate talk about purpose and risks.

"I wish you didn't have to go," she said.

"I wish I didn't either. But I feel that I must. Christ has a purpose for me in the east. I don't yet know what it is, but I do know that I need to accept the responsibility."

"I know you do. When I fell in love with you I didn't know what the future might bring. It certainly turned out different than I expected. But, I don't regret it! I'm very glad that you loved me and came for me in Alexandria. And when you became bishop I knew you would need to travel—I just didn't understand the risks that are involved."

"I won't take any unnecessary risks."

"I know you won't, and I love you for that. But you and I are not in control of our destinies. The Spirit is guiding you."

"The Spirit is guiding us. We have to have faith. We will be husband and wife always."

"I want my husband here on earth," she smiled. "Don't you ever forget that. Just promise me that you will return."

"I promise, my love. I promise."

"Four years ago, I made you promise that you would live until after my life is finished. Do you remember that?"

"Yes. I do remember."

"So, you have promised to outlive me and to return to me here on earth."

"I will. I promise I will."

As the ship left the Ostia harbor and put up full sails, Clement went up on the bow and looked around for white birds. There were none. He waited all day and into the evening, but he saw only a few gulls, and they didn't notice him.

On the Greek mainland, he visited the bishops of Larissa, Thessalonica, and Philippi. They were properly using the Christian texts and informed Clement that all was well in their regions. The only problems they mentioned were too minor to matter.

His next stop was Nicomedia of Bithynia, where he met and stayed with Bishop Evander. Like most bishops, Evander had been elected to a position of immense responsibility with few resources.

"The world considers this city the capital of Bithynia," he advised Clement, "probably because we are outside of the straights of Bosporus. But it is a vast region with hundreds of miles of coastline on the Black Sea, not to mention the extensive interior. We have so few presbyters that we send any willing missionaries to evangelize the towns. They labor diligently and bravely face great hazards, but our communities are small."

"Is it true that Andrew brought the faith to this region?"

"Andrew, the brother of Peter? Yes—that is what I am told. That tradition pertains more to the north shore, however. Andrew went through Byzantium and sailed to the mouth of the Danube and up the Dnieper River, then on to the Crimea."

Clement asked, "Are there people in the towns who read Greek? Do you have copies of the gospels?"

"Literacy is the greater problem. We have enough texts, but often no one to read them. Where we do have a catechist, the faith is gaining a solid foothold."

"Are there any cultural obstacles?"

"I don't understand what you mean."

"I was asking about the religious heritage in the area or any cultural factors that make it difficult for people to grasp the message of Jesus."

"These are people of the earth. They farm and fish. Their world is small, and the Greek and Jewish references can be hard for them to understand. Beyond that—there are pagan cults in some of the towns that get quite jealous when their people leave to join us."

"Has there been much violence?"

"We have lost two missionaries. Most of the violence is directed at those in their sects who become Christians."

"That seems to be common all over. I was arrested in Pergamum. They killed the local presbyter, but only ordered me leave town on the next ship."

"It is sad when even one life is lost," Evander moaned.

"Yes, it's sad, but Christ commanded us to preach the gospel to all nations."

"That is what keeps me going, even in difficult times."

Then Clement asked, "What cities do you suggest that I visit?"

"Just go along the coast and get off where the boat docks. Heraclea is the largest city, then Amastris, Sinope, Amisus, and Side, if you go that far. I will give you the names of who to ask for."

"Could I go to the Crimea? What is your advice?"

"The Crimea is in the Bosporan Kingdom now, but the region juts out into the sea, so there is some affinity to Bithynia and Pontus. We sent a catechist to Chersonesus, the largest city, about a year ago. His name is Haluk. I haven't heard from him since. You can go, if you can find a boat to take you from either Side or Trapezus."

"I will sail to as many places as there is time. I want to get back here within three weeks."

"Will you stop again and share what you find?"

"I will, Evander. On my way back I will stop and see you again."

"Go with God," the bishop prayed.

"Thank you, Bishop. I will pray for you too."

57

Romans and Greeks often find it chilling to sail through the straights of Bosporus. The channel is narrow, winds kick up strong waves, uncertain currents can push your vessel in the wrong direction, and from a western perspective, going into the Black Sea means entering a vast unknown.

The terrain was beautiful along the southern shore, and the winds carried the boat with little human effort. Clement felt no fear, only a passion for Jesus that he wanted purposefully to share.

The people spoke little Greek and were cautious of strangers, but knowing who to ask for made it easy for Clement to find the local presbyter. He just smiled and asked in two words, "Where (name)?" and they proudly led him to the correct house.

Clement stayed three nights in Heraclea, which gave the presbyter time to arrange a gathering. The man said that his people best grasped the gospel when he read from the stories in John. Clement guessed that this meant that they had a 'high' concept of divinity but liked stories about ordinary people. Clement was greeted by a roomful of blank faces, but he did his best to connect his thoughts with their own. He asked the presbyter to read the story of the woman at the well and then translate his comments from Greek, sentence by sentence, into the native Bithynian language.

"Jesus went to the city of Sychar, an ancient city where the people all knew one another but were suspicious of outsiders. Jesus had come from heaven in the form of an ordinary man, so when his group came to the city he was tired and thirsty, and he sat down by the well. No one was there because it was during the heat of the afternoon.

"Then a woman came to the well, who had been afraid to get water when the other women did. They liked to gossip about her and shame her. Jesus saw the goodness in her heart, though, and asked her for a drink. Did you like how she was willing to help him, even though he was a foreigner and didn't have a bucket? Jesus liked her too and offered her 'living water,' which was the grace of God that she thirsted for, but seemed to be unaware of. In fact, she didn't understand much about Jesus until he told her that he knew she had five husbands and the man she was with now was not her husband. Then she could see that he was a man of God. She said, 'Sir, give me this water, so that I may not be thirsty,' and Jesus gave her the truth of the gospel.

"The Christian faith came to Heraclea from afar, similar to the way Jesus came to Sychar. One day a missionary came and sat by your well. When one of you came there also, he spoke to you. He offered you something you didn't know you thirsted for—the truth of Christ. You said, 'Give me this water,' and he gave it to you. Do you see the similarity? He chose you to be the first in your city to hear about Jesus.

"So what did the woman do when Jesus gave her the water? She left her jar, ran into town, and told her friends. She told her friends, and the rest is history. Soon everyone in the city wanted to know Jesus, and he stayed with them for two days. And what does the gospel say…? Many more began to believe in him.

"Now—what should you do, now that you know about Jesus? What should you do…? Tell your friends. Tell your friends like the woman in Sychar did. And if you do, many more will begin to believe in him. Tell them what a difference it has made for you to have Jesus in your life. That is what they want to know. That is what they thirst for. That is what will bring them to the faith.

"The people of Sychar were joyful when they began to believe in Jesus. The people of Heraclea also will be joyful. And they will thank you for telling them what he has done for you.

"You have drunk from the well. You have tasted the living water. You have been blessed by the love of God. Now is the time for you to leave your jar and go tell everyone that you know Jesus Christ is the Son of God. And friends…Christ is counting on you to do it."

By the time Clement finished, the blank faces had turned to smiles. They were in touch with a sense of purpose, and they saw in the man from Rome the passion for God they had thirsted for.

The presbyter told Clement, "I never would have thought to put it that way. You have given me living water too. Thank you. Thank you for coming to Heraclea."

Now with more confidence, Clement continued his journey east, stopping for two days at Amastris, Sinope, Amisus, and Side, where the response was the same as in Heraclea.

I probably have time to get to Crimea, if I leave from here soon, he determined. *Let's see if I can find a vessel.*

Clement spoke the international language of travel—he held out two coins and said the word "Chersonesus." A man standing next to a boat nodded, took the coins, and pointed for him to get on board. They reached the destination in the late afternoon. Clement thanked the boatman, and asked some locals, "Where Haluk?" An old man with a cane led him to the house of the catechist, a slender young man with long black hair and a short beard.

"Hello. Are you Haluk?" he said in Greek.

"A visitor from the west?" he questioned. "It has been months since I heard your language."

"I am from Rome."

"From Rome, the center of the world. What brings you to this far region?"

"My name is Clement. I am the bishop there. I wanted to see how the faith is developing in this region, and your bishop Evander told me to look for you."

"It has been a year. How is the old man?"

"He is fine and sends his greetings. I told him I would stop there on my way back."

"You may tell Evander that you found me alive, although I don't know for how much longer."

"Is there danger here?"

"The faith was blossoming here a few decades ago, but our numbers have dwindled. Those in the old cults didn't like how their members were being taken away, and they began pressuring them to return. Many families went back to their former ways."

"That happens in many areas."

"Yes. But now the Bosporans have become determined to drive us out. First they mark the house of a Christian with a black cross. Then if the family doesn't give up the faith, they burn it down."

"Can they get away with that?"

"They do it at night, and the officials act like they are unaware. That is the hypocrisy. The magistrate should protect the people, but he doesn't."

"Have any been killed?"

Haluk lowered his eyes and nodded his head. "The worst case was just recently. It was at night. Before they lit the fire, they blocked the doorway. The man pushed his five children out the small window. They are orphans now."

"How terrible."

"It was awful. I heard the screams and tried to push away the barricade, but I was not in time."

"How do you encourage those who remain?"

"I help in whatever ways that I can, but I have little money. My words probably sound empty. They are strong people, but they are not prepared to withstand this kind of persecution."

"May I speak with them?"

"How long will you stay?"

"I can stay here until Sunday and celebrate the breaking of the bread."

"That will be greatly appreciated. They want so much to receive the Lord."

"And do you fear for your life?"

"I didn't expect the Bosporans to leave me alone for this long. I love these people, though. I'm not leaving Chersonesus."

In Rome, the emperor Domitian was hearing of clandestine conspiracies against his rule. Out of fear, he put to death all who could claim to be descendants of Vespasian, including his cousin, Titus Flavius Clemens, whose father had been prefect of the city under Nero. The charge against the high-ranking relative was atheism—Clemens may have secretly decided to become a Christian. But in any event, Domitian wanted all potential competitors eliminated.

The news frightened Sati. She hated staying in the house alone at night. When Cassius saw how afraid she was, he had Valerianus, one of his unmarried sons, move in with his aunt until Clement returned.

"Thank you, Cassius. It's hard for an old woman to stay alone."

"When do you expect him back?"

"Soon. Within three weeks. I'm grateful for Valerianus to stay with me."

"You are most welcome. It's the least we can do for you.'

Giving her brother-in-law a warm hug, she added, "I worry too much, I know."

When word circulated that the breaking of the bread would be celebrated for the Christians of Chersonesus, the house overflowed on Sunday morning with eager, smiling faces. People greeted Clement warmly, although he couldn't understand many of the names, let alone remember them. He felt filled with energy when the liturgy began.

Haluk read a passage from the gospel according to John, translating it into the native language:

> *Jesus said to his disciples, 'As the Father loves me, so I also love you. Remain in my love. If you keep my commandments, you will remain in my love, just as I have kept my Father's commandments and remain in his love.*
> *'I have told you this so that my joy might be in you and your joy might be complete. This is my commandment: love one another as I love you. No one has greater love than this, to lay down one's life for one's friends. You are my friends if you do*

what I command you.

'I no longer call you slaves, because a slave does not know what his master is doing. I have called you friends, because I have told you everything I have heard from my Father.

'It is not you who chose me, but I who chose you and appointed you to go and bear fruit that will remain, so that whatever you ask the Father in my name he may give you. This I command you: love one another.

'If the world hates you, realize that it hated me first. If you belonged to the world, the world would love its own, but because you do not belong to the world, and I have chosen you out of the world, the world hates you.'

People listened attentively to the reading. Then Clement spoke while Haluk translated.

"What we just heard were some of Jesus's parting words to his disciples at the Last Supper. They also are his parting words to us.

"He calls us his friends. He laid down his life for his friends, and he asks us to be prepared to do the same. Not all Christians are called to martyrdom, but we all are called to be prepared to die, and we all are called to lay down our lives in some way. That's what it means for him to be our friend and for us to be his.

"We must never forget that he chose us. We didn't choose him; he chose us. He chose us when he sent the apostle Andrew to this region. Andrew, the brother of Peter, gave his life to Christ to come through the straights and bring the gospel to you. Andrew was prepared to die for Christ, and in fact he did, up the river to the north, on a cross like our Savior. Yes. Christ chose us—he chose us to go and bear fruit—fruit that will remain long after our lives are done— fruit that will bless this land and its children for all time.

"On many days, it feels like the world hates us. Jesus said the world does hate us because it hated him first. My friends, the world will continue to hate you and you can't stop it. All you can do is love it. All you can do is love the people who hate you.

"I can't tell you how to live your lives. I can only tell you how Christ wants you to live them. He tells us right in this gospel: Remain in his love—do what he commands—and love one another. That is what Christ expects of us, and that is what Christ is counting on us to do.

"Our lives all will end in some way. It really doesn't matter how. What matters is, did we live in his kingdom? Did we bear fruit that will last? Did we love one another? Did we prove to be true friends?

"Do not fear. Do not fear, my friends, because fear closes off the fountain of love. Love opens the flow—love opens the gates to great joy.

"You have had joy. Being a member of his Body has brought you great joy. Bringing your friends to Christ has filled your souls with joy. His joy is in us, and our joy will be complete when we join his eternal banquet in heaven. So remember your commitment to Christ. Remember what you vowed at your baptisms. Remember how you feel when you receive his Body and Blood. He lives in you.

Christ loves you. Christ is in you. Christ lives in you and makes your life complete. He calls you to be his friend, and he will give you everything you need to remain in his love. We just have to do our part, day after day. We just need to love one another and let him take care of us. So be sure to love one another."

Then Clement bowed his head and prayed, "Lord Jesus, you showed the world that hate and fear cannot overpower divine love. You showed us that joy and love build up your kingdom in the only ways that bear fruit, in the only ways that remain. Hold these people in your hands. They are fine people. You chose outstanding people to tend the soil here in the Crimea. Bless their lives and bless their work. Help them to know how pleased you are with their dedication. Help them to know that no matter what threats may come their way, your love remains. Help them always to remember that you are their Savior—and you are their friend. Amen."

Everyone sat in silence, thinking about the days ahead in light of the graces they had received. A family brought forward a tray of bread and a large cup of wine. Clement blessed the gifts and, with his hands extended, prayed that the Holy Spirit would change them into the Body and Blood of the Lord. As the devoted followers came forward and received the consecrated bread and wine, they showed through the gleam in their eyes how grateful they were to have been chosen for their personal destinies.

58

After the last had gone home and the light of the day had begun to dim, guards came and arrested Haluk and Clement. Neither offered any resistance. They walked peacefully to the office of the magistrate, who informed them that some Bosporans had charged them with the crime of atheism.

Haluk asked, "When will the trial be, where we can speak in our defense?"

The magistrate answered, "The trial is going on now. There is no need for you to speak. We know what you do."

"But we have a religion. We are not atheists," he pleaded.

"Your despicable cult is too new to be valid. It is not acceptable to Bosporans."

Then Clement professed, "I am a Roman citizen. The Christian faith has spread all over the empire."

Haluk translated what Clement said.

"So, you are a Roman citizen?" the magistrate asked.

"Yes. I was born in Rome, and I live in that city."

"Why are you here now?"

"I am—visiting."

"You should not visit here. This land is not in your empire."

"It has been, and it may be again. You have no right to hold us."

"Hmm." The magistrate paused to consider the statement.

As he was thinking, a man entered the room and whispered in the magistrate's ear. Then turning to the prisoners, he stated, "You have been found guilty. But I must check with my superior before I execute a Roman citizen. That should take no more than a week."

Neither man protested. Anything could happen during the time it would take the magistrate to travel to the mainland and return.

"I will keep you here. Do you have money to pay for your food?"

Clement reached for his sack, but Haluk touched his arm. "I have the local coins," he offered.

"Fine, you shall not starve. Now follow me to the cellar. I will inform those waiting that the execution must be postponed until I return from Odesa."

The cellar was dark but dry. As they passed the thick door, both men noticed that it could be secured with two bars. They descended the steps, after which the magistrate pulled on a counterweight that raised the ladder up out of reach. Then the door slammed, and they heard two thumps as both bars were dropped into place.

A tiny line of light came in from a vent at the ceiling opposite the ladder. Haluk paced around the dungeon, feeling the cold stone walls with his fingers. "I can't see any way out," he stated.

"All we can do is pray," Clement answered. "If the Lord has more for us to do, he will provide the way."

When the light from the vent dimmed, they heard the door open. A young guard appeared at the landing with a basket. Lowering it on a rope, he shouted, "Here is food and water. Take it out so I can raise the basket. If you remain peaceful, I will bring your food each morning and evening." As soon as the two prisoners retrieved the contents, the guard pulled up the basket and double-barred the door.

"We have nothing to do but remain peaceful," Haluk muttered.

"Remain peaceful and pray," said Clement.

"Bread and water," the young man observed as he broke the loaf in half.

"Did you expect more?"

"No. This will keep us alive until they put us to death."

The days passed slowly as the two penned-in Christians observed the cycles of meals in the basket and light from the vent. They prayed, both together and silently, but without a glimmer of a response from their Savior.

"What are you thinking about?" the bishop asked the young missionary one day.

"How my life could have been different, if I had settled down and conformed in Nicomedia."

"Do you regret becoming a Christian?"

"No. I could have done nothing else. After I heard the stories about Jesus, my heart burned."

"Do you have a wife?"

"No. There was a girl. We were interested in each other. But…"

"What happened?"

"Her father would not allow her to marry a Christian."

"Oh my. Such a dilemma."

"Actually, it was for the best. If we had married, I could not have come here."

"So, you are glad that you came to the Crimea?"

The young man stood up and paced to the opposite wall, then he turned and stated, "If I had not come here when I did, the faith in this city may have died. Now I believe that even if I die, the faith here will live on."

"You have done well, my son. The Lord will bless your work."

The young man paused to picture the scene the bishop had painted, and then coming closer to Clement, he asked, "Do you have a wife?"

"Oh, yes. A very beautiful wife, who will be devastated if I do not return."

"Do you have any regrets, Bishop?"

"That is the only one. If I could, I wouldn't change one other thing in my life. I gave my life to Christ. No, I don't have any regrets."

"What do you think about when it gets dark in this cellar?"

"Last night I thought about Peter, my mentor. He spent his last nights in a dungeon."

"I heard he was crucified."

"He was...crucified. I went there and saw him grimace in agonizing pain at the end. Then I helped bury his body. We at least know where it is."

"Were you afraid?"

"At the time I didn't notice my fear. I just did what I knew I had to do."

"Are you afraid now?"

Clement paused. "I didn't think about that until you asked. I don't think I have been afraid—except for my wife—and I don't feel any fear now. I am at peace."

Then they heard the familiar sound of the door being opened. It was not time for the food basket. The guard shouted down at them, "The magistrate has returned, and the people are gathering for your execution!"

59

Evander, bishop of Nicomedia in Bithynia, to the family and friends of Clement, bishop of Rome: greetings.

I was saddened to hear of the death of Clement of Rome. He stopped to visit us in Nicomedia and gave us an inspiring message that will sustain us in troubled times. He was a fine man, truly devoted to the Lord and dedicated to Christ's mission on earth.

I thought that perhaps you might like to know the circumstances. Clement arrived by ship and wished to visit the cities where we have communities in Bithynia and Pontus. He also was determined to visit the Crimea, where a once-flourishing faith has been dwindling because of persecution. We had a brave, young catechist in the city of Chersonesus, whom Clement sought and apparently stayed with. I expected Clement to return here over a week ago, but I heard that he had been executed and received confirmation today that Haluk, the catechist, was killed as well.

I pray for them both, and I pray that your loss may be consoled by knowing that he died serving our Lord, Jesus Christ, right up to the very day of his demise. May God have mercy on his soul.

When Evaristus received the letter from Nicomedia, he walked with a heavy heart to the Capitoline Hill to break the news to Sati. She had only to look at the sadness in his face to know that something was drastically wrong.

"I am very sorry to have to tell you, Sati, that we received a letter concerning your husband."

"Is he…?"

"He is dead. I can read the letter to you."

Evaristus read the letter slowly and with compassion, pausing only when Sati shrieked or sighed in anguish.

"I can't believe it," she sobbed, dropping into a chair. "He promised me…"

"What did he promise you, dear?" Evaristus asked.

"It doesn't matter now. No…it doesn't matter anymore."

"I can stay with you, if you wish."

"It doesn't matter."

"I felt that I also should share the letter with his brother, Cassius."

"Yes, you should do that."

"I can bring it back later in the day."

"It doesn't matter when you bring it back. Cassius can bring it."

"Will you be all right?"

"I don't know. Anyway, it doesn't matter. My life is ended. I have no reason to go on."

Evaristus rushed to the house of Cassius but was told that he was working. Hurrying down to the warehouse, he found him stacking crates with his sons. Cassius was surprised to see the presbyter on a workday.

"Is something wrong?" he asked, expecting the worst.

"It's about your brother. I received a letter concerning him. I have already shared it with his wife."

Cassius scanned the letter and sat down on the loading dock to read it again. "I must go to her," he murmured. "I must go to her at once."

Cassius thanked Evaristus for informing him and quickly reviewed with his sons what work needed to be done. Then he ran up the hill to get his own wife and rushed to see Sati. He found her seated in the chair where Evaristus had left her.

"Oh, Sati, we are so sorry," Lucilia consoled, taking her hand.

Sati tried to force a grateful smile but simply couldn't do it. Instead she broke down in tears.

"We came as soon as we heard," Cassius said as he caressed her shoulders and kissed her forehead. "We will do everything we can for you."

"Thank you," Sati managed to say, but she had no further words.

"We can stay the night, if you like," Cassius offered.

"Valerianus will be here."

"We will stay and cook dinner," Lucilia announced.

"That's fine. It doesn't matter. I won't eat much."

"We will pray with you."

"I already did that. But it didn't bring him back. I prayed for him every day he was gone, but it didn't do any good."

Lucilia searched the shelves, while Cassius stayed close to Sati.

At the same hour, Evaristus met with as many of the presbyters and deacons as he could gather. They could tell by the expression on his face that the news was not good.

"Brothers, I must sadly inform you that a letter has been received from the bishop of Bithynia, stating that our Clement has been executed. This happened while he was visiting the Christian community in the Crimea."

A murmur quickly broke out in the room.

"Did the letter say anything else?" a presbyter asked.

"The letter was brief. Apparently a young Bithynian catechist was put to death as well. That is all that we know."

"How is the bishop's wife?" another inquired.

"I went first to Sati. She was devastated, as you may expect. I also spoke with Clement's brother, Cassius. He is with her now."

"Will there be a memorial liturgy?"

"I am sure that there will be, but it is too early to plan it. We can hold the memorial on whatever date the family wants—there is no body to be interred."

Another presbyter brought up a delicate subject, "When should we hold an election?"

"There is no hurry on that, either," Evaristus replied. "We are not in a state of crisis. The election can wait until after the memorial—don't you think?"

They all agreed. The news was so sudden—there was no urgency to elect a new bishop.

The next morning a deaconess came to visit Sati. "May I come in?" she asked at the door.

"Oh, Jillian. Yes. Come in. May I offer you anything?"

"That is my question for you," she answered. "How are you?"

"I am very tired. I couldn't sleep. This is all so—unreal. It's like I am in a dream, but I know it's not."

"No."

"I am in a daze. Everything is a blur. I don't know what will happen next."

"Evaristus or someone will ask you when you would like to have the memorial liturgy. The next few days will be busy."

"I will do my best to hold up through it. But after that—I don't know. I don't know how to cope without Clement. He was my life."

"You loved him very much."

"We loved each other—with a love forever."

"Then, whatever happens, you still have your love," Jillian shared.

"That is true, but it's not like having him here beside me."

"You could grow closer to him now, more than ever."

"How do you mean?"

"Every memory you recall, every memory you treasure, can bring him closer to you."

Sati protested, "It won't be the same."

"Not exactly the same, but in some ways even more precious. Mary did that, you know."

"Mary did what?"

"Mary first had to give up Joseph, and then she had to give up Jesus, her son."

"I don't know how she coped with all that loss."

"Well, she did, and you will too. Mary knew from the time she and Joseph brought Jesus to the temple that she would have many sorrows to bear. Simeon told her that, and she kept those things, pondering them in her heart."

"I guess I never expected to have Clement go before me."

"No one does. Mary may not have either, but she accepted what came. She accepted what is part of a great mystery."

"It is a mystery—how we meet someone—how we fall in love—how devoted we both can be. Are you saying that parting belongs to that mystery?"

"Yes, I am. Mary learned that, and you will too. It will be different, but you will still have each other."

"Thank you, Jillian," Sati sighed. "You have given me a glimmer of hope."

At the memorial liturgy, Sati held her head high. She tapped into an inner strength that Mary and women through the ages have discovered to sustain them through the tragedy of loss. Everyone commented on how strong she was. She didn't feel strong, however, and almost fainted during the service.

The line of people who wanted to give her a hug or a word of kindness seemed endless. Sati simply said, "Thank you," to each, in what felt like a monotonous blur. She told herself, *I need to get off of my feet. I will be glad to get home.*

Clement was surprised to find the house empty. He was tired from the long sea voyage, and found the walk from the docks up the Capitoline Hill exhausting. "This is just as well," he muttered. "I'll have time to wash up and put on a clean tunic. I certainly need to shave, if I have time."

After freshening up and with still no one home, he poured a small cup of wine and sat down to wait. He took a sip and noticed a folded sheet of white papyrus on the table. *I wonder what that is?* he asked himself, as he picked up the letter.

Then he jumped up and shrieked, "My God! I never stopped at Nicomedia like I said I would. My boat went to Byzantium, and I sailed directly here from there. Evander thought I was dead!"

Then he slumped back into the chair. "Oh, no! Everyone here thinks I was executed! Oh my God—my Sati. Sati must think I am dead! Oh, Jesus! Oh, God, she must be in pain. I didn't want to hurt her!"

Sati came in the door with Cassius and Lucilia, who stopped frozen in their tracks. Sati shrieked and began to faint, but Clement ran to her and pulled her into his arms. "I am home, dear. I was not executed. Because I am a citizen, they let me go free. I am so sorry to have worried you."

Sati slumped against his chest.

Cassius picked up the letter and read again the sentence, '*I was saddened to hear of the death of Clement of Rome.*'

"What did Evander hear?" he blurted. "He says he had heard of the death of Clement of Rome, but he didn't know what happened to the catechist until the day he wrote the letter."

Lucilia exclaimed, "Do you suppose that he heard of the emperor's executing Clemens and thought it was Clement?"

"Flavius Clemens?" Cassius replied in amazement. "That's crazy! He is Domitian's cousin, not the bishop of Rome."

"Evander was a thousand miles away, and he could have made the mistake."

Clement cut in, "This is my fault. I was supposed to stop at Nicomedia. When the boat took me to Byzantium, I should have gone to Evander before returning here. It would have only taken one more day. I'm so sorry. I'm so sorry that I caused you so much trouble."

Sati put her fingers to her husband's lips. "Hush! Don't talk about what might have been! I have you back; that's all I care about." Then removing her fingers, she kissed him tenderly. "You kept your promise, Clement. You kept your promise, my love, and I thank God that you did."

EPILOGUE

St. Clement of Rome did not travel again that we know of. Issues of disunity in the community at Corinth, similar to those in the time of St. Paul, led the bishop to write a lengthy treatise on church unity and governance in the form of a letter from "the church of God which sojourns at Rome, to the church of God sojourning at Corinth." Some presbyters or bishops had been deposed, and Clement called for their reinstatement along with obedience to the authority of bishops and deacons as established by the apostles. The epistle ranks as one of the earliest Christian documents outside of the New Testament. It was publicly read at Corinth and was found included with the Gospel of John in a fragmentary early Greek and Coptic papyrus. Clement's epistle met the criteria for New Testament scripture, except that when the canon was finalized, it was deemed to have been composed too late to be included among the inspired writings.

Domitian was assassinated on September 18 of the year we know as 96 AD, in a conspiracy by court officials. Minerva, the Roman goddess of wisdom, had appeared to him in a dream and foretold the date of his demise. A steward of Domitian's niece, who had been wearing a bandage for several days to conceal a dagger, suddenly stabbed him in the abdomen. During the attack, the steward and the emperor struggled on the floor, where he was stabbed seven more times and died within minutes. Domitian's memory was condemned by the senate, and the view was propagated by Tacitus, Pliny, and Suetonius that the unpopular emperor was a cruel and paranoid tyrant.

The troubled emperor was succeeded the same day by his advisor Nerva, whose reign was marred by a revolt of the Praetorian Guards that forced the elderly statesman to adopt an heir. Nerva chose Trajan—a young and popular general—to be his successor, and then died of natural causes after only fifteen months on the throne.

History does not tell us with certainty what happened to Clement, although the official lists of bishops of Rome show the papacy of Evaristus as beginning in 98–99 AD. Whether or not Clement outlived his wife is known only to those in heaven.

The oldest sources we have on Clement's life, the Christian historians

Eusebius and Jerome, note nothing of his being martyred, but according to lore dating from the fourth century or later, Clement was banished from Rome to Chersonesus during the reign of Trajan and was set to work in a stone quarry. Finding on his arrival that the prisoners there were suffering from lack of water, he knelt down in prayer. Then looking up, he saw a lamb on a hill, went to where the lamb had stood and struck the ground with his pickaxe, releasing a gushing stream of clear water. This miracle resulted in the conversion of large numbers of the local pagans and his fellow prisoners to Christianity. The legend relates that St. Clement was martyred by being tied to an anchor and thrown from a boat into the Black Sea, and every year a miraculous ebbing of the sea revealed a divinely built shrine containing his bones.

A number of writings have been attributed to Clement of Rome, which scholars today believe were composed well past his lifetime. The Second Epistle of Clement is a second-century homily describing Christian character and repentance. Two Epistles on Virginity were traditionally attributed to Clement, as were some in the ninth-century collection known as the False Decretals. St. Clement also was the hero of a Christian novel known as the Clementine literature, where he is identified with emperor Domitian's cousin, Titus Flavius Clemens. In about 869 AD, St. Cyril brought to Rome what he believed to be the relics of Clement—bones he found in the Crimea buried with an anchor on dry land, which are now enshrined in the Basilica of San Clemente in the city. Scholars today are unable to vouch for the credibility of the late legend or the authenticity of the relics.

Many emperors have ruled and died since the days of Clement, and the persecution of Christians has burst and ebbed, but never ceased. The dream of empire continues to bedevil those who thirst for power, along with the vast numbers willing to trade their humanity and liberty for the security that a strong ruler can offer.

After years of clashes between Jews and Romans in Palestine, combined with Emperor Hadrian's restrictions on Jewish religious observances and his intention to found a Roman colony at Jerusalem, a bitter struggle ensued. The forces of Bar Kokhba, who led the second Jewish revolt, proved no match against the methodical and ruthless tactics of the Roman military machine. With another bitter siege of Jerusalem, the rebellion was crushed in 135 AD, and Jews were forbidden to even enter the Holy City.

The theological issues that surfaced in the time of Clement grew into full-fledged heresies in the second century, as Docetism and Gnosticism spread throughout the empire. Groups that followed Marcion of Sinope believed that

Christ was so divine that he could not have been human, since God lacked a material body and could not physically suffer. They taught that Jesus only appeared to be a flesh-and-blood human. Other groups held that Jesus was a man in the flesh, but Christ was a separate entity who entered Jesus's body in the form of a dove at his baptism and abandoned him upon his death on the cross. Adherents to Gnosticism, which also denied the incarnation, believed in esoteric knowledge as the pathway to salvation. Much of the writing by the Apostolic Fathers of the second century centers on countering these heresies.

The development of the canon or official list of New Testament books took place in a gradual but orderly process. References in 1 and 2 Corinthians, 1 Thessalonians, etc. show that Paul's letters were read in Christian liturgies—as scripture—from the earliest times. Both Polycarp, bishop of Smyrna, and Ignatius, bishop of Antioch, in about 110 AD, use the Old Testament expression "it is written" to refer to the canonical writings. We find multiple manuscripts bound in a single codex, such as the Chester Beatty P45 from about 245 AD, which contain our four Gospels and the Acts of the Apostles, but there are no cases of both canonical and noncanonical writings bound together. The Church was using a collection of writings as scripture amazingly early.

Justin Martyr, in 150 AD, cited the four Gospels, Acts, the Pauline letters, James, 1 Peter, 1 and 2 John and Revelation. Irenaeus, bishop of Lyons, in 170 AD cited the same works plus the letter to the Hebrews. Some scholars see Irenaeus as "inventing" the canon at this late date, but he does not seem to be presenting anything new. He states that the message of salvation and Christ's delegated authority were "handed down" by the apostles and signified in the laying on of hands to succeeding bishops. The Muratorian Fragment—the earliest canonical list from about 180 AD—confirms twenty-two of the twenty-seven New Testament books. In the period of the early Apostolic Fathers, the core of the New Testament clearly was seen as scripture, and apocryphal books that later were excluded, were not.

A consensus exists today among Catholic, Orthodox, and Mainline Protestant scholars that Mark was the first to put the gospel message in writing in the 60s AD. He was followed by Matthew and Luke in the 80s, who drew upon Mark, a collection of the sayings of Christ, and other sources to compose their narratives about Jesus. Then John added his contribution late in the first century to provide detail the others had not included.

We are blessed in our time with an amazing heritage of inspired writings and tradition that has been handed down to us from Peter and the other apostles through giants of the faith like St. Clement of Rome, which the Church has preserved for posterity. They felt their hearts burn with zeal for the Lord, they knew their purpose, and with the grace of God they succeeded against extreme odds to preach the gospel to all nations. We can only be humbly grateful as we embrace their passion and do our part to show the world that we believe.

NOTES

I wish to acknowledge the scholarship of Richard Bauckham, Professor of New Testament Studies at the University of St. Andrews, Scotland, for his detailed insights into the eyewitness testimony contained in the four Gospels, which helped me to identify and characterize Mark, Matthew, and Luke in this novel, and especially John the Evangelist in chapter 53 and Papias of Hierapolis in chapter 54. See Richard Bauckham, *Jesus and the Eyewitnesses* (Cambridge, UK: Eerdmans, 2006).

The development of the canon of New Testament books described in the story stems from the work of many contemporary scholars, in particular Michael Kruger of the University of Edinburgh. See Michael J. Kruger, *The Question of Canon* (Dowers Grove, IL: InterVarsity Press, 2013).

The most helpful research about St. Peter in his later years came from the contributors to *Peter in Early Christianity*, ed. Helen K. Bond and Larry W. Hurtado (Cambridge, UK: Eerdmans, 2015).

Two scholars helped me to separate fact from fable about Clement of Rome: John Chapman, "Clement I: A Biography," in *The Sacred Writings of Pseudo-Clementine Literature*, trans. Sir James Donaldson (Altenmunster, Germany: Jazzybee Verlag Jurgen Beck, 2012) and Kenneth J. Howell, *Clement of Rome and the Didache* (Zanesville, OH: CHResources, 2012).

The details of the Great Fire of Rome and the persecution of Christians under Nero in chapters 40 and 41 are from the *Annals* of the historian Tacitus, which can be found at earlychristianwritings.com.

The quotation in chapter 47 from Pliny the Younger in his *Epistle concerning the eruption of Mt. Vesuvius* can be found at www.u.arizona.edu.

Many of the other descriptions of historical people and places were derived from articles from the various contributors to Wikipedia.

KEY HISTORICAL EVENTS

0 AD	The birth of Jesus
30	The baptism of Jesus at the Jordan River
30-33	Jesus teaches and heals in Galilee and Judea
33	The crucifixion of Jesus in Jerusalem
36	The conversion of Paul
41	Claudius becomes Emperor
41	Peter leaves Jerusalem
42	Peter moves to Rome
48-60	Paul's missionary journeys
54	Nero becomes Emperor
64	The Great Fire of Rome
64-65	Martyrdom of Peter and Paul
65	Linus becomes bishop of Rome
66-70	Jewish Rebellion against Rome
66-68	Probable date of Mark's Gospel
67-68	Vespasian leads the Roman invasion of Palestine
68	The death of Nero
70	Vespasian becomes Emperor
70	The destruction of Jerusalem by Titus
76	Anacletus becomes bishop of Rome
81	Domitian becomes Emperor
80s	Probable date of Matthew's and Luke's gospels
88	Clement becomes bishop of Rome
90s	Probable date of John's gospel
98	Trajan becomes Emperor

MAP OF THE ROMAN EMPIRE (14 AD)

ABOUT THE AUTHOR

Dedicated religious educator and deacon Gene Vanderzanden writes for those who like to search for and discover gems of insight that deepen their understanding of scripture and connect their faith with their life experience. He holds Master of Pastoral Ministry and Master of Divinity degrees from Seattle University, and has served in parish ministry for more than three decades.

Gene's other books include *Mark's Passion: The story of a spiritual calling*, *Christ Speaks about Peace: His message for today*, and *How to Preach Peace: Ten tips for pastors*, available from Amazon.com.

For a free download of illustrations, maps and facts about the first century, or to learn what New Testament scholars are saying about the gospels today, go to the author's website at www.markspassion.com.

PLEASE SUBMIT A REVIEW

Did you enjoy this book? Did you learn what it is like to grow in faith and what life was like for Christians in the first century?

I will greatly appreciate your submitting an honest review on Amazon.com. Reviews help us authors reach more readers, and that helps to get the word out about Clement and the gospels. It will take you only a few minutes.

To submit your review, go to the Amazon page for *Passion and Purpose*. Then scroll down until you see Customer Reviews and click where it says Write a Customer Review. Hit the number of stars that you want to give the book and write a few sentences that tell how you feel about it.

The most helpful reviews are simple, honest and to the point. Simply say why you liked the story, what you learned, and what people can get out of it.

Thank you for expressing your opinion about *Passion* and *Purpose*.

Made in the USA
San Bernardino, CA
06 September 2017